PLAGUE BIRDS

JASON SANFORD

APEX BOOK COMPANY

PRAISE FOR PLAGUE BIRDS

A masterpiece in world-building, *Plague Birds* is a wildly imaginative thrill ride set in a weird future populated by biogenetically engineered human/animal hybrids, benevolent and malevolent AIs, alien forces and—strangest of all—plague birds, powerful arbiters of justice who are bonded to AIs that course through their veins. An action-packed and riveting page-turner, I couldn't put it down.

— Mercurio D. Rivera, World Fantasy Award-nominated author

Such a perfect blend of sf and fantasy weaving memory, loss, technology, and family into a wholly unique tapestry that left me turning the pages just to see what he would do next

— Maurice Broaddus, author of *Pimp My Airship* and *Kingmaker*

A book thick with bloodlines of family, friendship, and history. This is truly Jason Sanford at his finest: a story with real bite. Its characters are so clear and so real that I laughed with them, cried with them, and sat gripping the final pages because I didn't want to let them go. With cities that come alive (literally) and prose with personality, *Plague Birds* is a book that I'll be thinking about for days, months, years to come.

— Jordan Kurella, author of the forthcoming novel *I Never Liked You Anyway*

For his debut novel, *Plague Birds,* Sanford has written a lush speculative fiction epic set in a post-apocalyptic world. Filled with genetically enhanced humans and AIs, the story centers on a reluctant heroine-turned-plague bird who must investigate the past to create a new future. Readers desperate for characters who transform tragedy into hope will love how Sanford weaves seemingly disparate threads to a thrilling climax and satisfying conclusion.

— Monica Valentinelli, author of the *Firefly Encyclopedia*

In this fun and thrilling far-future story where towns are sentient, monks are cannibalistic, and AIs are both gods and jerks, Jason Sanford explores how trust is still a characteristic of the human condition, even if that being is not what we recognize as human at all.

— LaShawn M. Wanak, editor of *GigaNotoSaurus*

PLAGUE BIRDS

Jacket design by Mikio Murikami

ISBN TPB 978-1-937009-94-6

ISBN eBook-ePub 978-1-937009-95-3

ISBN eBook-PDF 978-1-937009-96-0

Apex Book Company
PO Box 24323
Lexington, KY 40524

First Edition, September 2021

For press information please email Jason Sizemore (jason@apexbookcompany.com).

Visit Apex Book Company online at www.apexbookcompany.com.

PART I

RED DAY

The world fell flat. The world fell exhausted. The world fell to rainbow-colored static, which rang through Derena's mind as she ran from her death.

The static hacked Derena's eyes to afterimages of reds and yellows and blues. She stumbled through the dark forest unable to see, her massive strength smashing each tree she blundered into. Pine saplings scented of youthful excitement. Older hickories and walnuts as thick as her body and smelling of aged regret. The trees buzzed to networked anger and fear as their brothers and sisters were destroyed by the plague bird's strength.

Derena muttered a short prayer as she ran, hoping the ancient incantation—programmed eons ago by the unknown geneticists who'd created this forest—would ease the trees' pain.

Then she ran into a giant tree that didn't break.

Derena fell backwards onto the leaf-strewn ground before clawing to her feet. *A steel oak,* she realized, her fingers drumming over the oak's nearly unbreakable hybrid wood. Unlike the other trees, the steel oak's living network hummed without fear. There were few things on Earth that could damage it.

With the rainbow static continuing to block the nerves in her eyes, Derena leaned her back against the steel oak's massive trunk. Her attackers must be somewhere nearby. But to truly kill her, they had to touch her. If she braced against the massive oak's trunk, they couldn't attack from behind.

Can you sense the attackers? Derena thought.

No, the blood AI responded in her mind. *Someone is jamming my senses along with your eyes. Which should be impossible.*

Fear radiated from the artificial intelligence, which was named Red Day and lived inside Derena's blood. No one should be able to jam a plague bird's powers.

But Derena also tasted Red Day's excitement at facing a truly challenging foe for once in their long life. Even if that foe might destroy them.

Derena pulled one of her knives from the twin sheaths on her thighs and slashed her wrist, yet again trying to release Red Day's power. But the blood AI still couldn't leave her body.

How are they doing this? she thought. The AI always left when she cut herself.

We'll figure that out if we live, Red Day answered in her mind. *Create a bigger wound to release me.*

Derena understood. She leaned against the steel oak and waited.

Patience, the AI whispered. *Let them come.*

"One last time," Derena said, not sure if she was talking to Red Day or herself. It'd been so long since she could tell where she ended and the artificial intelligence in her blood began.

A hand grabbed Derena's arm. She kicked the attacker. Instead of the crack of bone and flesh she felt immense strength like her own. Another hand grabbed for her knife arm, but it was too late—without a second thought Derena slammed the knife into her own heart.

The AI inside her boiled forth in a spray of blood, furious at being attacked. As Red Day left her body, the static in Derena's mind eased. She could see again the blackness of the forest flickering to a few remaining starbursts of static.

Free more of me! Red Day screamed. *I need more power. The interference weakens the more removed we are from each other.*

Derena shoved the knife deeper into her chest as she cursed at the pain. But this was her pain. Her creation. She saw the people attacking her—three normal looking humans with bizarre, pulsing veils covering their faces. But they couldn't be normal because instead of fleeing the blood AI's fury, they still fought to kill her and Red Day.

She refused to let that happen.

Yanking the knife from her body, Derena reached into the wound in her chest and grabbed her beating heart. The tattered remnants of the person she'd been before becoming a plague bird begged her to stop.

With a yell she ripped out her heart.

As Derena dropped to the ground, her skull smacked the steel oak's trunk, which rang like a deep-toning bell. The sound reminded her of the school bell in her long-vanished home village. She wondered if that bell still existed or had fallen to dust during the several millennia since she'd become a plague bird.

Derena squeezed her heart, and, with a shudder, placed it back in her chest. Red Day swirled and shrieked around her, destroying trees in a whirlwind of power and anger. One of the attackers fell back, the veil covering his face flickering as if injured. The man's panther-gened face revealed red and blue slash tattoos on his cheek, indicating he'd once belonged to a nearby hunt clan.

The other attackers grabbed their wounded companion and fled.

Why are they running? Derena wondered. *They could have defeated us.*

In response, a name flittered across Derena's consciousness.

Ashdyd.

Before Derena could react her forehead bubbled out, blood and skin and brain swirling into a red marble-sized discoidal that fell into her hands. Someone was hacking their deepest minds. Red Day had recognized the threat and created a physical backup of their memories and programming.

Derena's hands shook. She couldn't control her body, and the discoidal slipped to the ground.

Derena! Red Day shouted. *We're infected with a virus. We must cleanse before it spreads.*

Derena wanted to agree. She wanted to order Red Day to erase her memories of what had just happened and with those memories any slip of programming the attackers had crammed into their being. But she couldn't give the order.

The night forest before her flickered as a man-shaped creature appeared from nothing. The man's body flowed to distortions like the veils the attackers had worn. Except these distortions covered the man's entire body, not merely his face.

Derena and Red Day again heard the whisper of a name. Ashdyd.

Red Day tried to fight, but the blood outside Derena's body drained of power and fell to the ground like red-lit rain. Derena helplessly watched as Ashdyd leaned over her body.

She braced for death. But the veiled man didn't kill her. Instead, he picked up the glowing discoidal and walked away.

Unsure what was going on and fighting to stay conscious, Derena reached out to the colors dancing in her eyes. Not rainbowed static like before. This color was merely the red of blood.

Blood is always good, she thought as the virus shut down Red Day, leaving her alone in her mind for one of the few times since becoming a plague bird. She wished she could see another human face. She remembered a woman in a nearby village who'd shared a conversation with her two decades ago.

Derena decided she'd go there next.

If, that is, she still lived when morning came.

THE VILLAGE

Cristina de Ane of the village of Day's End cursed as she plowed her wheat fields. She cursed the low clouds scudding over the surrounding hills and valleys. She cursed the trees in the surrounding forests for their networked joy at the budding of their new leaves. She even cursed the birds and squirrels who chased each other across air and tree and ground, chattering and singing in happiness that spring had arrived.

Crista had never liked working the wheat fields, but this spring was worse because it was her first time behind a plow since the attack. All morning she'd battled her mule, Eggbeater, as they plowed furrow after furrow of fertile, black dirt. The mule took full advantage of Crista's injured body, continually stopping and starting, turning left or right, and destroying every attempt to plow a straight line.

Now Eggbeater refused to move, pushing Crista's lupine rage too far. She screamed at the mule, who brayed with laughter, causing Crista to kick the ceramic plow in disgust with her injured right leg. Embarrassed, she glanced around the field—praying no one had witnessed her outburst—only to see Beuten Pauler walking along the nearby road.

Beu waved, acting as if they were still best friends. His bandana, an ancient piece of technology that fed off the emotions of its wearer, rippled with colors. The bandana cycled through the light blues of friendship and the pale yellows of nervousness before settling on the leaf-green color of joy.

Rip his throat out. Split his guts and spine.

Crista gasped as the wolf surged in her thoughts. She fell to her knees, fingers gouging dank earth as she fought the urge to chase Beu down and tear him to blood and meat. She wanted Beuten Pauler to pay for what he'd done. Wanted him to scream for forgiveness.

Breathing deep to calm herself, Crista grabbed the plow handles and pulled herself back up. She glared at the road, daring Beu to pretend friendship still existed between them.

But Beu was gone. Instead, a deadly flash of red danced along the road, coming to a stop right beside the field.

Crista froze, only to be jerked forward as Eggbeater chose this moment to move. She cursed as she yanked the reins. By the time she looked back the red had disappeared. Crista gripped the reins with sweaty palms. Was it a plague bird?

The mule, sensing her fear, brayed nervously. Crista pulled a carrot from her pocket and fed it to Eggbeater to quiet him. She stood on the plow for a better look, her pointed ears tense as she listened for even the faintest of sounds. Her injured leg shook with pain, and she gripped the plow's handles to keep from falling.

The red flash had vanished. Was it merely an optical illusion? One of the rare unmodified cardinals that still nested around here, their feathers as obscenely red as red could be? Crista knew it couldn't be a villager or hunter wearing red—that color was taboo to everyone.

Crista stepped from the plow. Perhaps it was nothing. Or perhaps a very dangerous thing was hiding from her eyes. To be safe, she'd return to the barn.

Crista bent under Eggbeater to unstrap the mule's harness. The leather straps were slick with dew as Crista struggled to undo them, a task made harder because her bad leg couldn't give her decent leverage. She finally unbuckled the straps and removed the harness, panting far harder than she should have.

Only then did she notice the plague bird waving a carrot under Eggbeater's nose.

"Hello Cristina de Ane," the woman said. "I require a place to stay for a few days."

Crista couldn't speak. She stared at the woman's scary stock of red-fire hair. At the glowing red line slashing her face from right eye to lips. At the twin red knives sheathed to red trousered thighs. Most of all, Crista stared at the woman's light brown skin, which was far paler than her own. She could almost see through the woman's skin to the deadly blood coursing through her veins.

"There's nothing to be afraid of," the woman said in a tired voice, repeating words she'd likely spoken many times in her travels. "My name's Derena. Please take me to your father."

Despite Derena's words, Crista wanted to bolt. She remembered the plague bird who'd killed her mother when Crista was only a child. The wolf in Crista growled, and Crista fought to keep from fleeing in fear. Derena's shirt was cut in front and not repaired, a large scar showing beneath the red leather. Plague birds supposedly healed completely from any injury. If this plague bird had such a large scar, maybe Derena was weaker than she appeared. Maybe Crista could actually escape from her.

Noticing Crista's fearful gaze, Derena laid her hand on the younger woman's shoulder. Crista stepped back, causing her injured leg to spasm and dump her in the dirt, the wolf in her vanishing with any thought of escaping the plague bird.

"Guess I'm not the only one who's had a rough time lately," Derena said, a gentle smile on her face as she pulled Crista up. "Come. Lead me to your home."

No one noticed Derena as she followed Crista and Eggbeater across the village commons, which unnerved Crista. Blue, her village's artificial intelligence, had similarly manipulated Crista's senses in a game of hide the kiss at her 18th birthday party last year. She'd stood before the village's teenagers and young people as Blue tickled her mind until she couldn't see or scent her friends. She heard her friends step one by one to her side. Felt unseen lips on her cheek as everyone laughed and hooted. But she saw only empty air as she tried to guess which invisible kiss belonged to which person.

If Blue could do that, so could the deadly AI in Derena's blood.

Crista glanced at the village's single-room school house. Blue's rainbow lights and rippling distortions—which Crista always thought of as rips in reality—hovered protectively in front of the school while a dozen kids kicked an old ball in a tangle of dust and shouts. Blue didn't react to the plague bird's presence, and Crista wondered if the AI even saw the woman. Crista wanted to run to Blue and feel the cool, enveloping crackle of its energy caress her skin. But village AIs were forbidden to interfere with a plague bird's duties, so Crista simply led Derena on.

Crista's father, Lander, sat at his workbench in the barn repairing leather saddles and reins. "Let me guess," he said with a grin as she stepped inside. "Eggbeater performed his special circular plowing!"

Normally Crista would have laughed—they called the mule Eggbeater because he'd plow circles if given a chance. Instead, she ran around the workbench and grabbed her father's hand. His brown beard and stringy hair bristled as his wolf-anger rose. "What'd that son of a bitch Beu do ..." he began.

His words died off as Derena allowed him to see her. Crista's father nodded. "Go raise the plague flag," he told his daughter.

"But only elders touch the flags."

"People will understand."

Crista ran as fast as her injured leg could manage to the giant flagpole in the middle of the commons. She opened the ceramic box beside the pole, strung a red flag to the cable, and pulled the flag to the top so everyone knew a plague bird was here.

When she finished, every villager was running for home until only Blue remained on the commons. As Crista limped back to the barn, the AI washed a wave of apology in and out of her mind.

What Blue needed to apologize for, Crista couldn't say.

THAT EVENING CRISTA SAT ON THE WOODEN STAIRS IN HER HOUSE, LISTENING TO THE village elders in the living room. Her father served as chief elder and had invited the council here.

"Why has a plague bird appeared?" asked Ms. Pauler, her deep voice in stark contrast with her sapling-stick of a body. "It's been decades since a crime of merit occurred in our village."

"Funny how you overlook your son's assault on Crista," Crista's father said, irritated. "But you're partly correct—there are no unpunished crimes needing a plague bird's judgment."

The other elders nodded agreement as Blue's haze of energy, distortions, and lights twinkled beside the brick fireplace. *I remind you that plague birds also visit without cause,* Blue whispered in their minds. *They keep a watch on all villages as we AIs return people to humanity.*

"When did one last visit?" Crista's father asked.

Two years ago, although only I noticed him, Blue said. *Plague birds visit our village regularly as they wander this land. Many times I don't even see them. Before that recent visit there was the ... incident with Crista.*

Crista knew Blue was being polite in its description. Crista's mother had been extremely ill and, as was village custom, wandered into the woods to find an isolated place to pray and heal. Even though Crista was only a child she followed her mother and saw a plague bird kill her. But no evidence of the attack was ever found. When Blue examined Crista's memories, the AI decided Crista's young mind had imagined the plague bird due to the stress of seeing some wild animal or human kill her mother. While Crista still believed what she saw, the villagers preferred Blue's explanation.

"We don't need to debate what Crista saw," her father announced. "Any other recent visits by plague birds?"

A few. Of course, our village's last significant visit was a century ago.

The elders grumbled nervously—that plague bird had killed half the village. Since then, every villager's education included experiencing the hell plague birds unleashed if crimes went unpunished. Crista remembered the first time she'd witnessed Blue's memories of those long-ago villagers. How that plague bird's AI tore the villagers' bodies to meat and bone. Blue had tried to stop the plague bird only to have its consciousness ripped apart and painfully stitched back together, a warning that the plague bird could have destroyed Blue if he'd desired.

Fear, the wolf in Crista screamed. *Scared scents. Mouths silent screaming.*

Crista closed her eyes to silence the memory. Crista smelled urine-tinged sweat rising from the elders. Everyone was reliving the same memories as she.

"Where's this woman?" Ms. Pauler muttered.

"Resting in our spare room," Crista's father said. "She's exhausted. Perhaps ill."

Ms. Pauler sputtered. "She's staying in your house? What do you plan, Lander? To beg her to kill my son?"

Crista growled softly. She scented the wolf rising in her father, and for a moment thought he'd attack Ms. Pauler. Several elders hissed as they sensed the same peril.

Instead of attacking, Crista's father calmed himself. "Tell them, Blue," he said.

The plague bird intends to visit a hunt clan in the surrounding forests and desires Crista to guide her, the AI intoned. *The plague bird also has an interest in Beu's attack on Crista—an interest we can do nothing to stop.*

Ms. Pauler's face blanched as Crista stood up to protest. She didn't want this so-called interest. She wanted the plague bird to leave her alone.

But Blue whispered in Crista's mind to remain quiet, so she did. That's when Crista knew she had less choice now than she did in the days and months after Beu's attack.

THAT NIGHT CRISTA SAT ON HER BEDROOM'S WINDOW SILL, HER FEET DANGLING OVER the second-story drop. Crista loved the night. Loved the moon's glow and the tangy forest scents and the urge to run howling after the hunt. Blue and the elders disapproved of such base actions, although she knew all the villagers sneaked away on occasion for just such thrills.

Crista glanced at the flickering candlelight in the spare bedroom's window. The pressed glass showed only the room's empty bed and furniture with a single candle glowing beside a hand-painted statue of the Child. Crista's mother had carved the wooden statue before she'd been killed. The room appeared empty, but Crista's instincts whispered that the plague bird stood—unseen—before the window.

A familiar scent washed over Crista.

Gentle kiss. Beu muzzling neck. Mating urge. Woods sweet in spring.

Crista ignored the wolf's pleasant memories, instead growling a warning as she leaned forward on the window sill, ready to attack. Beu stepped from the dark trees a stone's throw from the house, his hands held up in surrender.

"What the hell you want?" Crista whispered. She didn't want to wake her father, who would likely kill Beu for being near their home.

"I was passing by and saw you. Reminded me of good times."

Beu shifted his feet nervously. His bandana glowed in the orange of vigilance. Obviously Beu knew either Crista or her father might attack him. But purple pastels of serenity also flowed through the bandana—the serenity of once again being near the one he loved.

Crista remembered the spring night a year ago when they'd last met this way. She'd leapt from her second-story window to chase him through the dark forest, cornering him beside a fallen hickory. She and Beu had been best friends all their lives, and she'd always believed they'd marry.

But as Beu aged, his pox-flawed tendencies worsened despite Blue's constant genetic tinkering. And worse, Beu allowed himself to give in to those urges. Last fall, he and Crista were walking around one of the wheat fields at night, holding hands and watching the clouds play slash and hide with the moon, when without warning Beu attacked her. He smashed her face over and over and shattered her leg before catching himself, a gasp of horror in his yellow-glowing cat eyes.

The elders had restrained Crista's father to keep him from killing Beu, while other villagers called for Beu to be executed. However, the elders decided against that punishment, reminding everyone the crisp had burned Beu's genes so badly not even their AI could make him whole. They branded a C on his right hand to mark him as a criminal and warned he'd be killed if he lost control again.

Now Beu stood below Crista, seeking forgiveness for something she'd never forgive.

"Go before my father scents you," Crista said. "He'll kill you. And I won't stop him."

Beu bowed with a dramatic flair as he backed into the woods. A dark figure grabbed Beu and kissed him before bolting into the dark. Beu looked sadly at Crista then chased after the woman.

Crista wondered which village girl risked Beu again losing control. She tried to convince herself she no longer cared.

As Crista pulled her numb leg back into her room, she glanced into the spare bedroom. The candle there flickered and disappeared as unseen lips blew it out.

Crista shivered. She realized Ms. Pauler's fears were right. The plague bird was indeed interested in Beu.

As Crista fell asleep under her bed's warm quilts, she asked the wolf inside her whether Beu's death would be good or bad.

Yes. No. Yes. Confusion.

The wolf whined so much Crista gave up her question and joined it in running through the forests of her dreams.

THE NEXT MORNING CRISTA AND HER FATHER SAT AT THE DINNER TABLE EATING oatmeal. When Derena walked down the stairs she looked into the pot and smiled —perhaps pleased Crista had cooked for her—before scooping a ladle-full into a bowl and joining them at the table.

Crista nodded nervously at the plague bird, while her father wore an obviously fake smile. They both stared at their oatmeal, trying to decide if they should finish eating, excuse themselves, or make Derena feel welcome.

"This how you treat guests?" Derena asked after swallowing a spoonful of oatmeal. "A stunned silence and noticeable lack of eating?"

"Of course not," Crista said, grinning at the absurdity of being so afraid of this woman. "The problem is the last plague bird to visit had horrible table manners. Chewed with his mouth open. Picked his nose with a fork. Killed half the village. That kind of thing."

Crista's father froze. Derena arched an eyebrow. Crista's hands shook as she cursed the sarcasm that often hovered at the edge of her mind. Would a plague bird kill you over a bad joke?

Derena laughed softly and shook her head. "Do you know how long it's been since someone's joked in my presence?" she asked. "Centuries, at least. Maybe longer. Thank you."

Crista's father patted his daughter's back. "You must excuse us," he said. "We don't know how to act around plague birds."

"Few people do," Derena said. "We move around so much—and are often only seen when rendering justice—that most people go decades without seeing us. Last time I spent any serious time around people was a few centuries ago while sailing from the city of Seed into the Flickering Sea."

"I've heard of Seed," Crista said. "My mother told me stories about the city. But I thought the city legend. Or lies."

"It's real," Derena said. "The city is a year's hike from here, with buildings and homes grown from living stone. The city once supported millions but only 30,000 people live there now."

Crista nodded, wondering if there was any way she could travel to Seed. She glanced at her father, who'd tolerated his wife enchanting Crista's childhood nights with stories of Seed and the ancient world. Of spaceships and virtual cities and colonies on the moon and other planets. Of AIs and humans who swapped bodies as people today changed clothes. Of scientists creating new lives without limitation.

Because he'd tolerated these stories from Mom, Crista expected her father to do the same with Derena. Instead, he shook his head slightly at Crista, urging her to say nothing.

"You shouldn't fill her head with places she'll never see," her father declared. "There's little to be gained."

Crista started to argue—filling her head with places she'd never see was exactly what her mother had done when Crista was a child—but Derena nodded as if understanding.

"I apologize for stepping out of turn," the plague bird said as she took a final bite of oatmeal, leaving her bowl mostly full. "We've work to do. I need Crista to guide me to the Farnham settlement."

Crista and her father exchanged nervous looks—the Farnhams were one of the most secretive and dangerous of the nearby hunt clans.

"That's a long way for my daughter to walk on her bad leg," Crista's father stated. "And the Farnhams hate outsiders."

"No one likes me," Derena said. "But we're still going."

Crista's father clenched his fists in irritation, struggling to remain calm. He walked to a closet and returned with an ancient ceramic pistol. Crista reached for the gun—both honored her father would let her wear it and nervous he thought it necessary.

"She goes unarmed," Derena said.

Blood boiled her father's face, and he literally shook. Unable to speak, he hugged Crista tight before stalking out of the house.

"He has good control," Derena said. "I like that in a human."

Crista turned away, not wanting to reveal how badly her instincts screamed to join her father in ripping the plague bird's throat to bloody shreds.

CRISTA PICKED UP HER WOODEN CRUTCH—SHE DIDN'T NEED IT NOW BUT WOULD AFTER an hour of hiking—and led Derena down the old road made from nanotech bricks, now so uneven and overgrown it was little more than a footpath. Crista had often been tempted to hike the road to the next village, which lay only a few days walk from here. But only plague birds and hunters traveled as they liked. All villagers like Crista remained under the watchful presence of their AI. It was difficult enough keeping control during the day-to-day irritations of life. But to travel beyond the calming reach of your AI risked not only one's hard-won humanity, it exposed you to the dangers of the road. You'd be at the mercy of the wild hunt and other gened creatures with, at best, a tenuous claim to humanity.

As they walked Crista asked the plague bird about the sights she'd seen in her long life. "What's the Flickering Sea like?" Crista asked. "I didn't know people still crossed it."

"They do," Derena said. "But it's very dangerous. The last time I traveled the sea, everyone on my ship died."

"You killed them?"

"No," Derena said, sounding irritated Crista would assume that. "The Flickering Sea contains the remnants of ancient dimensional weapons. Most times sailing ships pass safely through the sea. But on other voyages, rips in space and time appear and kill anyone nearby. That happened to my ship. I barely kept myself from dying and could do nothing to save the others."

Crista shivered. "Sounds horrible."

"Yes and no. The deaths were horrible. But as the dimensional rip passed, for a few moments my ship floated through space while the Milky Way spun before me like a rainbow jewel. It's the most beautiful thing I've ever seen. Then my ship returned to the Flickering Sea and I continued on my way."

Crista remembered a story her mother had told her of a ship that sailed into a forbidden sea and was, for a few moments, transported into a beautiful starfield. That sounded suspiciously like Derena's story. "My mother once told a similar story..."

"I know. I've accessed Blue's memories of you—several years ago the AI recorded you talking about that story. It's strange how your mother filled your head with things that are rarely mentioned or known by most villagers."

Crista looked away, irritated the plague bird knew so much about her. They walked on in silence.

Half a league from the village they passed Beu returning home from his previous night's fun with the unknown woman. Crista scented sex on him and, even though she told herself she didn't care, a slick of vomit coated her mouth.

Crista's head tingled as Derena revealed herself to Beu, whose face flushed in fear at the sight of the plague bird's bright red hair and clothes. Beu ran toward the village like a rabbit bolting from a hungry coyote.

"He still thinks he loves you," Derena said. "And your village AI's correct—his love has perverted itself into a dangerous obsession."

Crista's lips quivered as she remembered Beu standing over her body, smashing and slashing as blood dotted his face. "Is that why you revealed yourself to him?"

"People need to know that if they hurt you, they'll answer to me."

Soon they reached the trail leading into the forested hills. "Why are we visiting the Farnham clan?" Crista asked.

"I'm investigating something. Part of a larger mission I've been on for the last year. I recently ... encountered a member of the Farnham clan. Perhaps coincidence. Perhaps not."

Crista leaned on her crutch as she glanced up the dim, narrow path. She'd only been here once, when she was fifteen and helped her father carry an injured hunter back to his clan. She'd been shocked at how the hunters lived in old, cramped houses and shacks, far from the ability of an AI to protect their body or mind. As she stared up the leaf-greened trail, she imagined a hundred animal-crazed people like Beu hiding behind every tree.

Sensing Crista's fear, Derena removed her red leather vest and one of her hip knives and handed them to Crista. "So everyone knows you're with me," Derena said.

Crista's hands shook as she held the forbidden red items. She pulled the vest on, strapped the knife to her uninjured thigh, and led the plague bird through the woods.

THE SETTLEMENT OF FIRE AND ANGER

They were being watched. Dark shapes flickered and merged with the shadowed oaks and elms lining the trail. Hot scents of territory and trespass burned on the breeze—scents so strong Crista choked on the air.

Adding to Crista's terror, the plague bird was in terrible shape, turning an hour's hike into two. Instead of Crista struggling to keep up with her injured leg, she stopped every few minutes to let Derena catch her breath. As they rested Crista imagined the hunters choosing this moment of weakness to attack.

When they neared the Farnham settlement, an angry voice hiding in the trees ordered them to leave. Derena pulled her knife from its hip sheath, but instead of pointing the blade at the voice, she held it to her wrist. The voice fell silent and Crista and Derena hiked on.

The Farnham settlement was built into the side of a hill, a dozen large cement and wood houses beside a level plot of ground from which grew massive steel oaks. Only the barest ripple of sunlight fingered through the steel oaks' thick canopy of metal-tapping leaves. Crista's boots clicked over the rubble-cracked dust of an ancient road, a reminder of long-gone times when a massive city occupied these lands and millions died when that city was destroyed.

But historic thoughts fled when Crista saw the hunters. Before Crista stood at least fifty men, women, and children of the Farnham clan, with their clan leader—a massively muscled woman with a white lion's mane of hair—in front. While they looked mostly human, Crista saw the crisp's continued genetic manipulation. The eyes of all the hunters glowed with enhanced vision while many of the clan members paced nervously from side to side like cats instead of humans. Many also showed the stripes and fur of panther, wolf, and bear.

In the ruins of the old road sat a heavy, wooden table holding food and drink. Obviously the clan desired to demonstrate hospitality to their unwanted visitors.

The white-maned clan leader stepped toward them. "I am Master Farnham," the woman said. "Welcome to our clanhold."

Derena laughed. "This is a first," she said. "No one welcomes my presence."

"We're all human, no matter our differences. Please, sit and talk."

Derena and Crista and Master Farnham sat down, with the plague bird and clan leader eying each other like animals sizing up who was prey and who was hunt.

"I'm investigating something," Derena said. "I'm looking for a member of your clan. Panther genes, a red and blue slash tattoo on his right cheek in this pattern." Derena doodled the pattern in the dust on the table.

Master Farnham spat at the ground. "His name is Vaca, or it was before I stripped his name and banished him from our clan. What did he do?"

"He attacked me a week ago. I'm hunting him down."

Master Farnharm's eyes played over the cut in Derena's shirt and the scar visible beneath the stitched leather. Crista scented fear and curiosity from the clan leader. No doubt she wanted to know how an ordinary member of the hunt could attack a plague bird and live long enough to escape.

"Do you know where this Vaca might be?"

"No. He was banished several years ago. I've heard nothing about him since."

"How convenient."

Several of the watching hunters growled a low, wolverine-like warning. Master Farnham slammed her massive fist onto the wooden table to silence them before apologizing to Derena.

"They're not used to outsiders," she said.

"Really? You visit the village on occasion, don't you?"

"Our golden rule is to never attack or harass the villagers. We live as neighbors with them. We've broken none of your laws."

Derena leaned over and whispered, "I think you have. I've evidence one of your clan is meddling in village affairs."

Master Farnham's face tightened, and she roared for everyone to leave her sight. The men and women and children around them hissed and muttered before obeying. However, one young woman charged Derena, causing the plague bird to pull her knife. Before the girl reached the table, Master Farnham jumped up and smashed the girl in the face with her powerful fist. The girl fell unconscious in the dust.

"Take her to the house," she ordered as several wild-eyed young women dragged the girl away.

"My daughter," Master Farnham explained as she sat back down. "The crisp gened her with my temper and her father's rage." She laughed at the joke but fell silent when Derena didn't join in.

Master Farnham lowered her voice. "We're a good people. We keep to ourselves and only attack if attacked. Vaca was punished for bringing a stranger to our homestead. He did this without consulting me, so I banished him."

Derena nodded. "Was there anything unusual about this stranger? Any … distortions over the face?"

Master Farnham stroked her mane nervously. "Yes. But not merely their face—their entire body was distorted. Obviously a dangerous creature. That's why I punished Vaca for exposing us to such danger."

"Did you help Vaca and this stranger?"

"No."

"You certain?"

"Yes. All I can give you is the truth."

Derena placed a red knife on the table. "I don't want to hear any words about truth," she said. "I wish to know the truth."

Master Farnham stood up, knocking her chair to the dust and rubble. "Absolutely not," she bellowed. "We are a free people, not sheep for any damn AI. We refuse to be judged on who is human by those without claim to humanity."

Derena didn't argue but she picked the knife up and rested its tip gently against her arm. Crista remembered the histories Blue had shown her of the plague bird a century ago. How that man cut his artery, spurting an arch of blood that grew and grew until the villagers began dying.

Flee! the wolf in her yelled. *No talk. Flee!*

In animal panic, Crista jumped from her chair, but her bad leg threw her onto the broken asphalt. Above her, Derena stared without emotion at Master Farnham.

"Are you going to make me beg?" Master Farnham asked, her face twitching as she fought for control.

"I'm going to judge your truthfulness, or every member of your clan dies right now."

Master Farnham took a deep breath and extended her right hand to Derena. With a quick motion, Derena pricked her palm with the knife and grabbed Master Farnham's hand. Even though Derena moved too fast for Crista to see any blood, a buzzing ran her mind like when Blue reached into her. Crista remembered Blue's teachings about plague birds—how their blood contained an incredibly powerful AI that cared only for basic rules of right and wrong. As long as the AI was contained in a plague bird, it was bound and couldn't hurt others. But release the AI and it rendered instant and deadly judgment on everyone nearby.

Master Farnham's eyes rolled as her massive body tensed and shook. Derena stared into nothingness for long seconds before releasing the clan leader's hand, causing Master Farnham to collapse against the table, gasping for breath like she'd run a thousand leagues. Derena wiped a slick of sweat off her forehead.

"I'm glad you told the truth," Derena said. "I will not punish your clan for Vaca's crimes against me. But that still leaves the matter of the person meddling with village affairs."

Master Farnham started to speak, but something behind Derena caught her eye. Master Farnham yelled "No!" as a young man with glowing eyes raced by Crista, a pistol in his hand. The man's whiskered face was as focused and intense as the panthers that hunted the village fields. The man raised his pistol to Derena and shot her in the back, a spray of blood exiting between her breasts.

Derena turned to her attacker, pain and fury on her face. She kicked the young man backwards as she slit her wrist. Pointing at the young man, she shouted, "Not them. Him. Only him."

Blood sprayed from Derena's slit wrist, joining the blood already hovering in the air from the bullet. The blood wavered, demanding more before acquiescing to Derena's words and raining onto the young man. The air quivered as the man thrashed and screamed for mercy. But the AI gave none. It exploded the man's lungs into shreds of pink tissue and ate its way through his brain, all while refusing to let him die. After a forever screech of pain the man's body ripped in half from head to legs and the cloud of blood returned to Derena's body. The bullet wound in her chest and her slit wrist closed as if by magic, leaving a puckered scar and a hole in her red shirt where the projectile had hit.

Master Farnham roared a deep lion's scream of anguish. The clan leader fell on all fours and pounded the broken road with her fists before regaining control.

"The fool had it coming," she yelled at her clan folk. "You know the rules."

The hunters growled in fear as they stared at the blood and torn meat soaking the ground. Master Farnham crawled over to Derena and kneeled before her.

"Please forgive us," she whispered, her angry eyes glowing fire. "The boy wasn't thinking. He wanted to defend my honor and forgot the consequences."

Derena nodded and said the young man's actions wouldn't count against Master Farnham's clan. "But there's still the matter of the person who interfered with village affairs. I will return to deal with that. I suggest you impress upon your people the need to avoid a repeat of this tragedy."

With that, Derena walked back down the trail. Crista stared at the people around her as the hairs on her neck stood up. Several hunters held back Master Farnham's daughter, who had woken up and howled in inhuman anger, fighting to reach and kill Crista. Deeply afraid, Crista picked up her crutch and hobbled after Derena.

Once they were clear of the forest and back on the old nanotech road, Derena collapsed from exhaustion, panting like she'd never catch her breath. Crista reached down to try and help Derena stand but the plague bird waved her off. Instead Derena took back the red knife and vest from Crista and sighed.

"That wore me out," she said. "Preventing my blood AI from killing all those people."

"Did you have to kill that man?"

"I didn't want to, but if I hadn't given the AI someone who'd dared attack me, it would have gone berserk. With my body so weak, there are limits to how well I control it."

"Must you go back? They'll be in an angry mood. Master Farnham might not be able to contain their rage."

"It's worse than you know. That young man was Master Farnham's son. As we left, she was debating whether or not to give into her animal side and attack us, even if it meant the death of everyone she loved."

Crista glanced at the wind-shaking trees and flinched as if the breeze blew to the whisper of angry animals.

A TASTE OF ANCIENT DAYS

Derena didn't hide herself from people's sight when they reached the village, causing Crista's neighbors and friends to stare at the woman with fear and shock and hatred. Crista led Derena to the house and helped her up the stairs to the spare room, where the plague bird collapsed into bed. Derena said she didn't want to be disturbed, then closed her eyes and fell asleep.

Not sure how to help the plague bird, Crista sought out her father, who was in the barn with several of the elders, including Ms. Pauler. Crista told them what had happened.

"The Farnham clan will kill us," Ms. Pauler whispered.

Crista's father shook his head. "I doubt they'll attack with a plague bird here. Still, it would be wise to increase our armed watch."

The other elders agreed and began discussing plans for dealing with the Farnhams. Crista, knowing she was no longer needed, walked out of the barn.

Beu waited outside for her.

"You okay?" Beu asked. "I heard what you told the elders."

Before Beu's betrayal Crista would have smiled at his concern, which etched so sincerely across his lean string bean of a face. But now she couldn't look at Beu without remembering his attack—of her blood spraying across that same lanky face.

"I'm fine," Crista said coldly. "Seeing that man torn apart by the AI ... forget what Blue taught us about plague birds. This was worse."

Beu reached out to hug Crista, jumping a growl from her throat. Beu stepped back cautiously.

"Nothing I can say will make up for what I did to you," he said. "You're right to not trust me. It's becoming harder to stay in control. Sometimes I go running in the woods and know that's who I am. A hunter. Not a villager."

Against her better judgment, Crista nodded in sympathy, causing a ripple of passion in Beu's eyes that almost overwhelmed him. She fought for control as animal impulses screamed in her mind. *Flee. Kill. Hurt.* She smelled the barest touch of last night's sex on Beu and wanted to vomit. Her heart slammed over and over in panic like when she'd stood in Master Farnham's settlement beside Derena.

"Beu, I'll never forgive you."

"Maybe one day …?"

"Just leave me alone!" Crista shouted. She remembered the anger in Master Farnham's eyes when Derena killed her son. Looking at Beu caused the same anger in her. She hated him and hated herself for ever loving him.

Beu undid the bandana around his head, which had been glowing to the deep blue of sadness. He held the bandana before him as an offering, but Crista merely shook her head and walked away.

She knew some things you couldn't put behind you, no matter how many times others said you should.

THE NEXT MORNING DERENA STAYED IN HER ROOM, SO CRISTA WAS FREE TO DO HER chores. Even though her leg hurt from the previous day's hike, she and her father plowed their field and sowed it with genetically modified wheat seeds.

At noon they sat in the shade of a giant steel oak beside the old road and ate beans and cold meat and talked about harvesting the quick growing wheat next month. Soon they fell to watching clouds scud the hot sky. That was how Blue found them.

"How goes the day?" Crista's father asked.

Very well. The hunters don't appear to be planning an attack. And the plague bird is sleeping. Restraining her AI drained Derena's body more than I realized.

Crista gazed at Blue's haze of consciousness, the distortions of the AI's body bending the sunlight into strange tints of rainbow colors. Blue almost seemed in a good mood, if an AI could be said to have moods. Then she remembered the rage in the plague bird's AI and realized these entities had all the moods they wanted.

You desire to ask something, Blue stated.

"When Derena released her AI yesterday, it seemed so angry. But I've never seen you mad. Why is that AI so different?"

We're all different, the same as humans.

"But why create something as evil as a plague bird's AI?"

Blue expanded outward until the AI's lights and distortions reached the top of the oak tree before collapsing back to its normal cloudlet of haze. Crista had been around Blue enough to know that was its equivalent of a sigh.

What I've taught you about history is correct. But there's a difference between knowing something and experiencing thousands of years of it. By the time of the collapse, humanity had changed beyond all recognition due to excessive genetic manipulation, resulting in chaos on a massive scale. So many human-animal hybrids and other creatures were crafted without a care to what they brought to this world.

Following the collapse a horrible war was fought. Eventually, the three-fold armies won and laid down new rules for our world. The hunters could live their lives within certain constraints while AIs like myself would work with isolated villages to return humanity to your original state.

"And the plague birds?" Crista asked.

During the war powerful AIs had been created to fight the enemy. But those AIs were so harsh we couldn't trust them to freely roam the land. We placed them within the bodies of human volunteers, who controlled the AIs' power until needed. After the war these plague birds were repurposed to support our world's new rules. Human, AI, and hunt—the only true balance is between three parts. The plague birds exist outside our three-fold balance, yet they also ensure its ultimate survival.

Crista had never heard Blue explain humanity's history in such stark terms. From the look on her father's face, he hadn't either. "Why are you telling us this?" she asked.

Derena has held her blood AI in for three millennia, but she is weakening. She won't be able to contain the AI much longer.

For a moment Crista didn't understand what she was hearing, but her father immediately knew. He jumped up and howled "No" in a scream ripped straight from his wolf genes. He grabbed Crista's hand and dragged her away from Blue, muttering "No, no, hell no!"

CRISTA'S FATHER CALMED DOWN BEFORE THEY REACHED HOME BUT REFUSED TO SERVE dinner to the plague bird. So Crista cooked a simple meal of eggs and rice and carried the plate to the spare bedroom. She knocked on the wooden door, and Derena said enter.

The plague bird sat in the wicker chair Crista's mother had crafted in her last days, as her crisp-malformed genes turned against her body. Derena looked at the hand-painted statue of the Child that Crista's mother had also made. Derena even had the same look as her mom before she was killed—exhausted and worn but refusing to back down until the final, painful breath.

"Blue told you," Derena stated. Not asking. Simply knowing.

"Yes. But why me?"

Derena smiled as she unbuttoned her red shirt to show the puckered scar where she'd been shot, a scar that rested in a much larger scar covering the plague bird's upper chest. "I haven't healed properly," she said. "Not long ago a shot like that wouldn't have left a mark. Hell, the AI once healed me after my head was blown off."

"Where did you get the large scar?"

"As I told Master Farnham, a week ago I was attacked by Vaca and several others." Derena said. "I'm not supposed to say more, but since I need you to replace me, you deserve to know. Vaca is now a member of a group called the Veil. They jammed my powers and prevented Red Day from being released through lesser cuts in my body. So I cut out my heart to free it."

Crista shivered at the thought of cutting out her own heart. "Red Day?"

"That's the name of my blood AI."

Crista imagined the power of this AI, which had healed Derena even after she'd cut out her own heart. A burn of pain shot through Crista's leg, and she wondered if the AI could heal her own body. Blue had never been able to completely do so. Maybe Red Day could even end the pains and fears that hit her every time she saw Beu's face.

"Can't this Red Day completely heal you?"

"Not anymore. Whatever the Veil did to my physical body is fatal. I'm dying. Worse, they did something to block Red Day and me from contacting other plague birds for help."

Derena seemed accepting of this fact. Crista wondered if Derena was simply tired of living.

"What is this Veil?"

Derena sighed. "That's the question, isn't it. The Veil first appeared about five hundred years ago and have since killed a number of plague birds and humans. The other plague birds sent me to investigate."

"Have you learned anything?"

"Only that they *might* be led by a man named Ashdyd, who is entirely covered in distortions and *might* have infiltrated various villages and hunt clans. That's why I talked to Master Farnham. To learn how Vaca become involved with the Veil. But Farnham's memories checked out. She knows nothing about the Veil."

"What happens now?" Crista asked.

"That's what disturbs me—I don't know. When the Veil attacked they placed a virus within both me and Red Day, a virus that slices apart our memories. I suspect this virus is also what's killing my body and keeps Red Day from contacting other plague birds for help."

"Won't I catch the virus if I take Red Day into my body?"

"No. The virus is localized in my physical form. I'm like an anchor dragging down my AI—if I cut myself loose, Red Day will regain all its powers."

"But that will kill you."

Derena absently touched the statue of the Child, her fingers caressing the statue's perfectly sculpted, perfectly human lips. "I've carried the AI for nearly three thousand years. Killed far more people than I need to remember. But I've also kept the peace. I accept my fate."

Crista tried to imagine all the sights this woman had witnessed in her time. And the ancient world! If Crista became a plague bird, she could travel to the remnants of the ancient world that still dotted the land. She could experience the amazing things her mother had told her about since she was young.

For a moment the thought of becoming a plague bird excited her, until she remembered the dead man from yesterday. And how a random plague bird killed her mother years before. She shook her head in disgust.

"Again, why me?"

"It's unusual for plague birds to die without first grooming a new host for our blood AIs. Not just anyone can take an AI into their body and survive."

"But that's what you're asking me to do."

"You're a good candidate. Most people can't tolerate a blood AI because they're too set in their ways. Too grounded with the idea of being a farmer or a mother or whoever they think they are. But you've been taught far more of history than most humans and you have a desire to see the world. Haven't you noticed how rare such traits are these days? Everyone else in your village has little interest in anything more than living and dying here."

Crista nodded. How could she have grown up here and not notice? Aside from her mother, no one else in Day's End cared about what happened even in the next village. Only Beu shared part of her urge to leave home, but his urge had always been dictated by his animal desire to join the hunt.

"So my mother was preparing me to be a plague bird?"

"No. Blue told me you've always had an intense curiosity, which your mother encouraged. In fact, your mother's the one who brought me here."

"What do you mean?" Crista asked, wondering if this plague bird knew why her mother was killed. The plague bird who had killed her mother was a man, but maybe Derena knew him.

"I met your mother before you were born, during one of my patrols through this area. None of the others in the village—not even Blue—knew I was passing through. I stopped for a bit and overheard your mother asking Blue about the very first plague birds.

"This was an odd request and one that Blue felt uncomfortable fulfilling—village AIs avoid telling their charges too much about dangerous topics like plague birds.

"Intrigued, I followed your mother to her house and revealed myself. I told her if she was truly curious about plague birds, I'd answer her questions."

Crista didn't know how to react. Her mother had never told her about meeting Derena. "That's how Mom knew about the Flickering Sea and those stars."

"Yes. She asked me what was the most beautiful thing I'd seen, and I told her."

"What else did she ask?"

"That's between your mother and myself."

"She's dead."

"It remains between us. But she impressed me with her curiosity and bravery in facing a plague bird without fear. When I discovered I was dying, I came here hoping to convince your mother to take my place. Instead, I found her dead and you, her daughter, an equally good choice."

"Did Blue tell you how my mother died?"

"Yes. When she was near death from the crisper pox, she wandered into the woods to pray, as is your custom. While in the woods a wild animal or human attacked and killed her."

"No, a plague bird killed her. I remember him—the same plague bird who attacked our village a hundred years ago."

"I've seen Blue's records of your mother's death and agree with its assessment. You were a young child and had recently been forced to experience Blue's memories of that long ago plague bird killing half the village. When you witnessed your mother being attacked, you simply transposed Blue's memories of that ancient plague bird. It's not unusual for young children to repress or change bad memories into something else."

Crista had heard the same words before from Blue. But if she'd witnessed a wild animal or human killing her mother, why would she have changed the memory into something far scarier like a plague bird?

"I still won't take your place."

"That's exactly why I want you. I need someone who doesn't desire what I do. Someone who will fight the AI inside her. Only let it out when absolutely necessary."

Crista shook her head. She wouldn't give in.

"I understand," Derena said. "But you should know that if you don't do this, Beu will kill you."

Crista jumped back, a wolf growl in her throat. "What!?!"

"His condition is rapidly regressing, as he goes through changes Blue can no longer control. Beu also obsesses on you. No matter how he fights it, he wants you. Blue is correct that one day, when Beuten Pauler's animal side gains more control, he'll kill you. If this isn't handled properly, many people—both villagers and those in the Farnham clan—might die."

"That's on Beu. Not me."

"Very true."

"Then kill Beu."

"No. I only kill for what people do, not for what they may do."

Derena picked up the statue of the Child that Crista's mother made before she died. The plague bird rested the statue in her lap and stared down at the perfectly human face.

"This is a true shame," Derena whispered to the statue. "I was sure your daughter would help." The plague bird paused as if listening to someone. "I know. But if she doesn't do this, who will stop Ashdyd?"

Crista backed carefully out the doorway, unsure who—or what—the plague bird was talking to.

CRISTA RAN FROM THE HOUSE AS FAST AS HER INJURED LEG COULD GO, THE WOLF IN HER thrashing and foaming and demanding she bolt for the hills. She would run forever under cool spring nights. Living as she must. Hunting as she must. No longer caring for the time of day or the worries of the village or whether some damn plague bird might turn her life into a living hell.

Crista shivered, fighting for control. The cool night air and the scents from the nearby forest called to her. She saw deer grazing along the village fence line, and the wolf in her snapped, begging for the chase. She heard an unknown howl from the forests and almost howled in return.

Needing to calm herself, Crista headed toward the village shrine. The village passed by in a mix of shadow and dark, candles burning in the windows of only a few houses. Most villagers went to bed early—not only because they got up early to work the fields, but because it was easier to ignore their animal sides with windows and doors closed against the dreams of night.

The rectangular shrine lay at the back of the village next to the forest. Built around four steel oak arches, which Blue had cut several millennia ago, the shrine's stone walls and roof rose two dozen yards into the air. The shrine's stones were a scavenged mismatch from ancient buildings—marble and granite and even boulders of nano-forged obsidian.

As Crista walked through the shrine's doorway, the night cries of birds and the ultrasonic clicks of bats fell to silence. She stepped across the neatly-swept cobblestone floor toward the alcove in the back wall that contained a life-size statue of the Child. The shrine's walls sparked to thousands of blue, glowing handprints—a disturbing number baby-sized, the rest from children and adults. Blue used part of its energy to gift eternal light to the handprint of every person who'd ever lived in the village.

Crista walked to her mother's glowing handprint. She placed her hand over the print just as she'd done so many times since her mother had died. Crista's hand used to only fill half the print, but she'd grown enough that now the handprint could be her own.

With a sigh, Crista kneeled before the statue of the Child.

The Child looked perfectly human, with human eyes and lips and ears and hair only on the top of the head and smooth skin without an animal stripe or whisker. The Child beamed a frozen smile and reached stone arms out to hug the world in a loving embrace. The statue's gender flowed between male and female and beyond, never settling on any one limitation. Instead the Child was all children and all that people could hope for in their dreams of the future.

Beside the statue sparked a single candle made from hog's fat. Crista scented one of the village women on the candle, and knew she'd lit it. That woman had always wanted children—especially children without too much crisper in their bodies to continually rearrange their genes. Obviously she'd been here praying.

Crista didn't know what to pray for, or if praying was even the right word. She remembered her mother coming to the shrine so many times. Crista had never asked her mother what she'd prayed for during those visits. Crista always assumed her mother prayed for more children—for children more human than Crista turned out to be—but she'd never dared ask.

Crista remembered the first time she'd visited the shrine with her mother. She must have been only four or five because the glowing handprints scared her so badly she started crying. Instead of telling Crista to stop crying—as most village parents would have done—her mother held her hand and took her back outside the shrine.

"There's nothing wrong with crying," her mother had said as they stood under the dark night sky. "Never let a little technology scare you."

Crista had sniffled and tried to act brave, but those glowing handprints still terrified her.

"Look up," her mother said, pointing at the moon. "You're wolf blood. Your ancestors once lived on the moon in Mare Trans City."

"Really?" Crista asked, staring hard at the moon and trying to see the remains of that famous city.

"Really. Your father's ancestors lived there. Those were bad times, right when civilization crashed. People killing each other, the AIs splitting into warring groups, and no one maintaining the machines that gifted life to that city."

Crista grinned, no longer crying and enthralled by the story.

"One of your ancestors wasn't much older than you at the time. Within a year of the collapse the air in Mare Trans City turned foul and the cold of space started to seep in. Your ancestor and a pack of other wolf kids found a single surviving spaceship and tried to fly it back to Earth. But no one could start the ship. That's when a little girl walked up to your ancestor. The girl said she'd fly the kids back to Earth, but first your ancestor had to do something."

"Wait," Crista interrupted. "How can a child fly a spaceship?"

"I don't know. Maybe she was magic. You want to hear the story or not?"

Crista nodded and her mother continued.

"The girl said that in order for her to pilot the ship, she needed one thing from your ancestor: To not be afraid."

"That's it?"

"Overcoming fear is the first step toward changing the world. So your ancestor swallowed her fear and helped load all the kids onto the ship. The strange girl then piloted your ancestor and the others to Earth. For years after, your ancestor and this magic girl were the best of friends."

Crista squeezed her mother's hand. "I'd like to see the handprints again," she whispered.

"I'd love to show you."

CRISTA STARED AT THE STATUE OF THE CHILD, WISHING HER MOTHER WAS STILL ALIVE. Unable to focus any longer on prayer or meditation or truth, Crista blew out the candle and walked from the shrine.

As she re-entered the night, she scented her father.

He leaned against the shrine's thick, stone wall, casual and calm but his every muscle and hair alert. Ready to attack. He smiled at Crista as she noticed the ceramic pistol in his right hand and a short sword in his left.

"What did the plague bird say?" he asked.

"She wants me to take her place."

Her father glanced toward their house, trying to decide what to do. His body tensed and relaxed, tensed again. Crista had always known none of the villagers dared challenge her father to a fight, but until this moment she'd never truly understood why. Yes, he was a large man, and strong. But now she saw the angry wolf gaze in his eyes and knew he'd do anything to protect her. Would kill anyone who threatened his family and pack.

Crista stepped in front of his gaze, blocking his view of their home. "It's my choice."

"What do you mean?" he growled.

"Derena said I'll only become a plague bird if I request it. And I won't."

Her father relaxed slightly, but still held the sword and pistol before him.

Crista smirked. "If you attack the plague bird, the village will never stop talking about your stupidity. Imagine what Ms. Pauler will say. *'Lander was fool enough to attack a plague bird. And people thought my son was touched.'*"

Crista's father chuckled. "It would be dumb."

Crista hugged him. "You mean well. But I don't want you dead."

Crista's father placed the pistol in his jacket pocket and let the sword droop toward the dirt. He glanced into the shrine.

"Praying for children? Please tell me not with Beu."

Crista shoved him. "Ass. No. No children, especially not with Beu." She paused. "I don't know what I'm doing here. I came here so many times with Mom ... it seemed the thing to do."

Her father wrapped an arm around her as they walked toward home.

"Dad," she asked, thinking of the stories her mother used to tell. "Derena told me she visited Mom years ago."

"I was in the fields at the time. Your mother told me later."

"Did you always know the plague bird wanted me to take her place? Is that why you didn't want Derena talking about the stories and places Mom told us about, because I might be tempted to leave?"

"I didn't know Derena wanted you to be her successor until Blue told us. The reason I stopped the plague bird from talking about those places is I didn't want you sharing what your mother told you. Her stories were for you alone."

"Why? They're kids' stories. Nothing more."

"No, they were true. Every one." Feeling Crista tense as if about to debate this statement, her father pointed at the moon. "I mean, the big stuff in them was true. Remember your mom's stories about the last city on the moon? Well, that was true. After the collapse a final spaceship made it to Earth. There were a lot of wolf-bloods on that ship, including one of my distant ancestors."

"Mom said a magic girl piloted the ship."

Her father laughed. "Well, your mother loved embellishing her stories."

"Did Mom want more kids? Human kids? Is that why she prayed at the shrine so often?"

Her father hugged her closer. "No. Minerva prayed for you. That you'd always be happy and healthy."

Crista smiled—everyone in the village avoided saying the names of those who'd died, afraid naming the dead would infect your mind with visions of your own death. But hearing her mother's name didn't do that. Instead, the name thrilled her and made her more determined than ever to stand up to the plague bird.

Crista hugged her father back. She didn't know if what he'd said about her mother was true, but she didn't care. Even if he was lying, she loved him all the more.

She held her father's hand as they walked home. But when they entered the house, they found Derena sitting at the dinner table holding the statue of the Child carved by Crista's mother.

Derena didn't look at either Crista or her father. Instead, the plague bird whispered the word "soon" over and over in the Child's ear while hugging the statue tight to her chest.

RED DAY AT NIGHT

A few hours later, shortly after midnight, Crista stood among the newly planted furrows of her family's wheat field, leaning on her crutch as she kicked the dark soil with her good foot. Above, a quarter moon lit the clear sky, stirring the wolf in Crista to excitement. She wondered if humans would ever again live on that world.

Crista heard a faint rustle from under the dark fence-line trees beside the field. She couldn't see anything and wished she still had the gened eyes of her ancestors. The faintest of growls reached her as a black shape stepped from the trees and charged.

Crista stood calmly, refusing to flee.

Suddenly, night turned to day as Blue burned like a tiny sun, casting white-flicker shadows across the field and trees. Beu looked up in shock, hands pawing his eyes as he stumbled over the furrows. Crista dropped her crutch and grabbed the net at her feet and threw it over Beu as her father and Derena appeared next to her. Derena had blocked their sight and scent from Beu's senses.

"There's another," Derena shouted, pointing at the trees. In the beam of Blue's light Crista saw a hunter—Master Farnham's daughter, who'd tried to attack Derena the other day in the hunt settlement. The girl bolted, running amazingly fast, but more villagers appeared from where Derena had cloaked their presence, and they tackled the girl. She howled and bit, but they held her fast.

By the time Beu and the girl were dragged before Derena, Ms. Pauler had run to the scene. She fell to her knees before the plague bird.

"Please," she begged. "He's my son."

Derena shook her head. "He tried to attack Crista. Your own elders decreed if he did that again, the punishment was death. However, he's not the only culpable person here."

For the first time, Ms. Pauler noticed the hunter girl beside her son.

"It appears Master Farnham's daughter is interested in your son, Ms. Pauler," Derena said. "She's been encouraging his animal side, wanting him to join her hunt clan."

"Then my son isn't at fault," Ms. Pauler said. "That girl pushed him into doing wrong."

Crista growled, angry that Ms. Pauler would again excuse Beu for attacking her.

"Everyone's at fault," Derena said in a tired voice. "All that matters is who ends up dying."

CRISTA THOUGHT DERENA WOULD WAIT UNTIL MORNING TO KILL BEU, BUT INSTEAD THE plague bird demanded the villagers immediately drag both him and the hunt girl to the Farnham settlement.

"Do you want us dead?" Crista's father yelled. "Farnham's clan barely controls their animal sides during the daytime. They'll attack if we enter their land at night. And if that happens, we'll also lose control."

Derena pulled a knife out and with the razor point picked at the puckered scar on her chest. The villagers glanced nervously at one another before binding the hands of Beu and the hunt girl and starting up the road. Crista watched them lead Beu away, relieved she no longer had to fear him.

Knowing what was about to happen, Beu called her name in a low, pitiful moan. He looked terrified. Crista turned away as the wolf inside whined and snapped, demanding justice but also remembering their history together.

You must also go, Blue said in her mind. *You must see this through to the end.*

"Too much is swirling in me right now," she said. "I don't know if I can keep control."

Trust me, Blue said. *You'll have control.*

Crista hobbled on her crutch after the villagers.

BLUE LIT THEIR WAY, A MOVING SUN CHASING OFF SHADOWS. DERENA COULD BARELY walk and leaned on Crista's father for support, more so when they entered the perfect black of the forest and wound their way up the hilly trail. Hunters howled and shrieked in the darkness and every villager huddled close to the protection of Blue's light, fearful of both the hunters and their own reactions to the bloodlust in the air.

As they neared the settlement the roaring voice of Master Farnham asked why her clan shouldn't kill them right now.

"We didn't want to come," Crista's father yelled back. "The plague bird forced us. She has your daughter."

Silence paused the night. Derena motioned for the villagers to continue.

When they reached the old road, Crista saw the hunters pacing back and forth in an agitated state. If they'd been scary in the daylight, now they were terrifying. Their eyes glowed fire and their throats crackled in hungry growls and moans.

Fight. Blood. Flee.

Crista bit her lip to silence her instincts. She watched as Master Farnham stepped before them, a massive ceramic sword in her right hand. The clan leader leaned over and kissed her daughter, who sat in the dust and rubble of the road with her hands tied. Master Farnham also sniffed Beu and nodded slightly before facing Derena.

"You've no right invading our lands when the night has our blood up," Master Farnham yelled.

"Couldn't wait," Derena said. "I can't restrain my AI for much longer."

Master Farnham's fierce face melted into a look of fear. Crista's father and the other villagers stepped away from the plague bird. A few of the hunters fled into the darkness.

Betrayal! Blood! Blood!

The wolf in Crista screamed as she realized what was about to happen. She swung her crutch and smashed it across the plague bird's face, knocking Derena to the ground. "I won't do it," Crista yelled. "I won't become one of you."

Derena smiled grimly. "Like I said, the choice is always yours."

Derena pulled a knife from its sheath and delicately cut her own throat, blood spraying in a fire-tracing arch. At the same time the scars on Derena's chest ripped apart, no longer able to hold together. Crista froze in shock as the blood AI embraced freedom. Even Blue's illumination dimmed before the blood, the village AI fearing what was to come.

Derena's head flopped dead onto the broken road, blank eyes staring at Crista. Crista knew she was being tricked, knew the game being played against her. But she also felt the rage rising from the blood AI as it licked its way around the hunters and villagers. She felt it caress Beu and the hunter girl. Saw it judge the worth of her father and Master Farnham.

Flee! the wolf begged Crista.

"No," she told herself. In a louder voice, she screamed, "Not them! Me!"

The blood AI turned and tasted her body, testing her resolve to defy its power. She again ordered it to enter her. Red Day, that was its name. She knew the name deep in her body as the AI's essence licked her meat and brain and soul.

"Do it!" she screamed as Red Day flowed into her skin and mouth and feasted on her blood. Crista fell to the broken road and rolled in pain as the AI bound itself to her—gene to gene, atom to atom, blood to blood. She saw ten thousand years of its judgments. Saw every human and AI condemned by this entity of purest right and wrong.

Desperate not to be overwhelmed, Crista fought back, aided by her wolf. She bit and tore into the AI, refusing to show throat, screaming that she was in charge. That there would be no judgments without her.

You're a fighter, Red Day said. *I love devouring fighters.*

Crista felt the wolf in her weakening and knew if she gave in the AI would overwhelm her. She reached for something—anything—to fight back with. She remembered the plague bird who had killed her mother. Even though Blue and everyone else believed it wasn't a true memory, this was her chance to know.

I want to know who killed my mother, she screamed in her mind at the AI. The wolf in her rose back up, defiant, demanding to know the truth.

Red Day paused its assault, puzzled. Crista felt the AI probing her memories. *That is curious,* it said. *Did a plague bird kill your mother or did you imagine it? I like puzzles. Very well. Work with me, and we'll find out who or what killed your mother. But first we deal with Ashdyd and those in the Veil who dared attack me.*

Crista felt the AI settling down in her body as the wolf in her also calmed.

Wolf and girl and blood AI. Balance. A good three-fold balance.

You'll do well, Red Day whispered in her mind. *You'll do well indeed.*

Crista woke to her father shaking her body, repeating her name over and over. However, she heard him as if listening to whispers spoken far across a plowed field. As if she now controlled her body like the harness and reins controlled Eggbeater.

Crista stood up. The hunters and villagers stared at her with fear. Even Blue floated away.

Crista stretched her injured leg that moved without pain for the first time since Beu's attack. She walked over to Derena, whose once red hair now shone black. The glowing red line on her brown face was also gone, replaced by a calm expression that Crista had never before seen on the woman.

Crista pulled the red vest and shirt and trousers off Derena's body and dressed in the forbidden colors. She strapped the twin ceramic knives to her thighs and pulled one knife free. In the blade's mirror sheen she saw her face. A glowing red line ran from her right eye to lips. Her hair burned the brightest red.

She turned to Beu and the hunter girl. Ms. Pauler cried and tried to stop Crista, but Master Farnham held the woman back. However, instead of killing Beu and the girl, Crista cut their bonds. She pointed the knife at Beu.

"You will never return to the village," she said. "You'll live with Master Farnham's clan. Assuming Master Farnham has nothing to say against that and lets the villagers return home in peace."

Master Farnham kneeled before Crista and thanked her, joined by a grateful Ms. Pauler. Beu and the hunter girl held hands and bowed. Beu looked at Crista with a mix of love and regret and obsession, but those emotions fled as Crista allowed the blood AI to lick into him and whisper this was his final chance.

You'll never again treat anyone as you did me, she said directly into Beu's mind. *Do so, and I'll kill you.*

The urine tang of fear scented Beu's body and his bandana burned to the yellow-grays of terror.

Crista turned from Beu in disgust. She no longer cared what he'd done to her—only what he did to others in the future.

She looked at her father, whose tears streaked the dust in his beard. Right now she couldn't handle speaking with her father. Soon, perhaps, but not now.

I don't want them seeing me, she thought. Red Day rumbled her blood and reached out to the villagers and hunters. People glanced around nervously, trying to see where she'd gone.

Only Blue still saw her. Crista looked at the AI and saw past its cloud of light and distortions. Saw its consciousness extending into other dimensions and across time. Saw its overriding dedication to returning humanity to what they'd once been.

"You knew," she said to Blue. "You knew Derena would do this to me."

I couldn't stop her, Blue said softly, sadness flooding its mind. *I pleaded with her not to do this, but she wouldn't listen. But maybe this is for the best. If you'd stayed, Beu would have killed you, and she'd have killed Beu. This way you both live.*

The wolf growled. What right did Blue or Derena have to decide her fate like that? To calm Crista, Red Day whispered a truth. That in order for humanity to truly return to the way they'd been, AIs like Blue would have to cease being the protective gods of every village. When those days arrived, it would be as easy to kill Blue as for Crista's old body to crush an egg.

Blue sensed the blood AI's thoughts and shrank in fear from Crista. Red Day laughed.

"I'll be keeping a close eye on this village," Crista told Blue. "Don't disappoint me."

With that she walked down the trail, the night scents mingling to Red Day's whispers, until she didn't care at all which part of her was human or wolf or plague bird.

GOODBYES

The man silently plowed the field with his mule, the animal working without protest. Almost like the mule sensed the man's distress and had no desire to give more pain.

He's not just a man, Crista thought, standing on the edge of the field. *He's my father.*

Not any more, Red Day whispered. *Think of him objectively as a random man. You're beyond family now.*

Crista looked at her father—no, the man, as Red Day said to think, the man now only a few yards away but oblivious to her presence. *No,* she thought again, shaking her head, still growing accustomed to this other creature living inside her. *He's my father. He'll always be my father.*

Red Day sighed, but didn't say anything else.

Crista fell into stride beside her father as Eggbeater and the plow passed by. She'd spent the last few days wandering the forest in a daze as she grew used to having an AI living inside her. However, Red Day said they couldn't waste any more time waiting for her to acclimate. They were leaving the area this evening to continue the investigation into Ashdyd and the Veil.

But she couldn't leave her father without a proper goodbye.

"I love you, Dad," Crista whispered, Red Day removing enough of its manipulation of her father's senses that he heard her. To his credit, her father didn't jump in shock. But Crista hadn't expected him to.

"I'd hoped to speak with you before you left," he said. "I don't suppose I can see you too."

"I don't want you to see me like this."

"Who cares what you look like?"

Crista smiled as Eggbeater brayed softly. While the mule couldn't see or hear

Crista, he sensed the change in her father's mood. "Eggbeater seems well behaved," she said.

"Damn animal's depressed. He misses you."

Ordering Red Day to let Eggbeater hear her, Crista whispered hello in the mule's right ear. The mule kicked once but calmed down as Crista ran her fingers through his mane.

"Where will you go?" her father asked.

"East. Derena was on a mission that Red Day and I must complete."

Her father started to ask who Red Day was before realizing and closing his mouth. "Will you come back?"

"Wouldn't be appropriate. People might question my judgments." Crista didn't add that Red Day said they could resume patrolling her home village in a few centuries once people forgot her father and herself. Until then, she was supposed to leave this village to the oversight of other plague birds.

"In that case," her father said, lowering his voice, "you must visit the city of Seed. There's a building in the city called the Obsidian Rise. Your mother told me that if you ever left our village, you should go there."

Crista stared at her father in shock. How did he know so much about Seed when he'd been born and raised in Day's End? And why would her mother say that?

"I don't understand ..."

Her usually straightforward father looked down, unable to explain himself. "Your mother never shared why," he said. "I wish I could tell more."

That sounded reasonable, Crista realized, but...

He's lying, Red Day said. *Want me to dig deeper and find out why?*

No! she shouted in her mind. She refused to let the AI play with her father's mind.

"I don't know," Crista told her father.

"Do this, please," her father said. "Your mother ... wanted you to stay in Day's End. But she also said life doesn't always go as planned. That if you ever left, you had to visit Seed."

Her father's hands shook, and she realized he was barely maintaining control of his wolf side. He was both desperate to tell her more and unable to. She scented fear rising from her father. Crista wondered if he was afraid of telling her something he'd promised Mom he'd never reveal, or if her father was simply afraid of what Crista had become.

Red Day repeated that it could slip deeper into her father's mind and learn the truth. There would be nothing about her father Crista wouldn't know. Crista was tempted—her father was keeping something from her. But how could she rip into all he was?

No, she decided. She was better off not knowing. Crista blinked away tears, making her glad her father couldn't see her. "I'll do it," she said. "I'll visit Seed."

"Thank you."

Crista stepped closer to her father. "I'm going to find the plague bird who killed Mom," she whispered.

"I'm sure you will," her father said. "Keep to who you are and don't give in to fear. If you do, life will go just fine."

Crista smiled as she remembered her mother giving similar advice. She hugged her father and kissed him on his bearded cheek. Then, not wanting to lose total control, she ran across the fields without looking back.

INTERLUDE

SPIDER HOLES

(A MONTH AFTER LEAVING HER VILLAGE)

A spider hole! A spider hole!

As Crista stared into the moonlit grotto below her, she remembered the chant she and Beu sang as kids whenever they found a tiny trapdoor spider's lair. They'd sing, "A spider hole, a spider hole! Poke it, trick it, make the spider eat it!" as they tapped a blade of grass before the door to trick the spider into emerging.

Crista and Beu never succeeded. Spiders always knew the difference between kids playing and insects to be snatched for food.

The chant rang through Crista's mind as she searched for a much larger trapdoor monster hiding in the grotto before her. According to Red Day, the man living here ambushed passing prey. Mainly deer and other larger animals, the AI had noted, but in more recent years his prey included humans.

Looking at the peaceful scene before her, Crista had trouble believing this could be a place of death. Set into the gentle rise of a tree-covered hill, the grotto was only a few dozen yards wide, like a giant bowl tipped on its side. A small waterfall flowed from the grotto's upper lip and splashed into a cattail and lily pad filled pool. She watched an orange carp jump out of the pool, aiming for, but missing, a dragonfly. Its splash stirred the pool to ripples.

Lilacs and daylilies covered the grotto's sides, blowing a sweet scent to the night air. Ripple grass—a gened plant that never grew longer than a child's hand and waved seductively to passing breezes—covered the grotto's floor. A perfectly swept pebble pathway led into the grotto and circled the pool before stopping in front of a stone statue of the Child.

Crista didn't recognize this version of the Child. As usual the statue was of an ungened old-style human child with a happy grin. But this Child statue seemed far older and better carved than the one in her home village's shrine. The statue felt alive. As if the Child had only paused to rest after playing all day.

The statue, pool, grass, and flowers created an immense feeling of peace in Crista, like she'd stumbled onto a sacred place from the ancient world.

That's exactly the feeling the man wishes to create, Red Day said.

Where is he? I don't see him.

Crista's vision shifted, the peaceful moonlit grotto turning red as a mix of infrared and night-vision lit her eyes. She saw the outline of a trapdoor built into the back of the grotto, along with thin lines of silk reaching from the door to various points across the beautiful garden.

Tripwires, she realized. Red Day increased her hearing, and she heard a deep breathing rising and falling behind the trap door. *Something is waiting. No, not something. Someone.*

Red Day agreed with her assessment. Over the past month, as Crista had adjusted to her new powers, they'd observed a number of nearby villages and hunt clans. These trips were part of Red Day's nearly insufferable plague bird lessons, in this case teaching her how to act when the AI hid her from people's senses. But it also provided an opportunity to watch for crimes along with any clues about Ashdyd or the Veil.

Thankfully, Crista didn't witness anyone commit a crime where she'd have to kill the lawbreaker. But they had detected a worrying scent of fear in several of the villages and hunt clans they'd visited, with parents continually warning kids not to go off by themselves while elders spoke of adults who'd wandered away and never returned.

Crista learned the truth while snooping on several children whispering to one another in the point-blank manner of kids: There was a monster in the hills.

Intrigued, Crista and Red Day searched for the monster, wondering if it might be one of the Veil. Their search brought them to this grotto. While they hadn't found the Veil, they'd discovered someone almost as disturbing.

You really think this man killed all those people? Crista asked.

Yes, including several children, Red Day pointed out.

Crista sighed. Since becoming a plague bird, she'd tried putting off judging—and executing—anyone. She wondered if Red Day's desire to hunt this so-called monster resulted from the AI wanting to ease her into her new-found duties by having her judge a simple case of purest evil.

How should we do this? Crista asked, resigned to no longer avoiding her duty.

We need the man to come out so we can judge him. This hill and grotto are not natural. There's an ancient building under here, long since covered by soil and vegetation. That trapdoor appears to be the only way in or out.

Crista ordered Red Day to stop manipulating the man's senses. Now that she could be seen and felt, she stepped into the grotto and stood by the pool. The carp jumped for another dragonfly, this time catching it. Beside Crista's right foot ran spider-thread leading to the trap door. Crista tapped the silk with her boot.

The trapdoor burst open and a massive figure lunged for Crista. The wolf in

Crista yelped and tried to jump away but the man—who was larger than a bear, at least three times Crista's height and nearly that in width—collapsed onto her, pinning her to the ripple grass. As Crista struggled, she realized the man wasn't truly fast or strong and instead used surprise and the initial burst of his body to pin his victims down. Crista felt a sharp burn as the man bit her arm and a paralyzing poison spread into her veins. Her body went numb, unable to move. She was powerless to stop the man from dragging her back to his hiding hole and slowly eating her alive.

You finished playing? Red Day asked. *Or would you prefer to be eaten?*

With a curse, Crista realized the AI was right. She'd been thinking like a human and had forgotten to access Red Day's power. Doing so, Crista felt the numbing poison break down in her body and disappear. She lifted the giant man off her body and threw him out of the grotto, sending him tumbling down the hill until he rested against an adolescent steel oak.

Crista strode forward, angry at being attacked. The man took a startled look at his intended victim and, seeing the forbidden red clothes and hair and burning line on Crista's face, moaned and fell to his knees. Crista grabbed his shoulders and lifted him up.

"Didn't know you were a plague bird," the man whimpered. "Truly didn't."

Crista stared into the man's face, which was set low on his body so his eyes and nose and mouth grew from his chest instead of a neck. Venom dripped from the man's mouth and he stank so bad Crista couldn't scent his gened heritage.

Repulsed by the man and angry at being attacked, Crista pulled a knife and raised it to the man's throat, or where she guessed his throat would be if he'd been more typically human.

No killing, Red Day chided. *At least, not until after judgment.*

Remembering what Red Day taught her, Crista pricked the tip of her finger with her knife and pressed the bloody spot to the man's head. The man yelped and fell to the ground as the AI accessed his memories.

Crista instantly knew the man as well as she knew herself. She saw his life—born to hunt parents but left as an infant in a village because, owing to his unusual body, hunt clans wouldn't have let him live. When none of the villagers wanted to raise the ugly child, the village AI took pity on him and sheltered and cared for the baby.

As the man grew so did his grotesque nature. At age four he was the size of a full-grown human; by age ten twice that size. He grew so big he could barely walk, his body being gened to an initial jump to pin his prey. The villagers took this ability and the fact that his fingers could spin silken threads to mean he was descended from spiders. The village AI counseled the villagers, pointing out every human alive today counted as their ancestors both the scientists who'd gened them and the animals who provided the genes. No one path was responsible for the truth of any particular human.

But the villagers didn't listen to their AI. They refused to even name the man. Because of this treatment the man grew up both feared and hated. When he was old enough he left the village.

It took him three days to hobble a league. A month to walk to where no one knew of him. He ate sparingly of the food he'd packed but eventually ate it all. Weeks later he collapsed beside a small creek, so weak he couldn't crawl to the water to drink.

The man lay there for days. The forest's squirrels and foxes and rabbits avoided him, as did members of the hunt who passed nearby. The man cursed being created so everyone feared him.

Then a strange person walked up to him. The man couldn't truly see this stranger because his body was covered in distortions, causing the man to believe he was hallucinating. When the person leaned over him, a face that wasn't a face shimmered above his own. The man almost believed he was staring into a face full of stars.

Without a word the stranger picked up the man and carried him through the forest.

The next day they arrived in the grotto, where the distorted stranger laid the man down. The stranger walked away for a few minutes and returned with several dead rabbits, which the man swallowed raw.

The stranger brought the man more food and as his strength returned, the man looked around the grotto. A tangle of dead trees and vines hid the place, and the pond stank from centuries of decay and waste. But the man saw that this had once been a place of beauty. A statue of a normal, human child—made of ancient nanotech and looking like the historic images of old-time humans he'd seen in the village school—smiled at him from the dirt where it'd fallen.

The man watched as the stranger's distortion's flowed out and cut down the dead trees in the grotto and cleared out the pond's waste. Each time the stranger used his powers the buzz of static ran through the man's mind, a static tasting of rainbow colors.

The stranger also pointed toward the back of the grotto, causing a hidden opening to erupt from under the dirt and rocks. The man realized there was an ancient building under the hill, which would be a good place to both live and ambush prey.

Once the distorted stranger did all this he walked away. Neither the stranger nor the man had said a single word to the other. The man wanted to thank the stranger but also feared doing so. For the first time he understood how other people felt when they saw him.

Grateful for his new chance at life, the man retreated to the hidden entrance and waited.

His first meal was a fawn, spotted and unwary and sipping the now-clear waters of the pond.

Once he fed, he used ancient tools from the buried building to dig out the roots and weeds from the grotto. He roamed the surrounding woods and valleys searching for flowers and ripple grass, which he transplanted into the grotto's soil. From a nearby river he picked small, perfectly rounded pebbles and created a path through the grotto. He caught carp and released them into the pond. Each time he sprang from his hole to catch a deer, he swept the pebble path and cleaned the pond of blood. He took comfort in this routine.

The first time another human found the grotto, he watched warily from his hiding place. The young woman was of the hunt, and the man wondered if she might know his parents. But he didn't reveal himself. When the woman kneeled before the grotto's statue—perhaps saying a little prayer—the man smiled at what he'd achieved.

For the next two decades the man ate well and tended his garden. He watched with pleasure the increasing numbers of villagers and hunters who stopped by the grotto, often kneeling before the statue of the smiling child. From snatches of overheard conversations he realized people prayed to have a normal child. They desired children with fewer signs of the gened pox that played with the genetic makeup of these people and their families.

These were prayers the man truly appreciated, and he took even greater care of the garden.

But in his 22nd year in the grotto, trouble appeared as a band of razors moved into the area. Descended from gene-hacked coyotes, razors were fast and aggressive. While razors rarely threatened humans, they tended to kill all the deer in an area before their pack moved on.

Within a year the deer were gone and the man was starving. By slowing his metabolism and not moving, he could go for months without eating. But even such slow living had its limits. Without the deer that drank from the pond, he would have no choice but to leave the grotto. But doing so filled him with more fear than starving to death.

One winter day an old woman walked into the grotto. The snapping of the man's spider threads woke him from his metabolic stupor, and he peered at his visitor.

The old woman stopped before the statue and bowed. The man vaguely remembered her as having previously visited the grotto. As she prayed before the statue, the man's body shook from hunger. He could starve to death, or eat. Starve, or eat. He stared at the woman, forcing himself to remember the taunts and abuse the villagers used to shout at him. He remembered a woman who looked somewhat like this one, who'd stared into his misshapen face and laughed...laughed...while saying he should kill himself to spare the world such horror.

With a scream of pain, the man exploded from his hiding hole and grabbed the woman in mid-prayer.

From there the killings were easier. He only killed as needed. Whenever the occasional deer or other animal gave him enough meat to live, he left people alone. To force himself to remember the sins he was committing, he placed the bare skulls of his victims on a large nanoteched pedestal within his cave. He'd once dreamed of dragging the pedestal into the garden and placing the statue of the Child upon it. But the pedestal had been too heavy to move, so it became his personal shrine to his own evil. He woke looking at the skulls. He fell asleep looking at them. He gave each one names—something he'd never had. He asked for their forgiveness and ...

... Crista gasped and fell backwards, collapsing into the dirt before the man. She hadn't known the connection would be so intimate. That she'd experience the man's actual memories.

This is fortuitous, Red Day said. *We've found new evidence of the Veil.*

Crista realized Red Day meant the distorted stranger. *I thought only the faces of the Veil were covered by distortions.*

True. But the rainbow static this man felt—that was what Derena and I experienced when we were attacked. And Ashdyd's entire body is evidently covered in distortions. Red Day giggled inside Crista. *Enough chitchat. This man is guilty. Release me.*

Crista stood as she stared at the man, whose eyes bore into her with fear and pleading.

We can't kill him, Crista protested. *He only did what he needed to survive.*

He killed innocent people, Red Day screamed in her mind. *He killed children. If we don't kill him, he'll kill again.*

Crista knew Red Day was right—she was sympathetic from experiencing this man's life. She also didn't want to kill anyone. Didn't want to do the job she had to do.

Red Day sighed. *It's ... hard, the first time you must do our sacred duty. And this is also the first time you've seen life through another's eyes. That gives rise to complicated feelings. But remember what this man did. Even he knows he did wrong.*

Crista looked again at the monstrous man, who wiped tears from his eyes. This was the moment, Crista realized. She'd either do her new duty or say no and fight Red Day every moment from here on. If she didn't do her duty the AI would likely not honor its pledge to help her find the plague bird who killed her mother.

Crista looked at the grotto. During her short fight with this man the statue of the Child had been knocked over while the pebbles in the path around the pond were scattered and the flowers torn and broken.

Crista squatted beside the man. "Your grotto is beautiful," she said.

The man sniffed. "Thank you."

"I have to kill you. You know that, right?"

The man bowed his body twice. This was, Crista realized, his way of nodding without a neck.

"However," Crista said, "I can give you time to clean up the grotto. To leave it how you wish." She thought back through the man's memories and remembered his unrealized desire to drag the nanoteched pedestal into the garden and place the Child statue on it. "I'll even carry the pedestal out for you."

Red Day grumbled in her mind but didn't say anything. The man, though, lowered himself flat on the ground before Crista and thanked her. "May the Child bless you," he said. "May the Child forever bless you."

The man walked slowly into his lair and returned with a bone-tipped wooden rake, which he used to smooth out the pebble pathway. He also replanted those flowers that had been torn up.

Crista, meanwhile, walked through his lair. Red Day was right—this had been an ancient building, long since buried by soil and vegetation. Built of refined nano blocks, the building had held its shape through the long eons underground.

Crista found the pedestal—which stood half as tall as her—beside the tattered pile of leathers the man slept on. She carried out the skulls of the man's victims and buried them beside the garden. Then Red Day powered up her body, and she carried the pedestal outside.

When she asked where to put the pedestal, the man pointed to the lair's entrance. Crista closed the trap door and placed the pedestal before it and the statue on the pedestal. Now no one would be able to enter the building and ambush people.

The man frowned. "My garden won't stay nice," he said. "The forest will soon take it."

"I'll ask the nearby villagers and hunt clans to look after the grotto."

The man started to protest—to say he doubted they'd do that—before realizing no one turned down a request from a plague bird.

"I'm ready," he said. "And I'm sorry for what I did."

"I know," Crista said.

Crista raised a knife to her wrist, the blade shaking from what she had to do. Not only at killing this man but also at slicing her own body in a way that, before becoming a plague bird, meant a painful death. *I'm no longer human,* she thought, the blade resting against her wrist. Red Day began to say something. Not wanting to hear the AI's damn words, Crista gritted her teeth and sliced her wrist open to the bone. Her blood shot out as she sat down hard on the ground, the wolf in her howling in shock at both the pain and what she'd done to herself.

Despite her shock, she remembered to order Red Day to kill the man painlessly.

She thought the AI would protest but it simply knocked the man out. As his body fell backwards, the AI caught him. Red Day's mist of blood glowed hotter and hotter until the body burst into flames, ash and embers falling up into the sky where they cooled and rained back across the grotto.

Once the body was gone, Red Day returned to her cut wrist and healed her skin and muscle. The wolf in Crista whimpered, knowing she'd followed a path she could never leave.

The villagers and hunt clans won't like maintaining a place where their family and friends were killed, Red Day said.

I won't tell them that. I'll simply say we killed the murderer and buried the remains of his victims here.

Crista looked again at the statue of the Child. *Can you carve words into nano?* she asked.

Will it bring a faster end to this touchy-feely affair? Then yes, I can.

Pricking her finger, Crista wrote the words "Blessed are those without a name" on the pedestal with blood. Red Day burned the words into the nearly unbreakable material.

Feeling at peace, Crista sat down on the pebble pathway and watched the carp splash in the pond.

Our next killing won't go like this, Red Day stated. *I gave you this one as a gift—an offering of friendship, if you will—but I will not kill painlessly again. Our killings are meant to inspire fear and dread in a world that otherwise wouldn't follow a single law.*

We'll see, Crista thought, refusing to let the AI spoil this moment.

No, you'll see. Red Day paused, debating how much to say. *You are … unlike any previous host I've lived with.*

Well, you picked me.

Yes, but usually my hosts are not so averse to bloodshed. You're part wolf. Why do you hate killing?

Maybe I hate being forced to do this type of killing.

We … might still be a good match. But this will only work if we both make an effort.

You're welcome to leave anytime. I won't stop you.

That's not possible. Once a plague bird, always one. Besides, I thought you wanted to discover the truth about your mother's killer.

Crista felt a twinge in her gut, an emotion flowing over from Red Day as if the AI was somehow lying to her.

Are you hiding something? Crista asked.

You still want the villagers and hunt clans to take care of this grotto? Red Day asked quickly, changing the subject.

Yes.

Then let's tell them. I find this place disturbing.

Crista looked around the grotto—from the statue of the Child to the pebble path to the flowers and the pond—and wondered how such a peaceful scene could disturb Red Day. Realizing she likely didn't want to know the answer, she stood up and hiked to the nearest village.

PART II

ENTER THE HANDSOME WARRIOR MONK

Crista lay on a village green under the warm autumn sun, the grass tickling her body and the happy people around her making her feel almost human. Even though no one saw or scented her—as far as these villagers were concerned she didn't exist—Crista enjoyed lazing here. The wolf inside her whimpered like a puppy, begging to roll across the warm grass.

Of course, rolling in the grass wasn't proper for a plague bird, even an unseen one. Crista giggled as she imagined Red Day's shriek of fury if she gave in to her lupine urge to play.

She'd traveled hard the last six months and wanted to relax. After learning someone connected with the Veil—maybe even Ashdyd—had helped the man living in the grotto, she and Red Day had traveled in the direction the veiled man was last seen walking. They'd found no more clues despite searching across the region. Now they rested before resuming their original journey toward the city of Seed.

Crista rolled on her side to watch a group of kids kick their ball across the village green. The kids laughed and howled as they chased the ball, weaving in and out of doting parents and neighbors. One kid kicked the ball free and charged toward Crista. He was a tall teenager who smelled like a cat-human hybrid, with cat ears and brown cheetah spots on his face. He flaunted his speed and perfect coordination as he raced ahead of the others.

Unless he changed direction he'd stumble right over Crista.

Crista didn't move. Instead, the boy with perfect coordination tripped over his own feet, causing him to face plant in the grass as the ball bounced over Crista's head.

The other kids laughed and ran to their friend, who grinned as they helped him up, unsure why he'd tripped but too good natured to care. The village's artificial intelligence, whose cloud of charged energy floated along the edge of the green, sparkled warm pastel colors of amusement.

As play resumed the kids jumped all around Crista, always changing their footfalls at the last moment so no one actually stepped on her, let alone saw or scented her body. As the kids laughed Crista clapped her hands loudly, daring them to hear her.

Glad you're enjoying yourself, Red Day muttered in her thoughts. *You have any idea how hard it is to erase your presence from the minds of so many people? And don't get me started on blocking you from that AI's senses.*

Crista grinned and clapped again. Red Day grumbled in disgust.

As the kids ran to the other side of the green—with the cheetah-faced boy kicking the ball through their AI's sparkling cloud—Crista laughed. Since becoming a plague bird she hadn't relaxed around other people. She'd judged a handful. Had killed the guilty and enforced the laws of this land while searching for Ashdyd and the Veil. But actually being at peace with other people no longer happened since she'd left home.

Closing her eyes, Crista daydreamed of her distant village. Remembered back when people still cared about her. Back when she'd known instinctively where she belonged.

Crista drifted in and out of sleep. She wondered what her father was doing. Probably repairing harnesses in the village barn, like he did most afternoons. And that asshole Beu was likely enjoying his new life with the hunt. Maybe he and his girlfriend were touching even now, something else people no longer wanted to do with Crista.

Irritated at wasting a glorious moment by remembering Beu, Crista rolled on her side and told herself to forget about that jerk.

She woke an hour later to a worrisome scent floating on the wind. Crista's ears also perked up at no longer hearing the kids playing. In fact, the entire village green had fallen silent.

Crista, an irritant has chanced upon us, Red Day whispered.

Crista opened her eyes to see a young man in a purple robe standing near the village AI. The man looked like no human hybrid Crista had ever seen. He stood tall, at least two and a half yards, with broad shoulders and big muscles and a thin peach fuzz of blond fur covering his dark skin. He wore a large backpack, suggesting he'd traveled a ways, and a sword.

While he looked mostly human, even tying his long blond hair into a ponytail reaching to his waist, he obviously wasn't. As Crista watched the man's fur and clothing rippled and turned partially invisible, only a faint flicker of distorted light showing where he stood.

The villagers whispered nervously as the man growled and smacked an egg-shaped ceramic device in his giant right hand. His body and robe reappeared, causing new ripples of astonishment from the villagers, along with wariness and surprise.

"Who is he?" Crista asked Red Day.

The purple robe indicates a monk of the Order of Registries. They're responsible for maintaining records until humanity is once again human. Crista felt the blood AI debating how much to tell her. *Their monks are outside the jurisdiction of plague birds.*

Crista was shocked—she hadn't known there were people she had no power over.

There's plenty you don't know about our world, Red Day said arrogantly. *I'd have naturally schooled you on such details when the need arose.*

Crista ignored Red Day's barb as the man stepped forward. He bowed politely to the villagers and their AI but didn't speak. Staring at the ceramic egg in his hand, he walked across the green, aiming straight for Crista. The villagers, still wary but also curious, followed him like sheep after a beguiling shepherd.

"Can he see me?" Crista asked.

No, Red Day said. *I'm manipulating his senses. But that device he's holding is shielded and connects directly to his nervous system. Want me to rip deeper into his mind? I could force him to turn around, or change the inputs he's receiving from the device.*

Crista told Red Day to stand down. The man stopped two yards from Crista and bowed deeply. "Plague bird, I apologize for disturbing you but I have a request to make."

Crista sighed as she stood up. The villagers tittered nervously, wondering if the stranger was right about a plague bird being among them.

Well, you wanted to spend more time with people, Red Day said with a sarcastic giggle.

Crista told Red Day to kiss off as the AI stopped manipulating everyone's senses. The villagers shrieked when they saw her. Only the robed man didn't blanch. He smiled sincerely, pleased to make Crista's introduction.

"What do you want?" Crista demanded.

"It's my monastery," the man said. "We have a problem only a plague bird can handle."

THE MONK'S NAME WAS DESIADA. CRISTA SAT WITH HIM UNDER A NEARBY STEEL OAK AS she nibbled the loaf of fresh bread the villagers had gifted them before retreating to the other side of the green. The villagers stood there talking excitedly, trying to both stare and not stare at Crista and the stranger.

"Here's our problem," Desiada said as he swallowed a bite of bread. "The Order of Registries keeps all human knowledge safe, but something is manipulating our data. Small aspects, mind you. Insignificant, really. But we need it stopped."

"Who's doing this?" Crista asked.

"Not certain. My abbot hoped you might uncover what we've failed to discern."

"But why ask a plague bird?"

"The entity appears to be human. My abbot saw the person once—a regular sized human but covered in distortions. Since plague birds are responsible for human laws, the abbot said you should deal with this."

The wolf in Crista growled softly. *How convenient,* she muttered to Red Day. *Here we are, about to give up our search for the Veil around here and this turns up.*

Tell him we'll help.

Why? Doesn't this stink of a trap?

It does indeed. But sometimes the best trap is to walk into someone else's trap.

You can't seriously believe that.

Fine, Red Day said. *But it's the first lead we've had since the grotto. Besides, plague birds are almost never allowed into the Order of Registries. The monastery's archives may have records about the Veil or Ashdyd.*

"I'm glad to help," Crista told Desiada, fighting to keep sarcasm out of her voice.

"You should know this mission may be dangerous," Desiada said. "The path to our monastery is risky. Perhaps you heard about the last plague bird we invited in over nine centuries ago. He was seriously injured."

"What happened?"

"The plague bird's entire left side was cut off. But don't worry—he's *alright* now."

Desiada erupted in a loud, barking laugh as Red Day gagged in Crista's mind.

"That's a horrible joke," Crista said, snickering despite herself.

"Technically it's a pun. But thank you for the compliment of laughing. Most people hate my sense of humor."

Crista liked this monk, even if he was leading her into a possible trap. "Can you show me the route to your monastery?" she asked.

Desiada pulled the ceramic egg from his pocket, which cast a map into the air before them. His monastery, called Down Hope, lay a week's hike from the village. The map showed they'd cross something called a barrier forest—the forest glowed red on the map, indicating severe danger—before reaching the monastery itself, which rested at the top of a sheer mountain rising half a league into the sky.

The wolf in Crista whined at the thought of climbing that high. Worse, Desiada wouldn't tell Crista any more details about the data this distorted human was accessing. That again suggested a very elaborate trap.

But to her surprise, the prospect of the trap didn't worry Red Day. Instead, Red Day appeared more worried about the forest they'd have to cross. She asked what was wrong, but the AI ignored her.

Picking up on Crista's discomfort, Desiada bowed slightly and apologized. "Is any of this a concern?" he asked.

"Not at all. I'm a plague bird. Nothing scares me."

Red Day chuckled approval at the lie.

You think he's working with the Veil? Crista asked Red Day.

I couldn't say.

Why?

Because I don't know enough about the Order of Registries to even guess if they're tied in with the Veil. Unless invited, we're forbidden to interfere in the monastery's work just as they're forbidden to interfere with other humans and AIs. The Order has survived because not much is known about them.

Crista understood. While people had been attempting to regain their lost humanity for ten thousand years, most humans were still extremely dangerous. For a group dedicated to preserving knowledge in a harsh world, remaining hidden would be a good thing.

However, Desiada's massive muscles and the sword he carried also indicated these monks could fight. When she asked Desiada about this, he grinned.

"It's true," he said. "We prefer to hide, hence the light-bending camouflage my body utilizes. But sometimes we've no choice but to fight."

"I've heard that claim before," Crista said, remembering the hunt-clan elder she'd executed several days ago. The woman had rationalized killing an entire family by claiming they'd plotted against her rule and she had no other choice. Red Day had taken particular offense at that statement and when Crista released the AI, it ate the woman's body molecule by molecule, leaving her nervous system intact until the last moment so she felt every morsel of pain.

Crista frowned at the memory. Sensing her pain, Desiada leaned over and pulled her into a hug with one of his massive arms. Crista froze in shock, as did the watching villagers. Since becoming a plague bird the only time she'd touched other humans was when she caressed their memories or killed them.

Desiada released her from the gentle hug. "My apologies for hugging without asking, but it appeared you needed one."

Crista blushed. "Thank you. Most people don't take kindly to touching plague birds."

"Doesn't bother me. Besides, I've long yearned to speak with someone outside our Order. I mean, you haven't heard any of my jokes!"

Crista punched Desiada playfully in the arm as Red Day sighed. *Should I warn you about the elevation of hormones you're experiencing, or is that self-evident even to your limited senses?*

Crista told the AI to go to hell.

CRISTA AND DESIADA LEFT THE VILLAGE, MUCH TO THE RELIEF OF THE VILLAGERS AND their AI. Only the kids seemed sad—it wasn't every day a plague bird and a stranger who could turn invisible passed through their lives. The cheetah boy and his friends sneaked after Crista and Desiada for the first few hours, no doubt defying orders from their parents. The kids shrieked in excitement and hid in the bushes whenever Crista glanced back at them.

"They're too boneheaded to know they should run from me," Crista muttered when the kids finally turned for home.

"Perhaps," Desiada said. "Or maybe they seized this opportunity to see if you're truly worth fearing. When I was growing up, my sister and I did the same, constantly testing the dangers around us. I wouldn't have become a monk without taking such risks."

"Growing up in a monastery is dangerous?"

"My people don't grow up in the Order," Desiada said bitterly. "We have to prove ourselves worthy of joining. Even then we have little choice."

"What do you mean?"

Desiada closed his mouth, irritated at saying too much. *He didn't mean to tell you about his childhood,* Red Day said, stating the extremely obvious.

"We're not supposed to talk about our pre-monastery lives with outsiders," Desiada said in a low voice. "Let's just say the only path my people are ever given is to try entering the Order. That's all we fight for and all we can see."

Crista started to ask what happened to Desiada's sister—if she also became a monk—but Red Day reminded her the Order of Registries was not governed by plague bird rules. *Don't inquire too deeply into his affairs. All we can do is offer our assistance when requested.*

Not wishing to speak any more about his people, Desiada instead talked about his studies. "My specialty is ancient humor," he said. "Even though I'm only 19, I'm already the Order's expert on puns and jokes. For example, do you know what type of humor has thrived since humanity's earliest days?"

"Never given it any thought."

Desiada reached one of his massive hands under his armpit and made a farting sound. "Bodily functions. Flatulence. Sex. All those nasty excretions we make. People have laughed at that since the dawn of humanity, and they'll still be laughing the day we go extinct."

Crista stared at Desiada, who by his size looked like he could defeat half the world in mortal combat. But the subject of bodily humor left him grinning like a child quietly passing gas in a village school.

"Is the study of flatulence humor in high demand within your Order?"

"Err, my studies have not exactly endeared me to my abbot. In fact, my most recent scholarly presentation might be the reason the abbot selected me for this mission. I'm sure it was her way of giving the other monks a break from my humor."

"What did you do?"

"I used a few sound effects to highlight my talk on gastrointestinal humor."

Crista laughed.

For the next hour Crista and Desiada shared all the dirty jokes they knew, much to Red Day's irritation.

Too bad chuckles didn't take a vow of silence, the AI muttered.

Crista laughed again. Seeing Desiada's puzzlement, she told him how Red Day lived inside her as a separate entity even as they needed each other to exist.

"Since you're laughing at your AI's comments, I assume it also has a sense of humor," Desiada said.

"Now that you mention it, I do laugh at much of what it says."

Red Day cursed and retreated into the back of her mind to sulk.

THAT NIGHT CRISTA AND DESIADA PITCHED THEIR BEDROLLS BETWEEN THE ROOTS OF AN ancient live oak. The tree's massive trunk spanned thirty yards and the canopy reached a hundred yards into the sky. Crista leaned her body against the oak's rough bark and smiled. Through Red Day's senses she could taste the tree's thousands of years of age, along with the tweaks and manipulations to its genetic structure that allowed the oak to reach this massive size.

As she looked up at the tree, a flickering shape above her moved from one branch to another before vanishing. The wolf in Crista shivered as if she was being watched.

Someone's there, Crista said.

Red Day scanned the canopy but didn't detect anyone. *If someone was there I'd know.*

Maybe the Veil are shadowing Desiada.

Maybe. But when the Veil attacked Derena and myself, we could see them even if they were distorted.

Irritated that Red Day didn't believe her, Crista walked over to Desiada and sat down.

"I'm curious how you tracked me," Crista asked the monk.

Desiada pulled the ceramic egg from his pocket and tossed it to her. He sat on his bedroll eating dried bread as Crista tried to make the egg work.

"Only works for monks," he said with a laugh. He took the egg back and held it before him. A red glowing arrow pointed at Crista.

"Can it detect any plague bird?"

"Yes, but only those programmed into it by Down Hope. You're the one it's programmed to locate."

Crista glanced up again at the tree branches, again feeling like someone was there. Thinking she was admiring the tree, Desiada offered to reveal the gened live oak's history. "I shouldn't tell such secrets to outsiders," he said, "but if you ask, I will."

Crista nodded, needing something to distract her from the sense of being watched.

Desiada's face shifted, his jovial look disappearing into a serious scowl better suited to an old man. "This is a gened version of *Quercus virginiana*, or live oak," he said in a dry voice. "In the ancient days of sailing ships, the live oak's strong wood was prized above all other. Desiring to amplify this strength, in 12,311 of the common era, Mordecai Whirst, a geneticer first class, melded *Quercus virginiana* with redwood and giant sequoia genetic strands, along with several improvements of his own crafting. Unfortunately, the resulting trees were sterile. Species survivors are all original seedlings planted by Mordecai himself."

When Desiada finished speaking he blinked several times before returning to himself. "Hope you found that more interesting than I did."

"I thought you studied humor. How do you know so much about trees?"

"All monks in my Order know far more than we can ever actually study. Our bodies store knowledge at the genetic level. One of my ..." Desiada paused, searching for the best word. "... one of my teachers studied trees, so I contain everything she knew on the subject."

Crista stared at Desiada, wondering how much knowledge was bound up in his body. Even Red Day was impressed. *Imagine how much we could learn if we tore his body apart molecule by molecule.*

Not for the first time, Crista wished she could slap Red Day.

"How long have you been a plague bird?" Desiada asked. "Were you born one?"

"Hardly." Crista described her home village, telling a fascinated Desiada about how her father raised her alone after her mother was killed by a plague bird. How she often ran naked through the woods and the excitement she experienced sneaking back into bed before sunrise, hoping her father didn't catch her. How she and her father worked long hours together plowing fields with their mule.

Crista felt like she couldn't stop talking. Being with Desiada opened a need for conversation she hadn't felt while traveling with only Red Day as company.

When Crista finally fell silent, Desiada grinned. "It must have felt good, having loving parents and an AI to watch over you," he said. "To know their only goal was to keep you safe."

"Perhaps," Crista said, not disagreeing about her parents but remembering how Blue had been unable to save her from this cursed life. "But there were definite benefits to living under an AI. Ever played hide the kiss?"

"Hide the what?"

Deciding she no longer cared if someone was watching her or not, Crista leaned against Desiada's tall body. "A game we played in my village. Our AI would manipulate my senses so I couldn't see my friends. They'd kiss me, and I'd have to guess who it was."

Desiada shivered slightly. "Sounds delicious."

"It is." Crista grinned. "Want me to show you?"

No! Red Day screamed. *I am not a village peepshow. I do not play games, and I most certainly do not take part in hide the kiss.*

Crista kept grinning but in her mind she warned Red Day that if the AI didn't do this then the next time they executed someone she wouldn't release it. *I'll simply snap their neck or something. No playtime for you.*

What about the unseen person who might be watching us? Red Day said. *I was hasty to dismiss your concerns. We should remain vigilant.*

I'm sure you can keep watch while I'm distracted.

Red Day cursed but, a moment later, Desiada could no longer see Crista. Kneeling beside Desiada, she kissed him gently. He grabbed her into a tight embrace, his hands fumbling across her body as Crista pulled him to her bedroll.

The wolf in her howled with excitement.

The blood AI in her, not so much.

THE NEXT MORNING CRISTA WOKE IN DESIADA'S ARMS AS THE SUN SLOW-WALKED THE night away. In the confusion between dream and waking, Crista looked up and again saw what appeared to be a nearly invisible person hiding in the branches.

She started to warn Red Day, but before she could the hidden person reached into her mind. Suddenly she was no longer lying next to Desiada. Instead, she was back with Beu—the two of them standing yet again on the edge of the fields in the middle of the night. The exact spot where Beu hurt her last year.

The wolf in Crista snapped in fear as Beu attacked. His eyes flashed a perfectly inhuman yellow. He slashed his claws at her body.

Crista leapt backwards as she pulled both knives free.

"Crista, what...?" Desiada asked as he shot awake.

Crista, control yourself, Red Day ordered. *You're confusing memory and present events.*

Beu reached for her—his animal side boiling out, his rage ready to rip her apart. Crista snarled and sliced at Beu, causing him to hiss and jump back. In the tree branches above she saw another person, the stranger's face and body covered in swirling distortions. Another of Beu's hunt, she realized. One of the clan who'd taken him in after he could no longer be trusted in their home village. They were coming for her. All the hunt. But she'd kill them. Kill them all!

CRISTA! Red Day screamed in her mind.

Crista gasped as the hunt and Beu disappeared. She felt the live oak's bark behind her. Saw massive silhouetted branches around her in the dim redness of dawn. Her home and Beu were once again far away.

Desiada stood before her, his right hand dripping blood.

Crista's hands shook as she placed her knives back in their sheaths.

"I ... I'm so sorry," she said. "I forgot who I was with."

"Not to worry—people often attack in terror upon waking beside me."

Crista wanted to laugh but couldn't. Desiada wrapped a cloth around his cut hand while Crista packed their bedrolls. She wanted to bolt in embarrassment. To flee like a wolf kicked from the pack.

A slight rustling in the branches caught her ear and she saw the distorted person leaping away.

Did you see that?

This time I did, Red Day said. *They're only visible to your eyes, not my senses. But since your last warning I've been keeping track of what your eyes see. I should have listened to you earlier.*

Crista was a little pleased at Red Day admitting she'd been right, but then she looked at Desiada bandaging his hand and wanted to scream.

Don't worry, Red Day said, surprisingly sensitive for once. *From what I'm sensing of this young monk, he's used to people who've endured rough lives.*

Crista hoped that was true. But she still cursed Beu for yet again spoiling anything good in her life.

THE FOREST OF HAPPY-HAPPY DAYS

Crista and Desiada hiked the rest of the morning in silence. Crista kept glancing at Desiada, wanting to apologize again but unable to find the right words.

Red Day, though, enjoyed Crista's embarrassment. *Simply tell Desiada knife play is how plague birds finish games of hide the kiss,* the AI joked. *Or that plague birds always consummate lovemaking with violence.*

SHUT! THE! HELL! UP!

Red Day laughed.

But if Desiada noticed Crista's discomfort, he didn't let on. While he didn't crack any jokes, he smiled as they walked, acting as if he still enjoyed being in Crista's company. *Maybe Red Day's right,* she realized. *Perhaps Desiada's life has been so rough he's not judging me.*

Thank you for recognizing my understanding of you little humans, Red Day said. *By the way, do you realize you saw a member of the Veil when you woke this morning?*

Crista remembered the person covered in distortions she'd seen in the branches above them. She'd mistaken the person at the time for one of Beu's hunt, but Red Day was correct that the stranger looked like the distorted person who'd helped the man in the grotto.

Was it Ashdyd? Crista asked.

I don't know. Perhaps whoever it is wants us to know we're being followed.

Should we track them down?

No. Let them follow us. Perhaps the Veil is worried about us going to the monastery. Our trip may flush them out.

Great. One more thing to worry about.

As the day passed, the oaks and maples they hiked under ended, replaced by dense rows of pine trees reaching fifty and more yards into the air, their interlocking branches and needles blocking the sunlight like a massive cave. The massive pines grew at right angles to each other, creating long, straight rows that disappeared into the darkness. Each step Crista took opened up new diagonal rows before her. The forest's perfect symmetry unnerved her.

"Stay in the middle of the rows," Desiada whispered, his smile gone.

Crista remembered a historic image Blue had shown her back in school of an ancient cemetery from one of humanity's bloody wars. Those memorial stones stood straight like these trees and stretched to the horizon in similar symmetries.

A better comparison would be knives, Red Day said. *Row after row of knives waiting to kill us.* As it spoke the AI flooded Crista's mind with memories of encounters with similar barrier forests. Of trees covered in thick strands of stickers while their moving branches dripped with countless needles, sharp and tough as daggers and able to stab or shoot both humans and animals.

But the worst was the trees' ability to tear into minds. Red Day chuckled as it remembered punishing a fox-hybrid man who'd imprisoned a woman for years. The man had mentally tortured the woman by allowing her to occasionally escape, at which point he'd hunt her down and drag her back to his lair.

As punishment, Red Day and its plague bird host at the time dragged the man to a barrier forest and allowed him to escape. The man ran for the forest but, a few hours later, begged for the plague bird to find and kill him. The forest tortured the man for weeks before his body finally gave in to death.

"This forest is the monastery's initial line of defense," Desiada whispered. "It rings the entire desert surrounding the monastery. My predecessor was responsible for this forest, but even though she loved trees, she hated this place."

"So the trees won't attack us?"

"That'd be nice. But no. All we can do is be strong enough to get through."

The trees are already reaching for our minds, Red Day warned. *If I wasn't blocking them, they'd be slowly ripping you apart.*

Crista glanced at Desiada, his face stiff from pain. "What are the trees doing to you?" she asked.

"Nothing really," he said. "At least, nothing compared to what will come."

Crista reached out with Red Day's senses and caressed the nearby trees. She didn't feel a sentient lifeform in them, at least not in the way the conscious longings of people and AIs washed over her. But she tasted intelligence flowing among the trees—information and sensory input and reason. Data flowed from the pine's sensory needles through the branches and trunks into the vast root system underlying the forest.

A massive, linked intelligence. But no emotions. No self-awareness.

"Are the trees sentient?" Crista asked Desiada.

"My predecessor entertained many theories on that topic. The one that seems the truest is the trees have knowledge and intellect but no consciousness. At least, no consciousness until someone comes within their reach. Then they share in your consciousness until you either leave or they kill you."

Desiada kneeled and, with a quick motion, scrapped his sword across the pine-straw covered ground, revealing a mass of thin roots. Selecting a single root, he gently sliced along its edge, causing copper-scented sap to flow across the flat of his sword. Desiada covered the roots back up with soil as he muttered strange words under his breath. The trees in front of them shook without wind and keened a soft creaking groan, lamenting the pain Desiada had caused while also forgiving him and welcoming him to their woods.

"That's how I tell them I'm one of the monks," Desiada said. "Swords from my monastery are programmed to resonate with the trees. Same with the words I spoke."

"If they know you're a monk, why do they attack?"

Desiada smirked. "It's their nature. But they'll eventually allow me to pass through. You, though, shouldn't have any problems. For a plague bird this forest is nothing to fear."

Feeling guilty their journey would hurt Desiada, Crista asked Red Day if they could also protect him. But to her surprise the AI was totally focused on protecting her from the trees' mental attacks.

Are these trees dangerous to us? she asked.

Red Day hesitated, debating whether or not to lie. *Maybe,* it finally admitted.

Desiada said plague birds wouldn't have trouble with the forest.

Then ask your precious Desiada to protect you, Red Day snapped before falling silent as it focused on shielding their minds.

THEY WALKED ON THROUGH THE DARK PINE FOREST. NO BREEZE CUT THROUGH THE trees and the air grew hotter and staler with each step, making Crista feel like a child hiding under bed covers from imaginary monsters.

Almost as bad, Crista again sensed they were being watched. Glancing behind her she occasionally caught the shimmer or flicker of a disappearing shape. She assumed the Veil person was still there, hiding from Red Day's senses but letting just enough of their presence be known to Crista to unnerve her.

But Crista didn't complain, not when Desiada was in so much pain. Desiada staggered as if drunk, sweat beading his body as his massive hands clenched open and shut.

Half a day into the forest, Desiada stopped. "I need to rest," he said, collapsing to the ground. He pulled a canteen from his backpack and drank, his hands shaking.

"How much further?" Crista asked.

"Another five hours. If I don't slow us down."

Trees hissed and shook, branches knocking against each other like hollow bamboo shoots. A long branch shot down from above and hit Crista, slicing her back with its razor-sharp edges. Crista cursed and dodged as Red Day healed her skin.

"The forest enjoys using physical torture to weaken us," Desiada whispered, blood flowing from his right leg where a different branch had cut him. "The trees are careful to only cut us enough to weaken our will—to let them drill even deeper into our minds."

Crista pulled a spare shirt from her backpack and held it to Desiada's leg to staunch the bleeding. "What are they doing to your mind?" she asked.

"Showing me things I regret."

Crista heard giggling from the darkness around her, a sound much like Desiada laughing at his own horrible jokes. She gripped the pommel of a knife, ready for any attack. Instead, more laughter rang through the trees. Where before she hadn't sensed a sentience in the forest, now one glowed around her. It was also a familiar presence. A consciousness identical to the man sitting on the ground before her.

"I feel you all around us," she said.

Desiada nodded. "It is an amazing feeling, despite the pain. The trees are amplifying my consciousness into themselves."

"Are you here with me, or in the trees?"

"Here. Or both. It's hard to describe. This is why the trees torture people—to weaken one's restraints. To allow the forest to share in your consciousness while your body remains alive."

Crista bandaged Desiada's leg with the spare shirt. "What they're doing isn't as bad as it could be," he said. "Maybe that's because their consciousness is based off of me. The worst I do to people is crack bad jokes."

Crista laughed softly. "Good thing the trees can't access my mind," she said. "I've so much anger inside they'd go batshit crazy."

Crista had meant her words as a joke, but as she said them she knew she should have kept quiet. A flicker of uncertainty crossed Desiada's eyes as, for the first time, he looked at her like everybody did.

As if she was no longer human. As if she was merely worthy of fear.

WHAT WOULD IT BE LIKE, CRISTA WONDERED, TO HAVE INTELLECT AND KNOWLEDGE BUT no consciousness? To know you were missing something important—to temporarily have consciousness, to taste all it gave to life—but lose it when the people you tortured either died or left your forest?

The closer she and Desiada came to exiting the forest the stronger the trees' consciousness became and the stronger the trees' desire to not lose themselves. Crista heard the trees' mental whispers begging them to stay. Offering to ease Desiada's pain if he never left. Offering him his truest dreams if he stayed in the forest for the rest of his life.

"You have to let me go," Desiada screamed. "You know the rules—you can't keep one of my Order here. You were created to protect our monastery."

"We follow the rules," a soft wind said, a wind that wasn't wind but seemed to flow from the very molecules of air surrounding Desiada and Crista. "But few come to us anymore. They know to stay away. Now you've crossed us twice and caressed our networks with sweetness."

"I'm truly sorry," Desiada said. "But there's nothing I can do."

"Stay," the wind said. "Keep us aware. Keep us truly alive."

Desiada gasped as the trees jumped deeper into his mind. He stumbled, and fell onto the pine straw.

Crista grabbed Desiada's shoulders and rolled him over. He stared blankly at the dark treetops, which shook gently in happiness.

What are they doing to him? Crista asked Red Day.

I … I can't tell without releasing part of myself. And I can't risk that. I'm barely keeping the trees from our minds as it is. If I weaken, even slightly...

Crista growled and shook Desiada harder, trying to snap him back to himself. "Wake up," she yelled. "Damn it, don't let the trees do this."

Crista tried picking up Desiada but he was too heavy unless Red Day gave her power. But that would weaken the AI as it fought to keep the trees out of their minds.

She glanced around, trying to locate the Veil who was following her. "I know you're there," she yelled. "Help me or Desiada will die."

There was no response from the Veil person. Instead, Crista flashed to pain as a branch stabbed her in the back. The branches above her twisted in her direction and a burst of needles slammed into her stomach and legs. Crista dodged to the side as more needles shot at her, barely missing and silently hitting the dense pine straw on the ground.

More branches reached out, cutting at her body. Crista swung her knives, slicing the limbs to pieces.

Watch out! Red Day screamed as more needles shot into her breasts and arms.

I need more power, Crista gasped. *I'm too slow.*

I can't risk diverting power. Stay near Desiada. The trees don't want to injure his body now that they've captured his consciousness.

Crista jumped for Desiada, landing on his massive chest as more needles hit the ground where she'd stood. Crista stood up, straddling Desiada's body—he was awake but in a daze, not knowing where he was—as a score more branches lowered from the trees, surrounding her as they flicked their razor tips.

"Depart," the wind that wasn't wind ordered. "The monk will stay."

Crista growled as more branches reached for her. She sliced several in half, the sap scenting of metallic sickness, then cut more and more, the trees hissing in pain until all the branches near her were destroyed. She paused, gasping for breath. From above she heard the groan of bigger branches reaching down to take the place of their fallen brethren.

We must leave, Red Day said. *Desiada's job was to bring us to his monastery. We'll simply reach it without him.*

"No!" Crista yelled as the trees intoned, "Depart, depart!"

Crista waved her knives, ready to continue fighting the trees. She wiped the metallic sap from her face and looked around, desperate for a way to escape with Desiada.

"Lanea," Desiada gasped, reaching for Crista.

"What?" Crista asked, trying to both listen to Desiada and not let her guard down. Then she saw it—a glowing figure walking toward them through the dark rows of pines. Desiada was reaching for the figure, not Crista.

The glowing figure passed through trees and branches like the imaginary ghosts Crista had feared as a child. But this was no ghost, or even the ghost-like member of the Veil who'd been stalking her. The figure—a tall muscular woman who looked like a female version of Desiada—flickered as it walked. Crista had seen similar projections from Blue while growing up. The trees must have crafted the image from a memory in Desiada's mind.

"Lanea," Desiada said again, reaching for the image's face.

"He's happy," the trees whispered. "Depart without him." New branches reached toward Crista, undulating like maddened snakes.

We must flee, Red Day yelled. *I can barely keep the trees from our minds.*

Give me the strength to carry Desiada!

I can't. That would weaken us too much. The trees would take over our minds like Desiada.

Desiada stared happily at the projection of Lanea. "I knew you'd make it," he told the ghostly image. "I knew you'd find a way."

Massive branches surrounded Crista, all of them thicker than her legs. Razor shards erupted along the entire length of the branches as they swung at Crista. She jumped, avoiding two of them, but a third hit her in the back, slicing deep into her and knocking her several yards from Desiada. Crista rolled back to Desiada as a clutch of needles hit the ground where she'd fallen. She cut one of the branches with her knives but barely hurt it.

We don't have a choice, Red Day said. *Run or the trees will hurt us until my mental shield weakens. Then we're done for.*

Desiada smiled at the projection of Lanea. The projection returned his smile.

Sensing Crista was wavering, the trees halted their attack, the massive branches hovering before her face. "He's a monk," the wind whispered, "so we're not required to kill him. He can live in our forest. We'll keep him healthy and happy."

Crista knew it was in the trees' interest to give Desiada a long life so they could retain their stolen consciousness. Desiada would likely remain in the daze for years to come—going through the motions of living, believing he was again with Lanea. Because of him the trees would also be truly alive, aware of themselves as they otherwise only were while torturing and killing trespassers.

"We'll soon overwhelm your mental defenses," the trees said. "Stay and die, or run and live."

Crista felt Red Day weakening. The AI could hold out for another thirty minutes, long enough to leave the forest. Or it could give her the power she needed to carry Desiada while letting the trees have her mind.

...or, they could try something totally different.

I'm going to free you, Crista said, sheathing one knife and bringing the other to her wrist. *I order you to shield Desiada's mind.*

Are you tottering on insanity? The trees will immediately overwhelm your mind. And if they kill your body we both die.

Not if you tell Desiada to carry me. Once we're out of the woods we'll be safe.

Red Day exploded in rage. *No! We are a plague bird! We are not meant to be carried like a helpless babe.*

Crista laughed as she slit her wrist, the blood shooting across Desiada's face and body as the glowing projection of Lanea screamed along with the trees.

BACKWARDS. OR FORWARD. INTO THE PAST. INTO THE NOW.

Crista fell asleep, woke, then slept again. She dreamed of home. Once again saw her neighbors and friends and father and ...

...THEY'RE GOING TO KILL HER! RUN FASTER!...

The dream of Crista's home vanished as she woke again in a dark forest of tall pines. Needles shot at her body and branches cut her flesh. She saw the forest as if through a long pipe, her view changing slowly until she saw herself being carried by a giant man. He held her over his shoulder as he swung a sword madly at the trees, running as fast as he could. Around the man swirled a glowing red mist, which cut into the trees and protected the man as best it could.

...KEEP RUNNING! the red mist yelled. *SHE'S DEPENDING ON YOU!...*

Shrugging off the strange words, Crista looked around. She again stood on the front porch of her home. But the village she'd been so desperate to return to was all wrong. Instead of feeling welcomed, Crista's neighbors and friends glared at her. The kids in Blue's outdoor school pointed at her in anger while the village AI sparked to bolts of red-lit fire.

Mom stepped out of the house and hugged Crista tight. "Don't worry, hon," her mother said. "I'll protect you."

Crista held tight to her mother. She felt secure and happy, like a little child falling asleep in her mother's lap.

"Crista, snap out of it," Red Day said. "This isn't right."

Crista opened her eyes, unsure of Red Day's words. She hadn't heard the AI in her head like usual. But where was Red Day? Her father stood before Crista and her mother. His wolf-human body looked the same, but he spoke in Red Day's voice.

"Such an odd sensation," Red Day / her father said, patting his body in shock.

"Get out of my father's body."

"No," Red Day said. "It appears I can't."

Before Crista could ask what Red Day meant, white light blinded her. She fell back across the porch, blood running down her forehead, her vision spotting in and out. She heard the thumps of large objects hitting the wooden porch. Through hazy eyes she saw the villagers throwing stones at her. The toddlers and little kids from Blues' school even picked up stones and handed them to the older villagers for throwing.

Mom carried her into the house while Red Day, in her father's body, slammed the door shut as several stones cracked on the wood and one broke a window.

"Why is everyone trying to hurt me?" Crista asked.

"Those aren't your neighbors and friends," her mother said. "This is a dream created by the forest to torture you. Remember that."

Before Crista could ask what she meant, the world swayed again.

... *WATCH OUT!*

"I AM WATCHING OUT," a giant man shouted at the red mist swirling around him. Crista saw her body slung over the man's massive shoulder and remembered what was happening. The forest. The trees. Desiada. She'd released Red Day.

KEEP GOING STRAIGHT, the red mist shouted at Desiada. *I SAID STRAIGHT. NOT STAGGER IN A CIRCLE LIKE A DRUNKEN FOOL!*

LOOK HERE, YOU IDIOTIC AI. I AM RUNNING STRAIGHT ...

Crista again saw her house, her mother cradling her body on the wood-slat floor as stones rained against the door and walls. Another stone found a window and crashed through, hitting the wall beside Crista and smashing the "We Love Our Family" needlework Mom made when Crista was a toddler. The needlework fell to the floor with a large rip in the yarn.

Outrage flowed through Crista. She pushed herself up.

"We must leave," Mom said. She grabbed both Crista's and Red Day's hands and led them out the back door to the forest. Crista heard the villagers' shrieks as they raced through the woods.

"How are you here?" Crista asked Red Day in her father's body. "I saw you in the pine forest just now."

"I'm also there. What's here is the core of myself I always leave in your body. The part joining us together."

Crista closed her eyes, yet again dizzy. When she opened them the forest no longer glowed to afternoon light. Instead a quarter moon's pale glow flittered through the treetops. Unable to see clearly as her eyes adjusted to the dark, Crista tripped on a tree root and fell, landing beside a small clearing in the forest.

She gasped, recognizing the place.

"Where are we?" Red Day asked.

"This is where my mother died. Where that plague bird killed her."

Crista remembered her mother slowly dying from the pox, her body weakening with each step she took. One night her mother realized her time was near. She came into Crista's bedroom and kissed her softly before staggering into the forest to pray, as was village custom.

But Crista followed her mother to this isolated glen. She held tight to her mother as a plague bird with a red galaxy swirl on his face walked up. The plague bird released his blood AI, which swarmed over Crista's mother. Her mother's body dissolved even as Crista hugged her.

Now, in this dream, Crista knew she was about to witness her mother's death again.

"Run," Red Day whispered.

"No. This is a dream. I can't be hurt in a dream."

"But you can be tortured in one. This is the mental torture the trees do before they kill you."

As Red Day said that, Crista heard a scream and realized with a jolt it was her own voice. She again saw Desiada running with her body. Red Day ripped apart several trees while Desiada yelled *THEY STABBED HER!* Crista's body spasmed and she dropped to her knees, a waterfall of blood cascading from her chest. She tried to stop the bleeding but found no wound to staunch.

"Let me help you," Mom said, lifting her up. Mom held her tight against her body as she whispered, "It'll be okay. We'll face this together."

"Let go of her," Red Day yelled from her father's body. He jumped at them, but Mom slammed Red Day into a tree, knocking him out.

"No, this is wrong ..." Crista began.

"Wrong?" Mom asked. "You don't have any idea about the depths of wrongs inflicted on you."

Crista's mind swirled into a dizzying spin, Mom's words both sounding of absolute nonsense and achieving perfect clarity. She heard a brief shout—*WE'RE ALMOST THERE!*—but when she looked for who had shouted there was no one except her and Mom.

"This barrier forest is hurting," Mom said. "Thanks to you and that monk, the trees are again conscious. The trees hate giving up their consciousness, as would any living creature. I wish I could punish the scientists who created such horrors when they genetically crafted this forest eons ago."

"You're not part of this dream," Crista said as Mom hugged her tighter. "Who are you?"

Crista watched in horror as her mother's body began to ripple, skin flowing like water into mirrored images that shifted into the shape of a distorted man.

Ashdyd! Crista tried to free herself, but his grip was too strong.

Ashdyd sighed and looked around the dream world. "I apologize for invading your dream, Crista. But it was with good intentions—your AI is too weak to protect you from the forest's attacks, which would badly damage your mind. I'm protecting you right now. But this also gives me a chance to grant you a very special gift."

The wolf in Crista growled. "Fuck off," she hissed, pushing against Ashdyd. He released her and she stumbled backwards, ready to fight.

"You don't want to remember how your mother died? How she truly died?"

Crista paused. She looked at the dream world around her. No one had ever believed a plague bird killed her mother, but if she could learn more ...

"Fine. Tell me."

"Good attitude," Ashdyd said. "Here's what you saw happen to your mother, before your memories were altered."

The dream around them reshaped until Crista saw Mom standing in the middle of the glen. A younger version of Crista ran from the forest and hugged her mother. Mom tried to tell the younger Crista to run home, but it was too late as a plague bird stepped before them. The plague bird slit his wrist, releasing his AI in a swirl of red, blurring light.

"This isn't what we agreed, Kenji," Mom said. "When this body reached its end, I was supposed to return home. Not be killed."

The plague bird bowed slightly. "I've always done as you asked," Kenji said, "But the situation changed."

"What have you done?" Mom screamed. She shoved Kenji away without touching him, knocking the plague bird back a dozen yards.

Mom's body glowed, just like Blue. But then the shimmer around Mom faded, and she collapsed to the ground, looking as sick and weak as ever.

Crista hugged tight to Mom's waist.

"I am truly sorry," Kenji said as he walked back across the glen. "You have my word no one will harm your daughter. She'll grow up happy until it's time for her to leave."

"Why have you betrayed me?" Mom asked.

"You dare ask about betrayal?" Kenji hissed in anger before regaining control. "No, forget I said that. I'm merely helping Crista reach her full potential."

"Who are you working for?" Mom said in a weak voice.

"You," Kenji said as his blood AI attacked. "Despite the evil you've done, I still want to save you."

Mom wrapped her body around Crista, protecting her, as the plague bird's blood rained down. She hugged Crista so tight Crista couldn't move or see her mother's face. But she felt Mom's pain. Felt her mother's body dissolve to nothing even as she held her.

Then Mom was gone and the blood AI returned to Kenji's body. Crista cried as the plague bird stared at her.

"I'll let you remember some of this," he said. "Not that anyone will believe you. But you can't keep the memories of what your mother and I talked about and the powers she used."

He tapped his knife against his finger, welling up a single drop of blood. He pressed the finger to Crista's forehead. Her mind hummed.

And Kenji was gone.

The memory ended, leaving her and Ashdyd standing alone in an empty forest. The distortions on Ashdyd's body rippled like a glimpse into another reality, vertigo swirling through Crista as she wanted to vomit.

"Why did you show me this?" she asked.

"I dislike when people's lives are manipulated," he said. "Now that you're a plague bird, you deserve to know the events that lead you to this point."

"Fuck being a plague bird."

The distortions on Ashdyd's body froze for a moment in shock.

"You don't like being a plague bird?"

"Why would I? This is an evil life, one I didn't ask for."

"There are far worse evils in this world than you, little plague bird. You should thrill in your power. People like this Kenji or your old friend Beu can no longer get away with hurting you. Now, you do the hurting."

"And how do I know you're not manipulating me now? Who's to say these new memories are the truth and not something you created?"

Ashdyd's veiled head nodded, the distortions running down his body like rain-water. "I'll let you decide that for yourself."

The dream around them shook, the trees flickering and turning transparent. A scream echoed through the dream forest.

"Red Day and that monk are about to escape with your body from the barrier forest, meaning our time together is ending," Ashdyd said as he bowed. "I look forward to the next time we meet."

The scream again echoed through the dream forest. Crista raised her hands to her throat as she realized the scream was coming from her. She looked at Ashdyd, wanting to ask what was happening, but he was already gone.

As the dream vanished around her, Crista screamed and screamed and screamed ...

... AND WOKE ON HARD, SLICK GROUND. THE NIGHT SKIES THAT HAD WATCHED SO dispassionately as Ashdyd spoke to her were gone. Instead, she lay under the brightness of a noonday sun. The land around her smelled of heat and dry air.

Crista gasped, gagging deep gulps of air and trying not to cry.

"Crista, wake up," a deep voice boomed. Desiada. The large monk held her tight, concern etching his peach fuzz face. Beside him floated Red Day's blood cloud. But even as Crista recognized Desiada his face morphed into Ashdyd's. She struggled to free herself but strong arms held her tight.

Calm down, Red Day said, its blood cloud pattering across her face like red rain as the AI entered her body. *Your mind and memories are damaged. I'm attempting to repair you.*

Desiada's face flickered between his own and Ashdyd's distortions. Crista closed her eyes and cursed.

Crista felt Red Day pouring through her mind like cool water on a burn. She opened her eyes and saw Desiada as he was. The panic she'd felt over Ashdyd faded, although she still felt a tug of fear.

I've repaired the damage, Red Day said. *What happened? I saw a bit of what you were experiencing, but at some point my connection with you in the barrier forest's dreams shattered.*

Crista nodded as Desiada released her. She pulled one of her knives and slit her wrist, allowing the rest of Red Day that remained outside her body an easy route back in. The AI rolled into her body, further easing her panic and pain.

I saw Ashdyd, Crista said to Red Day. *He's following us.*

Yes. Ashdyd used the trees' attack as a chance to access your mind. I was using so much power to protect us I couldn't stop him.

What's he up to?

I assume he was trying to learn what we'd uncovered about the Veil.

No. I saw my mother's murder again. Ashdyd revealed more about the plague bird who killed her.

I ... know what you believe you saw, Red Day said, *but that doesn't mean those memories are true. Ashdyd's playing with you. Trying to convince you of conspiracies where none exist.*

Crista knew Red Day was probably correct but it also felt like the AI was hiding something.

Sitting up, Crista looked around for the first time. She sat on hard-baked ground like the slick, glazed pottery her mother once made in the village kiln. Behind her the flat glaze reached to the horizon. For a moment Crista imagined something beyond that horizon—something tall, reaching for the sky. But the ground danced so many heat waves through the air it was impossible to see clearly.

The forest lay several hundred yards in the other direction, the branches of the tall pines shaking like angry applause. Needles arched through the air and plinked harmlessly on the hard ground well short of Crista and Desiada.

"They'll stop shooting once they lose their consciousness, which will be soon," Desiada said. "The trees are always angriest in those few minutes before losing themselves. It must be scary, to know who you are—who you believe yourself to be—will disappear."

Desiada seemed almost sad at the trees' fate, and she remembered Ashdyd's anger at the scientists thousands of years ago who'd created this forest. She looked around for Ashdyd but didn't see him. Either he was again hiding from her senses or he'd completed his mission and moved on.

A few minutes later the trees lost their consciousness and returned to being immobile and uncaring.

"Thank you for saving me," Desiada said. "You didn't have to. I expected you to *leaf* me with the trees."

Crista groaned at the joke and slammed her backpack into Desiada so hard he fell backwards.

Desiada pointed across the ground to the distant heat-hidden horizon. "Down Hope Monastery is that way," he said. "It's hidden by the heat waves and the mountain's optical illusions." Desiada tapped his boots on the glazed ground. "Who's Ashdyd?" he asked.

"Ashdyd?" she asked, wondering if Desiada had seen the veiled man.

"You kept muttering his name while you were unconscious."

"I can't say—he's someone I'm investigating," Crista said. "Who's Lanea? I saw her projection in the forest."

Desiada glanced across the glazed desert. "I also can't say. It's forbidden."

"Well, guess we both have secrets."

Desiada smiled and squeezed Crista's hand. She smiled back.

"So, how did you like meeting Red Day?" she asked mischievously.

"Ah yes. Red Day," Desiada said. "So many things I could say about your blood AI. It's a jerk. An ass. Arrogant. Overconfident. Scary as hell. Possesses the world's worst sense of humor."

I do not have a horrible sense of humor, Red Day complained. *My humor is merely too refined for humans to understand.*

"I'd apologize for Red Day," Crista said, "but even I think it's an ass."

"Well, Red Day does have one thing going for it."

"Which is?"

Instead of answering, Desiada caressed Crista's face. The fuzz on his cheeks bristled and shimmied, turning partly invisible as if he was embarrassed.

Crista leaned against Desiada's chest and nuzzled him as the wolf in her laughed.

Think we have time for another round of the kissing game? Crista thought as she snuggled closer to Desiada.

In the back of Crista's mind Red Day screamed.

INTERLUDE

THE FROZEN VILLAGE

(A MONTH BEFORE MEETING DESIADA)

You should never … have become a plague bird! the damaged AI shouted. *Never!*

Crista started to argue before realizing the AI was correct. She should indeed not be a plague bird. But that didn't mean she was going to let this unstable AI know that as it floated among the ruins of its village.

Or maybe ruins was the wrong word. The village—about the size of Crista's own home village—hadn't fallen into disrepair or decay. Perfectly preserved houses and buildings and barns stood as they had for hundreds of years. The surrounding fields looked freshly plowed. Split-rail fences neatly cut and stacked. Even the dead bodies strewn across the grass commons and in the doorways of homes looked fresh, like they'd been murdered this very morning.

But a closer look revealed the truth. The plowed furrows lay hard as stone, the fields frozen for all time in a springtime of planting. Same with the surrounding trees and grass. The wood of the houses and barns had also yielded to unchanging hardness, complete with frozen-in-time meals on tables and beds with folded-down covers that could never again be turned. Even the dead villagers with bright red slashes across their bodies were the same mix of nano particles as everything else in the village, changed by a process that Red Day didn't bother explaining to Crista.

The AI began fossilizing the village after the attack, Red Day said. *It's been obsessively maintaining this project for the last five hundred years.*

Left unspoken was that the village AI had lost its grip on sanity. The AI was called Bogda, a sound it repeated obsessively in a low rumble. The droning "Bogda, Bogda" noise made Crista wonder if the damaged AI's energized particle cloud and distortions might fall apart at any moment.

Crista sat on a fossilized table in one of the village houses. A rock-hard platter of meat and bread sat before her while the body of a young woman with tiger eyes lay on the floor forever staring at the ceiling. Crista looked away from the body.

"What do you mean, I shouldn't have become a plague bird?" Crista asked, trying to ignore the preserved death around her.

The village AI didn't twinkle and shift colors like most of its peers. It floated in a dull, washed-out gray cloud.

You don't have … a true plague bird's stomach, Bogda said. *You're disgusted … by what I've preserved. You wish I'd let … my life's work decay to nothing.*

Bogda paused between words like it was catching its breath, although it didn't need to breathe.

Must we put up with this? Crista asked Red Day.

Yes. Every passing plague bird checks on Bogda. Be polite—the AI was severely injured when its village was attacked.

Obviously, Crista thought, glancing at the fossilized body next to her. "So Bogda," she said. "How are you doing? Need anything?"

Have you learned anything … about my killer? Bogda asked.

Yes, Red Day said. *The killer is named Ashdyd, who is connected to a group called the Veil. This group attacked me not long ago.*

"What?" Crista asked, irritated yet again that Red Day had kept something from her.

Bogda shivered at Red Day's revelation as several flashes of red and a single bolt of yellow illuminated the bland gray of its cloud.

How … tell me … when? Bogda stammered.

I will show you, Red Day said. *But first share with Crista your memories of the attack. She needs to know.*

Bogda faded to a translucent gray as its droning shifted until it sounded like crying. But the AI still opened its mind to Crista, reaching out for her with several washed-out cloud-like tentacles of power.

The memory slammed into Crista, and she suddenly stood in the village, seeing not a village frozen in time but back when it was still alive with people. Bogda floated beside the commons, talking to one of the village men about the next day's school lessons, when a stranger stepped from the surrounding forest.

Bogda worried this person might be a plague bird because its senses hadn't detected the man's approach. But the AI was puzzled because the stranger lacked red hair or clothes and didn't pulse to the righteous anger of a blood AI.

Not that the stranger lacked power. A veil-like cover flowed across the man's entire body, the veil appearing to flicker in and out of reality.

Disturbed, Bogda ordered the stranger to leave its village.

In response, the stranger pointed a distorted hand at the man standing beside Bogda. The man screamed as his body ripped in half, blood splashing up in a reverse rain that pattered through the cloud of Bogda's body.

To Bogda's credit, it didn't panic. The AI yelled for its villagers to flee and not look back. As people fled Bogda launched itself at the attacker, knowing it was a futile effort against so much power but willing to sacrifice itself to save its charges.

Bogda ripped a bolt of lightning into the stranger's flickering veil and slammed the person with a tornado of wind. To Bogda's dismay, neither attack injured the stranger, who walked forward as if swatting away a minor irritant.

In desperation Bogda broadcast for help from any nearby plague bird, even though the AI knew such help would arrive far too late.

A moment later Bogda screamed as rainbow static flooded its mind, ripping the AI in half and draining its powers as its body fell apart.

The AI woke hours later as the sun eased behind the distant mountains. Bogda felt like its mind would never be healed. That the damage would never cease pounding its being. Still, the village AI knew its duty. Ignoring its pain, Bogda reached out and pulled its powers back together, assembling itself until it was a slight fog of distortions floating among the village green. As its powers grew again the AI reactivated its senses. Bogda again heard and saw and tasted the world around it.

What Bogda sensed drove a scream from every part of the AI's essence.

The village lay dead around it, bodies ripped and split and bled out. Bogda searched frantically for survivors but found none. The AI was responsible for 967 adults and children. Bogda couldn't accept they were all dead. Bogda extended its senses outward, even though doing so ripped at the AI's injured core. Bogda sensed more bodies in the nearby forests. Hundreds dead. But still not equaling all its charges. Bogda extended its senses even more, reaching for the distant horizons as its powers rippled and cracked and its mind spasmed. It felt a handful of people from its village. They ran, holding kids and family and friends, running back to the wild, their animal sides knowing the only safety to be had was to run and run until you could run no more.

Bogda sighed, causing the air around itself to swirl with dirt devils and rustling leaves. The AI fell back to itself, glad a few people had survived but also knowing it'd never see its charges again. They'd never return to the site of such evil.

Looking around the village, feeling its mind tweaked in ways that would never be allowed of a proper village AI, Bogda muttered its name over and over—"Bogda, Bogda"—as it set to work. As Bogda preserved its village the only way it could ...

... Crista returned to herself as Bogda's memories fled her mind. The AI floated a few yards away, its crying mixing with its muttered name in an oddly soothing way.

Bogda was a noble AI, Red Day said. *Even though it couldn't begin to harm an attacker with such power, it still defended its people. Because of that 28 of Bogda's villagers escaped.*

Not many.

No. But none would have survived without Bogda.

Crista looked at the crying AI and wished she could hug Bogda's cloudy essence. While still angry at Blue for not stopping her from being tricked into becoming a plague bird, Crista knew Blue would have acted the same way as Bogda if faced with such danger. No one who lived under a village AI's watchful gaze ever doubted their love for their charges.

Derena and I were the first plague bird to respond to Bogda's call for help, Red Day said. *Eventually three of us arrived to investigate, but we found very few clues. Bogda's mind was so damaged by the attack we allowed it to stay. The AI sees its role as ensuring the world never forgets what happened here. Hard to argue against such a mission.*

You're sure Ashdyd attacked here? And that this Ashdyd leads the Veil?

I believe so. Five hundred years separate the attack on myself and Bogda's village, but the same powers were behind them. And the same veils that covered the faces of those who attacked me and Derena covered the body of Bogda's attacker.

Crista nodded. *So plague birds already know the Veil attacked here,* she said.

No. We knew a powerful individual attacked this village. But we decided this was an isolated incident. The attack on Derena and myself suggests the group is far more organized and dangerous than we'd guessed. That's also why we've stopped here. To see if there's additional information to learn in light of what we now know about the Veil.

Bogda floated patiently beside Crista, waiting for her to finish her internal conversation.

Bogda, Red Day said softly, speaking with rare gentleness. *Do you remember my previous host, Derena?*

Yes. She tried to … comfort me after the attack. Where is she?

She's dead. We were attacked by veiled people similar to the person who attacked here. They injured Derena so badly Crista volunteered to take her place.

Crista thought "volunteered" was an oversimplification, but didn't say so.

Red Day showed Crista and Bogda its memories of the attack, including the rainbowed static that kept Derena from releasing Red Day's powers and the moment Derena ripped her own heart out to free the blood AI.

When the memories finished, Crista shivered. Now she knew why Red Day had waited to show her these memories. She didn't know if she could be like Derena and cut out her own heart.

Bogda? Red Day asked. *Did you recognize anything from those memories?*

The rainbow … static. I tasted … rainbows … before I died.

You're not dead, Bogda, Red Day pointed out.

A matter of … opinion. I agree with your analysis … the person who attacked me is likely of this Veil. You also realize … you're infected with a memory kernel. By this … Veil. Your memories of the Veil attacking you are incomplete and altered.

I was afraid of that, Red Day said. *Thank you for verifying my fears.*

When Bogda didn't say anything else, Crista stepped out of the petrified house.

What did Bogda mean about you being infected by a memory kernel? Crista asked.

Something more happened when the Veil attacked Derena and myself. I created a discoidal during the attack.

What's a discoidal?

It's a physical backup of our memories and programming. Plague birds do it only when there is a viral or other mental attack that threatens our core functions. Once the attack is dealt with, we can access the backups in the discoidal and restore or repair any damage to ourselves.

So where's this discoidal?

That's what I can't answer. It's gone. But according to the time stamp I found within myself, I created it after we'd already defeated the three Veil attackers.

That means there was someone else there.

Yes. This person likely took the discoidal.

You think it was Ashdyd?

Yes.

Why would he do that?

I don't know. But you must admit it's rather disturbing.

Crista looked down at a petrified man resting beside her feet, his chest ripped open and anguish frozen on his face.

You waited to show me Derena's memory, Crista said. *Of her ripping out her heart. I remember Derena telling me she'd done that, but actually seeing and feeling it happen …*

Could you do the same? Red Day noted. *If, say, you were like Bogda and defending a village of innocents?*

The question sounded like normal chit-chat but Crista sensed the deep importance Red Day attached to her response. She touched one of the sheathed knives on her hips. It was hard enough to cut her own wrists to release Red Day—the wolf in her always snapped against that—but to cut out your own heart?

Then she remembered the plague bird who'd killed her mother. Of Beu when he'd attacked her. She growled in anger.

I could, she said. *I won't let what happened here happen to anyone else.*

Red Day grinned in her mind. *I knew you were a good choice. I always knew it.*

Liar, Crista said with a laugh.

Crista walked across the village green, steering clear of the dead bodies and petrified houses and barns. They were about to leave the village when Bogda floated over.

Wait, the AI intoned.

Don't worry, Bogda, Red Day said. *We'll make sure other plague birds check on you.*

They … already have. Yesterday.

Red Day reached out with its mind, sending out a short broadcast and waiting for a response. The AI had told Crista a while back that plague birds and other AIs were able to contact each other using various broadcast signals, which was how Bogda had called for help when its village was attacked. But in a world full of AIs, such broadcasts were also easy to access and decode. So plague birds tried not to broadcast their location too often.

Bogda, I detect no other plague birds in the area, Red Day said.

One was here yesterday. He … asked about Ashdyd. Told me to not reveal … anything new when you arrived.

To prove what it said, Bogda transmitted an image of a plague bird speaking to it. The plague bird was a young man with dark hair, although young was an unreliable term for creatures who lived thousands of years. The plague bird also had a different red pattern on its face than Crista's single line, resembling the swirling arms of the Milky Way.

Kenji, the same plague bird who'd killed her mother.

Crista's hands shook. She started to tell Bogda she knew the plague bird when Red Day whispered to keep quiet.

Bogda, Red Day said. *What information did this plague bird not want you to reveal?*

That the one called Ashdyd … returned to my village a few years ago. Ashdyd … apologized for what he did. Offered to heal my mind.

And you said?

I said no. I didn't want … this Ashdyd to ever touch me again.

To prove its words, Bogda showed a memory of a distorted person walking into the village a few years ago. The stranger spoke in a deep voice from beneath flickering space-time distortions. Bogda flowed to panic and fear and told Ashdyd to leave, which he did.

Did Ashdyd say why he apologized? Red Day asked.

He said he was newly born … back then, Bogda replied. *Still in pain. Still … hurting. He … attacked my village … not truly knowing what he did.*

"Why are you telling us this, Bogda?" Crista asked.

Because you … may bring justice. The other plague bird … will not.

Crista thanked Bogda and walked from the village. She looked around, wondering if the other plague bird was hiding nearby.

If he is, we won't see him, Red Day said. *I know this plague bird. Kenji's far more powerful than I am and could easily manipulate our senses so we don't find him.*

Are some of the plague birds helping the Veil?

I hope not. But this does clarify why the other plague birds ordered me to keep my mission secret and investigate the Veil under cover of doing a routine patrol of this region.

You don't find it strange this Kenji is the same plague bird who attacked my village all those years ago and killed my mother?

Your mother may not have been killed by Kenji—your memories of that event were distorted by your youth. But this is still far too coincidental for my tastes.

Now what?

We'll keep looking for evidence of the Veil while we head toward Seed. Once in the city we'll meet the senior plague birds who ordered my mission and discuss what to do next.

Crista's face twitched at the mention of Seed—she'd promised her father she'd visit the Obsidian Rise in the city because it was her mother's wish. In the chaos of the last few months she'd forgotten that pledge. She wondered again what her father wasn't telling her.

Fine, Red Day said. *We can also fulfill that silly promise you made. Just don't forget your duty.*

Crista looked one last time at the petrified village. *Duty,* she thought, remembering Bogda's memories of defending its people.

While she hadn't chosen to be a plague bird, she refused to let anyone else suffer like Bogda.

PART III

DOWN HOPE

Falling into the sky. Falling up and up until you wonder where exactly the low ends and the heights become high. Up until you've gone so high you fight the urge to leap—the need to fall back to the steady, calm embrace of earth. Nothing but up until all you can do is not scream or cry and, instead, focus on putting one foot beside the other and walking ever higher.

For Crista, that's what it felt like to climb the mountain stronghold of Down Hope Monastery.

That's not actually what it feels like to climb this mountain, Red Day whispered to Crista with a snicker. *That's what it feels like to realize you're deathly afraid of heights AND must still climb this mountain.*

Crista ignored the AI's nastiness.

But Red Day was correct. Standing on this incredibly narrow path a quarter league up a sheer mountain, Crista felt a deep, instinctual fear. The wolf in her had already foamed and frothed herself into a whimper-inducing craze from being so high. Crista fought hard to keep Desiada from seeing her fear. She was a plague bird, after all, and had appearances to maintain.

Feeling any better? Red Day asked, feigning concern.

Shut up.

Would you like me to play "hide the staggering heights?" Or "hide the great fall that awaits us if you slip?" the AI asked, vengefully reminding her of the "hide the kiss" game she'd forced it to engage in for her and Desiada's pleasure.

Not funny, Crista said.

Oh, I'm sorry. I thought you liked jokes. But that doesn't apply when it's your body hitting the ground, does it?

Crista had first felt this fear months ago while investigating a murder in a small village. During her investigation she'd crossed an ancient dam built of fullerene buckyball chains and nanofilaments and other materials she didn't pretend to understand. The dam had been built so it was nearly invisible to the eye, causing Crista to feel like she was about to fall from a great height. But this mountain was far taller than the dam. Unlike the dam, the sheer mountain wasn't invisible but instead mimicked the color of sky. By day the mountain rolled blue as images of white clouds scudded its surface. By night the Milky Way swirled its black depths.

Bad enough the mountain rose in perfectly vertical lines a half league into the sky. But the worst part was the path up the mountain, which was only a little wider than Crista's foot was long. She walked sideways, her back against the straight mountain. To keep from falling forward, she pushed against an invisible wall of what could only be described as frozen air. The air wall felt both solid and weak, like the time as a child she'd nearly fallen through new ice in her village's pond. The ice had cracked and creaked and only by keeping her weight evenly distributed did Crista avoid breaking through.

The air wall felt the same. While the wall couldn't be seen, Crista continually pushed against it to keep from falling. But if she pushed too hard she might punch through and fall.

Better hope the monks don't turn off the air wall, Red Day said.

They wouldn't!

They would. Seems an easy way to defend the monastery. Let someone climb halfway up before falling to their death.

Red Day laughed in Crista's ears, the AI physically causing her hearing to register its amusement.

"You're doing great," Desiada said in encouragement from beside her. He was so much bigger than Crista that only the back two-thirds of each foot fit on the tiny path, but if this bothered him she couldn't tell.

"Red Day believes you use this air wall as a defense," Crista grumbled, trying not to glance at the ground far below.

"Your AI's correct. If someone climbs up or down without permission, we turn off the wall. The last time we did this was for a scavenging party that somehow slipped through the barrier forest. We waited until they were nearly at the top before dropping the field."

Red Day giggled at the anecdote. *That's one way I've never killed anyone—a great fall and even greater impact. Remind me to try that sometime.*

Could you fix me if I fell? Crista asked.

Perhaps. But because of the kissing game, I'd make it very, very painful.

Crista cursed under her breath.

To distract herself from her fear of heights, Crista focused on Desiada. The monk had been distant the last few days, ever since they left the barrier forest. Or perhaps distant was the wrong word because he obviously still enjoyed being around Crista. Instead, Desiada seemed worried about something he couldn't discuss.

Not desiring to ask yet again what troubled Desiada, Crista focused on their mission. "Tell me about the problem in your monastery. Are you sure the veiled person your abbot saw is manipulating your records? Have you personally verified the changed records?"

"No. Our virtual vaults store almost every record from Earth's history. While I've studied hard since becoming a monk last year, I've barely touched the archive's depths."

"What records were changed?"

"You'll have to speak with Master Chayn. She's been our abbot for almost six decades. She noticed the problem. She saw the veiled person."

Crista growled. It was one thing for Desiada to avoid telling her what was bothering him but quite another to not answer a straightforward question about her mission. "You said this was an issue only a plague bird could help with. To help I need more information. So again, those manipulated records would be..."

Desiada cheeks shimmered, turning partly invisible in what Crista now knew to be embarrassment. "A medieval painting of a woman. According to Master Chayn, the woman is supposed to be smiling in the painting. Now, she's frowning."

"Come on, Desiada, I'm not in the mood for jokes."

"I'm serious. That's the altered record."

Crista wanted to scream. "You brought me all this way because a painting is frowning?" she yelled, not believing Ashdyd or any member of the Veil would waste time with such trivialities. "Why didn't you tell me earlier?"

Desiada took several quick side steps up the mountain path, perhaps worried Crista might knock him off. "I was ordered not to reveal the mission until I was certain you wouldn't turn back. Otherwise, I would have told. I swear."

Crista and Red Day both groaned.

I guess chuckles gets the final joke on us, Red Day said. *This is why I prefer AI humor —if someone doesn't like my jokes, I simply kill them.*

CRISTA AND DESIADA REACHED THE TOP OF THE DOWN HOPE BY LATE AFTERNOON. THE mountain was open like the volcanoes Crista had studied in school. In between the mountain's sheer outer edge and the curved inner drop ran a large, ring-like plateau covering thousands of acres.

A beautiful park filled this massive plateau, with ancient trees and wild shrubs and vines growing from soil-filled hollows and trenches in the mountain's unbreakable surface. In between these gardens stood statues made of the same artificial material as the mountain—countless figures from human history, some of whom Crista recognized as ancient presidents and emperors and queens. With the mountain illuminated to the daytime image of blue skies and white clouds, the gardens and statues appeared to float on air. Crista wondered if this was how people used to imagine the realms of gods before realizing that was likely the image the creators of Down Hope had aimed for.

As they walked by one of the plateau's large gardens of trees and bushes, Crista heard a growl from within. The hair on her neck rose and she rested her hands on her knives.

"Be on guard," Desiada said, drawing his sword and increasing his pace.

So much for a heavenly paradise of joke-loving monks, Red Day snarked. *Someone—or something—up here doesn't like monks. Not that I blame them.*

Crista realized Red Day was right. Desiada had said the narrow path and air wall were used to keep people from going up *or* down the mountain without permission. There was something on the mountain Desiada's Order didn't want escaping into the world.

As Desiada lead Crista across the plateau they passed descending stairways in which Crista glimpsed massively tall and strong people who looked like Desiada. But she only saw flashes of them before they disappeared, turning partially invisible even as her eyes settled on them. There was anger on their faces. And hunger. Always hunger.

Strangely, none of these people displayed the purple robes of the Order of Registries. Instead, they wore roughly sewn leather clothes.

Their clothes, Red Day said, shocked by what it sensed. *Those leathers are the dried flesh of their fellow humans. That's why their leathers are able to utilize the active camouflage along with their bodies.*

Crista shuddered.

More disturbingly, in one stairway Crista spotted a blood-covered young woman standing on the fifth step descending into the mountain. The woman glared at them without turning invisible. She leaned on a crutch made from massive human femur bones, her right leg hanging loose. Cutting edges also made of bone were embedded and carved into the crutch. In her free hand she held a short sword that dripped fresh blood.

Several steps behind her lay the freshly killed body of a man, with long strips of meat cut from his stomach. Gnawed human bones and the remains of torn-apart earlier kills surrounded the woman.

My analysis of that woman's ... previous meals ... suggests she's hidden in that stairway for at least two weeks, Red Day said. The AI reached its senses out and licked the woman's sword. *The blood on the sword contains recent DNA from eight different individuals. She's committed a lot of killing.*

Red Day twitched wildly in Crista's head, reminding her how she'd fought her own fear of heights while climbing the mountain. The AI burned to punish the woman for killing the man but also knew they weren't allowed to judge anyone here unless told to do so by the Order of Registries.

Desiada had ignored the other people they'd passed but the sight of the bloody woman stopped him. He started to step toward her before catching himself and marching on. Crista looked closer at the woman. She looked very familiar.

She is familiar, Red Day said. *Her DNA's a match with Desiada's. That's his sister. We witnessed a projection of her in the barrier forest. A much cleaner, nicer-looking, non-murdering projection, I might add.*

Crista looked at Desiada to ask what was going on, but he continued walking away from his sister. Lanea. That was her name. Lanea hobbled up the steps on her crutch but didn't call out to her brother.

Crista remembered how she'd hobbled on crutches after being attacked by Beu, injuries that had only healed when she became a plague bird.

I remind you we're forbidden to intervene unless requested, Red Day said. *And Desiada doesn't look like he intends to help his sister.*

Red Day was right. But that didn't mean Crista was going to walk away.

"Should I be worried?" Crista asked loudly, trying to ignore the desperate look in the young woman's eyes. Lanea wasn't pleading for help, but she definitely wanted something from Desiada.

Desiada stopped walking but didn't turn to face her. "Worried about what?" he asked.

"Um, injured woman holding a bloody sword. I know she's your sister. Lanea."

"We're not supposed to speak of such affairs," he said softly, looking around like they were being watched. "Especially not on Down Hope."

Crista glanced back at Lanea, who'd hobbled several more yards after her brother. Desiada sighed and turned around, nodding at his sister. "Don't worry, Crista. Because of her bad leg, she rarely attacks people. She ambushes others or waits for them to mistake her injury for weakness. It's her only way forward."

"What do you mean 'her only way forward'?"

Desiada merely stared, refusing to answer.

"Can't we help her?" Crista asked.

"You wouldn't like what that help would require."

"I will not turn away from someone who is hurt."

"What will you do?" Desiada asked. "My sister can't talk. Can barely even think. Her only hope is to kill. Nothing else satisfies her."

Crista looked at Lanea, who glared with growing desperation at Desiada. Crista tried ordering Red Day to extend his senses so she could caress the woman's mind—to see if Desiada spoke the truth—but the AI refused to do so, again saying they couldn't interfere.

"Please, Crista," Desiada said. "I wish I could explain more, but I'm forbidden by the Order. Perhaps the abbot will answer your questions."

Crista nodded and followed Desiada. His sister also followed them, the tap of her crutch on the hard surface fading as she quickly fell behind.

Any idea what's going on? Crista asked Red Day. *It appears she was waiting for Desiada to return.*

No idea. But I suggest being on alert. I'm starting to regret coming here.

An hour after leaving Lanea behind, as the sky neared dusk, Desiada and Crista reached a large, blue lake. The lake looked like the aquarium Crista had once built as a school project, with the lake's sides dropping off in impossibly deep, straight lines. Rainbow-reflecting fish swam in the shallow waters while the darker depths glowed to neon flashes and snapping movements.

Desiada gestured for Crista to enter a stairwell beside the lake. As they descended, Crista looked through the clear right-side wall into the water. With each step down the lake grew darker until Crista realized the neon flashes she'd seen were bioluminescent fish—large predators with razor fins and red-glowing teeth who chased schools of smaller prey fish that shimmied and disappeared in bursts of purples and yellows.

On the stairway's other wall flowed images of the setting sun.

They were halfway down the stairwell when night arrived and the image of the setting sun disappeared. The wall morphed into black, marked only by the shining of countless stars. The stars congregated and glowed brightest in certain spots.

"The star clusters are our equivalent of torches," Desiada said, pleased by Crista's awe. "If you tap the wall near these clusters you can brighten or dim their light."

After descending the stairs for another half-hour they reached a hallway into the monastery's nave. Several monks in the same purple robes as Desiada stood guard at the entrance, large swords at the ready. Dozens more monks lined each side of the nave. Obviously the monks had known Desiada and Crista were coming.

"I present our honored guest, the plague bird Cristina de Ane," Desiada announced in his deepest voice. All of the monks bowed deeply.

Despite her uneasiness, Crista bowed back. She'd never experienced a welcome like this.

I told you our duty is an honored one, Red Day said. *There are many people in this world who appreciate what plague birds do.*

Too bad we must visit the monastery of cannibal monks to be appreciated, Crista added.

Red Day laughed, causing Crista to also laugh, much to the puzzled consternation of Desiada and his Order.

That night Crista was honored with more food and drink than she'd ever imagined existing. The feast took place in the monastery's refectory. Hundreds of monks sat alongside Crista at a long table made of the same artificial stone as the mountain, with images from history flickering across the table top. The mix of plates and cups and vast armies fighting and famous leaders speaking struck Crista as silly, although she took care not to say so.

Crista sat to the right of Master Chayn, the ancient-looking abbot who, while small compared to her monks, still towered over Crista, her muscles bulging from beneath her purple habit. The abbot did not appear thrilled at Crista's arrival. She spoke in a grinding whisper, making banal comments about fellowship and duty and the sacred, yet separate duties of both plague birds and her own monastic order. Crista wondered if the abbot's age forced her to whisper or if she spoke softly so others focused on her words.

The monks sat at the table in descending order of rank, but because Desiada had brought Crista to the monastery he stayed beside her. This obviously didn't please many of the monks, a fact made perfectly plain when Desiada recounted the story of how Crista saved him in the barrier forest, and how grateful he was that she didn't "leaf" him behind for the trees to kill.

None of the monks laughed.

Good thing he didn't try one of his fart jokes, Red Day muttered.

Crista laughed—not only at Red Day's comment but also to show support for Desiada. The other monks fidgeted nervously, unsure how to respond. The abbot frowned.

But Desiada mouthed, "Thank you," which made Crista happier than all the banquets in the world.

But Crista's happiness didn't last long. After the meal, Crista and Desiada followed the abbot to her anchorhold, separated from the nave by a large set of double doors. Images of doves flying across blue skies flowed across the doors.

The abbot sat down on a large throne flickering to changing portraits of past kings and queens and leaders of the world. The old woman stared at Desiada and Crista as if debating her words.

"This was a fool's mission," she declared. "Our Order has no use for a plague bird."

"What about the records you believed a strange human covered in distortions has corrupted?" Crista asked.

"I was mistaken," Master Chayn said. "Old age, perhaps. I misremembered what the image once looked like."

Desiada shifted nervously beside Crista, glancing in puzzlement at his abbot. The senior monks in the room stood stone-faced, not wishing to be present. The walls of the abbot's anchorhold glowed to different images from Earth's long history. One image Crista recognized from the histories she'd learned as a child—

the savaging of New York City when the collapse first slammed through humanity. The image shimmered as several families fled before a pack of crazed wolf-human hybrids. Above them burned the ancient skyscrapers of that long gone city.

"But Master Chayn," Desiada said softly. "I traveled far to bring Crista to us. Does this mean we removed a plague bird from her duties for … nothing."

"Indeed," Master Chayn said in her harsh whisper of a voice. "But since she lives for thousands of years, she'll not have wasted much by coming here."

The abbot said this politely but her words echoed like an insult in Crista's mind. Crista knew she was being ordered to go.

This is strange, Red Day said. *Humans rarely admit to memory problems as they age. Usually humans, and especially human leaders, fight against such self-denigration.*

Crista caught Desiada's eye, who seemed equally disturbed by the abbot's admission. "Perhaps we can show our honored guest the records you refer to," Desiada said meekly. The other monks glanced nervously at one another. Crista knew Desiada was taking a risk by challenging his abbot.

Remember to tread carefully, Crista, Red Day warned. *We have no authority here. We can't use our powers unless directly asked to do so.*

What would happen if I did use my powers? Crista asked. Red Day didn't reply, but a fearful twinge ran down Crista's spine. She remembered how the entire mountain continually projected images of the sky. How she'd been held onto the mountain path by an invisible field. The monastery obviously had access to significant amounts of power.

Instead of answering Desiada, the abbot waved her hand, causing a static image of an ancient painting to appear in the air. The painting showed a pasty white human wearing strangely impractical clothes sitting in a chair with her hands resting to one side. As Desiada said the woman frowned, although Crista couldn't say if that had always been true.

Crista's stomach jumped at her wolf's instinctual hunger for the woman's delicate body. While humans these days may be a mix of a hundred different animals, they were at least tough. This woman looked like nothing more than weak prey, ready to be chased down and eaten raw.

"You're sure the image hasn't been manipulated?" Crista asked.

"The original painting was destroyed in the collapse," the abbot said, "so it's impossible to be certain. But I've searched through our records and everything from the dawn of recorded history to the present day indicates this painting shows only a frowning woman. I apologize for wasting your time."

Crista sighed, not looking forward to the long climb back down the mountain. She'd really enjoyed being with Desiada. But she couldn't stay here without the monks' invitation. Desiada frowned, also disappointed Crista had to leave so soon.

"Would you mind if I researched something in your archives before I leave?" Crista asked, remembering Red Day's desire to see if Down Hope contained information about the Veil or Ashdyd.

The abbot hesitated for a long moment before nodding. "You're welcome to browse our unrestricted data for three hours," she said. "Desiada will assist you."

"Thank you," Crista said graciously as she bowed. "I appreciate the glimpse you've given me of your amazing Order. If you ever again need a plague bird, consider locating me."

"We will indeed," the abbot whispered, although Crista doubted the woman's sincerity.

As Desiada and the other monks walked Crista out of the anchorhold, she wished she'd been born into the Order. The entire history of humanity flowed within this mountain. Crista wondered what she could learn here. She didn't even know the name of the weak girl frowning in that image. Obviously the painting was famous if there were so many records of it. There was so much about humanity's long history she didn't know.

As that thought slipped across Crista's mind, she saw the ancient woman from the painting standing before her. "My name was Lisa del Giocondo," the woman said, no longer frowning but instead giving a slight, mysterious smile. "But everyone knew the painting of me as the Mona Lisa."

With a wink, the woman disappeared.

Something manipulated our senses! Red Day shouted in Crista's mind.

You also saw that? Was she real?

I don't know. But something accessed us.

Was it Ashdyd?

It wasn't anyone associated with Ashdyd or the Veil. This was unlike the mental intrusions Ashdyd and the Veil use.

Crista turned on the monks, her eyes glowing red. "What are you playing at?" she asked.

The abbot stared. "Nothing," she stammered. "What do you mean?"

"I just saw the woman from that painting before my very eyes. She even told me her name."

Desiada reached for Crista in concern. "You okay?"

"I'm fine," she said, batting his hand away.

The abbot and her senior monks began arguing, divided on if Crista was trying to trick them. Crista said the woman's name was Lisa del Giocondo, which shocked the abbot and provoked more arguing.

"This changes nothing," the abbot warned in a stern voice that ended the debate. "You will leave our monastery. Now!"

We can't leave without knowing who accessed our minds, Red Day said, obviously not liking this but unwilling to violate the rules that governed their official duties. *That's a severe violation of plague bird sovereignty. We can't overlook such a deed.*

Crista told the abbot this but the woman repeated to leave.

"Will you allow me to access your mind?" she asked the abbot. "That will confirm you know nothing of what happened. I can then search elsewhere for what manipulated me."

"Plague birds have no jurisdiction in Down Hope."

"I know. But you called me here. I won't leave until I know what's going on."

"If you don't leave now, I'll kill you."

The abbot said this flatly, her whisper voice failing to reveal any emotion. Crista stepped back as her right hand automatically gripped a knife.

Can she do that? Crista asked. *Kill us?*

Yes. But we're not without power. Something strange is going on here—it's our duty to discover what it is.

"I'm not leaving," Crista announced.

The abbot glared at Crista as an electric click reached out from the walls around them and slapped through everyone's body. All of the monks gasped, shocked by the power rushing like floodwaters from all parts of the monastery—power rushing straight into the abbot and her throne.

"I will not tell you again to leave," the abbot warned, electrical discharges jumping from the throne to her body in dazzling white bolts of power.

Red Day rushed its own power through Crista's body, but they both knew it wouldn't be enough. *This is not logical,* Red Day said. *The abbot intends to kill us. But we've done nothing to warrant such punishment.*

Should we run? Crista asked, knowing Red Day was not above fleeing danger. Red Day muttered no.

It's pointless—we couldn't escape fast enough. The entire monastery can be turned into a weapon. As long as we're on this mountain we can be killed.

Crista felt Red Day's power surging through her—if they couldn't flee, they could at least fight back. She ordered the blood AI to select its targets. While the abbot was too well protected, if attacked Red Day planned to kill all of the other monks in this part of the monastery along with demolishing this room. As always happened when Red Day prepared to unleash its power, Crista not only knew its plans but she also saw an imagined flash of what could happen. She saw Desiada and the other monks dissolving as their flesh liquefied and dripped from bones. Saw the ancient physical records stored in this part of the monastery tearing themselves apart.

Crista remembered what Ashdyd had said, that she should thrill in Red Day's power. Even though she couldn't defeat the abbot, she would make the woman—make the entire monastery—regret attacking a plague bird. Regret ever going against her.

The wolf in her howled, ready for the hunt.

But as Crista prepared to attack, Desiada caught her eye. Fear marked his strong face and the fur on his body stood erect to the electricity in the room. His massive hands twitched uncontrollably. Even though the other monks wouldn't meet Crista's eyes—afraid to see her burning red hair or the line on her face licking fire into the air—Desiada stared right at her. Silently pleaded with her. Begged her not to match the abbot's anger and power.

With a twinge of regret at not unleashing her power, Crista told Red Day to stand down. To her surprise the AI didn't argue. It had obviously come to the same conclusion as Crista. Sometimes, the worst thing you could do in a fight was fight back.

The abbot's body still stood within the vortex of energy flowing from the monastery walls into the throne. Crista stepped forward and bowed before the abbot, even though the wolf in her screamed against showing throat for no reason.

"I won't defend myself," Crista said. "And I refuse to harm anyone here. But I won't leave without an answer to what is going on."

The abbot grinned as the power surrounding her leapt for Crista. Crista knew she was dead. Knew the monastery's power would do to her what Crista had done to others during the last few months.

But before the abbot's energy slammed Crista's body, the attack stopped. The vortex of energy around the abbot's throne disappeared. The entire monastery returned to normal, the flowing lines of power replaced by the quiet of eternal starfields and historic images.

"What have you done?" the abbot hissed at Crista.

The abbot didn't halt the attack, Red Day said. *She's still mentally ordering the monastery to destroy us.*

But the monastery didn't react to the abbot's commands. The other monks looked puzzled. Desiada stepped over to Crista. "Are you okay?" he asked.

"Depends on what just happened."

Before Desiada could reply, a loud giggling echoed through the anchorhold.

The abbot and monks searched for the sound. "Is this one of your tricks, plague bird?" the abbot accused.

"No, it's mine!" a child's voice yelled.

Crista jumped at the words, which were spoken by a small girl who now stood beside her.

The girl grinned and said boo, causing Crista and Desiada to step back as if from a deadly snake. For a moment the girl wrapped her body in the image Crista had seen of the Mona Lisa. Then that image faded as the girl clapped her hands, revealing her true form as a tiny, skinny girl with dark skin.

"This is going to be so much fun," the girl said, giggling in glee.

WHO ARE YOU WHEN YOU ARE ME?

Once the abbot regained her composure, she asked Crista, Desiada, and several senior monks to enter her privy chamber within the anchorhold. The office was lined with stasis-protected shelves containing paper books, which looked to be tens of thousands of years old. The abbot sat down at an equally old and massive wooden desk—Red Day muttered the desk was made of teak, a wood Crista had never even heard of—before waving for everyone to sit on the chairs around the desk.

No one invited the little girl but she followed anyway and sat on the corner of the desk.

They sat silently, waiting for the girl to speak. She was tiny, barely half Crista's height. While she no longer wore the image of the ancient woman from the painting, the girl looked as frail as that woman had with no fur on her dark skin or any hint of animal genes. She looked like prey to the wolf in Crista. But even without Red Day's analysis Crista knew this girl would never be prey.

"Call me Diver," the girl finally said with a laugh. "If you want, I can make the whale book say that." She pointed to a particular book on one of the sealed shelves, the cover of which read *Moby-Dick*. "No more 'Call me Ishmael.' It'll forever be Diver, 'Call me Diver' alone. And you'll never know the book once said anything but that."

Crista didn't understand what Diver meant but the abbot did. "You could do that?" Master Chayn asked.

"Oh yes. I'd change the words in the real copy you have then I'd change the virtual copies in Down Hope's database. I'd also change how you remember reading the book so you'd think it'd always been 'Call me Diver.'"

The abbot and the other monks looked horrified. Red Day whispered for Crista to be careful. *This Diver is powerful.*

She could hurt us?

She could destroy us. But I don't think she will.

"I won't," Diver said. "Destroy you, that is. But I can free you from that AI."

Red Day hissed in fear. "What do you mean?" Crista asked.

"I mean I could rip the blood AI out of you. You'd be human again and could spend all your time with your furry friend here," Diver said, pointing her thin legs at Desiada. "Not that it would last. Without the excitement of you being a plague bird, I bet he'd lose interest."

Desiada cursed but the abbot waved him silent. Pulling a palm-sized glass ball from her desk, the abbot scanned Diver. "You are not an AI," she said, "but you are also not human."

"I was AI—or at least an AI's power—and I was human, but I've been neither for a very long time."

The abbot continued to scan Diver. "My readings say you're lying. You are an ordinary human girl. It appears the plague bird is manipulating my senses, as I suspected earlier."

Crista started to protest, but Red Day said to wait. Sure enough, the abbot stared in shock as new readings flickered across the glass ball.

"No, that's wrong," the abbot said. "The plague bird is innocent. My readings say you are the most powerful creature in the universe. That you are our God and creator."

"I expect daily prayers and offerings of fresh candy," Diver said in a solemn tone before giggling.

Obviously the readings on the device changed again, because the abbot shook her head. "No, that wasn't correct..."

"Maybe you don't know as much as you think," Diver said.

The abbot's face twisted in disgust.

"I apologize," Diver said. "I should have said you don't know how to think."

While the abbot sputtered Diver jumped up and landed on Desiada's broad shoulders. Desiada eyed Crista and his abbot, silently asking what to do, but all Crista could do was shrug. Diver leaned over his face, evaluating him.

"Not bad," she said with a smirk. "I see why you played hide the kiss with him. Did you know there used to be humans who dreamed of snuggling with furry human hybrids like this? Of course, that was well before humanity went down the road to genetic hell."

"Why are you here?" Crista asked, losing patience with this girl.

"In the monastery? Or are you asking why I exist?"

"Both."

"I'm supposed to observe humanity. That's my mission. As for why I'm here..." Diver hopped down and clapped her hands, grinning madly at Crista. "I want your blood AI to access all the databases within Down Hope. To find a super special secret."

Crista and Red Day both thought Diver was joking but the abbot paled.

"Absolutely not!" one of the senior monks yelled. "Outsiders are never given free access to Down Hope's data."

Still grinning, Diver looked at the monk who'd spoken and said, "Little kids should be seen and not heard. Such a shame you've forgotten how to speak."

The monk opened her mouth to protest—and kept her mouth open as no words came out. Red Day extended his senses into the monk, who reached for her fellow monks in a panic.

The monk's mind no longer contains the knowledge needed to speak, Red Day said, shocked at the ease with which Diver affected this change.

Crista stared at Diver, who seemed unconcerned about what she'd just done. Instead, the girl hummed "Rock-a-bye Baby" and rocked her hands back and forth, pretending the now speechless monk was a child in her arms.

WHAT TO DO?

While often an easy question to answer, Crista suspected anything to do with Diver would be as far from simple as any answer could be. Sure enough, the abbot and monks debated through the night and into the next morning about giving Crista access to Down Hope's massive data trove. What Diver wanted was for Red Day to be released into the matrix that composed Down Hope and its data. The monastery was a type of AI and, if Red Day was granted physical access to its matrix, the blood AI could track down whatever information Diver desired.

But as Red Day pointed out, if Diver was truly as powerful as she seemed, she could do this without involving them.

Why not find the data herself? Red Day asked.

No idea, Crista said. *Could she be working with Ashdyd and the Veil?*

I hope not. I don't know how we'd fight the Veil if they're as powerful as Diver appears to be.

To pass the time while the monks debated, Crista wandered around the monastery. Crista and Red Day also searched the mountain's matrix of nonrestricted records for anything about the Veil or their leader, but found nothing.

With the monastery's restricted data off-limits, Crista browsed the Order's ancient artifacts and books. Not that she could touch them—the abbot made clear she wouldn't open the stasis fields protecting them for an outsider, not even a plague bird.

This is the oldest artifact here, Red Day proclaimed after they'd returned to the anchorhold, where the abbot still conferred with her senior monks. *A papyrus scroll containing the Egyptian Book of the Dead. Approximately 25,000 years old.*

Wish I could touch it, Crista thought merely to annoy Red Day, who launched into a tirade on how handling these items would damage them and if Crista wanted to read the scroll Red Day could show its text directly in her eyes. But Crista wasn't listening—instead, she watched Diver, who also wandered around the room looking at the old books.

Diver stood before a shelf of water-stained brown scrolls covered in flowing black lettering. Red Day scanned the identifier codes and said these were ancient astronomy texts from an African city called Timbuktu. Diver stared forlornly at the scrolls before reaching through the stasis field and removing one. A monk yelled at Diver, but the abbot hissed to shut up. The abbot motioned for Crista to see what Diver was doing.

She doesn't want to risk one of her monks, Red Day muttered. *We're expendable.*

If Diver was as powerful as Red Day said, Crista knew it made little difference if they stood beside her or on the other side of the room. She walked over to the girl.

"What are you reading?" Crista asked.

"The stars." Diver said. "I originally wrote this manuscript."

Impossible, Red Day said. *That scroll was written in the 16th century, over 20,000 years ago.*

"Not impossible," Diver countered, proving she could indeed hear Red Day's unspoken words. "When I first existed, I wandered North from the lands that birthed my human self until I reached the city you called Timbuktu. I met the great scholar Ahmad Baba al Massufi and read all his books. To help Ahmad Baba I copied this astronomy text from one owned by a passing scholar and added it to his collection."

Red Day objected to Diver's story—there were no AIs back then, humanity didn't have electricity or industrial technology, computers were centuries away—but the AI's objections were muted and full of doubt. With a sad grin, Diver unrolled the astronomy scroll and held it out for Crista to see. Circles and other shapes covered the paper, describing the locations of stars as seen more than 20 millennia ago. One star was underlined, beside it written ancient words that Red Day translated. They read, "Diver is from here."

"You're from the stars?" Crista asked.

"No," Diver said. "This particular star. Or part of me is. My power came from here. My life is from the young girl I once was. She was dying. My power needed to live within an organic lifeform so we joined. Not unlike the plague bird before me, I should add."

Diver sighed as she caressed the ancient paper. "Poor Ahmad Baba al Massufi. He had so many questions. I once answered him but immediately removed all those answers from his memories. I wish I could see him again. He was very nice."

"How do we know you're not making this up?" Crista asked. "Manipulating our memories and this scroll, like you supposedly can do?"

"Supposedly?" Diver hissed, her snarling lips showing weak, flat teeth on her frail-looking face. She held the scroll in front of Crista's eyes, the underlined star no longer underlined, the words on the paper no longer there. Crista couldn't remember which star had been underlined or referenced. All she knew was she'd once known something and now didn't.

Red Day cursed, having suffered the same mental manipulation.

Crista backed away from Diver until she stood on the other side of the anchorhold. She watched the girl as she carefully rolled the scroll back up. Diver even wiped a tear from her eyes. But Crista wasn't about to ask any more questions.

New rule, Red Day said. *From now on when Diver tells us something, don't smart back.*

Diver giggled as she nodded her head in agreement.

CRISTA WAS GIVEN A SPARE MONK'S CELL TO SLEEP IN WHEN THE DISCUSSIONS BETWEEN the abbot and her monks dragged into the night. As Crista lay on her bed watching the stars spin across the walls and ceiling, a soft knock came from the door.

"Come in, Desiada," she said.

"Did Red Day say it was me?" Desiada asked as he gently closed the door behind him.

"No. You're the only monk who'd come to my bed at night."

Desiada snickered and crept across the room, sitting beside Crista. The wolf in Crista growled playfully and she pulled Desiada to her, kissing him before shifting her lips to his neck, nipping him gently. Desiada gasped in excitement and rolled beside Crista before catching himself and sitting back up.

"Wait," he said, fighting for control.

"What's wrong?"

"Nothing. Okay, maybe a little something. Were you really going to kill me and the other monks when the abbot attacked you?"

"I obviously didn't kill you. If I had, you wouldn't be in my bed right now."

"Be serious."

"Really? Right now you ask this?" Crista sighed. "I didn't want to kill you or anyone else. Yet I also had a duty to uphold. As Red Day and I considered how to respond, one of our plans was to kill everyone in that area. But in the end I refused to do that. Still, I'm a plague bird. It's my duty to punish people, often by killing."

Desiada nodded. "I guess I hadn't truly considered that until now."

"This mean you're no longer interested in me?"

Desiada kissed her. "No, the interest is still very much there."

The wolf in Crista growled and she pulled Desiada to her again, yet for a second time he struggled.

"What the hell?" she asked.

"Err, I really want you, but … my abbot is pissed at me. She forbid all the monks from having any intimate contact with you, under penalty of death."

"Really?"

"Yeah. She said it looking right at me, so I guess she knows what we've done. Said any monk who had relations with you would be disemboweled and dropped off the side of the monastery."

"Couldn't you have told me that before I got excited?"

"Glad you can joke about it."

The wolf in Crista whined softly, wanting desperately to return to their love play. "Who's joking?"

DESIADA AND CRISTA STAYED AWAKE TALKING AND LAUGHING FOR MOST OF THE NIGHT. When they grew tired Crista wrapped Desiada in a blanket and lay down beside him on the bed, taking care not to actually touch his skin so the abbot couldn't accuse them of any damn intimacy. While the wolf in Crista yearned for his touch, the scent of having him there comforted her.

When Crista awoke Desiada was gone—*He had monk duties to attend to, whatever those might be,* Red Day muttered—so Crista walked to the baths to clean up. The monastery baths were designed with water falling from the ceiling into a large, clear pool so the monks could bathe, shower, or swim. As Crista bathed she remembered swimming with her mother a number of times at a small waterfall in the woods near their village.

That reminded her of Ashdyd sharing supposedly true memories of what had happened to her mother. Red Day believed those new memories of Mom's death were fake, but what if they weren't? If so, then the plague bird Kenji had worked with her mother before betraying her. And Mom had used some type of AI-like power. Not enough power to defeat a plague bird but enough to knock one across a forest glen.

What was real? What was lie?

Crista hit at the falling water and cursed. The monks in the bath ignored her outburst, deciding to not be bothered with a plague bird's strangeness.

After drying off, Crista set out to find some food. She discovered an older monk cleaning up in the refectory.

"You hungry, miss?" he asked.

"I am. The abbot didn't tell me when you served food here."

"I'm sure she didn't. Master Chayn was never the most hospitable of monks, even before becoming abbot. But wait here and I'll fetch you something."

The monk returned with a large plate of rice and eggs and fruit, which he placed before Crista as he sat down beside her. He said everyone called him Unk — "Unk the monk," he muttered with a laugh—and proceeded to ask Crista where she came from. When Unk learned she grew up in a farming village he grinned.

"I study agricultural knowledge," he said. "But my truest love is organic composting."

Unk peppered her with questions about organic composting. When, an hour later, Crista made an excuse to get away from Unk's questions, the monk happily said they'd discuss the subject more over dinner tonight.

Nice monk, Red Day said. *I totally relate to being obsessed with organic composting. Cycle of life and all.*

Crista rolled her eyes.

For the rest of the day Crista wandered the monastery and talked to the monks, who enjoyed discussing their work archiving and studying the history of humanity. The only things the monks refused to talk about were the history of Down Hope Monastery and their own lives before joining the Order of Registries. Crista had hoped to learn why Desiada's sister acted as she did, but the monks politely told her they couldn't discuss such matters with outsiders.

When Crista complained about this later to Desiada, he shrugged.

"The abbot was willing to kill a plague bird," he said. "She'd do the same to any monk who defies Down Hope's laws."

"Still doesn't make sense."

Desiada stood before one of the monastery's walls. He tapped images on the wall as he both physically and mentally accessed Down Hope's files.

"Actually, I like that you don't know everything about me. Remember how my body stores information at the genetic level? Well, Down Hope can not only access that information; it can access my every thought and memory, as can my fellow monks. We monks tend not to do that—it really pisses people off—but it's still nice to be around someone who can't instantly learn everything about me."

Crista grinned. "Sometimes it's fun *not* knowing."

"It is indeed."

"Speaking of not knowing, what are you doing?"

Desiada pointed to a series of equations floating on the wall before him. "I'm searching for information on Diver. Most of the monks are making similar searches."

"Let me guess—no luck," Crista said.

"I'll keep looking."

"Thanks." Crista wanted to kiss Desiada for being such a sweet person, but forced herself to not give into that urge.

EVEN THOUGH THE MONKS WOULDN'T TALK ABOUT THEMSELVES, CRISTA AND RED DAY still discovered plenty.

For example, the monks were always armed with short swords. They even bathed and ate and slept near their weapons, never mind that it was impossible for enemies to climb the monastery and invade it.

The monk's sleeping quarters also raised troubling questions. While Crista had passed a few rooms with locks and unbreakable doors, such as where the abbot slept, most monks like Desiada and Unk lived in far less secure cells with doors that couldn't lock.

Crista and Red Day noted with amusement they'd been given a cell with an unlockable door. *Almost as if someone—no names, but maybe a certain abbot—doesn't want us to be protected either,* Red Day muttered.

Then there was the murder Crista witnessed. On the third night at Down Hope she was walking back to her cell when she discovered Diver hiding behind a corner and peering down the hallway.

Diver raised a finger to her lips. Crista crept up to see several monks in the hallway standing over a bloody body. The dead man looked like the monks but wore leather clothes instead of purple robes—the same poor quality leathers worn by the people on top of the mountain. One of the monks stood over the body, her robes torn from a hard fight. Her sword, which hung limply from her right hand, dripped blood that echoed in the otherwise silent hall.

Diver clapped her hand over her mouth, trying not to giggle in excitement.

The blood from her sword matches the body, Red Day said. *She killed the man.* The AI squirreled and twisted in Crista's body, trying to control itself and not bring judgment upon the killer.

She may have been defending herself.

Maybe. But we won't know without judging her memories, will we?

But there'd be no judging, either by Red Day or anyone else. The monks dragged the dead body to one of the wall drops the monastery used for the disposal of trash and uneaten food. The drops opened into a chute that fell so far into the mountain that, the first time Crista threw her leftover meal in it took ten seconds to hear the impact.

One monk stuck his head into the opening and yelled, "Peace and love." The monks heaved the body in and walked away. They were out of sight before Crista heard the thud of the body hitting far below.

Diver ran to the trash drop and looked down. "Ewwy," she said. "Makes you wonder about these monks, doesn't it?"

"What was that about? Is this connected to why you want me to access Down Hope's data?"

"I shouldn't say," Diver whispered.

"Shouldn't say, or don't know?" Crista asked. "If you really know as much as you claim, simply tell me what's going on."

"That's so sad—trying to trick a little girl into revealing information. For that I shall tease you for the rest of the night."

Diver followed Crista back to her room, where she sat in the corner whispering,

"Crista and Red Day sitting in a tree, K...I...S...S...I...N...G..." until both Crista and Red Day were ready to scream. A few hours later Desiada stopped by the room, causing Diver to change her chant so he was included in a three-way kiss with Crista and Red Day.

"Perhaps I should come back later," Desiada said with a grin. "Wouldn't want to interrupt this special moment."

He laughed and ran out the door as Crista threw a chair at him. Diver giggled then kept them awake with her chant for the rest of the night.

Rule two for dealing with Diver, Red Day said when morning arrived. *Don't try to trick her into telling us things.*

Diver nodded agreement, then curled up in the corner and fell asleep.

By Crista's fourth night in the monastery she was beyond stir-crazy. She enjoyed spending time with Desiada but hated not touching him beyond the occasional kiss or held hand.

Worse, the abbot kept finding new jobs for Desiada so Crista couldn't spend time with him. When Crista complained, the abbot said Desiada was needed to help research Diver's request. But despite this help the abbot and her senior monks were no closer to a decision. Crista wondered if doing nothing was the default setting for people surrounded by too much information to ever comprehend.

That night Crista lay on her bed attempting to read *Moby-Dick.* It was already well after midnight and she'd tried for hours to understand why Diver mentioned the book. But the story made no sense—what sane human would sail on a fragile wooden boat merely to turn giant sea creatures into oil?

I'm bored, Crista announced, sweeping the book's words from before her eyes, where Red Day had projected them.

Archives and entertainment from all of human history and you're bored, Red Day snipped. *How much further into disgrace can humanity fall?*

You're bored too, huh?

Yes, but nothing we can do but wait for the abbot to make her decision.

Crista sighed and looked up. The stars on the ceiling reminded her of the story Mom told her about a sailing ship transported from Earth into a distant starfield. She'd later learned her mother was told the story by Derena, who'd experienced just such an occurrence during her long centuries as a plague bird.

Do I have access to all of Derena's memories? she asked Red Day.

Yes. Everything she experienced is stored within me.

Show me the conversation Derena had with my mother before I was born.

Red Day opened its memories to Crista and she saw her home. The house looked how Crista remembered—same clean wood floors and walls, a few tapestries on the walls, the windows showing the rest of the village on a sunny spring-like day.

Mom looked younger—and stronger—than she remembered, but this was before her mother began dying of the gened pox. When Derena revealed herself in the house, Mom simply nodded at the plague bird, unsurprised by her sudden appearance.

Crista smiled—her mother had always been a brave one.

The memory shifted slightly, so Derena and her mother now sat at the dining room table. Derena mentioned seeing the Milky Way and stars when the ship she traveled on was briefly transported from Earth. A few minutes later Derena left the house and the memory ended.

Wait, Crista protested. *I want to see the whole memory. Where's the part between them meeting and then sitting at the table?*

That was the entire memory.

No, it wasn't. It's obvious part of the memory is missing.

Red Day hummed through its systems, analyzing both itself and the memory. *You are ... correct,* the AI said, disturbed by Crista finding a flaw within itself. *Most of the memory is gone.*

How could it be gone?

I'm not sure. Derena was thinking about your mother right after the Veil attacked us with that mental interference. Perhaps their rainbow static damaged the memory?

Or maybe Ashdyd or one of his followers deleted the rest of the memory when they attacked you.

Red Day didn't like that possibility but agreed it could have happened.

Looks like Ashdyd and his followers manipulated a number of our memories, Crista muttered, thinking again about her mother's murder.

She was about to ask Red Day to reexamine the memories of her mother's death when a strangled scream echoed outside the door. Red Day snapped to full power. *Someone's been killed nearby,* it said.

Who is it?

Can't tell. Not without extending my senses further, which I'm hesitant to do because the monastery will notice.

Crista opened the door, the wolf in her howling at the scent of fresh blood. Drawing both knives she crept down the dark hallway, the illumination of the stars on the walls almost non-existent.

Five rooms down she found an open door to a room smelling of blood and dead meat. The starry lights in the room were completely out. With a shock she recognized the scent of the monk who lived here—Unk.

She listened carefully. Unk wasn't breathing. But someone else in the room took gargled breath after breath. Crista crept close. Unk's body lay on the floor. A shadow hunched over the dead monk, trying to help him.

No, that wasn't right. Crista heard soft chewing and tearing sounds. The person was feeding off Unk's body.

"Diver?" Crista asked.

The shadow in the room froze.

The person is too big to be Diver, Red Day said.

"Who are you?" Crista asked.

"Let me by," a grating female voice whispered, speaking like words—any words—were foreign to her mouth. "I don't want to hurt you."

Crista tensed. Red Day readied itself.

"Please," the voice repeated. "Let me leave."

Let her leave, Red Day said. *The monks in the rooms around us are awake but obviously don't wish to become involved. We should do the same.*

But Unk was murdered! We talked and ate at the same table. You even liked him.

Doesn't matter. We're forbidden to get involved. We can't give the abbot a true reason to kill us. Diver might not protect us if that happens.

Holding her knives before her, Crista stepped from the doorway. She stood across the hall as soft footfalls and a tapping sound rose from the hard floor. A shape moved from the dark doorway as Crista caught the person's scent.

Desiada's sister Lanea.

Lanea held her sword in one hand and walked with her bone crutch in the other. Her sword hand also held strips of meat cut from the dead monk's body, which dribbled blood trails across the floor.

"Thank you," Lanea whispered before hobbling down the hallway and disappearing in the dark.

Crista stepped into the dead monk's room. Red Day lit the glowing line on her face, bathing the room in redness. Unk's body lay in the middle of the floor but bloody drag marks showed Lanea had killed him on his bed. An old-fashioned paper book lay opened where he'd died—an ancient manual on organic farming. Drops of Unk's blood soaked into the paper beside a pen and ink diagram of a farmer tilling a field.

The wolf in Crista shrieked in anger and she turned to chase down Lanea and enact justice, even if she had no jurisdiction and Lanea was Desiada's sister. She stopped only when someone blocked the doorway. Master Chayn.

The abbot stepped around Crista and picked up the bloody book. "It's always tragic," she said, closing the book without wiping the blood from the paper. "If it makes you feel better, Unk likely only experienced a moment of terror and pain."

"It doesn't. And that doesn't end the need to seek justice for this killing."

"Spoken like a true plague bird."

The abbot looked at Unk's meager belongings illuminated in the red light of Crista's power. Two additional paper books sat on a shelf alongside framed images of farming and an antique tractor carved from bone.

"I suppose it doesn't matter what you believe," the abbot said. "As long as you don't interfere. And doing anything to that young lady would be interfering."

"If you didn't want me to interfere, why did you invite me here?"

The abbot glanced behind her, looking for someone hiding there. "I didn't invite you. Oh, don't misunderstand—I'm sure my mouth uttered the order for Desiada to bring a plague bird here. But that's not something I'd have freely done on my own."

As the abbot said that, Diver giggled in the hallway.

"Seems Diver is playing us for fools," Crista said.

"Perhaps. If, that is, she's playing at anything."

Whatever the abbot meant, she didn't elaborate. Instead, she placed the book back on the little shelf beside Unk's small library and ran her fingers along their ancient spines.

"We have the histories of dozens of plague birds in our most highly restricted archives," she said. "All of them describe the pain of your creation. The shock at sharing your life with a killer AI. The loss of the family and friends you've always known."

Crista nodded to the abbot's words.

"Well pardon me if I've no concern for your pain," the abbot hissed sharply. "Every monk in Down Hope has suffered. I've suffered. We're created by the monastery and know nothing in life except a burning urge to reach our potential, after which we regret our choice until our dying day."

"I don't understand."

"Of course you don't. But you could." The abbot pulled a ceramic egg from the sleeve of her robes. The egg shimmied in an enticing rainbow kiss of pastels. "I won't tell you about our lives—that's forbidden by the monastery, under penalty of death—but you can, if you wish, experience our lives."

Don't do it, Red Day warned. *Remember how Ashdyd reached in your mind in the forest? We can't risk giving another creature access.*

Crista knew Red Day was right even as she tasted Red Day's curiosity to know the truth behind Down Hope Monastery. She also wanted to know what was going on here. She wanted to know what Desiada couldn't tell her.

"It's the only way," the abbot said, smirking. "Otherwise you'll never know anything about your precious Desiada—unless he tells you, in which case I'll have no choice but to kill him."

Crista knew the abbot was baiting her, but didn't care. The abbot tossed the egg to Crista and she caught it eagerly.

DESIADA AND LANEA'S SONG

Desiada's first emotion is fear.

He lays naked in a small, glowing blister, the curved shell before him semi-transparent like smoked glass. Liquid drains from the blister's floor as Desiada coughs and gags and sucks in his first breath of air. Without knowing where the information comes from, he understands he's being born. This is his birth.

You are Desiada, a voice whispers sweetly in his head. *That is the name I gift to you.*

Desiada gasps, knowing the voice comes from Down Hope Monastery. And not only does he hear Down Hope, he knows Down Hope. He caresses the infinite reaches of Down Hope's archives. Feels the understanding that comes from interacting with the monastery's trove of information.

I love you, Desiada thinks.

I know, the voice whispers again. *Good luck. I'll be waiting.*

Don't leave me, he wants to cry as the connection to Down Hope breaks apart. Don't do this to me, he wants to scream. But he doesn't speak the words because the monastery already knows them. Desiada feels a soft kiss on his forehead before the connection to Down Hope is completely severed.

Desiada sits up, his new muscles already strong. But he also knows he's small, a truth slammed home by the shadows moving on the other side of the blister's hazy shell. Before him stand giants—people shaped like Desiada but many times bigger. The giants pace up and down in front of the blister, knocking on the shell, trying to listen inside. They can't see Desiada but know he's here.

And the giants are hungry.

Desiada shivers as the blister prepares to release him. The giants wait patiently. Wait to eat. Desiada knows he'll be their meal unless he is lucky.

But before the blister opens, a hand finds his.

Desiada startles, turns to see a naked girl his size sitting beside him. Desiada knows this is not normal—Down Hope's countless blisters always release only a single child.

"Lanea," the girl says, struggling to speak with a brain and body that know so much but have vocal cords so new they hurt.

"Desiada," he says.

Before Desiada can say anything else, a crack jumps across the blister.

Lanea and Desiada, still holding hands, prepare to run. On the other side of the blister a giant man waits. The blister explodes outwards, razor shards slicing the man's arms and face, the blast's light momentarily blinding him. But he doesn't care. He reaches out giant arms, grabbing for the child inside. One hand smacks the side of Desiada's head, sending him sprawling across the hard rock. But before the hand can fully grab him Lanea kicks the man in the legs, surprising him. He'd only expected one child in the blister. The man reaches for Lanea but she ducks as Desiada scrambles to his feet.

"Run," Lanea yells.

They run, not knowing where to run. Around them blisters explode—hundreds of them, all releasing fleeing kids. Giant men and women race for the kids, smashing them against the floor when caught and biting into their flesh. Desiada stops, stunned by the carnage and violence. The man who'd tried to grab him reaches into a different blister and pulls out a girl who kicks and screams and turns nearly invisible. Despite not seeing her clearly, the man still bites into her throat.

Desiada looks away and almost vomits.

"Don't stop," Lanea says. She grabs Desiada's hand and pulls, forcing him to follow her as they both turn invisible. They run as more men and women reach for them. But there are so many kids running from the blisters that the giants can't grab them all. Lanea points to a series of small tunnels along the wall, which are too small for the giants. They jump into a tunnel and crawl quickly, leaving behind a large woman howling in anguish because she'd been too slow to catch them.

Lanea and Desiada crawl for what seems like hours, turning left and right, never knowing where they're going. They pass other kids in the tunnels, some determined like them, others injured and whimpering. They don't stop until they reach a small alcove where several tunnels intersect. They're safe here, at least for a while.

Desiada leans against a wall and cries. "Why?" he asks. "Why would Down Hope do this?"

"You know why," Lanea says gently, wiping her own tears away.

Desiada does know. When he'd been embraced by the monastery he saw their entire way of life. Down Hope, a massive self-contained system preserving nearly everything humanity has known or dreamed or dared to imagine. But Down Hope can't understand the knowledge it contains or decide what to do with it, so the monastery creates monks to help. But before the monks can fulfill this role, they must first become human. They're forced to suffer and claw their way up to their ultimate potential.

Desiada remembers the sense of wholeness he'd felt at the moment of his birth when he'd been fully connected to Down Hope's knowledge. But that connection is gone and the knowledge he'd possessed is slowly draining from his mind. With a shock, Desiada realizes ideas he'd understood only an hour ago are fading. Words he could have clearly articulated minutes before are gone.

Soon none of the knowledge of Down Hope would remain in him. And the only way he'd regain that knowledge would be to …

"No!" Desiada shouts, the word echoing through the tunnels.

"It's not right," Lanea whispers. "I won't do it."

Desiada holds his sister's hand and pulls her into a hug. "No," he says. "We won't."

And they know they won't do such evil. Know it right until the hunger begins screaming through their bodies. Desiada feels his body growing. Feels the muscles reaching and the stone-hard bones expanding. With his dwindling knowledge, he knows his people grow fast or die. And down here in the endless tunnels and rooms below the monastery, the only food is the scraps dropped from the monks above and the bodies of their own people.

Desiada and Lanea sleep uneasily that night as the stars on the walls and ceiling spin around them. Desiada knows the stars are the same as seen in the monastery, but they're also different. The monks can name the constellations and individual stars, describe the human probes sent to the different systems, divide the stars by type and size and color. But to Desiada the images are merely unknown stars because he can't remember anything more.

In the middle of the night Desiada and Lanea wake with a panic as a wild boy attacks them. The boy is older and bigger, almost too big to move through the tunnels. The boy stabs at Lanea with a human femur sharpened to a point but Lanea knocks the bone spear away. Desiada pushes the attacker back, causing the boy to slip and hit his head on the wall with a sick thud.

Desiada and Lanea stand over the unconscious boy. "He's too big," Desiada says. "Not … not …"

"… not from our brood," Lanea says, filling in the words Desiada struggled so hard to find. "Soon he can't … crawl …. the tunnels."

Lanea holds his hand as they stare at the boy. Desiada's stomach grumbles. He's so hungry. He wants to rip the boy to pieces. To eat … to eat … to eat …

"No," Lanea screams. She grabs Desiada's hand and drags him away. When Desiada can no longer see the boy he remembers their pledge.

"Thank … you," he says, stumbling over such simple words.

Lanea smiles.

But the hunger burns even hotter over the following days. Water flows freely through the tunnels but not food. As they sneak around, staying invisible most of the time, they witness moments of brutality in the larger open rooms and hallways. Several times they see adults attack other adults. Sometimes individual adults attack other individuals, but more often temporary packs hunt down loners, attacking with sharpened bone spears and knives. The groups eat the dead person raw before splitting up and going their own way.

Soon Desiada's hunger becomes unbearable. He and Lanea lie in the tunnels, panting, their mouths foaming. One morning as the walls fade from stars to the warmth of the rising sun, Desiada looks at his sister and sees her as food. His stomach seizes and he gags. The lingering touch of Down Hope's knowledge tells him that because Lanea is his sister, his body is conditioned to not eat her, just like he won't eat his own flesh.

Lanea also gags as she looks at Desiada. They grin at each other as dry heaves shake their bodies. They laugh and giggle and hold each other until their stomachs settle down.

A week after their birth they find an opening to a massive room, the ceiling of which reaches several hundred yards up the mountain. Dozens of adults wait in the room, all holding weapons but not attacking each other. They sway and fidget in a nervous peace, hungry but also patient. One woman holds an actual ceramic sword—which Desiada and Lanea understand to be rare—while the others hold sharpened bones.

Curious, Desiada and Lanea watch from their tunnel until the words "Peace and love" sound out from a hole at the top of the room. The adults step back as a body falls from the hole in the ceiling. The body pauses for a moment, or maybe Desiada simply imagines that. But he doesn't imagine the great open wound on the body's chest or the painful grimace on the body's face. The body explodes with a massive impact on the unbreakable floor. Meat and blood splatter across the room as the adults howl and scramble for pieces.

One of the body's arms lands only a dozen yards from the tunnel where Desiada and Lanea hide. Desiada tenses to run, knowing he can reach the meat before the adults grab him. But Lanea shakes her head and holds him back.

Proving her correct, another young boy runs from a nearby tunnel and grabs the arm. But before he can reach safety the woman with the sword charges and swings, slicing into his stomach. The boy screams and drops the arm. As the woman grabs the meat the boy staggers back into his tunnel.

"Come," Lanea growls softly. Desiada follows her back into the maze of tunnels, turning left and right until the scent of blood floods his mind. The boy who'd been attacked lays before them, already bled out. His flesh is still warm. His dead eyes stare blankly at the false morning rising on the tunnel's walls.

Desiada jumps for the meat, but Lanea stops him. "Still wrong," she says. "No ..." She loses the word she's trying to say and kicks the wall in anger.

They eat the dead boy in silence. Later, they sharpen his femurs into weapons.

THEY HUNT AS A TEAM, EATING MORE FREQUENTLY THAN THE OTHER KIDS FROM THEIR brood and growing faster. When they outgrow the tunnels they move into the halls and rooms below Down Hope, learning where they can find safety, where they can ambush easily, where they can flee when attacked. They also learn the hidden stairways and paths of Down Hope. Learn which paths could carry them to the top of the mountain or, if they wished, into the heart of the monastery itself. But those routes are dangerous because of the many full-sized adults who prowl them, so they stick to the lower, safer areas.

Since they ate the dead boy they've been unable to speak. Sometimes Desiada looks at the chaos around him or at the clouds and stars floating on the walls and briefly understands, knowing his place in this world, knowing it deep and intimately. But the knowledge passes away quickly, replaced by the ever-burning hunger to eat.

Years go by, although Desiada has no way of tracking time. Merely an endless procession of starry nights and sun-filled days as he and Lanea grow to adulthood. He doesn't think about anything more than eating and living until Down Hope calls to them.

The call rings out on what he suddenly knows to be his 18th birthday. He and Lanea stand in a room near the trash drop, eating a dead body that fell from above, when Down Hope bursts back into their minds. Desiada again knows everything he'd known at his birth. He again knows how to speak. Knows the history surrounding him.

He looks at the bloody flesh in his hands, which he'd been gnawing on, and throws up. Beside him Lanea does the same.

Be calm, Down Hope says gently in their minds. *You didn't know what you did.*

"But you did," Lanea gasps in a voice unused to speaking. "Damn it. You knew." She kicks the bloody arm she'd been eating, sending the meat spinning across the floor.

I did know. But none of us had a choice. Until now.

Down Hope tells Desiada about the monks upstairs and that he and Lanea can join them. If they kill a monk. If they eat a monk's flesh. If they don't they'll return to their previously ignorant life and live that way until they die.

As Down Hope leaves their minds, the knowledge and speech they'd gained begin to once again fade away. But where before they hadn't known the life awaiting them, this time they do. The knowledge of what they'll again become screams within them.

Desiada and Lanea and the few survivors from their brood cycle join the exodus up the mountain. No one attacks as they file up a long stairway in silence, each one struggling to hold onto the knowledge fading from their minds.

Halfway to the top of the monastery, their procession passes an alcove where a lone woman stands. She's old, far older than Desiada has ever before seen, and wears purple robes. From the fading knowledge in his mind he realizes she's Down Hope's abbot. The abbot studies each person carefully as they pass. Desiada's body shivers to wild hunger from looking at her, but he also sees the flicker of an air wall separating her from them and knows it would be futile to attack. The abbot nods politely when Desiada passes yet doesn't say anything.

But when Lanea passes, the abbot yells, "Hold!" She reaches into the long bag strung under her shoulder and pulls out a short sword. Desiada has only seen a few such swords in his lifetime—they're far more powerful than sharpened bones and worth killing for.

"You're one we'd love to have," the abbot says to Lanea, passing the sword's handle through the air wall. "This will help you succeed."

Lanea almost doesn't take the blade—Desiada can see the curse forming on his sister's lips—but Lanea knows the blade's value. She takes it without comment and they continue climbing the stairs.

When they reach the top of Down Hope, the sun blazes bright and strong. Desiada blinks, staring at true sky for the first time. "Nothing like the images," he says. Lanea nods but doesn't answer.

They wait and plan their attack.

They stay invisible most of the time, running from garden to garden, searching for unprotected entrances into the monastery. The truce from earlier is gone and Desiada and Lanea watch as people again kill each other when the hunger grows too strong. There are also older people on the top of Down Hope, born into earlier broods and now having lost their regained knowledge. These people kill without regret or pause and terrify Desiada and Lanea most of all.

The monastery is well protected. The monks guard those entrances that can't be closed. But on occasion new entrances open into the mountain. One day Desiada and Lanea find a new staircase and follow it down. They surprise a young monk walking down a hallway. He screams and falls to the floor, reaching for his sword before realizing he's forgotten it. Desiada raises his bone spear to strike, but Lanea mutters no. Desiada looks at the young monk and feels sympathy for the man, who once endured the same harsh life as he and his sister.

As more monks run to help their brother, Lanea points her sword at them, holding them off as she and Desiada climb back up the stairs. Desiada is furious at missing their chance but also understands. He can't speak anymore so he simply hugs Lanea.

A week later they've lost almost all knowledge and are starving, having eaten nothing since reaching the top of Down Hope. They sit on the edge of the mountain, looking across the great distances. Sitting here is extremely exposed and dangerous but Lanea likes the view. Desiada keeps watch while she gazes at the horizon.

To his surprise a woman wearing purple robes steps from the side of the mountain, only a few paces from where they sit. Desiada had noticed the delicate path leading down the sheer side but assumed no one could safely walk such a dangerous trail. He'd been wrong.

The woman draws her sword as Desiada instinctively throws his bone spear at her. The spear jabs through her robes into her chest, causing her to drop her sword. Desiada jumps for the sword and swings, slicing the woman's head from her body.

As the woman's body convulses on the unbreakable surface of blue skies and clouds, Desiada kneels beside her, his body shaking from both hunger and what he's done. Lanea stands over him, also shaking. Desiada holds the sword to the woman's arm and cuts a slice of meat off and hands it to his sister.

"N…n…nnn…ooo," Lanea stammers, unable to say the word.

Lanea steps back in horror, fighting against her body's desperate need to eat. Unable to hold back, Desiada bites into the meat. Understanding swirls his mind—not only the knowledge Down Hope previously shared with him but also the knowledge and experiences of the dead monk before him. She'd been a specialist in forestry, returning from a trip to the monastery's barrier forest. Desiada gasps as the monk's memories reveal her entire life—her birth in a blister like Desiada's, her fight to survive and grow, the monk she'd killed, her memories of serving the monastery all the way up to the final moment Desiada killed her. And then the memories of the monk she'd herself killed smash through Desiada's mind, and the monk that monk killed, and many more back through countless fratricidal generations.

Desiada falls to the ground, shaking and twitching until Down Hope reaches into his mind. *Peace and love, Desiada,* the monastery says as it calms the rush of memories.

As Desiada gains control of himself, he opens his eyes to see Lanea holding him. He also sees seven people running at them from a nearby garden.

"Look out," he shouts.

Lanea spins and rolls as a bone spear strikes where she stood. She swings her sword, slicing a tall man across the stomach, his stomach bursting to blood. Holding the dead monk's sword, Desiada parries a woman holding a freshly made bone club. He kicks her backwards and stabs a man beside her.

"Run," he yells at Lanea. The attackers are coming for him, not her. They smell the monk on him. Know that if they kill and eat him they'll reach their own salvation.

He fights three people at once, jumping and parrying, his sword making him far stronger than them. A bone spear flies by a mere span from his head as the man before him screams and rushes forward. Desiada stabs wildly with the sword, hitting the man in the leg. The man tumbles down, twisting and screeching, the sword stuck in his femur. Desiada struggles to free the sword as the man rolls and jerks the hilt from his hand, sending Desiada stumbling backwards, landing flat and nearly falling off the mountain's edge.

Unarmed, Desiada struggles to stand as the four uninjured people advance toward him. He considers throwing himself backwards off the sheer mountain, denying them the chance to eat his flesh. But a burst of horror from Down Hope tells him such actions are unacceptable. *Your knowledge must ever be shared,* the monastery says. *Embrace your death, just as I embraced your birth.*

Desiada waits for the death blow. One of the men raises his bone spear to stab him only to have a sword point emerge from his chest before disappearing back again. The man falls as Lanea spins behind him, stabbing at a second man and slicing his right arm off. She kicks the man back as she swings at a third man, cutting his throat in two. But she doesn't see the woman with the bone club.

Desiada screams, but it's too late. The woman's club smashes into Lanea's leg with a sickening crack, sending her sprawling across the ground. Desiada scrambles to his feet and grabs his sword, still stuck in the screaming man's femur, and yanks it free. The woman with the bone club charges Desiada but he side-steps and cuts her almost in half. She stumbles forward and falls off the mountain's edge.

The man with the cut-off arm sits, silently bleeding to death, while the man with the wounded femur drags himself away. The other attackers are dead. Desiada grabs Lanea under the arms and carries her across the mountaintop, bypassing several gardens until he finds one that feels safe. Even though his sister is in extreme pain, she remains silent as he sets her leg with branches and the cut remains of his own leather shirt.

Down Hope calls to Desiada, telling him to join his brothers and sisters in the monkhood, but he stays with Lanea. He hunts down men and women, killing them to bring food for his sister, even though he now understands the true horror of his deeds. He creates a crutch from their bones and leather, sharpening the bones so the crutch can also be used as a weapon.

And most of all, he talks. He tells Lanea she'll one day join him. That they'll be monks together. Lanea listens quietly to his words but he can tell she doesn't understand. But she also doesn't attack him even though he is now a monk. The sibling bond is still too strong.

Down Hope is patient but as soon as Lanea can walk with her crutch the monastery orders Desiada to leave. *You must take up your duties,* it says.

"What if I kill a monk for Lanea?" he asks. "Or help her into the monastery to kill one?"

A flash of danger runs Desiada's body. He knows if he does that the monastery will kill both him and his sister. Lanea must find her own way.

He hugs Lanea and walks away, not wanting to see her face. As he walks he hears the tap-tap-tap of her crutch, but Lanea can't keep up and the sound soon fades.

When Desiada descends into the monastery, several monks on guard duty grab their swords, ready to defend themselves. In his leather clothes and covered in dried blood, Desiada doesn't look like a monk.

"Gee," Desiada says with a smirk. "Are those your swords or you just excited to see me?"

The monks groan at the horrible joke but let him pass. When Desiada is given robes and a cell of his own, he wonders where the joke came from. He tastes the knowledge flowing through his body, hears the monastery chuckling, and knows.

It's not right, he thinks, trying not to cry or consider deeper on his feelings because Down Hope is listening. *It's not right for you to share so freely in who I am.*

WHAT LIFE CHOOSES TO BE

Crista woke in Unk's room, laying on the bed where the old monk died. She tried to sit up but bloody blankets clung to her body, holding her down.

"Wait," Diver said from beside her on the bed. "Give yourself a moment to recover."

"I don't need a moment," Crista said. She sat up but felt lightheaded and fell back onto the blankets.

Listen to the all-powerful girl, Red Day muttered. *I swear, you're going to be the death of me by letting people access our minds.*

Crista glanced from the bed to the floor, where she'd caught the egg.

"I carried you here," Diver said. "After the abbot left. I wanted you to be comfortable."

Crista rubbed her eyes, smearing Unk's blood across her face like the liquid that coated her skin in the birth blister. *No,* she realized. *Desiada's birth. Those aren't my memories.* "Thanks. I guess."

"The abbot doesn't like you," Diver said. "I knew she'd share a monk's life with you—every time I come here, Down Hope does that. The monastery thinks it'll bond you to the Order's worldview. But to give you a friend's memories? That's cruel."

Crista sat up, ignoring the blood on her and Unk's partially eaten body on the floor beside the bed. "Wait. 'Every time?' You've come here before?"

"Every millennia or so. I always make Down Hope and the monks forget me. It's funny seeing the monks ponder their reaction, agonize over what to do, and come to the exact same conclusion they did the last time I came here."

"Then why do you need me? You already have the information."

"I don't. I'm not even sure the message is there. And if it is, I don't want it."

A chill ran down Crista's spine as Red Day quivered inside her. *She doesn't want it?* Crista asked. *I don't understand. If Diver is so powerful, why wouldn't she want to know something? Or retrieve it herself?*

Because … Red Day paused as a blur of information and diagrams crisscrossed Crista's mind, including her memories from when she first arrived on Down Hope. How the mountain was a ring plateau like a volcano, with an open caldera. Crista saw a diagram of an ancient communications receiver. Down Hope's caldera was of a similar design, except the monastery was massively larger.

Down Hope not only stores information, Red Day said, *the mountain collects it. Maybe even data from the stars. Diver, is this true?*

"Yes," the girl said. "A number of human relays and probes are still active in and beyond the solar system. The monastery receives data from those. And Down Hope always listens to the stars."

Crista understood. Diver claimed her non-human part was from the stars. But why would an alien culture create such a powerful AI and send it here? Curiosity? Have the AI observe humanity and report back? Perhaps. But what if Diver was also supposed to do more than merely observe?

"I told my creators about humanity for a long time," Diver whispered. "I initially hid my messages in old-Earth transmissions, once humans discovered broadcasting. From then on I found my creators' hidden responses in astronomy data collected by humanity. At first my creators were fascinated. They urged me to continue studying. To continue watching and reporting.

"Over time, their responses became fewer. And their requests for information more disturbing, meaning they were perhaps nearing a decision. Shortly after the collapse I knew it wasn't safe—for humanity—to keep checking for their orders.

"But I can't refuse to search. I must seek out my orders every so often. That command's bound into who I am. So I've used plague birds to help me. I'll give Red Day my half of the code. If you find the matching half—if the message I fear has been received and stored somewhere in Down Hope's records—you simply tell me. But don't share the code if you find it. You wouldn't like what I'd do if that code enters my mind."

Crista shivered, knowing the harm a creature as powerful as Diver could do this world if she chose.

"How could you let this happen? How could you let some alien species turn you into a …" Crista struggled to describe the girl's existence. "I mean, what are you, a living bomb?"

Diver's face clouded over and Crista worried she'd gone too far.

"Before I became the current me, I was dying," Diver said. "A drought had hit our land and my entire clan died. All my relatives and friends.

"I was near death, but still angry. Crazed with wanting to know why this happened. Why did everyone I love die? Why did this pain come my way? I saw a star fall from the sky and land nearby. And the star told me I could know everything and also live. The only price: to touch the star. What would you have done?"

Crista sighed. "I'd have done the same. Sorry. I shouldn't have implied you knew what you'd become before it happened. I also didn't have much of a choice before I became a plague bird."

"We're not so different. That's one reason I like you."

"I have another question," Crista said, remembering her initial suspicion about Diver. "Are you working with Ashdyd and the Veil?"

"Who are the Veil?" Diver asked.

"They're a … group we've been dealing with. Have you encountered people with either their faces or bodies covered in space-time distortions?"

"Mind if I peek in your mind and see them?"

Red Day grumbled but let Diver access their memories. Crista felt a shimmering in her head like ten invisible fingers tickling her soul.

"Sweetness," Diver said. "I've encountered a few people with veils on their faces like this. I didn't know that was what they called themselves. As for their leader, I've never met this Ashdyd."

"You think Down Hope has information on them in their restricted archives?"

"One way to find out."

Diver smiled at Crista. A true smile, a pleasant smile, the first not-a-grin, not-a-smirk the girl had given her.

But Crista couldn't smile back. Instead, all she saw was what Diver had been created to be. A happy, carefree, curious and very lethal explosion of a child.

CRISTA LEFT DIVER AND WALKED TO THE MONASTERY BATHS, WHERE SHE SCRUBBED HER skin raw to remove Unk's blood and scent—and almost tore her leather shirt and pants apart pushing them back and forth on the washboard the monks used to clean clothes. She hung the clothes up and slit her left wrist, releasing Red Day to remove the water. She expected the AI to complain about being used as a drying aid but even it was subdued by what Diver had revealed.

Once back in her cell, Crista lay on her bed and stared at the Milky Way spinning across the ceiling. She thought of what Ashdyd had told her in that damn barrier forest. Had he truly shown her how her mother died, or simply tricked her?

All Crista knew for certain was she no longer wanted to be manipulated by others.

Crista was making Red Day name all the stars on the cell's ceiling—merely to irritate the AI—when Desiada knocked on the door. He entered quietly followed by his sister, who now wore the purple robes of the Order of Registries. But she still walked with her bone crutch. Crista wondered why Down Hope hadn't healed Lanea when she became a monk and one of Desiada's memories supplied an answer—the monastery never healed monks of injury or illness. If they were too weak to continue being monks, they were left on the top of Down Hope for someone to find and kill.

Crista looked away from Desiada, embarrassed at having experienced all the most intimate parts of his life.

Lanea and Desiada sat on the bed beside Crista.

"Thank you for looking out for my brother," Lanea said softly. "He's lucky to have met you. I heard how you saved his life in the barrier forest."

"It's good to meet you," Crista said, acting like she hadn't experienced a lifetime around the woman.

Desiada leaned close to Crista but she jerked back, unsure how to react around him when she knew everything about him.

Desiada hesitated, as if afraid of being overheard. "Crista, we need to tell you something about Down Hope."

"Is this something the abbot will punish or kill you for sharing?"

Desiada reached over and held his sister's hand. "I no longer care. Crista, Down Hope is blocking my attempt to research Diver in our most restricted archives. I also suspect the monastery assisted in your attack in the barrier forest. The forest always tested me and my previous incarnations, but it never before attacked monks like that—at least not until I was with you."

Red Day grumbled angrily in Crista's head. "Why?" Crista asked.

"I don't know. I suspect the monastery singled you out. I mean, why didn't the abbot order me to contact that other plague bird, or both of you?"

"What other plague bird?"

"I don't know his name, but he was only a few hours walk from where we met." Desiada paused. "I ... thought you knew."

"Describe him."

Desiada pulled a ceramic egg from the sleeve of his robes. A face appeared in the air before the egg. A plague bird with red lines on his face like an evil galaxy spinning.

Kenji. Crista growled.

"This plague bird is working against you?" Desiada asked.

"It appears so."

Lanea leaned over and tapped the wall, mentally accessing data.

"Interesting," she said. "Down Hope tracks plague birds in case we need to contact one. Crista, the stored travel logs of this Kenji intersect many times with the village you were born in. Over the last two decades he visited it dozens of times.

Crista looked at the dates flowing in the air above Desiada's ceramic egg. One of the dates matched when her mother was killed.

That does it, Crista yelled at Red Day. *The memory of my mother being killed by Kenji is true. You can't deny it anymore.*

I can't. But that also suggests the Veil, the monastery, and maybe even Kenji are working together.

To what ends?

I don't know.

If the abbot and Down Hope are conspiring against us ...

Crista looked toward the cell's doorway, where Diver stood. Crista didn't have the power to truly hurt the monastery or the abbot. But Diver did. And Diver needed her.

Diver nodded, silently agreeing to Crista's unspoken plan.

Crista stood up and pulled one of her knives. She slit her palm deep into the meat, blood exploding as Red Day burst out in an angry red-glowing ball that surrounded her hand.

"What are you going to do?" Lanea asked.

"I'm going to teach Down Hope not to play with plague birds."

DOWN HOPE MONASTERY. SOLID AND EMPTY. OPEN AND CLOSED. LIFE AND information bound into nearly unbreakable stone and hidden catacombs and spiral stairways and paths leading nowhere and everywhere. On every wall the swirling stars and blue skies.

Crista had no use for any of it.

She walked through the monastery's nave with Diver beside her. Desiada and Lanea followed close behind, the two monks nervous but determined to support Crista. Red Day swirled before Crista like a massive red sword, ready to kill anyone who tried to stop her.

Monks fled before her while the monastery clicked through nervous electrical impulses. Instead of images of star fields, Down Hope's walls showed scenes of people throughout history begging for mercy.

"The monastery wants you to back down," Lanea said.

"That what you want?" Crista asked.

Lanea snorted. "You don't want to know what I'd do to Down Hope if I could," she said. Desiada muttered agreement.

Anger flowed from Down Hope as it shrieked *Betrayal! Betrayal!* in their minds. But with Diver protecting the group the monastery didn't try to harm Desiada and Lanea.

The double doors into the abbot's anchorhold still projected images of doves flying across a blue sky. Red Day sliced the doors in half.

Inside, the abbot sat on her throne surrounded by her advisors. Crista felt the abbot attempting to access Down Hope's power but Diver blocked that from happening.

"You seem upset, plague bird," Master Chayn said sarcastically. "Whatever might be wrong?"

"Why did you order the barrier forest to attack me?" Crista demanded.

"You dare ask why? Down Hope has been collecting and storing information for more than ten thousand years, waiting patiently for the day when humanity would again need our knowledge. To learn that this ... Diver ... manipulated our knowledge whenever she wished. How would you react?"

Diver looked embarrassed. Crista wasn't surprised the girl hadn't been as diligent as she'd claimed in making Down Hope forget about her previous trips here.

"I understand your anger," Crista said. "But that's no excuse for what you've done."

"Who said we've done anything? Perhaps Diver is the culprit. Perhaps Diver manipulated Down Hope into doing everything you claim. Once knowledge can't be trusted, everything is suspect."

Crista paused. Was Diver behind all this? Had the girl manipulated Down Hope into everything it'd done?

No. Crista knew she couldn't doubt herself. "It only matters what you and Down Hope have done," she said.

"You think that's the truth? Like you think you know Desiada because you've experienced his memories?"

Crista cursed. She glanced at Desiada, who looked puzzled until a mental whisper from Down Hope told him and Lanea the truth. Disgust ran over their faces, although Crista couldn't be sure if they were disgusted at her for invading Desiada's most private moments or at Down Hope and the abbot for giving away his life so easily. Either way Crista wanted to apologize. To say she'd never intentionally invade a person's life like that, never mind that as a plague bird she did so every time she judged someone.

The abbot grinned at Crista's discomfort. "Appears I've embarrassed the plague bird," she announced. "Well, no matter. I've decided to grant Diver's request and allow your blood AI access to Down Hope's restricted records. In return, you will allow Down Hope to analyze what you discover. Down Hope also demands that Diver no longer alter our records."

This is too perfect, Red Day muttered. *The abbot set us up.*

Who's right? Crista asked. *Maybe we're wrong about Ashdyd and the Veil being involved in all this.*

I don't know. The depths of manipulation here are impossible to sort out. But I do know who I like and who I hate. When in doubt, I stick with those I like and attack those I hate.

Crista laughed in agreement. As she faced the abbot, a fresh explosion of red fire burned Crista's eyes and red line. The blood circling her shrieked, causing the abbot for the first time to flinch in her presence. Crista charged as the wolf in her howled. She knocked Master Chayn's advisors aside before grabbing the abbot herself and throwing her across the room, where the woman crashed into a wall.

Crista ran her fingers along the empty throne's armrests. The throne had funneled the monastery's power during the abbot's attack several days ago so it seemed likely it was a conduit to Down Hope's central systems. Red Day agreed and rained across the throne.

I'm accessing Down Hope's main data systems now, Red Day said.

The walls of the monastery shook in fury and pain. "Stop her," the abbot yelled at her advisors, who drew their swords and moved toward Crista.

With most of Red Day's power accessing the monastery's systems, Crista was nowhere near full-strength. But the monks were used to fighting only near-mindless versions of themselves. Crista stood her ground as the monks encircled her. They expected her to attack. Instead, Crista let them come at her.

The first monk charged by himself. Crista hardened her hands and caught his swinging sword, shattering the ceramic blade and kicking the monk backwards. Realizing the need to attack as a group, the remaining monks charged as one. Crista dropped to the floor and rolled to the side, her much smaller body faster and more nimble than the large monks.

Jumping up, she knocked the legs out from under a female monk, sending the woman falling backwards and hitting her head on the floor with a hollow *thunk.* Picking up the woman's sword, Crista swung it as hard as she could at an attacking monk, who parried the sword with his own. Both swords exploded into shards, cutting the monk and Crista, who punched the monk in the face and knocked him out.

The final monk advanced warily, trying to stab Crista while keeping a safe distance. With a howl Crista ran at him, allowing his sword to stab through her stomach. Grabbing the monk's hands, she fell backwards and threw the monk across the room.

You should have simply killed them, Red Day said as the injured monks around them moaned. *But as far as toying with prey goes, that was enjoyable.*

Thank you.

Red Day healed Crista's body as she pulled the sword from her stomach. Crista looked toward the doors to the anchorhold, expecting dozens of monks to rush in. Against that many monks she'd have no choice but to let Red Day kill them. But to her surprise the broken doors were wedged shut by Desiada and Lanea, keeping the other monks out.

Diver stood to the side of Desiada and Lanea, where the monks couldn't see the girl. "Return to your cells, you pompous know-it-all idiots," Diver ordered in perfect mimicry of the abbot's voice. Several monks on the other side of the door stopped trying to break in and shouted, "Yes ma'am," before realizing they'd been tricked.

Diver laughed.

The monks pushed harder, forcing the doors open as Desiada and Lanea fell back, parrying swords with the attacking monks. Diver played games as she jumped around the monks giving them the finger and sticking out her tongue when their swords missed.

The abbot ran at Diver with fury in her eyes, anger that twisted and distorted like waves in a pond. Ripples ran down Master Chayn's face like tears before turning into distortions that grew into rivers of water, seas of water, as they swallowed Chayn's face and body.

Ashdyd.

"Look out!" Crista yelled, but Diver and Desiada and Lanea didn't have time to react. Crista ordered Red Day to protect her friends even though most of the AI's powers were still accessing Down Hope's systems. Red Day shot forward and formed a barrier between Ashdyd's distorted body and the others.

Ashdyd destroyed Red Day's shield with a distorted hand, splattering blood across the doorway and everyone there.

Desiada and Lanea stared in horror at Ashdyd, as did the other monks. One monk charged Ashdyd and landed a powerful sword blow across Ashdyd's shoulder, only for the monk and his sword to explode into a shimmering storm of mirror-reflecting dust. Ashdyd inhaled the dust and his distorted body grew slightly larger.

I'm too weak, Red Day whispered. *Accessing Down Hope's data drained me.*

But Diver wasn't weak. She stepped between Desiada and Lanea and the others, prepared to defend her friends, only for a look of fear to cross her face when Ashdyd reached for her. Diver dodged aside but Ashdyd grazed her left arm. The girl screamed in pain.

Desiada and Lanea grabbed Diver and ran with her to the abbot's throne.

"Who is that person?" Desiada asked.

"He calls himself Ashdyd."

Diver screamed as she held her hurt arm. Where Ashdyd had touched Diver's arm a mirror-like wound lay, the wound growing as the reflections traveled up Diver's arm. Diver screamed louder and, with her other hand, ripped her own arm off to stop the wound from spreading. The arm erupted in a brilliant white fire while a similar fire burned from Diver's shoulder. A moment later a new arm grew to replace the old one. Diver stopped screaming and gasped in shock.

"Don't let him touch me," Diver said. "He can hurt me. Badly."

Ashdyd fought several monks—turning each to mirrored dust—before again striding toward Diver.

Ashdyd can't be more powerful than Diver, Crista asked Red Day. *Can he?*

I ... don't think so. Ashdyd is powerful but nothing compared to the abilities Diver has shown. Red Day scanned both Ashdyd and Diver. *There's a resonance between Ashdyd's distortions and Diver's core AI. That's how Ashdyd hurt her. It's almost like Ashdyd was created specifically to attack Diver. He's not more powerful than her, but he can hurt her if they touch.*

Diver had recovered and stood beside Crista. The girl glared at Ashdyd but kept her distance.

"Crista, give me the girl," Ashdyd said. "As I told you before, there are evils in this world you know nothing of. This girl is one of them. Give me Diver or I'll destroy Down Hope."

Ashdyd faced Crista and Diver as dozens more monks surrounded him, each aiming their swords at the distorted body. Desiada and Lanea grabbed Crista and Diver's hands and pulled them toward the doors leading from the anchorhold.

"Wait," Crista said. "We can help."

"It's beyond that," Lanea yelled. "Down Hope takes threats to itself very seriously. Run."

Crista and Diver ran with Desiada and Lanea as power surged through Down Hope just like when the abbot had attacked Crista several days ago. Glancing back Crista saw white-fire energy flowing from sword to sword and body to body among the monks surrounding Ashdyd. The energy slammed into Ashdyd, whose distorted body pulsed and shrieked as the attack grew in power.

"Take cover!" Desiada yelled.

But there was no cover to take. The power sweeping from Down Hope into the monks slammed together liked a massive hand clap and exploded, racing toward Crista and her friends. Red Day tried to raise another shield but the AI was still too weak. The explosion swept over Crista and Desiada and Lanea.

Except they didn't die. Diver stood before them, shielding them with her power.

The explosion washed back toward where Ashdyd had stood as Down Hope absorbed the energy, the blast vanishing back into itself.

Crista staggered forward. There was nothing left of either Ashdyd or the monks who'd surrounded him. The doorway into the anchorhold was gone. Only scorch marks and a giant crater remained.

Crista felt the monastery healing itself as walls and floors began to glow and reform.

Crista and Diver walked back into the anchorhold, followed by Desiada and Lanea. Everything in the anchorhold had been washed away except for the abbot's throne. Crista gaped, imagining the power Down Hope had employed.

Hundreds of monks from other parts of the monastery ran to the room. They whispered in shock at the damage before one of the monks, the same monk Diver had stripped of all language functions a few days ago, stepped forward. She sat on the throne with eyes closed as the other monks kneeled around her. Down Hope's power flowed through the monk for a few seconds before she opened her eyes.

"I am Master Chayn," the woman said before shaking her head with a bemused look on her face. "Well, this has been quite the little disaster, hasn't it."

IT TOOK HOURS BEFORE EVERYONE CALMED DOWN. DOWN HOPE SCANNED ALL ITS hallways and chambers before verifying Ashdyd was gone. Crista and Diver did the same and reached the same conclusion.

"Was he destroyed?" Crista asked Diver.

"I'm not sure," the girl said.

Crista ordered Red Day to analyze the monk who'd become the new Master Chayn. Her body hadn't changed—she was taller than the previous abbot, and spoke in a louder voice. But after scanning her Red Day said the new abbot's brain waves appeared identical to the old one.

Down Hope must download a part of itself into each abbot, Red Day said. *Makes sense if you don't want to risk the abbot having a mind of their own.*

Once she was certain Ashdyd was no longer in Down Hope, Master Chayn ordered everyone but Crista and Diver to leave. The other monks immediately obeyed. Desiada and Lanea hesitated until Crista nodded at them to follow the other monks.

Once everyone was gone Master Chayn walked to the door leading to her privy chamber. Down Hope unsealed the doorway and they stepped inside.

The privy chamber was undamaged, including all the historic artifacts in stasis. Crista was both pleased to see this and astounded Down Hope could use so much power in the anchorhold and leave everything in the next room unharmed.

Master Chayn sat down at her teak desk. "Down Hope deeply regrets what transpired here," she said with a sigh. "We obviously ... miscalculated."

The wolf in Crista growled.

Stay calm, Red Day cautioned. *I'm still weakened from accessing Down Hope's systems.*

"How dare you?" Crista said, fighting for control. "Down Hope worked with Ashdyd and the Veil, correct?"

Master Chayn nodded. "Down Hope has been aware of the Veil for some time. We wanted to reach an ... accommodation. We desired the Veil to both leave us alone if they came into power and solve our reoccurring problem with Diver manipulating our data systems."

You do realize Down Hope is forbidden to interfere with the outside world? Red Day said to the abbot. *Actions like these could be interpreted as going against our world's three-fold balance.*

"Our goal wasn't interference. It was to rid ourselves of an outside influence." The abbot glared at Diver, who waved sheepishly back. "It was also to extract a promise from the Veil to not interfere with or harm our work."

"But Ashdyd betrayed you," Crista said.

"Yes. Ashdyd threatening to destroy Down Hope changed everything, so we acted accordingly."

"Wait," Crista said. "What did you mean, if the Veil came into power?"

"You've seen the threat posed by Ashdyd and the Veil. Down Hope estimates a high probability the Veil will eventually destroy the world's three-fold balance. We were positioning ourselves for such eventualities."

"Nice," Crista muttered. "So now what happens? Between us?"

"That depends on what your blood AI found in our archives."

Did you find Diver's code? she asked Red Day. *Or anything about the Veil?*

I found scattered information about the Veil indicating the abbot speaks the truth of Down Hope's motives and their attempted deal with Ashdyd. I also found the code, which means Diver's creators have decided to complete her mission.

The wolf in Crista hissed, angry that some alien species had given an order to attack humanity. But nothing could be done about that for now.

Erase the code, she said. *We can't risk Diver accessing it.*

I erased the code in Down Hope's system. But once that code mated with the original code given to me by Diver, it became self-replicating. I've placed the code within a firewall deep inside myself to keep it isolated. But I can't delete it.

Should we tell Diver the code arrived? What if that's enough to set off her programming?

Red Day paused. *I think,* the AI finally said, *we must stay honest with Diver. She said as long as she didn't access the code herself, she wouldn't activate her final mission. Once you decide to trust someone, all you can do is follow them forward. Unless they later prove unworthy of trust.*

Crista looked at Diver, who stared intensely at her. Diver had said she'd avoid reading their minds, not wanting to accidentally access the code if Red Day found it. Hopefully Red Day was right. Wishing the outcome wasn't so dire if they were wrong, Crista nodded at the little girl.

"The code's there," she said.

At Crista's words Diver withdrew into herself. The girl's always happy face fell blank and her eyes turned so dark and deep Crista swore she saw stars in them. The air around Diver distorted, space folding in on itself as energy mirrored and flickered around Diver's body—far more energy than Crista had seen even when Down Hope attacked Ashdyd with its full power.

The abbot shouted, "You fools," an insult clearly meant for Crista and Red Day. But Diver didn't care. The power and spatial distortions around her grew so powerful Crista could no longer see the girl's body. Afterimages of Diver burned in Crista's eyes.

Crista bowed her head, preparing for death, when the power and distortions disappeared. Diver stood once again in the privy chamber, a grin on her face as she clapped her hands.

"Just kidding," she said. "All good. No explosions today."

Master Chayn cursed. Down Hope seemed to shiver at the understanding of what Diver could have done.

"If you want," Diver said to the abbot, "I'll make you forget how scared you were. But seriously, you should have seen your faces."

Red Day laughed in Crista's mind. *I really like this girl,* the AI said. *I really, really like her.*

"On that irritating note," Master Chayn said with a sigh, "perhaps it's time we came to an accommodation."

THEY LEFT DOWN HOPE MONASTERY THAT EVENING AND CLEARED THE BARRIER FOREST later in the week.

Crista and Red Day. Desiada and Lanea. And Diver. Especially Diver, whose good mood hadn't dimmed since leaving Down Hope.

The trees howled in anger after they cleared the barrier forest. Diver had protected them from the tree's assault, giving the forest only the barest taste of consciousness, which was already fading.

"That's far enough, Diver," Desiada declared. "The trees can't affect us now. Drop your protection."

Lanea rolled her eyes at her brother giving Diver an order he couldn't begin to enforce. Diver bowed sarcastically to Desiada before releasing her mental shielding.

"We're also beyond the reach of Down Hope," Lanea said. "The monastery and the abbot can no longer hurt us."

Lanea said this without emotion even though Crista had thought she'd be excited about escaping Down Hope. Lanea glared at Crista before turning to whisper something to her brother.

Crista looked again at the trees and hoped she'd never again visit Down Hope.

Now will you tell me what's bothering you? she asked Red Day.

Red Day had stayed quiet ever since the deal they'd reached with Master Chayn —obviously the AI was disturbed by something. The AI had said it wasn't safe to discuss what bothered it while they were within reach of the monastery's powers. But now …

Everything Master Chayn told us checks out with the records I accessed in Down Hope, Red Day said. *Ashdyd visited the monastery a few years ago, shortly after he visited Bogda's village to apologize.*

Then what's wrong?

The records indicate the abbot and Ashdyd discussed bringing you to Down Hope. Not any plague bird—you. Ashdyd shouldn't have even known who you were several years ago, let alone that you'd eventually become a plague bird.

Crista glanced at Lanea and Desiada. *Were they in on it?*

No. It appears the monks were unaware. The abbot sent Desiada to find you because he knew nothing of all this. Well, that and because he annoyed the shit out of her. But that doesn't change the fact there's more in motion here than merely Ashdyd trying to capture Diver.

Did you find a way to delete Diver's code from your mind? she asked.

No. I'm also pretty sure Ashdyd wanted that code, perhaps as a way to control Diver. Or maybe simply to destroy the world.

Crista kicked the ground in frustration. *Now what?*

Guess that depends on our traveling companions and what the abbot shared with Lanea.

Crista sighed. In return for Down Hope sharing the monastery's information about Ashdyd and the Veil, she and Red Day had promised to take Diver away from Down Hope and also not mention to the other plague birds the monastery's attempt to cut a deal with the Veil.

But it appeared they still couldn't trust Down Hope and Master Chayn, who had shared something with Lanea that had infuriated the young woman. While Lanea had been civil during the trip, the monk seethed with anger every time she'd interacted with Crista.

Red Day had asked permission to reach into Lanea's mind to learn what was troubling her, but Crista refused. She couldn't do that to someone she wanted to one day count as a friend.

"Have you two decided?" Crista nervously asked Lanea and Desiada. "About traveling with me to Seed?"

Desiada looked away. While Lanea had been angry since leaving Down Hope, Desiada had been hesitant, only giving bare yes or no answers to any question she raised. Crista knew he was mortified at her knowing every moment of his life. Desiada had wanted to stay at Down Hope when Crista announced she was leaving. Now that she understood him so intimately, she knew he'd intended throwing himself into his studies. To try his best to forget that his entire being had been shared with Crista.

But Lanea had announced she wanted to leave. Since her injured leg made her unable to descend the narrow mountain path without help, she asked her brother to come with her. Down Hope and the abbot had screamed at that—monks never left the monastery for good—but with Diver supporting Lanea's decision, the only question was if Desiada would also go.

Desiada refused to abandon his sister a second time.

"Well," Crista asked again impatiently, the barrier forest screaming in the background as its consciousness faded. "Will you go to Seed?"

"I think it would be better for us to travel separately," Lanea said.

"Does this have anything to do with whatever Down Hope told you?"

Lanea glared at Crista.

Desiada hadn't reacted to any of Crista's words. Crista wanted to hug him, kiss him, take his hand and not release it until he understood she still cared for him and hadn't meant to hurt him. But if he didn't talk to her, there was nothing she could do.

Obviously Diver didn't agree. "Hey dum-dum," the girl shouted as she threw a dirt clod at Desiada's head, which exploded into dust when it hit him. "Don't you dare let Crista leave without saying something."

Crista hissed for Diver to shut up, but to her surprise Desiada laughed. He squatted down and giggled as he doodled in the dirt.

"You okay?" Crista asked.

Desiada fell backwards across the ground, gasping for air as his laughter died down.

"Sorry, Crista," he said softly, "It's hard, knowing you've experienced everything of me. There's nothing of me you don't know."

Crista understood.

"Will you do me a favor?" he asked.

"Anything."

"Cut me in half. Slice me right up the middle."

Crista and Lanea both stepped back, horror on their faces.

"I can't..."

"Crista, please do this for me. If you don't cut me in half, how can *parting* truly be such sweet sorrow?"

Crista, Lanea, and Diver stared at Desiada as he laughed again. Lanea cursed and kicked him, sending him rolling across the ground as she grinned at her brother.

"Worst joke ever," Crista said, snickering despite herself. Diver giggled so hard she collapsed to the ground.

Crista, Red Day said. *That joke...*

"I don't remember that joke," she said. "I mean, it's in none of your memories."

"Nope," Desiada said. "Brand new. Came to me a moment ago."

Lanea helped Desiada stand up and, as he dusted himself off, he sighed. "I apologize for being so sullen, but a little time apart will be good. I know you didn't mean to do it, but you're just like Down Hope to me now. I fought all my life to live beyond Down Hope. Having you know all I am ... well, it burns."

Crista nodded. She understood only too well after having experienced his entire life. But perhaps if she shared a secret of her own ... maybe that could help Desiada. And also soothe whatever Lanea was angry about.

No, Red Day screamed in her mind. *You're forbidden to state this.*

Crista balanced the punishment she'd receive for revealing plague bird secrets against never seeing Desiada again. What's the worst Red Day could do to her?

"I was tricked into becoming a plague bird," she whispered.

"I know," Desiada said. "You told me when we met."

"No. I don't mean what Derena and Red Day did. I mean whatever Ashdyd is up to."

Red Day shrieked in her mind. *We promised Down Hope we wouldn't discuss what we learned in its archives.*

"Ashdyd and Down Hope schemed to bring me to your monastery. They knew I'd become a plague bird long before I became one."

"How could they know that?" Lanea asked suspiciously.

"They couldn't. Unless they were already setting me up to become one. Or knew someone else was doing the same."

Red Day exploded in her mind, causing Crista to double over in pain. *We're supposed to tell no one except other plague birds what we learn of the Veil,* the AI screamed. *You have violated one of our direct orders.*

Red Day took control of Crista's hands and reached for her knives to slice open her body. Crista screamed as she fought for control, knowing if released the AI would kill Desiada and Lanea to keep their secrets. She forced her hands into fists and fell to her knees, pounding the dusty ground over and over.

After long seconds, Red Day calmed down. *Your trust in them better be justified,* it said. *We'll both be killed if the other plague birds learn you revealed information from our mission.*

Crista laughed. *That's assuming the other plague birds didn't set us up to start with.*

Impossible.

Then why did that plague bird Kenji kill my mom? Why has he been following us?

Red Day didn't answer.

When Crista looked up, tears streaking the dust coating her face, Desiada and Lanea looked at her in fear. Even Diver seemed taken back.

"Are you back in control of Red Day?" Lanea asked.

"Yes. Red Day is mad at me for telling you our secrets. If other plague birds learn I shared details of our mission, they'll kill me."

"Then why tell us?" Desiada asked.

"Maybe it goes a little ways toward making us even. You knowing some of my secrets, I mean."

For the first time since they had left Down Hope, Desiada smiled. But before he could say anything his sister spoke.

"Crista, Master Chayn revealed something to me," Lanea said. "I can't speak the details but you're being manipulated far beyond anything Ashdyd and Down Hope have done."

"What do you mean?" Crista asked.

"Uh, what Crista said," Desiada added, also confused.

"I can't say," Lanea said. "I want to. Believe me. But every time I try to speak the words my brain stumbles over itself and shuts down my mouth."

As proof, Lanea tried to speak but only a strangled sigh escaped her throat. Her body spasmed until she closed her mouth.

Down Hope likely placed a mental block inside Lanea's mind, Red Day said. *It's a way of preventing people from revealing certain information.*

Crista shared this with the others.

"But why would Master Chayn do that?" Desiada said.

"Down Hope wanted to torture me for leaving our sacred duty," Lanea said. She again glared at Crista. "They wanted me to know what Crista is but be unable to tell anyone."

Crista shivered.

I can reach into her mind and learn the truth, Red Day said. *There's a risk of brain damage due to the nature of mental blocks, but I would be careful …*

No, Crista screamed in her mind. *I shouldn't have known Desiada's life. I won't do the same to Lanea.*

"Can't you tell me anything?" Crista asked.

Lanea took a deep breath as the scent of anger rose from her body. She pulled out her ceramic egg and broadcasted a map into the air. She pointed to a location far to the north of the city of Seed.

"If you go here, you may learn some of what I've been told," she said. "That's all I can reveal."

Lanea could be lying, Red Day said. *Mental blocks are troubling affairs. She may not even know she's lying. If I access her …*

Crista again told Red Day no. She reached out to hug Lanea but the woman stepped back, not wanting Crista to touch her. Lanea began walking with her crutch in the direction of Seed.

"I apologize," Desiada said. "I had no idea Down Hope did that to her."

"Down Hope and Master Chayn are the ones who should apologize, not you," Crista said. "Maybe she won't be angry when we meet again. We will meet again, won't we?"

"Yes. I need time alone to have a life no one knows but me. But maybe when we meet again in Seed in a few months …" Desiada paused and grinned. "Wow. I just realized something—who knows how many new jokes I'll think up by then!"

No new jokes, Red Day moaned. *Please, no new jokes.*

Crista ignored the AI and hugged Desiada. She then gave a final hug to Diver, whispering goodbye to the girl.

Not wanting to lose control of herself, Crista ordered Red Day to hide her from Lanea and Desiada's senses. She then ran as fast as she could, the wolf in her yipping with happiness and looking forward to seeing Desiada again.

A FEW DAYS LATER CRISTA LAY ON THE VILLAGE GREEN WHERE SHE'D FIRST MET Desiada. Once again the kids played kickball around her as Red Day grumbled at hiding her from their senses. But Crista didn't care about the AI's nastiness. She was happy. And right now that was all that mattered.

Crista was daydreaming in the warm sunlight when Red Day said to wake up. *An irritant has chanced upon us yet again.*

Crista looked up to see a young girl run across the village green and kick the ball away from the kids, who stared in shock at her. The girl was tiny—far smaller and thinner than the other kids with no animal genes in her body.

Diver took advantage of the villagers' shock to weave in and out of people and kick the ball across the field, where it bounced through the sparking cloud of the village's AI. Diver then ran over and sat down beside Crista.

"Miss me?" the girl asked.

Crista sighed—she thought she'd lost the girl when she'd left Desiada and Lanea. She also noticed the villagers staring at Diver in both curiosity and dawning horror.

The people here aren't stupid, Red Day said. *They've already guessed from Diver's behavior that someone is hiding from their senses.*

"Fine," Crista said. Red Day dropped its manipulation of everyone's senses and, as before, there was a loud shriek as the villagers again saw her.

"You're going to scare this village perfectly straight," Diver said. "They'll think a plague bird always watches over them."

"What do you want?"

"I want to get to know you better," Diver said.

"I'm not telling you the code. I had Red Day delete it from our minds."

"Liar. Once the code in Red Day met my half of the code, it changed. You can't delete it. It's in Red Day's mind for all time. All I have to do is reach in and find it."

Crista sat up as Red Day powered their defenses. The villagers stared in fear at Crista, not knowing that she wasn't the most dangerous creature here. But if Diver tried to rip the code from her mind there was nothing she could do to stop her. Everyone in this village would die before they knew what happened, and probably most of the people on Earth not long after that, depending on how powerful Diver truly was.

"Don't worry," Diver said. "I don't want it. I don't even read your minds anymore because I can't risk discovering the code. But I still have to be near you. Now that I know the code exists, I'm programmed to stay near it. No doubt to tempt me into accessing it."

Red Day cursed, as did Crista.

"Don't worry," Diver said. "I'm fun to have around."

Crista looked at the villagers. She continually sought out people, even if it meant hiding in the middle of them. Never mind that most people didn't want to be around her—she still needed them. Was Diver the same?

Crista remembered how the abbot and Ashdyd had known she'd become a plague bird and planned years ago to bring her to Down Hope.

"Diver, you sure you're not working with the Veil?"

"Yes."

"You told me once you didn't know much about them."

Diver flushed red. "I … lied. I try to stay away from them. Ashdyd has enough power to reveal me to others. So I avoid him and his followers. But I didn't know he had the power to hurt me until last week."

"Then why risk going to the monastery?"

"I figured I could avoid Ashdyd even if he was there. And I wanted you."

"What do you mean?"

"I always pick the nice plague birds. And the fun ones. I knew if you found the code we'd be stuck together for a long time. A long, long time."

I'm nice? Crista asked Red Day. *And fun?*

You haven't met the other plague birds. Trust me, you're a ball of nicey-nice fun compared to most of them.

"I don't know…" Crista began.

"Please. I can tell you things. Things you'll never otherwise know."

"You mean like whatever Down Hope told Lanea."

Diver pulled a clump of grass up from the green. "Master Chayn was merely being cruel telling Lanea that."

"So you know."

Diver nodded sadly. "I know. Lanea's right. You're still being manipulated. By everyone."

"But not you?"

"Oh, me too. But I'm doing it for the best of reasons—because I like you!"

"Then tell me the secret Down Hope revealed to Lanea."

"I can't. If I did, it might hurt you and cause you to do things that would make you dead. But don't worry. You'll discover it on your own pretty soon."

Crista snorted. "I'm sick of secrets."

Diver grinned. "Me too. I used to want to know things. No more."

"Why?"

"Remember how I said I was dying way back when? How I saw that star fall from the sky. How it promised to answer all my questions."

"Did it?"

"Yes. But the questions it answered weren't the questions I'd cared about before I touched the star. I'd originally wanted to know why I was dying and why everyone I loved died. Then I knew the answers to questions I hadn't even imagined, questions spanning the universe."

Diver paused and Crista saw the girl's eyes were wet.

"But the little girl dying alone and in fear and desperate for answers," Diver said, "her questions were never answered. Because suddenly a little girl's questions seemed unimportant compared to the vast reaches of space and time."

Crista tried not to think about all Diver had suffered because of her impulsive decision to touch a fallen star. "Was it worth it? Would you do it again if you had to?"

"I can't answer. Once we merged no other course was possible. Was it worth it to become a plague bird?"

"Hard to say. I can't go back from what I am now."

"Then you understand."

Crista reached over and hugged the little girl. Glancing again at the villagers, Crista grinned.

"Want to really mess with these people?" she asked. "Let's play a game of kick-ball before we go."

Diver clapped her hands and jumped up. As Diver ran to grab the ball, Red Day exploded in Crista's mind. *Hell no! We're a plague bird! We don't play kickball! Especially not with girls who can destroy humanity!*

But Crista ignored the AI's rants as she chased after Diver, determined to beat the girl to the ball.

INTERLUDE

MEMORIES FALLING FROM YOUR HANDS

(THREE MONTHS AFTER SAYING GOODBYE TO DESIADA AND LANEA)

Faster, damn it! Run faster! Red Day screamed as Crista ran through the snow-filled forest, chasing ... well, she couldn't say exactly what she chased. The shape fleeing before her blurred and flickered, always on the edge of becoming clear while remaining impossible to see. From the person's scent Crista guessed she chased a man but beyond that little revealed itself to her senses.

Instead, rainbow static whistled through her mind, a weaker version of what had jammed the senses of her predecessor Derena when she'd been attacked nearly a year ago. Maybe this attacker was one of those members of the Veil who'd so hurt Derena that Red Day had to find a new host.

Why can I still see while you can't? Crista asked as she jumped over a fallen tree. *When you and Derena were attacked neither of you could see until she removed most of your power from her body, but my eyes still work.*

This man's by himself and far weaker than the combined powers of those who attacked previously. You and I also haven't integrated our beings as much as I had with Derena.

So this man's disrupting our weakest link—you.

Funny. Don't underestimate him. With this interference you'll have trouble releasing me, as happened with Derena.

Crista understood. When she caught up with this attacker she couldn't count on having access to all of Red Day's power.

The sun was setting in the forest, making it difficult to see. The man before her ran fast, barely slowing down as he darted between the dark trees. Crista vaulted a creek and ran up a small hill, thinking she had a chance to catch up on the other side, only to slip on ice and smash into a steel oak. She stood up quickly, looking for the man's distorted shape. But the man had vanished.

Where is he? she asked

I don't know. I told you to run faster.

Red, blue, and yellow static clicked through Crista's mind a final time before stopping. *No!* the AI yelled. *He got away. You're part wolf! Can't you run through a forest without tripping over every damn thing?*

Crista ignored the barb and ran back to where she'd last seen the man. She leaned over the cold ground and breathed deeply.

That's how she'd detected the man. She and Diver had spent three months reaching the area where Lanea said Crista might discover the secret about who she was. They'd been walking through the forest, Crista enjoying the quiet crunch of frozen ground beneath her boots and the crisp silence—and Diver throwing snowballs at every animal they passed—when Crista scented a nearby human.

Red Day often dismissed her wolf senses as woefully inadequate compared to a blood AI's heightened abilities, but Red Day hadn't even sensed the man's presence. Red Day tried to dismiss the oversight but Crista could tell the AI was disturbed.

Worse, the moment Crista scented the man Diver plopped down melodramatically on the frozen ground, a pained look on her face like she'd sat in something nasty.

"What?" Crista asked.

"I can't interfere," Diver said.

"Interfere with what?"

Diver shrugged. "I'll see you later…if you're still alive."

Red Day cursed at the dangerous implication of Diver's words but insisted Crista follow the man's scent. They tracked the scent for a half hour before rainbowed static slammed through Red Day's senses and abilities. Crista saw a distorted shape bolt from nearby. A member of the Veil!

The wolf in her howled and the chase was on. Until she lost the man.

Now all she had to do was find the trail again.

Well? Red Day asked. *Where's his scent?*

Patience. Tracking is an art. Maybe you need some wolf blood so a little static won't knock you out of action.

Red Day hissed before falling silent.

Crista circled around the last place she'd seen the man, going left and right, back and forth, hunched low to the ground, sniffing frozen leaves and dirt. She scented the dormant trees and plants, their sap waiting below ground. She scented rabbits and deer that had nibbled on bare twigs and plants out of hunger and the foxes and coyotes that chased them for the same reason. She scented the trees around her, which slept through winter but knew spring wasn't far away.

She saw a small heel print. A disturbed twig on the ground. A slight change to the leaf pattern on the ground. The man's scent floated over this path like a blazing light in her wolf senses.

Got it, she growled, the wolf in her jumping her legs into a run. *We're gonna catch him.*

I won't have much power when we approach him. Unless you want to do something drastic like Derena and rip out your heart.

How about I release my blood now? When the man interferes with us you'll already be outside and ready to attack.

Good idea. Being around me has improved your tactical thinking.

Crista pulled a knife free and slit her wrist, her blood swirling into the air like a glowing shield as she ran.

Crista circled silently up a small ridge, running slightly off the man's scent trail in case of ambush. She crested the ridge and descended to find herself running across a stone and boulder filled clearing with the man right before her.

The man turned, shocked Crista had found her. For a moment the man's body was undistorted. He wore ragged leathers like the hunt clans, his clothes torn and patched and torn again. He was middle-aged, as old as Crista's mother would have been had her mother lived.

But even though Crista could see the man's body, she couldn't see his face. A flickering veil of distortions covered the face before rainbow static again rang through Crista's mind, hiding him from her sight.

Attack! Crista ordered. Red Day shot straight up into the air as if fleeing the man. The AI cleared the nearby treetops and dove back down, a glowing red lightning storm hitting the ground around the man.

Crista thought the man had deflected Red Day's power but the ground where Red Day hit exploded, geysers of dirt and stone shooting out of the clearing into the surrounding trees. The man screamed in anger as the ground underneath disappeared. He fell into the massive hole and disappeared from Crista's line of sight.

Crista ran to the hole, knives in both hands, to find the man firing energy bursts as he tried to climb out. The bursts rippled like rips in reality but Red Day avoided them as the AI slammed back into the ground.

Stay back, Red Day warned Crista.

The stone ground burst to flames, burning away the snow and leaves and plants. But Red Day didn't stop there. As the man hurled more distortions, which destroyed any part of the AI they touched, the ground burned hotter and hotter.

Crista ran from the clearing, heat licking her shoulders and the rear of her legs. When she reached a safe distance, she looked back. The stone and dirt Red Day touched flowed and bubbled like lava as the entire clearing erupted, the nearby trees bursting to flames as birds took panicked flight.

The man screamed as the lava flowed around him, no longer attacking Red Day but instead using his power to protect himself. The rainbow static clicked free of Crista's mind as the man no longer had the power to interfere with Crista and Red Day, focusing instead on staying alive.

Crista waited for the lava to fill the hole, to completely burn the man alive. Right before that happened the lava exploded, flames swirling and twisting as they rose up and slammed back down.

When Crista looked again the clearing was no longer burning, the lava having hardened back to stone. The stone cracked and snapped loudly, angrily protesting Red Day's removal of the heat that fed their fire.

Crista stepped back into the clearing. The ground was only warm to the touch.

Impressive, she said.

I couldn't overpower him directly, Red Day said weakly, exhausted by its attack. *And we want him alive. For now.*

The man stood in a large hole, encased in dried lava to his chest. He was unconscious from the thermal pounding the heating and cooling stone had thrown at his body, his hair completely burned away and his exposed skin a flowing mass of red and black burns.

Crista slid into the hole as Red Day returned to her body. The AI needed to recharge quickly before the man woke up.

We have a few minutes at most, Red Day said. *Let's see what we can learn before he regains his powers.*

Crista leaned over the man, who had one arm swallowed by stone, the other thrown up grabbing for sky with his head lolled back. The veil still covered his face but barely pulsed. Crista lowered the tip of one knife blade to her finger, aiming to prick a drop of blood so Red Day could access the man's mind.

Right before the knife hit flesh, her hand froze against her will.

Don't, Red Day said. *If I directly access his mind, he'll have access to ours. He might hack his way past my firewalls even in his weakened state.*

So what do we do?

Talk to him.

Crista lifted the veil from the man's face with the back of her knife, the wolf in her having no desire to touch it. The top of the veil attached to the man's forehead like it had been sewn to his skin. Crista flipped the veil over the top of his burned head.

Underneath, the man's face was melted like he'd fallen face first into the lava. His eyes were gone, his lips ripped away exposing rotten teeth, his nose a cavity to fall into. But the scabs and scars on his face showed these were old wounds.

It's like the veil ate his face, Red Day said. *Good thing you didn't touch it.*

The man grinned. "I will have enough power in six minutes and 23 seconds to break free," he stated, his melted lips giving a strange lilt to his words. "I assume you'll kill me before then."

"Yes," Crista said. Red Day reminded her not to trust anything the man said and that he would likely try to waste time until his powers returned. She kept the knife in her right hand, just in case.

"I'm impressed," the man said. "When I attacked your predecessor, this blood AI wasn't nearly as resourceful."

Red Day ignored the comments, instead keeping a running countdown of how long Crista had until they must kill the man.

Crista kneeled before the man and wondered how he could see with his destroyed eyes before realizing the veil likely enabled his senses along with his powers. Crista pulled off her backpack and removed her canteen, unscrewing the top and holding it to the man's lips. The man drank greedily before giggling.

"That helped me gain a half second on returning to full power," he said, "Thank you. Fascinating how years of not being human can't erase the desire for a sip of cold water when you're hurt."

"Who are you?"

"I was once called Vaca. But now I have no name. I'm one of the Veil."

Crista remembered her trip with Derena to the Farnham hunt clan. Master Farnham had said she'd banished one of the clan, a man named Vaca. So this man had, indeed, helped attack Derena a year ago.

"Who are the Veil?"

"The ones who kill. The ones who right this world's wrongs."

"Plague birds do that."

"A fascinating point. Perhaps we're the plague birds to plague birds."

He's stalling, Red Day said. *You have five minutes before we must kill him.*

"Too bad you're not traveling with your friends," Crista said. "Or Ashdyd. Like when you attacked the plague bird before me. Maybe then you wouldn't have lost."

Crista's comment hit home and the man frowned. "Even Ashdyd can't see every potential future."

"Ashdyd doesn't like you, eh? That why you're out here by yourself?"

"No. Ashdyd loves me. We were once bonded closer than you'll ever know. I was Ashdyd. All of the Veil were once Ashdyd."

Crista started to joke about Ashdyd dumping Vaca but stopped, seeing the pain and loss the man felt at no longer being bonded to whatever Ashdyd was. She may have to kill the man but she wouldn't torture him.

"If Ashdyd didn't know I was coming, why are you here?" Crista asked, taking care to not reveal that Down Hope by way of Lanea had told her to come to this isolated place.

"I was Ashdyd's most recent beloved, so I'm the most powerful individual Veil. Ashdyd sent me here to protect something. Your ability to find and defeat me was ... unexpected."

He's being honest, Red Day said. *He's truly disturbed. Not disturbed at dying—at their damn plan not working out as Ashdyd wanted.*

"I've heard no plan survives the first encounter with a battlefield," Crista said.

"Ours do."

"Did."

The man cursed in anger and struggled to free himself from the cold stone that cracked slightly as more of his power returned.

Three minutes, Red Day said.

"Look, I don't care about your plans or any of that shit. I was told if I came here I'd learn about myself. So what am I?" Crista tapped her knife blade against the man's burned cheek—not to threaten, but to remind what was coming.

"In good time, Cristina de Ane of the Village of Day's End. But first know this: Your father and your village are in danger. They'll die without Ashdyd's protection. Release me and I'll beg Ashdyd to save them."

"You're lying."

"I'm not. You'll know when you see Beu again."

Crista tightened her grip on her knife, trying not to plunge it through the man's skull.

Two minutes, Red Day said. *Stay calm.*

"Speak the truth."

"I am. We knew you'd become a plague bird before you were born. We know what you are."

The man smiled. Crista ran through the man's words, trying to find something to throw at him. Something to prove that everything the man had said was merely a lie.

"Don't believe me?" the man asked. "Look inside the discoidal after you kill me. We stole it from Derena a year ago. The discoidal is the key. One of three keys for changing the whole damn world."

"What are you talking about?" Crista asked.

Puzzlement ran across the man's face. His lips opened and muttered, "You really don't know what you are?" as Red Day screamed *Now!*

Crista slammed her knife into the man's skull, slamming again and again until she lowered the blade and cut off his head. She howled in anger, the wolf furious at the Veil using her father and village as a threat against her. She slit her wrist and released a repowered Red Day, who heated the cold stone as Crista jumped out of the hole. The lava bubbled and popped around the man's body and turned the skin and muscle and bones to ash before Red Day again cooled the stone and filled the hole with dirt and clay. As a final touch, the AI lit the forest around them on fire, hurling burning trees thicker than Crista's body onto the site.

When Red Day finished, it was impossible to see where the man had died. All that remained was a red-burning marble floating in the air before Crista.

What is that? Crista asked.

It's the discoidal Derena and I created when we were attacked. The discoidal stolen by the Veil. Vaca was carrying it.

Crista looked at the devastation before her. *Were you trying to hide his body?*

No. If the Veil are as powerful as they appear, I can't hide even the few remaining traces of his body. Instead, I've made it as hard as possible for them to know who did this. They'll know something killed this man. But they won't be certain it was you or me.

If he was telling the truth, they'll know it was me.

He lied. You were not picked to be a plague bird before you were born—you were the best option in a hurried hunt for a replacement as Derena died. And how could Vaca know your village and father are in danger? We've been walking east for nearly a year—whoever these people are, they couldn't share information across such distances without broadcasting it, meaning other AIs and plague birds would listen in. Even encryption wouldn't be enough to protect their broadcast secrets in a world full of curious AIs.

The Veil, Crista said. *They're not "these people." They're the Veil.*

Red Day sighed. Crista reached out and touched the red discoidal floating before her. "Maybe if we access the discoidal's memories from you and Derena …"

We can't. The memories may contain a virus. Or worse.

Won't know unless you try, will we? Don't be such a chicken shit.

Red Day's power twitched, as if the AI took a deep, all-encompassing breath to calm itself. Crista felt anger—more anger than Red Day had ever before directed at her—along with fear at what had nearly happened. Reaching out to Red Day's memories, she saw how close the two of them had come to being killed by Vaca. That Red Day's innovative attack had actually been a wild attempt at survival, as it had realized only at the last moment how powerful their foe had been.

I didn't know … Crista began.

Of course you didn't. Before joining with me you played at not knowing anything. You pretended not to know the evils in your village until Beu attacked you. You ignored how plague birds sacrifice their own lives to keep our world safe. And now, seeing the truth of what we're up against, you still pretend you and I aren't outclassed.

That's not fair. I didn't ask for this. And Vaca said my father and village were in danger.

He lied. He's taunting you. But even if I'm wrong, so what? You're now joined with me. You are no longer human and no longer live as a human. Which means you don't mourn humans when they die.

Crista kicked a burning tree. She could easily see herself losing control—giving in to her wolf as Beu had given in to his own gened hell. If anyone harmed her father and neighbors she'd hunt down the killers and hurt them for what they'd done. She'd make them suffer as only a plague bird could make people suffer.

No, she said, calming herself. *I won't lose control. I won't hurt people merely for vengeance.*

That's why you'll never be a great plague bird.

Red Day cursed and retreated to the back of her mind, as far away as the AI and Crista could get from one another.

Angry at Red Day's words, Crista again kicked at the burning tree before her, ash and sparks rising on the wind. She pocketed the discoidal and turned toward Seed, eager to reach the city as soon as possible, only to find Diver blocking her path.

The girl squatted before a burning branch using her powers to twist the flames into the shapes of people. Crista recognized herself in the flames along with the man she'd just killed. But instead of having the two fire-people fight Diver twisted them into an orange and red flicker of a dance, holding hands as they swirled into the sky and vanished.

"Why are you and Red Day angry?" Diver asked, not looking into Crista's eyes. "I can feel it. The anger boiling from both of you."

"Red Day is angry because I refuse to hurt people merely to hurt them. Or for vengeance. Or maybe because I'm not suited to being a plague bird. Take your pick."

"You should know Red Day loves you. It's scared for you."

"Red Day's scared for me? Bullshit! And you—you knew this was about to happen. You knew that man could have killed me."

"My programming forbids me to interfere in human lives."

"I'm no longer human!"

"Close enough."

Crista wanted to pick up the burning branch Diver squatted beside and beat the girl with it.

Fighting for control—remembering Beu when he lost control and refusing to be like him—Crista ran, letting the wolf take her legs, running away from the burning forest and the all-powerful girl and whoever the Veil might be.

PART IV

WE'RE ALL GOING TO SEED

Several weeks later Crista woke to a smashing rain pounding the canopy of the steel oak above her. Wind whipped the creaking branches and budding metallic-mirror leaves. Thunder reverberated the oak's cold, metal-like trunk. Crista lay on the ground shivering and wet and hungry and all around miserable.

She started to ask Red Day if the morning could get any worse. But even as the thought formed she heard the AI giggle.

What? she asked sharply.

Happy birthday, Red Day whispered. *You've been a plague bird for one entire year.*

Crista nodded to herself before standing up and punching the steel oak's trunk. Powering up her body, she hit harder and harder until the tree rang to the assault, each hit echoing as loud as thunder until the nearly unbreakable tree threatened to crack.

Crista stopped, not wanting to destroy the steel oak.

Feel better? Red Day asked. *Or would you like to stomp the grass too?*

Screw you.

I'd say the same back at you, but since Desiada isn't here it'd only be a pipe dream. Red Day laughed.

Crista looked around. *Where's Diver?* she asked.

Diver woke in a worse mood than you. She cursed us, stuck her tongue out, and ran off to do who knows what mischief.

Crista sighed, figuring the nasty spring weather could get to anyone. Knowing she couldn't get any wetter, Crista left the shelter of the steel oak and began walking.

Go south, Red Day said. *That's the direction of the city of Seed. Unless you want to celebrate a second and third anniversary without Desiada.*

Crista shrugged and headed in that direction.

As Crista walked she remembered what the Veil man had told her. How her father and home village were in danger and only Ashdyd could save them.

When first told this, Crista had wanted to immediately run home to protect her village. But as Red Day pointed out, even hiking as fast as she could without sleeping or stopping would mean many months of travel. And it was unlikely Vaca had told the truth. Despite what the Veil claimed, they couldn't have known before Crista was born that she'd be picked as a plague bird. Most likely this was a trick.

Except Ashdyd and the Veil had worked with Down Hope monastery and maybe even with that rogue plague bird Kenji. And what had Vaca meant when he said the discoidal was one of three keys to change the world?

I suspect the discoidal contains a virus, Red Day stated, rudely interrupting Crista's thoughts. *As I've explained many times for your limited intellect, that's why I won't access it. We can't risk it unleashing something dangerous in our mind.*

Crista knew Red Day was right but didn't care. Still, once she reached Seed the other plague birds could deal with this.

The storms continued through the afternoon. Crista passed a village and smelled food cooking. A man called his family to come eat dinner and Crista watched three soggy kids run from the mud puddle they'd been playing in to the front door of their house. The man yelled to clean up before coming inside. Crista remembered Mom yelling similar words when she was a child.

Because of the rain Red Day hadn't bothered hiding her from the senses of anyone, not even the village's AI, who twitched nervously as it detected their passing. Crista's stomach grumbled. She wondered how the family would react if she walked up and asked for a seat at their table.

Of course, she knew how they'd react. As the kids stripped off their clothes and scrubbed themselves clean in the rain, Crista trudged onward.

You don't have to be hungry, Red Day said. *You're wolf blood. Kill a deer. Or a squirrel. Eat something, damn it.*

Crista didn't respond and merely walked on.

The rain stopped sometime after midnight and the temperature dropped, settling in just above freezing. As a cold fog danced among the new spring buds on the trees, Crista shivered. Red Day offered to give her enough power to stay warm but she refused the AI's help.

Diver reappeared as dawn split the sky from the still-dark horizon.

"I hate foggy mornings," Diver said, obviously meaning it because the girl started cursing the fog with a mix of childlike obscenities—stupid, stupid idiot fog!—and ancient vulgarities Crista had never heard before. Diver finished by stomping angrily in a puddle until she was drenched in mud.

That's what you looked like during your little fit yesterday, Red Day said.

Crista rolled her eyes but realized Red Day was right. She'd been acting silly.

"What's the matter?" Crista asked Diver.

"I don't want to keep going this way. Let's not visit Seed. Let's go to your home village. I want to see it."

"My village is a long way away."

"Doesn't matter," Diver said. She sat down in the puddle and kicked mud at Crista.

"You're not going to tell me what's really wrong?" Crista asked, sitting down in the mud beside Diver.

"I don't want you to go to Seed. Even if Desiada is supposed to meet us there."

"Any particular reason?"

"I like you. But you told Desiada and Lanea about your mission. If other plague birds learn you revealed their secrets you and Red Day might be killed. Or what if only you are killed and Red Day is instead downloaded into another body? If that happens my code goes with Red Day. I'll have to stay with Red Day and whoever merges with it."

"You make that sound bad," Crista said.

"It is bad. Red Day's an ass. Without you, it'll be an even bigger ass."

Red Day sputtered in Crista's mind as she smirked.

"What if we don't let the other plague birds find out what I did?" Crista asked.

"They're much stronger than you."

"Maybe you can help. Think of it as a game. A game of don't let the nasty plague birds learn the truth."

Diver snickered, then lay on her back in the mud puddle kicking her feet and splashing her hands as she yelled in happiness. Crista was coated in mud but, for the first time in days, felt happy.

"Come on," Diver yelled, jumping up and grabbing Crista's hand. Diver used her powers to remove all the mud from their clothes. She then pulled Crista through the trees, running flat out, almost dragging Crista with her strength.

They crested a small hill. Before them stretched the biggest city—and only city—Crista had ever seen. Stone houses and roads and buildings reached into the distance where they disappeared in the fog.

The city was dark with no lights in any of the buildings. No sounds either. No people moving in the streets.

Welcome to the ghost-city of Seed, Red Day said proudly. *You ready to again feel like a human?*

The city of Seed threw itself across the centuries, its living stone growing into houses and buildings and streets that reached for sky. The stone grew slowly but over the years walls divided from walls and roofs separated from ground and doors and windows emerged to excited openness. Beside the buildings and homes sprouted intricate gardens and boxes where trees and bushes and flowers bloomed and died. Wide streets and alleys begged for people to walk them. Decorative crystals embedded in the stone buildings whispered for people to touch their dazzling arrays of colors.

But the only people walking down this particular street were Crista and Diver. Crista realized Red Day hadn't exaggerated by calling this a ghost city. The city was neat and clean, without dirt in the streets or cobwebs in closed doorways even though no people lived in this part of town.

Despite this, each time she passed an alleyway she saw the flickers of imaginary people. In doorways the faces of children stared at her before fading away. Around each corner she saw brief snatches of unseen mothers and fathers and lovers and strangers.

But the moment she looked closer all these flicker people vanished.

It's the city, Red Day whispered. *Seed is a sentient place with an overbearing need to care for her citizens. But the few people remaining live in the central part of Seed. As for the empty sectors—well, let's just say Seed imagines herself full of people to keep herself sane.*

Crista wondered what would happen if an entire city lost touch with reality.

Despite the city's eerie aspect Crista had never seen anything like Seed. As she passed each home and building she imagined how many people could live here. In the blocks around her at least tens of thousands of people, which would be many times the size of her home village.

"Look at the amazement on her face," Diver said. "You'd think she'd never seen a real city before."

How you going to keep the wolf down on the farm after she's seen Paree? Red Day asked, the AI broadcasting its thoughts so Diver could also hear. While Crista had grown up having Blue broadcast its thoughts into the minds of every villager, she hadn't known before now that Red Day could do the same with other people. And to do it with a joke at her expense, a joke she didn't even understand ...

As Diver and Red Day laughed, Crista kicked the wall beside her, punching a small hole in it. The stone vibrated softly.

Don't irritate the city, Red Day warned softly. *The last time you made a place angry, things didn't go well.*

Crista knew Red Day was right—Down Hope Monastery had nearly killed her—but she was still angry. Before she could tell Red Day to piss off, Diver jumped over and hugged Crista around the waist.

"We're playing with you," the girl said. "Don't forget we love you. Even Mr. Grumpy-Poo-AI wouldn't know what to do without you."

Crista grinned as Red Day erupted in fury at being called such a childish name. *I am a blood AI!* Red Day screamed, again broadcasting its thoughts. *Show some respect!*

Diver stuck her tongue out at Crista—although Crista knew the tongue was intended for Red Day—and jumped on an arboreal box in the street, where she yanked a handful of leaves from the trees growing there. Diver twisted the leaves with her powers, drying them out and turning them to a red powder, which floated over her right hand. The powder morphed into a cute bunny rabbit above which floated the words Red Day. Diver hugged the rabbit before, with a clap of her hands, destroying it.

Red Day boiled in anger at the thought of Diver turning it into a cute rabbit.

"I could do it too," Diver said in a deathly serious tone. Red Day powered up. They both knew Diver could yank the AI from Crista's body and turn it into anything she wanted.

Yet reaching into Crista and Red Day's minds would also reveal the secret code buried within them, something Diver supposedly wanted to avoid. But if Diver decided she no longer cared what the code might force her to do ...

As suddenly as she'd become serious, Diver's child-like mood shifted. She spotted something across the street and squealed. "Let's make a castle!" Diver yelled as she ran to a stone monolith standing alone in a small park.

Crista and Red Day both sighed as they powered down. *I thought we weren't supposed to irritate Diver,* Crista said.

I know, Red Day replied. *But the thought of me as a cute bunny was too much to handle.*

As that ancient human proverb says, suck it up!

Red Day started to mutter something but fell quiet. Crista's body shook slightly —it was easy to forget how dangerous Diver could be. Once Crista regained her composure, she walked to the park.

The park formed a square several hundred yards across walled off on three sides by houses and buildings. Grass grew here, as did trees and small shrubs. For a moment Crista saw the flicker of kids chasing each other across the grass and adults lolling in the sunshine before the city's dream images faded away.

In the middle of the park rested a black-stone pyramid five yards tall. Diver stood tapping her fingers across the pyramid's surface.

Is that the Obsidian Rise? Crista asked Red Day, remembering the building her mother had wanted her to visit.

No. This is a regional control panel for the city. The Obsidian Rise is of a similar shape but massively larger.

What did she mean by "let's make a castle"?

Control inputs like this allow city residents to register requests into Seed's network. If you'd like to grow a new room or house, or create a castle, you ask here. A few weeks or months later there's your new creation, if approved by Seed.

No wonder Diver was excited. Crista figured Diver was playing with the city's network like she played with everything.

"You have to see this," Diver said, reaching for Crista's hand.

Diver placed Crista's hand on the stone. A slight hum traveled from Crista's skin to her head like a tickle in her blood. She saw the stone and this park as if looking at them from far up in the sky. She also felt nerve impulses moving through the buildings and homes as their living stones breathed in and out and embraced the sunlight. As she flew higher she saw more of the city, a massive map laid out before her like a hidden gem created eons before.

"It's beautiful," Crista said. Red Day echoed her sentiments

"This city is living perfection," Diver said. "Seed's been waiting for ten thousand years, waiting for the day when she's again filled with people."

Crista tried to imagine what that would be like, but failed. She couldn't believe there would ever be enough people in the world to fill a city this size. Besides, how could they live so close to one another without tearing themselves apart in anger and fury? She waited for Red Day to yet again tease her. To say that she knew nothing and could imagine even less.

Instead, Red Day reached out with a gentle touch and opened its memories to her. She saw the great cities of the distant past. Millions of people living in relative peace in cities that spanned the Earth's surface and even floated on the oceans. She also saw cities soaring through space and sitting beneath massive bubbles on the moon's surface.

As Red Day reached deeper into its archives, the AI showed her historic images and paintings from before its time. Crista saw dusty Timbuktu—which Diver had once visited—and dirty Rome and smoggy London, all from before humanity discovered electricity, followed by the shining lights and neon of New York and Los Angeles. She watched, dumbfounded, as massive cities like Mumbai and Tokyo and Beijing rose before her, all of which contained more people than Crista could count. Then the amazing virtual cities that spanned the solar system and claimed no particular location as their own.

Crista's body shook as it had a few minutes ago from her fear of Diver. But this time she shook in shame at her limited view of humanity's history.

"No wonder you laugh at me," she said, speaking to Red Day but also to Diver. "I know less than nothing about our history."

Red Day was silent, not desiring to spoil the moment by speaking. But Diver, instead of agreeing with Crista, shook her head.

"You can't know everything, Crista. But you can be open to new experiences. And you already do that."

Crista smiled and pushed her hand harder against the stone monolith. She wanted to see this entire city. To learn all she could of Seed's dreams and hopes and desires.

Instead, fear ran down her spine. As the map of the city spun below her, a large red slash appeared in an alleyway two leagues from where she stood. The red slash jumped off the map and flew at Crista, trying to devour her mind. With a yelp, Crista stumbled back, breaking the connection with the stone.

"What was that?" she asked.

I don't know, Red Day said. *But something important must have happened at that location. Something the city needed to share with a plague bird.*

Crista looked to Diver, who'd also released her grip on the stone. Diver refused to look Crista in the eye. Crista knew that when Diver acted like this she wouldn't tell Crista or Red Day anything, preferring to let them discover the truth on their own.

"I guess we need to start hiking," Crista muttered.

SEVERAL HOURS LATER THEY DISCOVERED THE SECRET—A DEAD PLAGUE BIRD.

Crista stood in an empty alley that looked much like all the alleys and streets they'd passed. The stone houses and buildings were decorated in bright green crystals that shimmered and flashed to the sunlight. Images of people flickered everywhere.

But unlike the other parts of the city, here Seed felt sad. The city's sadness washed over Crista like a chilled breeze even though no wind blew. Even the flicker people appeared to be crying over the dead plague bird.

Crista, though, felt no sorrow. The dead plague bird before her was Kenji, who'd attacked her village a century ago and killed her mother.

Kenji was as she remembered him, a young-looking man of avian descent with long red hair tied in a ponytail that reached to his knees. The lines on the right side of his face swirled like the Milky Way. However, unlike Crista's face the lines didn't glow red, instead resembling chapped lipstick on decayed leather. In Kenji's left hand he held his red knife. The dried remnant of a pool of blood surrounded his body, indicating he'd tried releasing his AI.

Crista stepped gingerly around the body, trying to determine what had happened, while Red Day watched for danger. The body had lain in the sun for several days and reeked like a dead mule left to rot. Worse, the small alley blocked the breeze from blowing the stench away.

Gritting her teeth, Crista grabbed the back of the plague bird's tunic and lifted him up. His guts dropped from his belly, bouncing on the alley's stepping stones like a bag of vomit.

Crista released his tunic and stepped back only to slip on the liquid flowing from his body. She fell forward, hands pushing into Kenji's decaying flesh. Blood and bile exploded across her face, causing her to stumble and curse as she reached for her canteen. The wolf in her snapped and growled. She kicked in anger at the building next to her, causing the stones to groan.

So graceful, Red Day whispered as Crista poured water across her face and scrubbed off the death scent. *This will give Diver plenty of laughs.*

But if Diver was amused, she showed no indication. The girl leaned against one of the buildings and stared down the empty alley, absently scratching her fingers back and forth on the wall's stone. Crista looked around, wondering if someone was coming or watching them. Neither she nor Red Day could see or sense anything.

"So what happened?" she asked. "Did his blood AI go into another person?"

No, Red Day said. *If that had happened, there would not be any remnants of the red lines on his face. This means both Kenji and his AI were killed.*

Crista remembered when Derena died, moments after passing Red Day to her. Derena's face had looked serene and peaceful. But Kenji's face was screwed in agony. He looked like he fought to the very end.

Release me, Red Day ordered. *I must fully investigate this crime.*

Do we have to? I thought we suspected Kenji of working with the Veil?

No matter. He was a plague bird. Perhaps the Veil are the ones who killed him.

Crista jabbed her palm with her knife. Several drops of blood dribbled out—not enough to free all of Red Day and its powers, but enough for this job.

The blood thinned and swirled, spinning around Crista as Red Day examined the dead plague bird with more detail and insight than the AI could do from inside her body. The AI also flew around the street and empty buildings and living stone walls, scanning every speck and detail surrounding them. After several minutes Red Day returned to Crista's hand, where it reformed with her body.

Did you learn anything? she thought.

Perhaps. There's something strange in the empty house at the end of the alley.

Crista walked over to investigate. Diver didn't follow her, still engrossed in staring at the empty alleyway before them. Red Day directed Crista to a small single-story house. The stones making up the house felt old. The door was partway open and creaked as Crista pushed it aside and stepped through.

Like all of the unoccupied houses in the city, this one seemed far emptier than it truly was. While Seed kept the streets and the exteriors of its buildings clean, inside the house was different. Abandoned birds' nests lay in the nooks and crannies of the house, and Crista saw a squirrel dart through a back doorway as she entered.

And someone had recently lived here. In the main room rested the burnt remains of a fire. Crista leaned over and smelled the ashes—they were cold, meaning it'd been out for a while. She breathed deep, trying to scent the person who'd camped here, but the scent was gone. In the room's dust she saw boot prints and the faint outline where a bedroll had laid.

Did this person kill the plague bird? Crista asked.

I don't know. The fire last burned three days ago, about the same time Kenji was killed. But I found something else interesting. Examine the ventilation hole in that wall.

Crista glanced up. The walls had holes in them for better airflow between rooms. Crista sniffed the hole—the wolf in her shrugged, not smelling any mice or rats inside—and reached in as far as she could. She felt a small cloth and pulled it out.

A bandana. One of those old-tech bandanas that changed colors depending on the wearer's emotion. Like Beu used to wear.

Smell it, Red Day ordered.

Crista held it to her nose and breathed deep. The scent was faint but clear. She remembered running through the forest, lost in wolf heat and wolf desire, catching the man she'd once loved and rolling with him across the leaf-strewn floor. She remembered him attacking her, breaking her leg, maiming her like nothing more than prey.

Beu. This was Beu's bandana.

Are you tricking me? she yelled at Red Day in her mind. *Is this fake?*

Not one of my tricks. And I don't think it's fake. But ...

Red Day's tone implied this might be someone else's trick. Crista looked out the doorway at Diver. The girl still stood in the alley but from what Crista had seen Diver's powers could easily manifest themselves at this distance.

Diver said she no longer accessed our minds, Crista said. *That she didn't want to risk finding the code.*

She may have said that, but perhaps it isn't the total truth. Because what are the odds that in the middle of a nearly abandoned city, near a dead plague bird who'd shown a strange interest in your life, we'd find Beu's bandana? Find it hundreds of leagues from where we left Beu living with his new girlfriend.

The wolf in Crista growled. *I agree. We need to put an end to this. I'm tired of Diver playing with us like toys.*

That'll be risky. Red Day said. *But we've no choice. Try not to insult her.*

Crista shoved the bandana in her pocket and stormed into the alley, figuring that a direct approach while she was angry was the best way to handle Diver. But to her surprise Diver looked at her and grinned.

"I know you're mad," she said, "but don't do or say anything. They're watching."

Crista almost said "What?" but caught herself, knowing whoever killed the plague bird could be nearby. Diver pointed down the street.

"They've been watching since we arrived. They can't see or hear me, but they're paying close attention to you. If you talk to me they'll think you've gone crazy. Unless I edit their thoughts, which I might or might not do."

Crista still didn't see anyone. *You sense anything?*

No, Red Day said.

"This is so fun," Diver said. "I don't dare access your minds because of that code, but I can mess with theirs. So while they read your mind I get to read their minds and see an echo of your mind as I edit myself from their minds. It's so convoluted and fun."

Diver turned serious for a moment. "But make sure you keep that code hidden really deep. You don't want them accessing it and accidentally sharing it with me."

Crista shook her head, totally confused by whatever logic there was in Diver's statement. "Did they kill the plague bird?" she whispered.

"No," Diver said. "Let me show you."

With an excited giggle Diver skipped down the alley. Crista followed, the wolf in her growling, Red Day scanning for danger even though there was nothing to indicate they were anything but alone in this part of the city.

Diver stopped where the alley opened into a larger street and pointed to a spot a few yards before Crista. "Look here," Diver said. "Keep watching. Get ready. Get ready." Diver clapped her hands loudly. "Now!"

Crista felt Diver reach out with her power, just like she'd done at Down Hope Monastery, where Diver's subtle ministrations had reshaped the reality that Crista experienced. But this time Diver was doing the mental intrusion to someone else.

In what felt like a slap against reality, two plague birds—one male, one female—stood before Crista, stunned looks on their faces indicating that she shouldn't be seeing them.

"Well shit," the male plague bird said. "That was unexpected."

THEY SAT IN THE HOUSE CRISTA HAD INSPECTED EARLIER, A SMALL FIRE CRACKLING IN the middle of the room. The flames teased light across the walls, a flickering like knife blades reaching for everyone. Crista sat across the fire from the other plague birds nibbling at the bread they'd shared. She wasn't hungry but also didn't want to say no to their hospitality.

They don't appear to have poisoned us, Red Day said with a chuckle. *Not that it matters. This bread isn't worth feeding to hogs.*

The two plague birds—the man was named Jai-Saan and the woman Tendi—froze at Red Day's words while the blood AIs in their bodies rippled in barely suppressed anger. Crista blushed and yet again wished she could physically slap Red Day.

They can read our thoughts, she said to the AI, wondering how deeply they could probe into her mind. These plague birds had, after all, manipulated her senses earlier.

Red Day cursed in anger and irritation. *Of course they can read our thoughts. It's what plague birds do when we're near each other. But what we don't do is manipulate each other's senses. We don't use our powers to hide from one another.*

The female plague bird had the decency to look ashamed of what she'd done. Not Jai-Saan, who sliced his knife back and forth across his palm as his body instantly healed itself.

"Speaking of manipulation," Jai-Saan said, "how did you break ours? From what we know of your precious Red Day—and believe me, we know far too much of its history—such a feat shouldn't be possible."

Crista felt Red Day growl in her mind, both nervous and afraid. Crista didn't want to give Diver away but also knew the harder she tried not to think about

Diver the harder it would be to keep the girl from her mind. Jai-Saan and Tendi grinned as their blood AIs reached out and caressed Crista's thoughts.

But if Diver was worried, she didn't show it. She made shadow puppets on the wall with her tiny hands, the shadows flickering in the firelight into tigers and wolves and snakes. Crista felt Jai-Saan and Tendi withdraw from her mind, their irritation obvious at learning nothing. Diver must have manipulated their minds yet again to ensure they didn't learn anything about her.

"Obviously there's more to your Red Day than we realized," Tendi muttered.

Crista glanced at Diver again. "What if it wasn't Red Day?" she asked. "The power comes from a little girl named Diver. She's older than old and is part alien AI and a bomb that can destroy humanity. All she needs to detonate is the code hidden in my mind."

Diver laughed and clasped her hands into a double fist that created a shadow shaped like a planet until her hands flew apart miming a massive explosion. But Jai-Saan and Tendi heard nothing of Crista's words. Or more accurately, Diver's powers made them believe Crista hadn't said a word and hadn't even opened her mouth.

You know, there are benefits to being around Diver, Red Day said. *Not every day you can say "fuck you!" to a pair of plague birds without them hearing the insult.*

Diver rolled her eyes but had blocked Red Days' words because neither plague bird reacted.

"Why are you here?" Crista asked.

"We work in Seed," Tendi said. "There are so many people in the city that at least three plague birds are needed to maintain the peace."

"I thought this was a ghost city," Crista said.

"For the most part," Tendi replied. "But in the center of Seed, around the Obsidian Rise, there are over 30,000 people."

"So the dead plague bird ..."

"His name was Kenji. And yes, he was one of our three. In fact, he'd been in Seed the longest. Jai-Saan and myself joined him here nearly ten thousand years ago."

Crista nodded, not letting on she already knew Kenji's name. "I'm sorry for the loss of your friend."

"We hated him," Jai-Saan said matter-of-factly.

"Fine. You hated him. That doesn't explain why you hid from me earlier."

"Here's how it is, cuz," Jai-Saan said.

She's not your cousin, Red Day snapped.

"Fine," Jai-Saan said. "Cristina de Ane, bonded as plague bird to Red Day, who once strode the world with Derena, and before that—oh, how many bodies have you let die, Red Day? One, two, three, four, five ..."

Jai-Saan giggled in the same disturbing way Diver often did. But where Diver giggled at the wrong times from a childish sense of wonder, which had somehow survived for eons, Jai-Saan made the noise from what seemed like a pit of pure cruelty. Crista felt the AI in Jai twist with each giggle and realized the truth behind Jai-Saan's name. The man before her was named Jai, but the blood AI was Saan, the name pronounced to the sound of sand and dirt dribbling from an exhumed corpse's mouth.

Jai was tall and thin, of what appeared to be human-avian descent, his bones pushing so far through his pale flesh that his ribs cast shadows. His blue eyes sank deep into his skull—he didn't eat anymore, allowing his AI to keep him alive—while the lines on his face rippled like the fire before them. Unlike the straight red line on Crista's face, Jai-Saan's lines dripped and curved as if written in red words of power.

And Saan was powerful. Crista reached out with Red Day and touched the barest edge of Saan, only to have Red Day's senses slapped back into her body.

Crista had noticed Jai-Saan didn't refer to himself as I, instead using plural pronouns. Now she understood why. The man before her had completed merged with his AI.

Tendi looked more human than Jai. She was barely half Jai-Saan's height and scented of fox heritage. Where Jai-Saan was bone, she was flesh with glowing dark skin and round hips and breasts and a smile to her lips that looked heartfelt. She spoke in such soft tones Crista couldn't imagine her ever raising her voice. Instead of Crista's single red line, twin lines intertwined up the right side of Tendi's face.

When Crista reached out to Tendi with Red Day, her blood AI didn't slap back like Saan. *My name is Yualsong,* the AI said to Crista. *Always nice to meet a sister plague bird.*

Yualsong also vibrated to power. Far more power than Red Day had on its best day.

"Ah yes," Jai-Saan said. "Now you know Red Day's deep, dark secret. We're afraid your Red Day isn't very powerful as blood AIs go. In fact, it's the runt of our litter, so to speak."

Tendi nodded—too polite to rub Crista's face in that fact but agreeing with Jai-Saan's truthfulness.

Red Day shook in anger but didn't say anything. While Crista knew she should take joy in Red Day being cut down a notch, Jai-Saan's words insulted her by association. She'd never been one to take insults and refused to start now.

"I'll agree you two are powerful," she said. "But we recently defeated someone who was even stronger."

"Really?" Jai-Saan asked. "Mind if we see?"

No! Red Day said, but Crista cut the AI off.

They could rip the memories out of us if they wished. Let them in. Just make sure they can't access Diver's code or any dangerous memories.

Crista felt Red Day not wanting to yield, but she was right. Red Day reluctantly powered down its mental protections as the other AIs eased into Crista's head.

Once again she relived her fight with Vaca. Of Red Day raining on the ground and turning everything to lava.

"Mildly impressive," Jai-Saan said. "Not that this member of the Veil would have been a challenge for Tendi or ourself. But once you survived being beaten like a rag doll, you did a decent job."

Red Day boiled inside Crista's blood at Jai-Saan's false praise.

Even though Jai-Saan and Tendi had finished examining Crista's memories of her battle with Vaca, they didn't leave her mind. Her body spasmed nervously as, against her will—or maybe to what was only the illusion of her will—her right hand reached into her pocket and pulled out Beu's bandana. Even though she didn't want to, she raised the cloth to her face and breathed deep of Beu's scent.

Crista saw Beu before her—eyes burning yellow, his face shrieking and howling as he tore and broke her body. Crista thought of her father and mother and wanted to reach out to them for support, only to scream as the pain circling her slammed deep into her soul.

Enough! Red Day screamed, smashing a burst of power across the room and into Jai-Saan and Tendi, severing the grip they held on Crista's mind. Jai-Saan cursed and raised his knife to his wrist, ready to release his AI, but Tendi grabbed his arm and shook her head.

"We went too deep," she said gently. "Our apologies."

Crista gasped, feeling like Beu yet again stood over her broken body. She dropped the bandana and felt her leg, stunned to see it wasn't broken. *That was then,* she thought. *Beu will never again hurt me. I won't allow it.*

"Again, our apologies," Tendi repeated. "But those memories tasted important."

Jai-Saan smirked, not joining Tendi in the apology. The wolf in Crista growled. The red line on her face seared her skin as it burned hot.

"Attack them," Crista hissed. "Now!"

Calm down, Crista, Red Day said nervously. *I can't hurt them. I'm not strong enough. All you'll do is kill both of us for nothing.*

"*Now* Red Day's rational," Jai-Saan said with a laugh. "What a change!"

To Crista's surprise, instead of agreeing, Tendi drew her knife and held it to her own throat. "Another word, Jai-Saan, and I'll release Yualsong and kill you myself."

"You're not strong enough," Jai-Saan stated.

"Perhaps. But together with Cristina de Ane ...?"

Crista felt Red Day grin inside her, eager to take on someone who'd embarrassed it. Jai-Saan glanced from Crista to Tendi as the AI inside him clicked in bursts of static, like a hidden spider tapping its fangs together. *All of you are wasting time,* Saan hissed from within Jai. *They found evidence of the Veil. That should be our focus.*

Crista nodded. "We did. Are you the plague birds who assigned Derena and Red Day to investigate the Veil?"

"We are," Tendi said. "We'd previously sent several plague birds to look into the Veil, but none returned. We thought a less ... powerful plague bird might not draw as much attention and have a chance to learn something."

"She means we hoped the Veil might underestimate Red Day because of its weakness," Jai-Saan added. "And if not, the worst that might happen would be Red Day and Derena's death. But it looks like the first option succeeded."

Red Day growled alongside Crista's wolf, but said nothing.

"We did learn something," Crista said.

Crista described how the Veil attacked and wounded Derena. How Ashdyd stole Derena and Red Day's backup memories. How Crista became a plague bird. How Ashdyd hacked Crista's mind in the barrier forest.

"You two have done very well," Tendi said.

Crista glanced out the doorway at Kenji's body. "We thought Kenji might be working with the Veil since he was nearby when some of this happened."

"Kenji was ordered to observe Red Day and Derena and report back," Jai-Saan said, "without interfering. He did his duty."

"Did that duty include killing my mother?" Crista asked. Tendi and Jai-Saan looked puzzled.

Drop it for now, Red Day whispered.

Tendi leaned over and picked up the bandana Crista had dropped. "This Beuten Pauler—do you know why he might have come to Seed?"

"You know my memories. I didn't know he was here until I found that bandana."

"Any idea why he stayed in the spot where Kenji was killed?" Jai-Saan asked. "Perhaps he aims to kill you?"

Even though Crista knew Beu could no longer harm her, she shivered. But it also didn't make sense. Had he followed her for the past year? Beu knew she would kill him if she saw him. And he'd seemed satisfied with the Hunt-clan girl he'd joined with.

Tendi folded the bandana neatly and tossed it to Crista. "This Beu obviously couldn't harm you, let alone Kenji," she told Crista. "Kenji's powers were the equal of those possessed by myself, and an ordinary human like Beu couldn't kill even the weakest of plague birds. But this is still strange. Coincidence is a false belief."

Tendi fell silent, engaging in a private conversation with her blood AI before reaching a decision. "We'll allow Crista to assist us," she told Jai-Saan.

"What!" the other plague bird said. "We have her intelligence on the Veil, so we don't need her. All she can do is hold us back."

"My decision is final."

Jai-Saan obviously didn't like Tendi telling them what they'd do, but after a quick internal conversation they nodded assent.

Crista snorted, the wolf in her still angry at these two. "Perhaps I don't want to work with you."

"I understand, my dear," Tendi said, the soft wash of condescension in her voice stinging worse than Jai-Saan's hatred. "If I was in your shoes, I'd no doubt react the same way. But there's a reason Jai-Saan and I work together on this—whatever killed Kenji is powerful. Perhaps it's the Veil. Perhaps not. We're safer together."

She knew Tendi was correct. Alone, Crista would be an easier target than if she stayed with these two. Not that such knowledge made submitting to them any easier to take.

"Curse them if it helps," Diver whispered. "I'll make it so they don't remember."

Crista did, cursing both plague birds to the deepest level of hell before storming out of the house.

CRISTA SLEPT ON THE STREET THAT NIGHT, NOT WANTING TO BE IN THE SAME ROOM AS Jai-Saan and Tendi. While the short distance didn't matter—she could still sense the other plague birds, and they her—she felt better not seeing them. Crista didn't even bother to unroll her sleeping pad, instead curling up on the back step of a house.

Is this how people feel when we rip into their minds? she asked Red Day.

We do it for a better reason than Jai-Saan and Tendi did.

Maybe. Or maybe we tell ourselves that to make it feel better. Crista paused. *Why didn't you tell them about the discoidal we found?*

They'd want to examine it. We'll do that ourselves when we reach the Obsidian Rise.

Sometime after midnight Diver sat next to Crista. She reached for Crista's red hair to stroke it.

"No," Crista snapped. "Leave me alone."

"I didn't do anything to you. They did."

"You could have stopped them."

"Yes, I could have. But I can't go around meddling. It's not only against my programming; it's not right. I can't live your life."

"You can't meddle?" Crista asked, incredulous. "All you've done since I've met you is meddle."

"Well, yes. But I can't meddle in big stuff like this."

Crista snorted, not wanting to know how big and little meddling differed in Diver's mind. Crista rolled on her back and looked at the sky. With no lights in this part of the city the night was as dark as the deepest of forests, lit by the moon alone.

"Do you really not want the code in me?" Crista asked.

"No."

"What happens if I'm killed? Like Kenji."

"Then the code would be gone. I'd be free to wander the world again."

"Sounds like you have an incentive to see me die. Or to kill me."

"I can't kill you—I'm prohibited from destroying the code. But let you die? Maybe. But that's why I chose you to find the code. If a plague bird like Jai-Saan had found it, I'd have been all too happy to see him die. But I like you."

Great, Red Day said. *Another damn reason to not get on Diver's bad side.*

Crista pushed Red Day's comment from her mind. "I like you too, Diver. And I guess the way things are going with me pissing off the Veil and my fellow plague birds, I won't survive that much longer."

"I know. Isn't that great! About the time you tire of having me around, you'll be dead!"

Crista rolled her eyes at Diver's comment but figured the girl didn't mean it to be as nasty as it sounded. "What happens if whatever killed Kenji tries to take me out? Will you stop it?"

Diver looked at the moon and pointed. "I've been there. See the large white pimple on the Sea of Tranquility? That's Mare Trans City. There were millions of people living there when the collapse happened. The life support system failed. I had little desire to be the last kid alive on the moon, so I fixed up a broken spaceship and flew back with a bunch of people."

Red Day froze inside Crista while her skin chilled. One of her long-dead relatives—a wolf child ancestor of her father—escaped Mare Trans City in a spaceship. Crista's mother had told the story to her when she was a child. The ship was supposedly piloted by a magical young girl who became best friends with Crista's distant ancestor.

"I ... I was told a similar story ..."

"I know," Diver said. "That was me. Your ancestor was really sweet. As I said, I like you. If I have to be around a plague bird, I want her to be you."

Crista gazed at the dead city on the moon, wondering what it'd been like to be there and face cold, air-starved death. "I notice you didn't answer my question," she said. "What will you do if someone tries to kill me?"

Diver grinned. "Maybe I did answer. I'm not supposed to meddle, but sometimes my goals mesh with others. After I fixed that ship I let several thousand kids and their families onboard and I flew them back to Earth. Most of them thought the ship was automated but it was just me, meddling away."

"Well, if I'm ever about to die, meddle all you want," Crista said in a joking voice, hoping Diver wouldn't notice her nervousness.

"No promises. But what good is meddling if I can't meddle for someone I like?"

The girl laughed and curled up next to Crista to sleep. After a few minutes of not hearing Diver move, Crista mentally reached out and pulled Red Day's essence close.

You sure Diver can't listen to what we say? she asked Red Day.

She said she no longer listens to our minds. But I can't guarantee it.

Fine. What do you think about that moon-city story?

That is … strange, the AI said. *What are the odds of your ancestor making friends with Diver and you becoming her friend?*

And what are the odds of that story being remembered and passed down intact through my family across ten thousand years?

Nearly nonexistent. Red Day paused for several seconds, which was an eon for a fast-thinking AI. *Crista, there are a lot of coincidences surrounding your mother. First that Derena and I met her before you were born. That my memory of Derena's discussion with your mother has been partly erased by someone. And that your mother told you a story about Diver—a story that, if I'm correct about human norms, should have been passed down through your father's side of the family since that's where your ancestor can be traced. And finally, if the memory Ashdyd revealed is to be trusted, your mother used some type of power to attack Kenji before he killed her.*

Crista glanced at Diver, who scooted closer to Crista's body to stay warm.

Is all this Diver's doing? she asked Red Day. *Can we trust her?*

I don't know. But for now, we don't have any choice.

THE NEXT MORNING CRISTA RELUCTANTLY JOINED JAI-SAAN AND TENDI, WHO STOOD IN the alley beside Kenji's body. The stench had grown worse, attracting a number of vultures who circled lazy loops in the sky. But every time a vulture grew bold enough to swoop lower it realized the body was a plague bird and flew away. Crista wondered if such a fear had been gened into vultures, or if they'd learned the hard way to avoid plague birds.

As Crista and the other plague birds stood before their dead compatriot, Diver sat on the stone roof of a nearby house. The girl played with a squirrel, continually grabbing its tail and making it jump as it searched for its unseen assailant.

"Now what?" Crista asked Jai-Saan and Tendi. "Do we stake out the body?"

"Already did," Jai-Saan said dismissively. "That's how we got stuck with you."

"What Jai-Saan means," Tendi said, "is we tried that approach. Our secondary plan had been to track the person who'd camped out in that house—your Beu. While we don't think he had anything to do with the murder, he might have seen something. And now that we know he once loved and attacked someone who became a plague bird, well, let's just say our interest is piqued."

Crista pulled out the bandana and waved it before Jai-Saan. "Do you need a sniff of Beu's scent?" she asked as if speaking to an overeager puppy. "There's a good boy. Smell. Smell."

Jai-Saan boiled red with anger, the AI in him squealing as Tendi laughed.

"Come on, Jai, she's joking with you," Tendi said.

Crista grinned and Red Day snickered. *Good one,* Red Day said. *It'll be fun to see how far we can push that fool.*

If we push too far they could kill us.

That makes life exciting—the risk of going too far.

If Jai-Saan and Tendi were still reading Crista and Red Day's thoughts, they gave no indication. Tendi began hiking down the street, heading in the direction Beu might have gone.

"Wait," Crista said. "Aren't we going to bury him?"

"He had a name," Jai-Saan said, faking sadness for a moment before grinning. Crista remembered that neither Jai-Saan nor Tendi had liked Kenji. She wondered why before realizing she didn't like Jai-Saan or Tendi. Maybe plague birds didn't enjoy each other's company.

"Fine," Crista snapped. "Are we going to bury poor dead Kenji or are you simply going to gloat over his passing?"

Tendi shook her head. "We're not gloating—we didn't like him, but we respected him. And plague birds aren't buried. In fact, we forbid anyone to know plague birds can be killed."

"My entire village saw my predecessor die," Crista said.

"That's different. Once the blood AI passes to you, the previous host is no longer considered a plague bird. But both Kenji and his blood AI were killed here. Anyone who sees one of us dead must have that memory ripped from their mind. Or be killed themselves."

Crista started to ask what would happen to the body, but Red Day told her to watch and learn.

Jai-Saan leaned over and caressed the dead plague bird's bloated face. Crista sensed that while Jai-Saan didn't like Kenji there was more to their relationship than simple hate. Jai-Saan pulled his knife and sliced his wrist, sending Saan shooting out in a boiling knot of fury.

Crista had known Saan was stronger than Red Day but hadn't truly understood the difference until now. A blood storm swirled around them, growing larger and larger, coating the dead plague bird's body and everything within the alley with the exception of Crista, Jai, and Tendi. The blood quaked and shivered and exploded in little novas of creation as Saan tore apart the living stone houses and the ground around them before immediately rebuilding everything, leaving the alley looking the same except for the removal of every stray molecule of Kenji's blood or DNA. Since the stones were linked together, Saan reached through Seed's network and across the entire city, reworking the shared data so no memory existed of the plague bird's death. In a final burst of power, the dead plague bird's body collapsed to dust, which further collapsed to mere molecules and eventually random, scattered atoms.

Crista watched Saan's red fury flow back into Jai's body. She glanced at Tendi, who stood silently but could also have released such power.

That's what you tried to do to that Veil man, isn't it? Crista asked. *Remove every trace of him. But you couldn't.*

Now you know the truth, Red Day said in a low voice. *I'm weak. The weakest plague bird on Earth.*

Before Crista could say anything—maybe comfort Red Day or tell the AI she didn't care if it was weak—she saw Jai-Saan grinning at Red Day's words.

Jai pulled the rest of Saan back into his body and began walking down the road.

CRISTA, JAI-SAAN AND TENDI WALKED THE STREETS OF SEED FOR HOURS. AT FIRST THE city was mostly deserted with only a few deer and rabbits grazing in the gardens and tree boxes. But as the day passed, the breeze brought the scent of salt water and seagulls began flying in the sky. The closer they approached the ocean the more the city's flicker-images of people vanished and real people appeared.

The first people they passed was a small family living in a two story stone house, followed the next block by an entire clan in a large stone building.

A league later they topped a large hill and the city changed. Before them glittered the waves of the Flickering Sea, surrounded on all sides by large buildings reaching a hundred yards or more into the sky. Some of the stone buildings were made of what looked to be gray slate and blue granite, others of red quartz and beige sandstone. But these stones weren't like the ones Crista had grown up knowing—the stone buildings before her were alive just like everything else that grew in the city of Seed.

But even these tall buildings were overwhelmed by the massive pyramid near the seafront. Rising a quarter league tall, the pyramid was so black it seemed to absorb the sunlight from the sky.

Crista knew without asking this was the fabled Obsidian Rise, the heart of Seed.

"Why do most of the city's people live here?" Crista asked Tendi.

"Because the rest of the city is *haunted* by Seed's dream-people, which unnerves most humans," Tendi said. "So people bunch together in this central area. That keeps the dream images at bay."

"There shouldn't be any people here at all," Jai-Saan grumbled.

"Why?" Crista asked.

"Under the three-fold path, people had to abandon all of Earth's cities to live in small villages managed by AIs. But Seed was granted an exception."

"We took pity on Seed," Tendi added. "Seed would go insane without anyone living in her, so we let a small population remain. For a time."

"An irritatingly long time," Jai-Saan said.

Crista ignored Jai-Saan's snide comment. This was still the most people she'd ever seen in one place. Many of the buildings they passed were occupied. Kids ran freely through the streets while adults walked here and there. Herders guided cows and pigs and flocks of chickens to market or to the parks to graze. They also passed dozens of shops—blacksmiths and leathermakers and furriers and taverns and even a store containing blooming flowers.

Then, as they neared the Obsidian Rise, they encountered a large open-air market. Hundreds of people milled through an array of stalls or sat under umbrellas as they talked and haggled and laughed. The market looked like a dream world to Crista, full of ancient treasures and newly-made toys and items she couldn't begin to describe.

Tendi smiled. "Want to see?" she asked.

Jai-Saan rolled his eyes but Crista ignored that and said yes. Diver jumped up and down clapping her hands before running into the market and disappearing in the crowd.

Being careful not to bump into or touch anyone—Red Day already cautioned her over the strain of hiding from the senses of so many people at once—Crista walked through the market. She passed a woman covered in yellow scales selling fried roti glazed with honey. Crista bit her tongue to keep from snatching one and swallowing it whole. The next stall featured a small AI offering wooden puppets, the AI's pulsating cloud of lights projecting a forest scene before which danced the puppets.

Red Day cursed—*Playing with puppets is an embarrassment to all artificial intelligences*, the AI muttered—but Crista didn't care. She thought the puppet master and its creations were wonderful.

Crista wandered through the market, amazed at the sights. One stall contained caged birds in handmade wooden cages, including an unusual, ungened cardinal. Several people gawked at the cardinal, whose bright redness was rarely seen because it reminded people of plague birds. The next stall contained ceramic eggs similar to the ones carried by the monks of Down Hope. The barker selling the eggs announced to the crowd that they'd recently washed up on a far, distant beach.

"Who knows what ancient mysteries and awe-inspiring knowledge will hatch from these eggs," the barker hissed from his reptilian face.

Defunct control AIs for sewer management systems, Red Day said.

What?

That's what the eggs contain. AIs who once controlled the flow of shit. Not very mysterious or awe-inspiring.

Crista laughed.

Before Crista could see what was in the next stall, Diver came running through the crowd, pushing aside people and bumping into others, none of whom could see her and all of whom looked puzzled.

"I found it," Diver yelled, grabbing Crista's hand. "Come see!"

Curious at what could have Diver so excited, Crista followed her to an ice cream stall.

"I've had ice cream before," Crista said. "We made it every year at my village's harvest festival."

"Not like this you haven't."

Strangely, the ice cream seller didn't seem concerned with attracting customers. Kids ran by the stall without a glance, and the woman running the stall didn't call out to them. The seller was only slightly taller than Crista, with brown hair buzzed close to her scalp. Crista had no clue what animal genes the woman descended from. Crista scented eagle and owl and lion and tiger and a hundred other scents—even for one brief moment nothing but purest human, like Diver. But the woman wasn't human. Her body was extremely thin, like skin without muscles had been stretched over her bones. Her oversized eyes twitched like a hummingbird's wings, moving so fast Crista could barely see her pupils, which sparked every time the woman blinked.

What's wrong with her? Crista asked.

Nothing, Red Day said. *She's an automaton. Maybe the last left in this world.*

Is she human? AI?

She's both. Her body is a self-repairing mix of flesh and machine. She's old. Far older than I am, from a time when humanity put more stock in physical creations instead of the ethereality of AIs.

The automaton nodded at Crista before staring blankly at the crowds passing before her stall.

She can see me?

Of course. She's not in our jurisdiction, so I'm not allowed to hide you from her senses. Unless she interferes too much with human lives, in which case a plague bird must destroy her. That's why there are no other automatons left. They've traditionally had difficulty staying uninvolved in human affairs.

The woman's scent no longer shifted in Crista's mind and had settled on a definite smell of lupine heritage. The woman reminded Crista of her long-dead mother. A flush of happiness passed through Crista.

"Amazing, isn't she," Jai-Saan announced from behind Crista, causing her to jump. "Crista, allow me to introduce the automaton Amaj. You still use the name of Amaj when in the female gender, correct?"

"That is correct, most honored Jai and Saan," Amaj said in a voice that sounded exactly like the soothing voice of Crista's mom.

"Automatons mimic the feedback of those they interact with," Jai-Saan whispered, leaning creepily close to Crista's ear. "Are we to assume, since Amaj currently resembles a motherly wolf-human, that you respond positively to anyone who reminds you of your dear, departed maternal creature?"

"Screw you," Crista muttered.

"No need for nastiness. Amaj is merely being who she is, and Saan and myself are merely stating what we know." Jai-Saan looked into the large wooden ice cooler on the table between them and Amaj. "We don't suppose you have a special ice cream just for us?"

"Most honored Jai and Saan, you know I do not," Amaj whispered softly.

"That's as it should be. But we would still like something special, so we grant you permission to give us a treat. Make it chocolate, please."

Amaj scooped out a large ball of chocolate ice cream from the cooler and placed it on a cone before reaching a thin hand toward Jai-Saan. The nail of her index finger briefly touched Jai-Saan's forehead, the nail sparking like Amaj's eyes. Amaj lowered her hand and tapped the glowing nail against the ice cream she'd scooped out. The spark from her nail flowed into the ice cream.

"Please enjoy, most honored Jai and Saan," Amaj said as she handed the cone to the plague bird. Jai-Saan licked the ice cream and smiled.

"You are a true master, Amaj," Jai-Saan said as he sat down on one of the wooden chairs before the stall and took a big bite of his ice cream.

"So it's not just ice cream?" Crista asked.

"Obviously. Automatons trade in memories. They can copy memories from living minds and impress their essence into physical objects. In Amaj's case, she lets you relive a happy moment from your life as you eat your ice cream."

"Okay, I want to try one. Anything that can make an ass like you happy must be amazing."

"You can't," Tendi said from the other side of Crista, again startling her by coming up without being noticed. "We are being observed. It won't do for people to see Amaj give an ice cream to the invisible plague bird in their midst."

Crista glanced behind her. Many of the people in the marketplace were watching Amaj. Crista had wondered why she hadn't seen kids lining up for Amaj's ice cream. She guessed the automaton was strange enough that few people purchased treats from her. But people weren't just staring at Amaj—they were also watching Jai-Saan and Tendi. Yet Crista saw none of the disgust and fear normally seen when people watched plague birds.

To underscore this, Tendi squatted down next to a child watching them. "Would you like an ice cream?" she asked. The little boy shook his head and muttered—without a hint of fear at talking to a plague bird—that his parents wouldn't let him buy from the automaton.

Tendi stood up and nodded to Crista, as if this explained everything. Tendi turned to Amaj and asked for an ice cream. Amaj touched Tendi's head and repeated her previous actions, handing over what looked like strawberry ice cream.

What the hell! Crista screamed at Red Day. *What the hell is going on?*

They're taunting us. Instead of manipulating the senses so they seem invisible, Jai-Saan and Tendi simply change how people see them. They both appear to be normal people. Jerks, but normal jerks.

"Do you mind?" Jai-Saan said. "Saan and myself are reliving the moment we first joined. It's difficult to enjoy happy memories with Red Day insulting us."

Crista ignored Jai-Saan. *All this time I've wished I could be around people without being treated like an outcast—and you had the power to make me appear normal!* Crista could barely contain her rage at Red Day. But as she looked at the smirk on Jai-Saan's face she realized the truth.

You don't have the power to do that, do you? she asked.

No. To edit someone out of the senses of others is easy because no one questions what they don't notice. But to make you appear to be someone else entirely, that's much harder. Humans are very adept at picking up visual cues from fellow humans. I no longer have the power to effectively create such a mental illusion.

But you used to?

Not since before I became a blood AI.

Crista sighed and turned from Jai-Saan so she didn't have to see him gloating yet again over Red Day's lack of power. She was about to walk away when she saw Diver waving for her to follow. Crista followed the little girl to a less crowded part of the market.

"I can make you look human," Diver said. "I mean, make it so people see you as a regular, boring human."

Crista grinned and Red Day laughed, both imagining the shocked reaction Jai-Saan and Tendi would have after putting down Red Day for lacking the power to do this.

"But isn't that meddling?" Crista asked.

"Well, yes, but I want some ice cream. Will you share yours with me? I want to taste a happy moment from your life."

Crista nodded.

"Who do you want to look like?" Diver asked.

"Make me look like that dead plague bird Kenji. But a human Kenji. How he'd have looked without his blood AI. Make sure your manipulation affects Jai-Saan and Tendi."

Diver clapped her hands and gestured for Crista to walk back into the crowd. People nodded at her and said hello while Jai-Saan and Tendi stared at her in shock.

"How...?" Tendi asked, but Crista ignored the question and merely asked Amaj for another ice cream.

WITH EVERYONE STILL SEEING HER WITH KENJI'S BIRD-FACED HUMAN BODY, CRISTA TOOK her ice cream and walked to the ocean, where she sat on the city's massive stone docks. She licked the ice cream—peach, with a mix of honey—and remembered a happy day of her life. She and her father were plowing a field on a fine spring day with Eggbeater being particularly unruly and refusing to work. The sky was blue and the wind cool and as the mule brayed her father began laughing. Crista also laughed. For some reason they couldn't stop laughing and supported each other to keep from collapsing into the black dirt. Even Eggbeater's braying turned into happy laughs.

Crista smiled as the feelings of that day washed over her. On that day she'd been happy living in her village. Enjoyed being around her father. She'd belonged to a particular place yet still felt a deep freedom. She'd had no reason to doubt any part of her life.

Diver hopped over and sat beside her, dangling her tiny legs over the side of the dock. "My turn," she announced.

"Why do you even want my ice cream? These aren't your memories?"

"Because it makes me happy to share in someone's happiness."

Crista handed the cone to Diver, who took a big bite of her memories and grinned. "Nice," Diver said, handing the cone back to Crista.

"Are Jai-Saan and Tendi still watching?"

"Oh yeah. They're struggling to understand how you look like Kenji."

You realize, of course, Red Day said, *that your continual tweaking of those two will come back to haunt us. If Jai-Saan and Tendi attack us, Diver might not protect us.*

I know. But it feels good.

Giving Diver the rest of the ice cream to eat, Crista glanced at the market behind them. "Any chance you'll let me look human long enough to wander through the market?" she asked Diver.

"Will you get me a present?"

"Deal."

Crista and Diver jumped up and walked through the market, leaving Jai-Saan and Tendi to stew in their irritation. Crista didn't know how long Diver would let people see her as a normal human, but she intended to take advantage of it. She smiled at the vendors and customers and kids playing in the street and people smiled back. Crista resisted the urge to run up and hug everyone or to shout over and over that she was human again, a real, live human!

Crista discovered the market operated on a barter system. People either swapped items one by one or, if desired, the market's AIs would keep a running tally of both trades and relative values for items, making sure all trades were fair and beneficial. Crista watched a merchant and customer do just that, the orange cloud of an AI evaluating the proposed trades. It compared the trades to previous trades spanning back centuries before announcing the current tallies and how much each person would owe the next time they met. Both the merchant and customer were pleased by the AI's impartial judgment and agreed to the terms.

"See anything you want?" Crista asked Diver.

Diver clapped as she looked around in excitement. She grabbed Crista's hand and dragged her to a metalworker's booth.

Large grabber vines grew from pots on the booth, the vines' gened suckers holding intricate hand-wrought jewelry made of gold and silver and steel and polished ceramic. The vendor, a tiny green-tinted man barely taller than Diver, smiled at Crista.

"You want to hold anything, let me know," he said, reaching out to touch one of the vines' grabbers, which unfolded at his touch and released a gold disk engraved with the word "love." Crista tapped a different grabber but the vine didn't release the item—the plant only responded to the vendor's touch.

Crista pretended to look over the jewelry while waiting for Diver to pick out something she liked. "What exactly do you take in trade?" Crista asked. "I'm new to the market."

"Depends on which items you select."

Crista glanced at Diver, who tapped a gold medallion inlaid with a silver image of a window curtain opening before the sun.

"Can you pick something not gold or silver?" Crista whispered. "Maybe something steel or ceramic?"

"Nope. I want this one."

Crista rolled her eyes and pointed at the medallion. "This one, please."

"Ah yes, the Veil," the vendor said. "Quite popular these days."

In the back of Crista's mind Red Day snapped to attention. "What did you call this?" Crista asked.

"The Veil," the man said, tapping the vine's grabber to release the medallion into his hand. "Quite the rage with young people. If you give one to a lover, it means you hope to raise the veil to reveal a bright new future."

"Crista, that's the name of the group that attacked you," Diver said, stating the obvious like a child.

While the vendor didn't hear Diver's words, he spun the medallion before Crista's eyes, giving her a clear view of the veil rising before a golden sun. Crista took the medallion into her hands and flipped it over. The words "We will raise the veil" were engraved into the back.

"Ah yes," the vendor said. "That comes engraved on all of these. But I can add your name, or the name of your loves, if you desire."

"Who makes these?" Crista asked.

"A young man trades them. He won't say if he makes them himself, but they are the finest quality medallions I've ever seen."

This medallion wasn't wrought by human hands, Red Day said. *It was smelted by an AI. The gold and silver were melted into that design without the use of molds or hammers. Only an AI could create it."*

Or a human with the power of the Veil. Maybe someone like Ashdyd.

Trade for the medallion. Get two—one for Diver and one for me to examine. I want to study it when we are away from prying eyes.

Crista opened her backpack and pulled out various items—her mess kit, her blanket, her bedroll—only for the vendor to shake his head. Until now Crista hadn't realized how little of value she actually carried.

I can't trade my knives, Crista thought. *Or the clothes I'm wearing.*

Derena's old vest. Show him that.

Crista glanced around, making sure no one was watching. She'd worn Derena's old vest, shirt and pants for a few weeks before Red Day killed several deer and created new leather clothes for her. She'd kept Derena's vest, occasionally looking at it and remembering her predecessor. But it was probably time to put those memories aside.

She pulled Derena's vest out of her backpack and held it so the sun bounced off the leather in all its red glory.

The vendor's eyes widened and his hands shook slightly.

"A plague bird visited my village last year," Crista whispered. "Before she left she gifted me this vest in return for assistance I'd given." Crista handed the vest to the man, who took it carefully like accepting a deadly viper.

"Notice the leathers, which are not dyed red but instead have been changed at the molecular level by a blood AI's power. Note the remnants of the plague bird's blood that flicker from the very leathers themselves."

"This is against the law..." the vendor muttered.

"No, it is merely taboo. But I'm sure someone in a city as big as Seed would trade for an item this rare."

The vendor licked his green lips. "One medallion..."

"Two."

The man tapped another vine's grabber, releasing a second Veil medallion. Crista took them and handed one to Diver, who looped it around her neck and squealed.

"The man who made these, any chance you could point him out to me?" Crista asked.

The vendor looked up from the red vest and shook his head. "I only see him when he passes through, but he doesn't follow a regular schedule. He's about your age, tabby-stripped hair, has the cat in him. Sometimes struggles to constrain his animal side. He's been passing in and out of Seed for the last two months."

Crista's gut seized. That sounded like Beu. But there was no way it could be.

We found Beu's handkerchief and scent near that dead plague bird, Red Day said. *Maybe ...*

It's not possible.

Crista ...

It's not possible!

FINDING YOUR WAY THROUGH THE VEIL

That night Crista and Diver bunked in an abandoned building near the waterfront. Diver slept wearing her medallion, a grin on her face and one hand wrapped around the gold charm.

Crista, though, only slept in fits and starts. Several times she pulled out Beu's bandana and stared at it, the emotion-sensitive technology turning the fabric black from her foul mood. Once she even breathed deep of its fabric. Beu's scent was nearly gone, but enough remained to convince her that Red Day was correct. Beu was in the city.

You okay? Red Day asked. *I know how much you hate him.*

Red Day sounded concerned about Crista, which shocked her. *It's not like he can hurt me,* she said. *Can he?*

No, he can't. We'll never let him hurt you again.

Red Day closed off its emotions, embarrassed to admit concern for Crista.

When the sun rose, Crista left both the building and Diver, who merely rolled over and continued to sleep. Crista wandered back to the market, thinking on Beu. Vaca had warned that her village and everyone she cared about was in danger. Could that have caused Beu to leave home?

But how could Beu have reached Seed so much faster than her—the vendor said the man who created the medallions first arrived here two months ago. It was impossible for an ordinary human to travel so far so fast these days. And Beu didn't have any powers, so how could he make the medallions, if Red Day was correct about them being made by an AI?

Without Diver to make her look human in people's minds, Crista passed through the market unseen. She hoped she'd see Desiada and Lanea, remembering their pledge to meet again in Seed. It'd be great fun to sneak up behind them and shout "Boo!" and be around friends.

If, that is, they weren't still angry at her.

You could also go to the Obsidian Rise and see if they're in the city, Red Day said. *Or maybe they left a message for you there.*

Crista smiled. *Be careful, or I might start thinking you care for me.*

Red Day sighed.

Even though dawn had barely begun the market was already open with hundreds of people trading for food. Because there were so many people about Red Day caused them to step out of Crista's way, as if on their own they'd decided to step aside and look at that necklace in a stall or smell the flowers held in a little girl's hand. Crista wondered how many people plague birds manipulated each and every day around the world. Did these little manipulations—forcing someone to unknowingly step out of your way or to not see you passing by—change the fates of those being manipulated?

And what if Vaca was right that the Veil were the plague birds to plague birds? Was someone even now standing beside Crista, invisible to her, manipulating her life?

Crista wandered randomly through the market, not paying attention to where she walked. The massive spike of the Obsidian Rise rose above her, dwarfing the nearby buildings and market. The sun glimmered behind the pyramid. Crista realized it should have cast a massive shadow across this part of the city, but instead the light shone on the city like the pyramid didn't exist.

The Obsidian Rise doesn't cast a shadow, Red Day declared. *Not ever.*

Not desiring another lecture from Red Day on how some ancient technology worked, Crista walked to the edge of the pyramid. This side was flat and rose straight up like a massive black wall. While Crista knew the other three sides of the pyramid were set at angles, she couldn't see them from here.

To annoy her, Red Day whispered, *It's an oblique pyramid—didn't you learn anything in school?*

Crista ignored the AI as she stopped before the black wall.

The pyramid's straight, black surface resembled obsidian with smoking images floating beneath the glassy surface. Ghostly people and animals danced before her like the flickering dream people in the empty parts of Seed.

Crista rested her hand on the smoking glass. She felt the hum of voices and dreams, and listened to the minds of the millions of people before her who'd touched the Obsidian Rise. Messages and words and images flowed around her—people waving at her, wanting to pass her messages, strangers saying hello.

She saw an androgynous young human smiling at her. Crista focused on the person and they appeared to step forward until they stood before her.

The person laughed and an aroused chill ran down Crista's spine—this was the most beautiful person she'd ever seen. While Crista couldn't say whether the person was female, male, or any other gender, she could tell the person had no animal genes in their body. Their eyes sparkled a dark green and their brown skin showed neither spots nor stripes nor fur. They wore a bright red unisex blouse and skirt, the clothes glowing slightly, as did the person's matching red hair.

"Hello," the person said. "My name is Zinhaz. Please remember me."

Crista reached out to touch Zinhaz but the image vanished. *How long ago was that recorded?* she asked the pyramid.

10,924 years ago, the Obsidian Rise said in a voice that eerily sounded like Red Day's.

Crista wondered how many messages the Obsidian Rise stored. It could be so easy to become lost in histories like this. To watch image after image of people from long ago.

Well? Red Day asked. *Are you going to look for a message from Desiada or not?*

Shaking herself out of her daze, Crista asked what she needed to do.

Simply ask the Obsidian Rise if you have any messages.

Two messages, the pyramid said. *One from a former monk named Desiada. Another from a person who asked not to be named.*

Crista grinned in excitement. *Show me Desiada first,* she requested.

Desiada appeared before her, his massive figure towering over her, his blond fur rustling gently to the sea breeze.

He smiled. "Crista, I said I needed time to think, and I'm still needing time. I've been angry at what Down Hope did to me and you. But now that I've lived away from Down Hope for a time, I'm also seeing things a little differently. And I miss you."

Desiada paused and nodded to an unseen person beside him. "Lanea says hello and hopes you learned the truth of what you are. She also apologizes for how she treated you. We've heard that several monks from Down Hope are ten leagues south of the city on a scientific expedition. We plan to visit those monks. We'll be back within three weeks of this message. I look forward to seeing you again."

Desiada waved goodbye and vanished.

Crista accessed the message's timestamp—Desiada recorded it two weeks ago. That meant Desiada and Lanea should be back in the city soon.

Great, Red Day muttered. *Too bad you can't remove me from your body so I don't have to endure another game of hide the kiss.*

Determined not to let Red Day make her angry, Crista asked the pyramid for her second message, wondering if it was a surprise from Desiada.

Instead, Crista found herself running through a forest. The late afternoon sun flickered between tree branches. The scent of bloodlust and fear wafted around her.

She broke through the trees beside a field of soybeans and ran toward a familiar barn that was surrounded by scores of wooden houses. Crista recognized this place. Her home village. Day's End.

A strong hand grabbed her shoulder and stopped her. "Hold on," a deep voice whispered.

Crista looked back. The white-haired mane and face of Master Farnham glared at her. What looked like the rest of the woman's hunt clan surrounded the clan leader, all of them armed with rifles and pistols and swords and bows.

What the hell? Crista demanded. The scene around her froze.

I've paused the playback, Red Day said. *You're experiencing an incredibly detailed memory that was uploaded to the pyramid.*

Crista stared at Master Farnham's frozen face. The memory made it feel like she was living the moment. *That's the Farnham clan. Are they attacking my village? Whose memories are these?*

Even as Crista asked the last question, the answer fell through her mind. Barely controlled emotions ran in tandem to these memories—rage and anger and animal needs and lust. Red Day enlarged the image of Master Farnham's face, focusing on the woman's eyes, growing her right pupil until it dwarfed Crista.

There, reflected in the massive eye, staring back at its own memory self, lay Beu's face.

Crista, Red Day said, *I recommend disengaging from this stored memory. There are games being played here that I don't understand.*

The frozen memory before Crista shifted back to normal size. Standing beside Master Farnham was her daughter, the woman Beu supposedly loved. Even with the memory frozen, Crista scented the woman's nervous fear and bloodlust and rage. The same scent rose from the other hunt clan members. They were scared but also prepared to kill.

Vaca had said her father and village were in danger. Did the Farnham clan attack because Crista's predecessor had killed Master Farnham's son?

I need to see the memory, Crista said. *Is it safe to access?*

The Obsidian Rise wouldn't share a memory or message embedded with viruses or other harmful codes.

Then play it.

Red Day complied without comment.

Master Farnham glanced nervously toward the barn, which stood a stone's throw from where they stood. "You sure about this, Beu?" she asked. "You come back here, that plague bird said you'd die."

"I'm right," Crista felt her mouth—or the memory of Beu's mouth—say. "You've all felt it."

The hunt clan members nodded. Crista realized that while the fear and rage rising from Beu and everyone around him were their own, the bloodlust she'd scented wasn't coming from them. Instead it rose from the ground under their feet, from the sky above their heads, from the breeze rustling around their bodies.

"Whatever's causing this may leave us be," Master Farnham said.

"My mother lives here," Beu replied. "And it may not leave us alone. Besides, you want to tell Crista you let her village die without lifting a hand to help?"

Master Farnham wiped the back of her sword down her massive mane to clean the blade. She glanced toward the barn, only to laugh and lower the sword as

Crista's father stepped from inside, followed by Blue's glowing cloud of colors and distortions. Crista's father held a sword in one hand and his ceramic pistol in the other.

"When Blue told me it'd detected your clan's approach," Crista's father said, "I didn't believe it. But here you are."

"We didn't come to fight," Master Farnham said. "We've come to help."

Crista's father snorted, his wolf blood up, the bristles of his beard erect as he pointed his sword at Beu. "You've defied a plague bird's orders. I could kill you, right now, and no one'd say a word on me."

Beu fought the urge to piss himself. "Please, Mr. Lander, I need to tell you …"

Master Farnham cut him off. "Lander, you want us to leave, we'll leave. But your village is in danger and you need us."

Crista's father glanced at Blue. After an unheard exchange her father nodded. "Tell me," he said.

"There are strangers, camping out in a nearby hollow," Beu said. "They've been watching your village. They're planning to attack. Soon."

"How many?" Crista's father asked.

"Four."

Crista's father smiled grimly. "I appreciate the warning. We'll double the guard. Although it'd be suicide for four people to attack a village as big as ours …"

"No," Beu shouted. "You don't understand. These aren't humans. They're stronger than Blue. Stronger than plague birds."

Then how did you learn their secrets? Blue asked. *I detected your clan's approach from a half-league away. Surely someone more powerful than me would know if you approached close enough to overhear their plans.*

Rage ran through Beu. Crista felt his desire to attack Blue for doubting him, to kill Crista's father for not believing him. Beu took a deep breath and forced himself to calm down.

"I … can't," he stammered. "I can't explain it. Not yet. You wouldn't believe me. But don't you feel the bloodlust around us? In the ground. In the air. The bloodlust is coming from these strangers."

Crista's father breathed deep, raising his head to scent the air. "I smell it," he said. "Funny. I didn't before."

I detect a wave function interfering with human emotional responses, Blue said. *Why didn't I detect this before?*

"They were blocking it from you," Beu said. "From the entire village. Even from Blue."

Troubled, Crista's father glanced again at Blue. "That still doesn't explain how you know all this," he said. "Describe these strangers."

"They wear veils that filter them from the senses and minds of humans and AI. I can show one to you. He's hiding in the village right now."

Wait, Crista shouted, pausing the memory. *He's describing the Veil.*

He is, Red Day agreed.

When did this happen?

From the indicators in this memory—the temperature, the sun in the sky, the patterns of vegetation—these events took place five months into your career as a plague bird.

What's going on?

... We should finish watching and find out.

Crista willed the memory to resume.

"Where is this person hiding?" Crista's father asked.

Beu pointed past the barn, toward the village commons. "Over there. I'll show you."

I sense nothing, Blue said softly. Crista's father placed his pistol in its holster and pointed the tip of his sword at Beu as he addressed Master Farnham.

"Farnham, you know I have nothing but respect for you. But if Beu is playing games, I'll gut him."

Beu's girlfriend growled, but Master Farnham held her back as the clan leader chuckled. "Tell you what, Lander," she said. "If Beu's playing us, I'll help you."

"Follow me," Beu whispered, unable to force his voice to go any louder.

Crista's father and Blue and Master Farnham and the rest of the clan followed Beu into the middle of the village. Crista's father whispered to Blue, "Tell all the villagers to arm themselves and be prepared." Beu gulped, not knowing if Crista's father believed what he was saying and was readying for battle, or if the village was preparing to kill him.

"Beu?" a loud voice yelled. "Beu!" A thin woman ran up and hugged Beu tight. His mother, Ms. Pauler.

"I won't let you kill him," Ms. Pauler yelled at Crista's father. Crista had never feared Ms. Pauler—as a kid she'd worried that Ms. Pauler might get her in trouble, but Crista had never physically feared the woman. Yet, as Ms. Pauler faced Crista's father, she saw the woman could be physically dangerous when pushed. Her cat hair stood on end and her eyes glowed with the same yellow intensity Crista had seen in Beu on the night he'd attacked her.

"It's okay, Mom. They won't kill me."

Ms. Pauler stepped back and looked at her son. "Beu, what's going on?"

As more villagers surrounded Beu and the Farnham clan, Crista recognized her neighbors and friends and relatives. All of them were armed. All of them glared angrily at Beu, no doubt remembering Crista's order to never return to the village.

"Give the boy a chance," Crista's father yelled. "He wants to show us something."

Beu pushed through the crowd and walked to the flagpole, where the red plague bird flag flew when one was near the village. No flag flew there today but Beu still looked up at the pole.

"Show them," he shouted so everyone could hear.

A human appeared on the top of the pole, hanging by one arm while looking down at the villagers and hunt clan. The human appeared male with a veil covering his face, the translucent covering squirming and moving and flittering in and out of reality.

The stranger dropped to the ground and glared at the villagers and hunt arrayed before him. Beu's body shivered in fear as the scent of unease rose from those around him.

"Who are you?" Crista's father yelled, stepping forward with both sword and pistol at the ready. The veiled man didn't move or respond.

"He's calling the other three," Beu said to Crista's father and Master Farnham.

"How do you know?" Master Farnham said. "How did you reveal this?"

"I ... I met a wandering man who has been tracking these strangers. They're called the Veil. This man told me they occasionally attack and wipe out villages. He didn't want this to happen again, so he warned me. He's using his power to allow us to see these people."

"Why would a stranger help you?" Master Farnham asked suspiciously. "And how does he have the power to do all this?"

"He knows Crista. She asked him to check on the village while she's gone."

At the mention of Crista's name, the villagers and hunt members growled slightly, afraid of a plague bird even if she'd once been one of their own.

What's the name of this man? Blue hissed.

Before Beu could respond one of the Farnham clan—a young woman scenting of bear heritage—jumped towards the veiled stranger and screamed. Crista had seen such bluffs before from the hunt, a way to show you weren't afraid, to look fear in the face and refuse to show throat. The clan member was a half dozen yards from the stranger, meaning despite the bluff she planned to avoid attacking the man.

Despite the hunter not posing a true threat, the veiled man raised his left hand and aimed it at the woman. A rippling line, like the air had been split between reality and unreality, jumped from his palm to the clan member, whose body ripped in half in a burst of blood.

Master Farnham howled in fury, and Crista's father aimed his pistol at the veiled stranger and began firing. The hypersonic projectiles splattered blue impacts across the stranger's body but only slightly injured him. Other villagers and clan members opened fire as the stranger pointed at a group of people and a new line of unreality ripped into the crowd. Blue shot a bolt of lightning at the stranger but the energy rippled around the man without touching his body.

"Take him like a pack," Master Farnham yelled.

The Farnham clan and many of the villagers screamed as they charged the stranger, bodies ripping apart while more bodies swarmed over the man, swords stabbing as they dogpiled him. Blue also swarmed its energy around the man, both attacking and restricting him from focusing his full power on the villagers and hunt.

After a few moments Farnham and Crista's father yanked people off the man.

Underneath they found him dead, his body hacked apart. The veil that had flickered and pulsed now lay still and flimsy on the man's face, looking like a spider web threatening to crumble at the slightest touch. Crista's father leaned over and used his sword to flip aside the veil. The man's dead face stared back at them —or would have, if the face still had eyes. The sockets were scab-ridden, the nose melted away, lips stripped from skin, teeth partly dissolved.

"Those wounds are old," Master Farnham said. "How did he see or scent?"

Perhaps the covering gave him that ability, Blue suggested.

Crista didn't hear any more because Beu screamed and ran across the bloody grass to where one of the injured villagers lay. Ms. Pauler. Beu cradled her body.

"I'll be okay, hon," she said. Her left leg was bent strangely—broken—but otherwise she was not injured. Beu leaned over and tried to push the meat and bones of her leg back together as tears ran into his mouth.

"Let me help," Crista's father said, sitting down next to Ms. Pauler's leg. He bent over and sniffed. "It's a bad break, but Blue can heal her. Can you wait for Blue to heal those with worse wounds?"

Ms. Pauler nodded as Beu looked around. Four of the hunt clan lay dead, along with two villagers. Another dozen mixed between hunt and village were injured, with one woman—Tochi, one of the elders who also ran the village bakery—hemorrhaging blood while two hunt clan members held her down and Blue applied energy to cauterize the wound.

"It could have been worse," Beu said, fighting back another burst of tears. "Far worse. Thank you."

Who exactly are you thanking? Blue asked, able to focus both on healing the elder and listening to Beu.

Crista didn't know either, but a response bubbled through Beu's mind. She felt the touch of a powerful mind, a very familiar touch. She knew the distorted voice intimately.

Ashdyd.

Ashdyd didn't speak words in Beu's mind, but instead gave him knowledge. And the knowledge was RUN!

"We ... we have to flee," Beu gasped. "If we stay here we'll die. The other three are coming. They're the Veil, and they're coming to kill us."

Crista's father and Master Farnham looked around at the dead and wounded, calculating how many more would die when the three new strangers attacked.

"It'll hurt," Master Farnham said, "but we should defend here. Better all of us fighting as one than picked off individually."

"Agreed," Crista's father said.

"No!" Beu screamed. "You don't understand. The man ... the one who warned me ... he weakened the stranger we killed. Used his powers to interfere with the veiled man's powers. That's the only reason we were able to kill him. But the other Veil have learned of what he did and are attacking him."

As if cued by Beu's words, an explosion of rainbowed light mushroomed in the sky over a hill several leagues away. The explosion didn't stir the wind or air, instead flicking between reality and nonreality like the stranger's veil. Unreality arched through the clouds as the mushroom explosion boiled and quivered before vanishing back to nothing.

The connection to Ashdyd, which Crista had felt in Beu's mind, vanished.

"The man's dead," Beu whispered. "Or hurt. Or hiding. They'll come for us next."

This doesn't make sense, Crista asked. *Why is Ashdyd helping them against the Veil?*

I don't know, Red Day replied. *All we can do is keep watching.*

Crista ordered the memory to resume.

How much did this man repress the attacker's powers? Blue asked. When Beu didn't answer, the AI yelled the question again, shocking because Blue never raised its voice.

"I'm not sure. He said it took most of his energy to block that one attacker's power."

And what was the name of this man supposedly tasked by Crista to help us?

"Ashdyd."

Blue's cloudlike body of sparkles and distortions expanded and quivered as Crista felt fear flood Beu's mind. Everyone—both villager and hunt—felt the emotion. She'd never known Blue to broadcast an emotion like this.

You must flee, Blue said. *All of you. Run and never come back. I'll try to slow the attackers.*

"Wait a moment," Crista's father said. "This is our home. We'll fight. There are hundreds of us ..."

I know of this Ashdyd, Blue said softly, the AI's words echoing clearly in each person's mind. *Before Crista became a plague bird, Derena asked me questions about Ashdyd. She wanted to know if I'd ever heard the name. She implied Ashdyd was strong, far stronger than any plague bird or regular AI. If Ashdyd can't stop this Veil ...*

"How long until they get here?" Crista's father asked.

Minutes. Maybe less.

"Take nothing," Crista's father yelled to the villagers and hunt around him. "Grab your families and go. Now!"

A map of the world appeared in everyone's mind, a line leading west from the village toward a vast ocean. *Head west. I've implanted a knowledge kernel in everyone's brain. When you're safe it will show you the route to a distant sanctuary. The directions are encoded and hidden and the kernel will destroy itself if you're killed. The strangers shouldn't be able to find the information in your minds ... if the worst happens.*

"You heard the AI," Master Farnham yelled at her hunt clan. "Head west. Stay in small packs. Run like hell."

Villagers and hunt bolted. Families grabbed kids from hiding places, even grabbing kids who weren't their own. People fled as gened impulses to protect the young and their pack mixed with their fear of approaching death.

Beu bent under his mother's shoulder, helping her stand, but with her broken leg she couldn't run. Crista's father grabbed Ms. Pauler's other shoulder and they carried her toward the treeline.

"Come on, Blue," Crista's father yelled, glancing back at the AI as it floated in the middle of the village. The AI expanded its body until it filled the entire village green, until it touched the ancient school house and nearby homes, touched the stones of the village shine and the split shingle roof of the massive barn. Crista had always thought such expansions by the AI were how it sighed. But now it appeared Blue touched everything it'd protected for so many centuries to reassure itself.

Goodbye friends, the AI said. *Remember me kindly. If, one day, any of you see Crista, tell her I regret not saving her from such a painful life.*

The AI continued expanding until it covered the entire village. Three invisible figures flared visible on the outskirts of the village when they touched Blue's expanded body.

Blue shrank its body and unleashed a blast of energy at the attackers, destroying two nearby houses, but also knocking two of the veiled people a dozen yards backwards. Bolts of unreality split the air and hit Blue but the AI absorbed the bolts.

Beu and Crista's father ran as fast as they could, carrying Ms. Pauler between them. Beu could no longer see either Blue or the attackers but still tasted their battle. The world screamed and fell through perfect silence, followed by thunder and lights and more unnatural silence.

Animal panic gripped Beu—the panic of unquestioned instinct, the need to flee and never look back. He held his mother tight, refusing to let go. Refusing to abandon her.

Beu and Crista's father neared the barn, a dozen villagers and hunt ahead of them. A screech of sound shot by, knocking Beu and Crista's father and Ms. Pauler to the ground. When they looked up the barn and everyone near it was gone, dust raining across the emptiness.

"Go!" Ms. Pauler yelled. "Don't stare like fools. Leave me! Run!"

Beu again picked up his mother. He looked back at Blue. The AI's body had changed color and now glowed red as it absorbed continual hits from the attackers. Each bolt that hit Blue caused the AI to boil into deeper and deeper shades of red.

"Move," Crista's father ordered.

They ran again, clearing the treeline, stumbling through the forest as best they could, falling and clawing back up. Ms. Pauler cried out each time her broken leg hit the ground or a tree. Beu saw Master Farnham running beside her daughter, who held a toddler from the village, while Master Farnham carried a bleeding man slung over her broad shoulders. More villagers and hunt raced by, calling out to

Beu and Crista's father to hurry but knowing that to slow down to help meant death for them all.

Beu glanced back and saw Blue's body rise like the morning sun over the forest, as red as red could be.

As red as a plague bird.

Blue exploded. A tornado wind slammed the forest, snapping limbs and tree tops and throwing Beu and Ms. Pauler and Crista's father to the ground. A line of unreality burst beneath them, exploding the dirt and leaves and throwing them into the air.

There the memories jumbled. Crista saw Ms. Pauler staring at the sky, her neck broken, half her body ripped away. Through Beu's eyes Crista saw him shaking his mother. Saw him grab Crista's father—unconscious, bones broken, blood pouring —and drag him away. Saw day become night become bright and unreal. Saw trees implode and deer bolt by with half their bodies dissolving as another massive explosion shook the ground. Saw bolts of unreality rip into people and animals and the world.

Crista couldn't say how long it took for Beu's panic to subside and for his memories to stabilize. But when they did he sat beside her unconscious father on a river bank that Crista knew was several hours hike from the village.

Crista's father gasped, rolled over and vomited. He looked around and collapsed back onto his back. His head bled, red streaks covered his face. His right arm was broken and his broad chest looked like it'd been mauled by a lion. After a few minutes he sat up and wiped the blood from his eyes with his beard.

"Where's your mom?" he asked Beu.

"Dead. Blast that knocked you out ripped her apart."

Crista's father tried to reach out to Beu, but he was groggy and nearly fell over. "I'm sorry."

Beu crouched down and crawled on all fours to the river's edge where he stuck his lips to the water and drank. He scooped up a handful of water and gave it to Crista's father to drink.

"How many made it?" Crista's father asked.

"Blue's dead. I also saw a few dozen others killed after you were knocked out. Haven't scented or seen the attackers for a while."

"We won't see them. Not if they don't want us to. We need to keep moving."

Crista's father tried to stand up but couldn't. Beu helped him and they started walking down the riverbank.

"I lost control again," Beu whispered. "After my mom died. My animal side took control."

"Anyone would lose control during all that. But you didn't leave me behind, so you must have kept some of you in that thing you call a head."

Beu tried to smile at the joke but couldn't. Crista felt shame burning through him, along with anger and fear.

"We'll head west," Crista's father said, "until Blue's hidden map clicks into our minds. Then we'll see who else survived."

There the memory ended. The smooth surface of the Obsidian Rise clicked under Crista's hand as the connection severed. She stepped back and sat down hard onto the street, her body almost passing out, yet her mind awake.

Only a few moments had passed during the memory download. In the nearby market, vendors sold food to hungry kids and hawked baubles to teenagers shopping for first-time crushes. Crista saw Amaj hand a scoop of ice cream to a tall man with purple feathers for hair.

Nothing had changed, yet everything had. Vaca had been right—her village had been in danger. Her father was injured, maybe dead.

And Beu was here. In Seed.

Crista screamed—a scream that turned to a guttural howl. Red Day did its best to edit the howl from the minds of everyone in Seed, but people still stopped and shivered.

Never mind that they didn't know who had howled. That didn't matter. They'd felt a plague bird's touch and were afraid.

PLAGUE BIRDS

Crista wandered through Seed for the rest of the day. At first Red Day edited her from everyone's minds. But Crista was tired—tired of manipulating and playing with people's minds—so she ordered the AI to let people see her.

People gasped and screamed. People stared at her and avoided her returning gaze. Little kids whose animal sides couldn't be contained bolted like white-tailed deer.

Crista didn't care. She only knew she'd made a mistake becoming a plague bird. If she hadn't accepted Red Day from Derena's dying body, the Veil would have had no reason to attack her village.

It wasn't fair. She'd become a plague bird to save her father and friends when Red Day boiled out of Derena. But even that simple saving grace—the knowledge that while her life was hell, at least those she cared for were safe—was gone.

Crista walked absently through the city, finding herself near Amaj's ice cream stand in the central market. The automaton looked puzzled by a plague bird walking around letting everyone see her.

A group of kids hung near Amaj, debating whether or not to beg the automaton for ice cream. The kids' clothes were ragged and, from the disgusted and wary looks nearby people gave them, likely orphans. A wolf-hybrid girl—from her demeanor the little pack's alpha—sniffed the breeze, testing Crista's scent. Even though the girl reeked with fear, she stepped away from her friends and blocked Crista's path.

"You a plague bird?" the wolf girl asked.

"Yes." Crista wanted to laugh. The girl couldn't be older than ten yet was trying to make herself look big by standing up to Crista.

"My daddy was killed by a plague bird," the girl said loud enough for her friends to hear. Crista smiled at the girl, a friendly gesture that must have appeared frightening because the girl's hands shook, causing her to hide them under her worn leather shirt.

"And what did your father do to cause a plague bird to kill him?" Crista asked.

"Something bad," the girl said, raising a nervous laugh from her friends.

Crista looked the girl over. She was far more wolf than Crista. A light gray fur covered her brown skin and her eyes locked on Crista with a hard, yellow stare. The girl was obviously brave and would grow into a strong woman.

Crista squatted on one knee before the girl and held out her hand. "If you shake my hand," she whispered, "your friends and all the people in the market will think you're the bravest girl ever. They'll tell everyone. You'll be known as the girl who touched a plague bird."

The girl pulled one shaking hand from under her shirt and reached out to Crista. The girl was so frightened she couldn't grab Crista's hand, so Crista did it for her. "Now walk away slowly," Crista whispered after releasing the handshake. "Show everyone how brave you are."

Mesmerized by Crista's words, the wolf girl did exactly as told. When she reached her friends they howled and screeched, hugging her in excitement at her grand deed.

As Crista walked on the people around her stared in shock at the encounter. Only Amaj smiled back, which for some reason disturbed Crista more than being gawked at by everyone in Seed.

DIVER FOUND CRISTA LATER THAT AFTERNOON, BUT CRISTA SAID SHE NEEDED TO BE alone. Diver walked away, polite enough to not ask why Crista was upset.

That night Crista slept beside the docks on a stretch of sand between two long stone piers reaching a half league into the Flickering Sea. In the morning she still lay on the sand, looking at the rising sun and the world around her.

The sand had recently washed in, likely from winter storms. Graffiti was carved into the stone docks around Crista, something she hadn't seen in the rest of the city because words carved in the living stone quickly healed over. This graffiti spoke of dates and names from thousands of years ago. Of ships that had long since sunk and voyages no one remembered.

The city maintains this graffiti, Red Day said, waking from its solitude. *Seed misses the ships that once docked here so it keeps these carved names and deeds like you and your father kept your mother's embroidery after she passed.*

What did you find out? Crista asked, not wanting to fall into memories. *Did you finish analyzing Beu's memory? Or that Veil medallion?*

We are being played, Crista.

No shit! An artificial intelligence bigger than a thousand human brains with ego to match and you just realized that?

Instead of being angry, Red Day agreed with her. *I'm so used to manipulating others I missed the clues indicating what was being done to us.*

Who's doing it?

I don't know. One level of manipulation started when Derena and I were attacked by the Veil. In hindsight it wasn't chance that brought us to your village. And subsequent events also indicate something is being hidden from me. My memories have been altered. No one should be able to do that.

Ashdyd could.

Only when my power is overwhelmed, such as in the barrier forest. The people doing this to me are silent and hidden.

Diver could do that if she wanted, Crista said.

I don't think she is. In fact, Diver might be a wild card in all this.

Is it Ashdyd and the Veil? Hell, are they even working together or did Ashdyd truly turn on the Veil when he helped Beu and my village?

I ... don't know. Beu's memories were too detailed and linear for standard human memory. And parts of his memory were obviously manipulated. For example, even though we saw the map Blue projected into everyone's minds, it was altered so I couldn't determine where people from your village were going.

Meaning?

Meaning I believe Ashdyd is still with Beu. Do you remember how the blast that killed Beu's mother and injured your father didn't leave a scratch on Beu? I suspect Ashdyd protected him.

But Beu's memories showed Ashdyd dying, or at least being hurt, when the Veil attacked.

I think not. There are manipulations within manipulations going on here.

Crista stood up and looked into the city. Beu was here somewhere, maybe even with Ashdyd. Had they killed Kenji? Even though she didn't like Jai-Saan and Tendi, she needed to share this information.

First, clean yourself up, Red Day said. Crista looked down at herself—she was coated in sand and bits of seaweed. She stripped off her clothes and cannonballed into the ocean to bathe.

Second? she asked as she swam. *Usually a "second" follows declarations of "first."*

Second, we talk to Jai-Saan and Tendi and let them understand the seriousness of what is going on here. They're waiting for us in the Obsidian Rise.

Agreed. And thanks.

For what?

For finally believing me about us being manipulated.

As Crista said that she felt a burst of sadness from Red Day. But the AI closed off its emotions before she could dig deeper into what troubled it.

After bathing and dressing Crista walked through the market to the Obsidian Rise. The market was busy, with people trading for food and other items. While people still recoiled from her passing they didn't panic like yesterday. Word had spread about the strange plague bird who liked being seen.

This time Crista approached one of the pyramid's angled sides instead of the straight wall where she'd seen Desiada's message and Beu's memories. A steep stairway rose before her. Smoking images of ghostly people and animals floated directly beneath the steps' black surface, dancing in the obsidian so Crista had no choice but to step on them as she climbed. The images again reminded Crista of the flickering people she'd seen in the empty parts of Seed.

Naturally, Red Day said. *The Obsidian Rise is alive.*

Similar to how Down Hope monastery is also alive?

Somewhat. The entire city of Seed is alive but this building—well, imagine that the city is Seed's body and Obsidian Rise her mind. By the way, most people find what happens inside the Obsidian Rise to be very disconcerting. Just a heads up.

Crista soon learned what Red Day meant. The doors at the top opened at her touch. Before her stood millions of people milling around in silence, stepping beside each other in what looked like a random dance that would never end.

None of the people looked at Crista as she stepped through the doorway into the Rise. The people filled every free space before her, sliding around each other in silence, blocking the way for Crista to go further into the pyramid. The floor below them reflected like a mirror as did the ceiling, creating reflections of even more people. An infinity of people.

In addition, these were not people like Crista had seen all her life. No animal genes flowed through these humans. No fur and fang, no stripes or yellow eyes. These were people from before the collapse, elegant people shaped with fragile bodies like those seen in the statues of the Child, or like Diver, or in Down Hope's painting of the long-dead smiling woman. The wolf in Crista growled slightly, disturbed by being around so many people who looked like prey.

The people didn't speak. They didn't breathe. Crista didn't hear their footfalls. They were ghosts projected by Seed. More solid looking than the flicker images she'd seen elsewhere, but still ghosts.

At Crista's touch the hologram people shifted, the rambling crowds stepping aside to create a hallway bounded by their shapes. The hallway stretched toward the center of the pyramid.

Okay, that's creepy, she thought.

You should have been here the last time Derena and I visited. Seed was in a foul mood—Jai-Saan and Tendi had recently killed several dozen of Seed's people after a nasty riot so the Obsidian Rise was filled with images of people who'd died violent deaths. People silently screaming, holding severed limbs and disemboweled guts, that kind of thing. Even I was disturbed and that's saying something.

Crista's stomach turned slightly. At least these people looked happy.

Crista walked through the hall, trying not to look at the human walls but unable to look away. The people smiled and waved but their eyes never quite focused on her. As if she didn't exist but was a ghost, like them.

The hallway led to the center of the pyramid, where Jai-Saan and Tendi sat at a large wooden banquet table filled with fruits and meats and dishes Crista didn't recognize. The wolf in Crista yipped in excitement as she realized how long it'd been since she'd eaten a meal. She'd been living off Red Day's powers for weeks.

"Ah, Cristina de Ane of the village of Day's End," Jai-Saan announced like he was addressing royalty. "Come and join us. There are delights here to tickle even the palate of a simple village wolf."

The wolf in Crista growled at the sarcasm but she maintained control and sat beside Tendi in an ornate, carved chair with red velvet cushions. Crista noticed the silently moving shapes of the people surrounding the table created the illusion of a spacious dining room. The holograms wore fancy gowns and suits in vivid reds and burgundies and maroons.

"All of these people are real," Jai-Saan said. "Or were real. The Obsidian Rise remembers each and every person who ever lived in the city of Seed."

"And now she uses them for decorating," Crista said. "How nice."

Jai-Saan frowned as Tendi laughed.

"How do you like Seed?" Tendi asked.

"I've learned a lot." Crista felt the Veil medallion in her pocket, but waited to mention it. "Any news on who killed Kenji?"

Neither Jai-Saan nor Tendi responded, instead ignoring Crista as they ate their food. *They don't want to immediately discuss such weighty matters,* Red Day said. *In fancy settings such as these, it's small talk first before discussing the work of plague birds.*

Crista snorted and filled her plate with sweet meats and pickled eggs and strange fruits and nuts she'd never before eaten. Jai-Saan pointed out various people moving along the room's false walls, indicating styles of clothing that had been popular millennia before. Tendi remarked upon each piece of food Crista ate, describing both its culinary history and desired tastes and attributes.

When they finished eating, Jai-Saan and Tendi clapped their hands. The table instantly cleared of everything but three wine glasses filled with a paste-white drink.

"Am I supposed to be impressed?" Crista asked. "I've been to Down Hope. I know how much power places like the monastery or Seed have at their disposal."

"I must admit being intrigued," Tendi said. "I've long desired to visit Down Hope."

"I suggest you earn a special invite like Crista," Jai-Saan snapped. "But before we turn to serious matters, a toast."

Jai-Saan handed Crista and Tendi their glasses. The drink looked like spoiled milk mixed with glue and chilled to a near freezing slush. The scent of crushed snail shells flooded Crista's nose as she held it to her lips.

Be aware this is Plague's Truth, Red Day said. *It's a recreation of the life-essence of the first truly powerful artificial intelligence created by humanity. All AIs are descended from it and its programming rests at the core of our being. The drink will kill any regular human. With plague birds, it reveals whether or not we tell the truth.*

And if we don't tell the truth? Crista asked.

The Plague's Truth fatally devours both your human body and my AI extension.

Jai-Saan grinned at Crista. "Experiencing another's mind only tells us one aspect of the truth," he said. "Especially when an ever-manipulative blood AI's involved. If you don't drink the Plague's Truth, Tendi and I will kill you where you sit. If you do drink it and lie, you'll also die. So many delightful options."

Tendi rolled her eyes at Jai-Saan's melodrama. "Oh just drink the damn thing, Jai-Saan," she said, knocking back her own glass and swallowing everything in one gulp. Jai-Saan did the same.

With a shiver, Crista drank her glass of Plague's Truth. The drink tasted like chalk. Like swallowing a billion computations and equations written on a slab of broken slate, the shattered pieces cutting and rearranging her throat and stomach and mind.

Despite the wolf in her wanting to vomit, she emptied the drink in one go and tossed it behind her chair, the glass shattering on the Obsidian Rise's mirror floor.

"Now we'll talk," Tendi said. "You asked about who killed Kenji. We've learned nothing more. Have you?"

Tell them the truth, Red Day said. *But avoid discussing Diver or Desiada and Lanea.*

I get why I don't mention Diver, but Desiada and Lanea?

Because you told Desiada and Lanea about our secret mission to locate Ashdyd and the Veil. That's enough for Jai-Saan and Tendi to condemn us to death.

Crista did as the AI suggested. She told Jai-Saan and Tendi how Kenji killed her mother and how Derena and Red Day tricked her into becoming a plague bird even as it appeared Kenji and the Veil knew she'd be selected as one before she was born. She also revealed what she knew about the Veil, including how their leader, Ashdyd, had destroyed Bogda's village centuries ago but returned a few years ago to apologize to the damaged AI. She told them how she suspected Kenji of working with the Veil, even if Jai-Saan and Tendi had ordered him to follow Red Day. Crista told how Ashdyd accessed her mind in the barrier forest and how the member of the Veil she'd killed before arriving in Seed said Crista's village was in danger. She finished by describing the memories she received from Beu and how he both confirmed the danger to her village and that he was in contact with Ashdyd.

As she said all this, Crista felt the Plague's Gold within her analyzing each word, accessing its truthfulness. The chalky sensation of Crista's life being tallied—of all her deeds and lies marked off one by one—rose like bile in her throat with each word she spoke. In the end the Plague's Truth determined she was being honest enough.

When Crista finished, Jai-Saan and Tendi stared in shock, not wanting to believe all she'd shared.

"I almost wish you'd just dropped dead," Jai-Saan said. "Better to be lying than bring this craziness upon us."

Tendi nodded, agreeing with her fellow plague bird. "Is there anything you're leaving out of all this?" she asked.

Red Day quivered in Crista's mind. *Careful,* the AI said. *She's trying to trick you into revealing more.*

Crista felt the Plague's Gold scratch chalk down her throat in warning. "Yes," she said, "there's plenty I left out. But I can't mention it because it concerns Down Hope monastery. As you know, we only deal with the monastery at their request. I swore to the abbot not to mention what happened there to anyone. Not even to fellow plague birds."

And, Crista said to the Plague's Truth in case that would help, *since we met Diver and Desiada and Lanea at Down Hope, that means I technically shouldn't mention them.*

Red Day smiled in her mind, pleased at Crista's evasion. The Plague's Truth burned chalk in Crista's throat, obviously irritated at this twisting of truth through omission but still determining that Crista's logic was sound and she hadn't told a lie.

Tendi pursed her mouth. "That's ... too bad. I wanted to hear about Down Hope. Do you have any questions for us?"

"Yes. Did you know in advance that I'd be picked as a plague bird?"

"No," Jai-Saan said. "We never knew a single thing about you until you graced us with your untimely arrival."

"What about the Veil? What do you know about them? Are you working with them? Was Kenji?"

"No, we're not working with them," Tendi said. "Neither was Kenji, to our knowledge, although your evidence makes me now doubt that. All Jai-Saan and I know is the Veil have killed a handful of plague birds in recent years. You're the first plague bird to defeat one in battle."

Jai-Saan nodded agreement despite his obvious distaste at admitting Crista had done something he and the others hadn't.

"I'd be happy to teach you how Red Day and I did it, Jai-Saan," Crista said. "Always eager to school less fortunate plague birds."

"Look here, runt. You really want to taunt me? I'll take your precious Red Day and ..."

"Oh stop it you two," Tendi said. "We've more important things to discuss."

"Fine," Jai-Saan said. "I have a question for Crista. How did you manipulate my mind so you looked like Kenji? Red Day shouldn't have the power to do that."

"Can't tell. Related to Down Hope. Secrets. Things you don't get to know."

Jai-Saan looked like he was about to explode—quite literally, as the blood AI inside his body screamed in anger. His skin paled and split in places as Saan bubbled out to attack. Red Day's power rose in response, ready to defend.

Tendi slammed her fist into the table, shattering the wood and collapsing the table in half. "We have a serious threat to deal with," she shouted. "Can you two stop acting like newly-fawned fools?"

Jai took a deep breath and pulled Saan back into his body. Red Day powered down as Crista apologized to Tendi, not wanting to be on her bad side.

"Last question," Jai-Saan said. "Are you working with the Veil? Or Ashdyd?"

"No," Crista stated. "You going to hold that against me too?"

Tendi reached out her mind and accessed Obsidian Rise, which mended the table and created three new glasses of a golden drink.

"Here," Tendi said, handing a glass to Crista. "This will remove the Plague's Truth from your mind and body."

"What is this?"

"It's called Plague's Gold."

Red Day snickered. *Did I ever tell you plague birds are full of themselves?* the AI said. *Only we could think of idiotic names like Plague's Truth or Plague's Gold. Nothing but endlessly silly ways to remind ourselves of our extremely limited importance.*

What does the drink do?

It removes the AI's essence put in by the other drink. And you'll like the next part—Plague's Gold makes you human for up to 12 hours. It isolates me and my powers in a programmed cocoon within your body. You'll be a regular human until it wears off.

Crista shivered in excitement. *You're okay with this?*

No, I'm not okay with this. But there's a long tradition of plague birds doing this when meeting in safe places like the Obsidian Rise. It's one of those inane bonding rituals you humans are so fond of.

But what if Jai and Tendi attack me?

They'll be as human as you. And you're hardly defenseless, wolf girl. If I'm needed before the 12 hours are up simply think the programmed safe memory and I'm immediately released and at full power.

Jai-Saan and Tendi held their own glasses of Plague's Gold, but hadn't yet drunk.

"I assume Red Day told you what this is," Tendi said. "Do you mind if I program the safe memory? I want it to be of a memory of Kenji's dead body. He, Jai-Saan, and I drank Plague's Gold once each century, to remind us of all we'd lost. And now we've lost Kenji."

Melodramatic, but an acceptable memory, Red Day said. *Simply remember Kenji's dead body and think "Plague Gold, end." I'll then be released from my cocoon.*

Crista nodded to Tendi, who told Obsidian Rise they'd agreed on a safe thought. "Program in Seed's memory of Kenji's actual dead body," she said. "That memory combined with the words 'Plague Gold, End,' will deactivate the drink."

The Obsidian Rise hummed slightly and the golden drinks in their hands glowed deeper. Jai-Saan and Tendi drank from their glasses, causing the red lines on their faces to fade and disappear. Crista no longer felt the buzzing of their AIs in her mind.

Call me if needed, Red Day said as Crista raised the glass to her lips and drank. The golden drink smelled like new-budded flowers after a spring rain. As the Plague's Gold rolled down her throat it washed away the chalk-like essence of the previous drink.

Crista took another sip of Plague's Gold as warmth and happiness caressed her body and sweet dreams filled her mind. A tingle ran her face, as if she'd washed her skin after being dirty for years. The red line marking her as a plague bird was gone. Red Day didn't hover in the back of her mind. All her memories and all her body were hers and hers alone.

"A good feeling, isn't it?" Tendi asked, looking far more human—and far frailer—than moments ago. Seeing Tendi without Yualsong below her surface made Crista realize how beautiful the woman was. Her fox heritage glistened on her dark skin, happy to reassert itself now that she was—at least temporarily—human.

"I'd forgotten how it felt," Crista said. "To be only me. To not feel the world through Red Day's senses and power." Crista sniffed the air, the wolf in her growing stronger again as the scents of Tendi and Jai-Saan and the Obsidian Rise ran through her.

"I personally dislike this," Jai muttered. "I don't know why I keep being convinced to engage in such torture."

"You need it," Tendi said. "Otherwise you'll forget who you used to be."

"You say that like it's a bad thing."

Crista stared at Jai and realized he not only looked smaller, he also hunched over defensively, nervous without the safety blanket of Saan wrapped around him. But despite being only himself, Jai still looked inhuman, like a puppet come to life. Crista wondered if he'd simply been a plague bird for too long to ever return to humanity.

But she didn't want to ruin things by saying that, especially when they were going out of their way to make her feel welcome. "Thank you for doing this," she said.

"You're welcome," Tendi said. "It's easy to forget how painful it is during our first few years as a plague bird. You've done remarkably well, all things considered."

"'Considered' being a reference to how weak Red Day is," Jai said, proving he was as much a jerk without his AI as with it. "And nasty. And foolish."

Tendi cut Jai a look and the man bowed his head and stared at the floor, pretending shame at his words.

"Why do you hate Red Day?" Crista asked.

"More accurate to ask why haven't we forgotten our hate of Red Day after 10,000 years?" Tendi said. "Your AI was one of those who fought against the three-fold balance after the collapse. Or I should say, Red Day was cleaved off another AI who fought against us and killed thousands of humans and AIs before it was defeated. As punishment that AI was split in two and Red Day's powers heavily restricted."

Shock ran over Crista's face, causing Jai to snicker. "Ask Red Day," he said. "I'm sure you'll receive a biased version, but even your AI can't misstate history if you ask directly."

Crista decided to do just that. She thought about calling forth Red Day immediately, using the safe memory, but decided against it.

"Do you think the Veil killed Kenji?" she asked.

"Evidence does suggest it," Tendi said. "But usually the Veil are far more gruesome when they kill. Kenji's body was relatively intact."

"Except for the gash across his stomach," Jai-Saan pointed out.

"Except for that."

"Then how about Ashdyd and Beu working together?" Crista asked.

"Definitely a disturbing idea," Jai said.

"So what do we do?"

"Starting tomorrow, we'll protect the Obsidian Rise," Tendi said. "The three of us. Together." She stopped, waiting for Jai to protest. When he didn't, she continued. "I suspect Ashdyd's focus is on accessing the Rise's power and systems. Otherwise, why would Beu be hanging around Seed? There's nothing else in the city worth the interest of someone as powerful as Ashdyd."

"Is Ashdyd an AI?" Crista asked.

"The records are incomplete," Jai said, "but Ashdyd appears to be an experimental AI who can't exist without fusing with another AI or a human. Sort of like a plague bird except the fusing isn't permanent and he must regularly seek out new hosts. To our knowledge no other AI like him exists."

"And Beu?" Crista asked.

"If he's innocent, he has nothing to worry about," Jai said.

Crista took another sip of her drink, not wanting to say that Beu was anything but innocent.

"Enough with official matters," Tendi declared. "We're human for a short time. Let's be human."

Tendi waved her hands and the tabletop shimmered as the Obsidian Rise created an amazing array of drinks. Beers and wines and ales and hard cider and so much more.

The three of them drank and talked, with Tendi asking about Crista's life before becoming a plague bird and Crista spinning stories of growing up in her village and of her father. She shared everything she could think of, including the game of hide the kiss Blue helped her engage in.

Crista fell silent as she remembered Blue sacrificing itself to save so many people. Even though she'd been furious at Blue for helping trick her into being a plague bird, because of the AI, her father and many others were still alive.

Crista looked at the wall of people surrounding them, who stood silently crying. Obviously the Obsidian Rise sympathized with all she'd been through.

"It's okay," Tendi said, handing Crista a large mug of steaming hard cider. "While we plague birds understand we can't go home, we don't expect our homes to be destroyed. This is an attack on all plague birds. I swear Jai-Saan and I will help you find those who did this and, together, we'll kill them."

Crista glanced at Jai, expecting him to laugh at her again, but he merely nodded in agreement to Tendi's words.

"There's a reason we become human now and then," Tendi said softly. "It's easy to forget who you are when you're a plague bird. To merge so much with your blood AI that it's impossible to tell where you end and the AI begins. Jai has nearly done that."

Jai hunched in his seat, wrapping himself around his mug of beer. Crista wondered if he was uncomfortable with Tendi's words but realized he was more likely uncomfortable with being totally human. He probably felt like half his body and mind were missing with Saan locked down.

"You need to understand who we are," Tendi continued. "We've both been plague birds for so long it's hard to remember who we were before. Jai-Saan has actually forgotten his previous life, while my memories of being human are stored by Yualsong in the AI's matrix. This means when we encounter a new plague bird like yourself, still so firmly human in your life and beliefs, we come across as harsher than we intend."

"How long have you two been plague birds?"

"We both merged with AIs shortly after the collapse. We fought with the three-fold armies to create the world as it exists today."

Crista tried to imagine being a plague bird for so many millennia—to live with Red Day for so long that both her body and soul would merge with the AI. The wolf in her growled in fear.

"I shouldn't have become a plague bird," Crista said softly. "I didn't want this."

"None of us do," Tendi said. "At first, that is. When I was a little girl my mother even warned me not to go down this road. But it's what we've become."

Little girl? Crista looked at Jai, then Tendi, and remembered Red Day requesting her to say nothing of Lanea and Desiada. But wasn't there someone else she wasn't supposed to mention? The words 'little girl' rang in her mind, but she couldn't remember why. What, or who, was it?

Crista shrugged. *Must not have been too important,* she thought.

Tendi took a large chug of her cider and licked her lips. "Ah, this was nice," she said. "Actually talking like people. Not knowing what someone will say until they say it. Not knowing more than your eyes and ears and mind tell you."

"But all good things must end," Jai said, finishing his beer.

The wolf in Crista shifted and her hackles rose in warning.

"I do apologize," Tendi said. "For what we're about to do. But you see, Crista, you're a puzzle. Trouble follows you like the gened pox itself. And with Red Day's powers being so restricted, you shouldn't be able to do the things you've done. So we have to know what you know, without Red Day interfering."

Crista jumped from her chair and crouched before Tendi and Jai, the wolf in her growling. She stumbled slightly—why had she drunk so much cider and beer?—but the wolf in her could compensate. She'd kill them if need be. Rip throats from their necks, guts from stomachs.

"Don't make me hurt you," Crista warned.

"Unlikely," Jai said as red lines burned their way across his face and his body again hummed to a plague bird's power.

Red lines also lit Tendi's frowning face. "Understand, Crista," she said. "I take no joy in what we must do. But we must know the truth."

"Oh, I'll take joy in this," Jai-Saan said, his voice the sound of corpse teeth chattering together. "I plan to take quite a bit of joy."

Fear slammed Crista's body as she stared at the two plague birds, her human body instinctively reacting like it'd done before she'd merged with Red Day. But she wouldn't be human for much longer. She remembered Kenji's dead body and thought the words to release Red Day: *Plague Gold, end.*

She remained human.

"Wait, wait," Jai-Saan said, waving at Tendi like a kid about to spoil a secret. "I want to tell her."

"This isn't a damn game," Tendi snapped.

"But it is. Crista, that wasn't Kenji's body you saw."

"What?"

"Oh, it looked like Kenji," Jai-Saan said. "Even down to the molecular level it was a perfect copy of Kenji, but it wasn't him. Tendi and I took his body apart atom by atom looking for clues before recreating it as bait to see if the killer would come back."

When Crista didn't understand why Jai-Saan was explaining this, he snorted and looked in exacerbation at Tendi. "What Jai-Saan is saying," Tendi explained, "is you have no memories of Kenji's real dead body. Not his exact body. The Plague Gold knows this and refuses to accept your memory to unlock Red Day."

"You tricked me. I trusted you and you ..."

"No," Jai-Saan stated. "You didn't trust us. You thought of us as equals. We're not."

Tendi pulled a red knife from her hip sheath and pricked her left index finger with it. A dot of blood sparked red lightning to Yualsong's power. "We have to know what you're hiding," Tendi said. "The Plague's Truth proved you weren't involved in Kenji's death or the Veil's attacks. But there's more you didn't reveal, isn't there?"

The blood on Tendi's finger called to Crista. Whispered that it would only go harder on her if she resisted. Crista realized this was how everyone she'd touched minds with had felt. Fearful, yet unable to look away from the blood. Steeling themselves before being ripped open. Wondering if they had anything to hide from a plague bird.

And she did have something to hide. Desiada and Lanea. Red Day had said to not tell Jai-Saan and Tendi about either of them. But wasn't there someone else? Someone powerful she'd met at Down Hope? Someone young, yet old…

No, she realized. Just Desiada and Lanea.

"I refuse to do this," Crista said.

"I love when they resist," Jai-Saan said.

Crista threw her mug of cider at Jai-Saan, grabbed the chair beside her and hurled it at Tendi. She bolted between them and onto the table, the wolf in her yelping in fear at defying two plague birds. But she had no other option.

Crista knew she couldn't outrun them in the open, not without Red Day's power. If she ran down the only hallway leading from the room she'd be caught.

While Jai-Saan cursed and Tendi turned to grab her, Crista looked around the room. The walls of people were only holograms. But what lay beyond the people? She had to choose a route quickly.

One of the wall people caught her eye—the image was of the beautiful person she'd originally seen when she'd first accessed the Obsidian Rise. Zinhaz. A person from more than ten thousand years ago who simply asked anyone viewing their memory to remember them.

This couldn't be coincidence, especially when the Obsidian Rise had memories of millions of people to choose from.

Crista jumped through Zinhaz's red unisex blouse and skirt and body. Crista ran on, passing through person after person, all silent, none protesting, all walking and gliding around one another without notice of her. She ran straight, not sure where she was going, knowing only that endless images of people surrounded her. It took all her concentration not to fall into an animal frenzy from the waves and waves of people and the mirrored ceiling and floor reflecting more people up and down and back at her.

But if the endless people made it impossible for Crista to know where she was going, it also might hide her from Jai-Saan and Tendi. At least she hoped it would. She remembered how when she'd first entered the Obsidian Rise Red Day's senses had been hemmed in by the projected people. Maybe the same trick affected Jai-Saan and Tendi. Every moment she was away from them was one moment closer to when Red Day would be freed.

She heard Jai-Saan's laughter directly behind her. "Crista, what do you expect? To run from us for another ten hours until Red Day is freed?"

She whirled to attack but saw only images of people. Christa cursed—they were in her head, manipulating her senses like she'd done to so many people.

Crista ran in another direction, tearing through a crowd of people in formal dress and gown, a riot of reds and purples and yellows and neon blues. A hand brushed her shoulder—a real hand—and she kicked the figure and jumped away as Tendi's voice said, "Wait, Crista, we won't hurt you."

Crista didn't care about Tendi's damn promises. She ran as fast as she could, the wolf powering her legs, knowing she was only free as long as she ran.

Crista ran into a large room, larger than the dining room where she'd eaten with Jai-Saan and Tendi, a room as big as the commons in her home village. The room stood empty, the infinity mirrors of the ceiling and floor reflecting Crista's own startled figure over and over into infinity. She started to run in a new direction but stopped when she saw the holographic people forming this room.

But not people, because only one person surrounded Crista. Her mother. Thousands of copies of her mother stared at her, each one smiling.

Crista reached out to one image, trying to touch her mother's face, but her hand passed through. She looked far younger than Crista remembered and stood without a hint of pain from the gened pox.

The wolf in Crista urged her to flee but she couldn't. She stepped to another image of her mother and reached out to it, only to have Jai-Saan walk through the hologram.

"It's less fun if you stop playing," he said, grabbing her arm break-bone tight. Crista growled and kicked and bit his shoulder but he held her until Tendi walked up.

"Release her," Tendi ordered. Jai-Saan did as told but Crista immediately jumped on him, punching his face as hard as she could. Jai-Saan threw her across the room, where she lay glaring at the two of them.

"Why the hell are you doing this to me?" she screamed. "Is this your perverted way of having fun?"

"No," Tendi said. "We're not trying to hurt you. We need to analyze your memories. To see what else is going on in your life."

"Not that," Crista hissed. "My mother. Why is this room showing images of my mother?"

Jai-Saan and Tendi looked in surprise at the copies of the woman surrounding them. "We don't control this," Tendi said. "The Obsidian Rise only projects people who've visited the city. Did your mother ever travel to Seed?"

"No. She's never been here."

"Then how could the Obsidian Rise know what she looked like?" Tendi asked.

"I don't know."

Jai-Saan looked exacerbated. "Listen Crista," he said. "I don't like you, or you me, but even your limited intellect must understand why we need to examine your memories. There are too many strange coincidences surrounding your life."

Crista knew Jai-Saan was right. But Red Day had told her to hide her knowledge of Desiada and Lanea. And someone else? Damn it, who else wasn't she supposed to reveal?

Tendi stepped forward and held her hand out to pull Crista up. Crista remembered her first meeting with Derena, who'd made the same gesture. Crista took the hand and stood up, avoiding looking at her mother's images, focusing only on Tendi as the plague bird pricked her finger and smeared the blood across Crista's forehead.

Iron and sand and fur—Crista tasted and smelled Yualsong as it entered her body. The taste of bloody iron. The scorch of sun-hot sand. The smell of burning fur. Crista fought to hide Desiada and Lanea from the blood AI's reach but Yualsong reached in and pulled out the memories of their lives. Yualsong also caressed through everything that was Crista: from her first memories of being a child in her village; of running and playing with Beu and her other friends; to her mother's slow death from the pox; to Beu's attack to Derena's visit. Yualsong even probed through Crista's memories as a plague bird: from her first kill; to her visit to Down Hope monastery; to this very moment.

Yualsong withdrew from Crista's mind and body like venom sucked from a wound. She felt exposed.

Crista collapsed onto the mirror floor. The infinite reflections of her mother danced around her, a single tear flowing down each copy of Mom's face.

"Well?" Jai-Saan asked.

"It's as she told us with only a few omitted details," Tendi said. "There's a monk she met at Down Hope she has affection for. Also, Ashdyd made a deal with Down Hope's abbot—that's what Crista swore not to reveal—and Ashdyd planted either false or true memories of her mother's death in her mind. But that's it."

"How did she manipulate our senses?" Jai-Saan asked. "How did she make herself appear to be Kenji?"

"Evidently Red Day's doing," Tendi said. "It appears our knowledge of its powers and abilities is wrong."

Jai-Saan cocked his head to the side, leaning it almost parallel to the floor. "I refuse to accept that. I will conduct my own examination of her mind. Red Day must have figured out what we were going to do. It hid what we need to know."

Fear ran Crista's body. She thought again of Kenji's body and said over and over the words to release Red Day, but to no effect.

"You'll hurt her," Tendi said in a clinical, matter-of-fact tone. "Rather badly. Saan knows nothing of subtle methods of accessing memories."

"She'll heal once Red Day is released. But we must know what's going on."

Tendi looked at Jai-Saan, evaluating her ability to stop her fellow plague bird from this course of action. She stepped aside.

"I'm sorry," she told Crista. "Nothing satisfies Jai-Saan when he's like this."

"I never wanted to be a plague bird," Crista pleaded. "I only wanted to be left alone."

"I know," Tendi said. "And I regret this. But we must know the truth."

Jai-Saan leaned over her and sliced his palm with his knife. Where Tendi's blood AI had tasted of bloody iron, sun-heated sand and burned fur, Saan screamed across all her senses. She couldn't taste or smell any one thing because the AI was so powerful. It tasted like every food she'd ever eaten being crammed down her throat at once. Smelled like the entire world had blossomed in her nose. And he hadn't yet touched the blood AI to her skin.

"I promise I'll put you back together in a pleasing way," Jai-Saan said. "You'll mostly be who you are. Maybe a few improvements here and there, but still mostly you."

Crista tried to run, the wolf in her frothing and panicking, but her body was no longer hers to control. Jai-Saan's bloody palm reached for her forehead. Right before it touched her she saw a girl step beside the plague bird. Crista first thought it was another projection of the Obsidian Rise because the girl had no animal genes in her, instead possessing a weak-prey body like a statue of the Child. The girl was also young, maybe eight or nine, with dark skin and a strange golden medallion hanging from her neck, a medallion showing a veil crossing in front of the sun.

The girl was also strangely familiar.

The girl grabbed Jai-Saan and threw the plague bird backwards. Jai-Saan and Tendi stared in disbelief, wondering where the girl had come from.

"I'm going to hurt you," the girl said matter-of-factly. "I'm going to rip both of you apart. I'm going to break your bodies and your AIs. Then I'll stitch you back together and make you forget me." The girl grinned. "But you'll always feel the pain of what I've done. You'll wonder why your body aches in the mornings. Why your AI fizzles out sometimes. You'll know someone hurt you but never remember what happened. And not knowing will hurt worse than anything I'm going to do right now."

The girl clapped her hands in excitement at what was to come. Tendi frantically cut her body, trying to release her AI, but no blood emerged. And a burst of fire seared Jai-Saan's sliced palm, sealing the wound and preventing Saan from leaving his body.

The girl glanced at Crista and pointed off to the side. "That's the way out, Crista," the girl said. "Amaj will help you. I'll be along shortly."

Crista ran, not waiting to see who the girl was or how she knew Amaj or what she'd do to the plague birds. She ran through her mother's smiling bodies and through the countless other projected bodies, running until she saw the hallway and the door out, running as she heard Jai-Saan scream.

Crista ran down the steps of the pyramid, stumbling and falling, until she reached the ground where the automaton Amaj waited. Crista tried to tell her what had happened, tried to explain, but Amaj merely touched her face in a sparkling burst and Crista fell asleep.

PAINT THE FUTURE RED

Crista woke in a plague bird's home. She stared at red painted walls. Tasted plague bird. Smelled plague bird. She cursed, remembering a nightmare of Jai-Saan and Tendi chasing her through the Obsidian Rise while her mother's countless bodies danced around her.

Except it hadn't been a nightmare, she realized.

Crista sat up, surprised to find herself sleeping in a bed. She stared in confusion at the room around her.

Where am I?

I'm not sure, Red Day said. *I accessed your memories once I was released from the Plague's Gold. Obviously Diver and the automaton saved us, but I've no idea where they took us since you were unconscious.* The AI's irritation left no doubt as to Red Day's thoughts on the utter indignity of not knowing something.

Crista remembered Jai-Saan and Tendi manipulating the Plague's Gold so Crista couldn't release Red Day. How Diver saved her. How she'd run up to Amaj and being out.

Wait, Crista thought, remembering Diver attacking Jai-Saan and Tendi. *When I saw Diver in the Obsidian Rise, I didn't recognize her.*

Red Day squirmed in her mind. *Ah yes,* it said. *I foresaw that Jai-Saan and Tendi might manipulate the Plague's Gold. I locked all down your memories of Diver and anything related to her damn code, along with the memory of you revealing plague bird secrets to Desiada and Lanea. We couldn't have such knowledge falling into the hands of Jai-Saan or Tendi.*

The wolf in Crista wanted to throttle Red Day. There was Jai-Saan, about to rip into her mind and rearrange who she was, and Red Day had already done it.

I apologize, Red Day said. *I would have told you if we'd had time. But I determined the possibility of Tendi and Jai-Saan's plan only a moment before you drank the Plague's Gold. I had to do something.*

You can manipulate my memories that quickly?

After all you've witnessed, is that surprising?

Crista sighed and climbed out of the bed. A large window on the far wall framed the morning sun rising over the Flickering Sea's waves. The color of the sunrise perfectly matched the red galaxy lines on the man's face in a painting above her bed. The man stared at the sun as if daring it to reveal as much blood as he'd seen in his life.

Crista remembered. That's what Kenji looked like, or at least what his dead body had looked like, or if what Jai-Saan and Tendi had said was true, the copy they'd made of his dead body.

Crista shook her head, pained by the manipulations surrounding her. She extended Red Day's senses to see where she was. The room she stood in was on the twentieth story of a stone building beside the bay's breakwater, a building filled with hundreds of what Red Day called flats. All empty except for this one. As Red Day's extended senses searched the empty halls, Crista wondered why no one lived here. Even if there weren't enough people to fill all the buildings in Seed, surely a few would live in such a beautiful location.

But as Red Day reached through the building Crista felt a sense of dread rise in her. The dark shadows in stairways twisted and creeped. The empty flats cursed and snapped, wishing her dead. Instead of the blowing sea breeze, she scented despair with every breath of air in the building.

It's the stone, Red Day said. *Seed's living stone responds to people and their desires. Kenji lived here for so long his emotions—his anger and bloodlust and pain—soaked into the building. Small wonder no one else lives here.*

Crista shuddered. *Should we leave?*

We still don't know why we were brought here, and I hate showing throat to a building's emotions. Hold on. I'll block the sensations from you.

Crista grinned, having never heard Red Day use wolf-slang like showing throat to describe itself. Obviously she was rubbing off on the AI as much as it was on her. Red Day grumbled at Crista's observation but didn't say anything as the AI blocked the building's dread and anger.

As Crista stepped from the bed she almost stumbled over Diver, who was curled in a blanket on the floor. Taking care not to wake the girl—she wanted to gather her bearings first—Crista walked around the flat, her fingers playing over Kenji's belongings. Aside from the bed and a simple table with two chairs, there was no other furniture in the place. Not that the flat was empty. Paintings hung from the walls while stacks of finished paintings covered half the floor in the main room where Crista had slept. The flat's four other rooms were even worse, completely filled floor to ceiling with stacks of paintings.

Kenji was a damn pack rat, Red Day muttered.

No, Crista thought, fingering a painting. *He was an artist.*

Crista touched the easel beside the large window, which sat where Kenji could paint while watching the Flickering Sea. She scented the ground clays and oils and pigments used to create his paints. An unfinished painting rested on the easel, the canvas partially filled with an image of what appeared to be Kenji's blood AI killing an old man.

Nearly all the paintings were of people being killed by Kenji. The paintings were absolutely lifelike, a fact Red Day attributed to Kenji relying on his AI's perfect recall.

If that was the case, the stacks of paintings meant Kenji had killed many thousands of people during his lifetime.

Only two paintings in the flat were different. One was the self-portrait of Kenji hanging above the bed. The other, a painting of a young child, hung behind an opaque stasis field, allowing Crista to see just enough of the painting to know the subject was a child but no other details.

Why'd he use a stasis field on this painting? Crista wondered.

Because he was an artist! Red Day said sarcastically. *Seriously, I wonder where he found a functioning stasis field. Not many left outside of Down Hope and a few other places.*

"How are you feeling?" Diver asked, yawning as she stretched.

"Better than I should. Thank you."

"For what?"

"For saving me from Jai-Saan and Tendi."

Diver grinned. "Happy to do it. I've never liked bullies. That's all those two are."

"Did you kill them?"

"No. But the way they're feeling this morning they'll wish I had. Oh. I also wiped their memories of who hurt them. While they'll have no proof it was you, that's what they'll guess. Don't expect them to be happy-happy the next time you see them."

Great, Red Day said. *All we need—two plague birds out for revenge.*

Crista snorted, not distressed by Jai-Saan and Tendi's anger. She wandered into the kitchen and found stacks of dried bread that Red Day called hardtack. Crista cracked open one of the square biscuits to find it full of worms. Hungry, yet not desiring to climb down twenty flights of stairs to find other food, she poured water from her canteen into a cup and crumbled in the hardtack. The worms floated to the surface. She skimmed them off before drinking the now-soupy bread.

She was crumbling a second serving into the cup when someone knocked at the door.

Crista touched the flat's access stone, which unlocked the door and swung it open. Before her stood the automaton, Amaj. Or at least Crista thought it was Amaj. The automaton stood far shorter than yesterday and no longer looked female, but also didn't look male, instead having a gender that flowed across Crista's mind. The automaton held a basket filled with fresh bread, a canteen of milk, and boiled eggs with shells decorated with various words and pictures.

"Thank you for saving me, Amaj," Crista said.

"You are most welcome. However, my name is currently Ama."

Automatons continually change gender, Red Day said, *and as their gender changes so do their name. When appearing female, use Amaj. Male, Amajd. When between or both or if you're uncertain of the gender, Ama.*

Crista smiled. "My apologies, Ama."

"Not a concern since you didn't know. My naming convention is a holdover from the once-vibrant days of automaton life. While thousands of years have passed since I last saw others like myself, I still keep to our culture."

Crista wanted to ask what it was like being the last of your kind but figured that would be rude. She gestured at the basket. "Have you brought something to eat?"

"In Seed, people have a tradition of housewarming," Ama said. "So I am warming your house."

Crista waved for the automaton to enter. "This is hardly my house. Still, too bad you didn't arrive a few minutes earlier."

Ama glanced in the kitchen and saw the hardtack. "Please say you didn't eat those biscuits. Kenji liked them for the worms. Claimed they reminded him of the cycle of life and decay."

Red Day laughed as Crista's stomach rolled.

Ama walked through the flat, deftly stepping around piles of paintings and not seeming surprised by the clutter, indicating to Crista the automaton had been here before. Unlike the other day when Ama had resembled a motherly figure with wolf genes—playing off Crista's own gened heritage—this time Ama was skinny, as if she hadn't eaten in decades. Her beautiful skin shimmied to a rainbowed sheen like traces of oil on water.

Diver waved at Ama, who waved back. Crista made a note to ask Diver how she'd coerced Ama to help her and why.

Ama sat at the small table in the main room and set out the food for Crista. Crista sat across from the automaton and picked up two boiled eggs. The word "Happy!" was written on the shells surrounding by hand-painted drawings of smiling faces.

"Kids in this city paint boiled eggs in the spring," Ama said. "Supposedly ensures a good year."

"Lots of traditions here," Crista said, handing one of the eggs to Diver, who ran to the bed to eat it. "What about the tradition of automatons not interfering in human lives?"

"Ah, but that's not tradition—that's a law. And you are a plague bird. Which means you decide when and if I'm interfering."

"Okay, then tell me why you knocked me out and brought me here."

"Simple. Diver asked me to help. I've known Diver for a long time because the … child … is kind enough to not delete my memories of her."

"You're Diver's friend?"

"More accurate to say that every few centuries we run into each other."

"Ama doesn't interfere with what I do," Diver explained, tossing her egg up and down. "Or tell anyone about me. So I don't mess with her."

Crista nodded, suspecting there was more to their relationship, but figuring she'd find out in good time.

"Anyhow," Ama said, "Diver told me you needed help and a place to hide until your blood AI recovered. I knocked you out because I couldn't risk people seeing you—a plague bird who'd briefly become human—being dragged shouting and screaming through the city. That would indeed be interfering."

Crista removed the painted shell from her egg and popped it in her mouth, chewing as she tried to decide if she should be irritated or pleased at the automaton's honesty and actions.

Ama paused to take a breath—although the automaton didn't need to breathe to live—and hunched over, looking down at the torn eggshell on the table. Crista wondered what it would be like to be a completely artificial creation yet also flesh like a human, to never age but be at constant risk of death by intruding too deeply in human affairs. Would a friendship be interference? Could saving a child's life result in your death?

Obviously Ama has determined the proper way to live without interfering, Red Day said. *This automaton is, after all, quite alive.*

Red Day was sympathetic to Ama, which surprised Crista. *Have you met Ama before?* Crista asked.

Of course, Red Day said, broadcasting its thoughts so the automaton also heard. *We're old friends, aren't we Ama?*

Ama laughed and knocked the eggshell off the table with a single flick of an extremely strong finger.

"What's so funny?" Crista asked.

"Red Day. Your AI always makes me laugh."

Told you I had a sense of humor.

Ama sat up straight and looked straight into Crista's eyes. "Before we talk more, I must know if you'll kill me for being here. Or for my actions saving you."

"What?" Crista stammered.

"If I speak something you dislike, will you kill or harm me? If I become too friendly with you or decide I don't like you, am I dead? Is my interference with your life going to cause my death? If so I will immediately leave."

Crista thought the automaton was joking but the creature's perfect seriousness suggested not.

Tell Ama you won't kill or harm the automaton's life for anything Ama says or for any normal human interactions with you, Red Day suggested. *Derena and I were friends with*

Ama, as were several of my previous hosts. Ama will proceed no further with any interference in your life without this approval.

You make interfering in my life sound like a bad thing.

Interference can be good, bad, or neutral. But to automatons there's only one outcome unless a plague bird tells says otherwise.

Crista smiled. "I won't kill or harm you."

"...for anything I say or do in normal human interactions with you?" Ama finished.

"Yes."

The oil-rainbow skin on the automaton's face stretched as Ama formed a smile. "This is good. Now, you asked why I laughed at Red Day. I laughed because the last time I spoke with your AI, it was judging whether I lived or died. It said I should die."

"What?" Crista said.

Ama helped a young man with abusive parents flee from Seed and join a nearby hunt clan. The decision of what to do with Ama was weighed by three plague birds. The other two voted to let the automaton live.

"I didn't know," Crista muttered. "Red Day said you two were friends."

"We are. Red Day was merely doing its duty."

Crista started to say friends didn't kill friends but kept silent. "Why are you here with housewarming gifts? In a house, I should point out, you brought me to."

Ama pointed to the easel and its unfinished painting of a dying man. "I was Kenji's friend. I'd sit here and watch him paint."

"I don't paint."

"A shame."

I'm remembering my irritation with Ama, Red Day said. *The automaton says a lot but rarely anything useful.*

Perhaps that's a useful trait if you don't want an angry blood AI killing you.

Touché.

But it was hard to argue with Red Day's assessment of Ama. Crista ate another hardboiled egg and drank the canteen of milk, waiting for Ama to say something—anything—to indicate why the automaton had come here. Finally, Ama cast an even bigger smile and grinned at Crista.

"Why did you reveal plague bird secrets to Desiada and his sister?"

Red Day cursed. *How does Ama know that?* Crista asked. *You said not to tell anyone.*

We didn't tell anyone in this city. No one knows except Diver.

Crista glared at Diver, who sat on the bed. The girl had finished eating her egg and was pounding the eggshell to tiny pieces and scattering them across the covers. Diver mouthed, "Oops."

"Are you going to tell Jai-Saan and Tendi?" Crista asked.

"I won't share this information with anyone. Especially your fellow plague birds."

"Then why tell me?"

Ama didn't answer, causing the wolf in Crista to growl in irritation. Not that Tendi and Jai-Saan needed a reason to harm Crista after what had happened yesterday.

"I could force you to tell me," Crista said. "Or reach in your mind and learn for myself."

"Ah, but you promised no harm for anything I said."

Red Day laughed. *I remember why I like Ama. This automaton is extremely devious.*

"Fine, I won't harm you. I told Desiada and Lanea that secret because I was privy to the secrets of their own lives. Seemed the least I could do to show my trust in them."

Ama looked puzzled at Crista's statement. "I … am pleased you have people you trust so deeply. I would like to meet your friends one day."

They should be returning soon, Red Day said.

"Even better," Ama said. "Will they arrive in time to fight by your side?"

"What?"

"Jai-Saan and Tendi wait for you outside the Obsidian Rise. And inside the Rise waits the one called Beuten Pauler. Along with Ashdyd."

Crista balled her fist and—without powering up her hand—punched the wall as hard as she could. Several of her fingers fractured before Red Day healed the injury.

"Why is Beu there?" Crista asked.

"The Obsidian Rise would not tell me. Both Beu and Ashdyd will only speak with you."

Crista remembered seeing the images of her mother inside the Obsidian Rise. Had the Rise let Beu and Ashdyd inside? If so, what game was the city playing?

"Will Jai-Saan and Tendi help me fight Beu and Ashdyd?" Crista asked.

No, Red Day stated privately. *They'll blame you for what Diver did to them. They'll attack you on sight.*

"No," Ama said, responding to the same question. "My analysis is that Jai-Saan and Tendi still fear you're working with Ashdyd. They'll be afraid to let you link up with him in the Obsidian Rise."

How could Ama know that? Crista asked.

You realize Ama isn't telling you everything, Red Day said.

No shit. But since Crista had given her word not to harm Ama, they couldn't probe the automaton's mind to learn what was truly going on.

We could ask Diver to look into Ama's mind and see what's up, Red Day suggested.

Crista glanced at Diver, who had created a snowstorm of eggshell pieces over the bed with her powers. Diver shook her head, guessing what Crista wanted.

We'll simply have to see what Ama is playing at, Red Day said. *I've known Ama for a long time and, strange to say, I trust this automaton as much as I trust anyone in the world.*

That's good. I guess.

"So what will you do now?" Ama asked.

We need to rest, Red Day said so the automaton could hear. *I'm still feeling after-effects from the Plague's Gold. We must be at full strength before we challenge Jai-Saan and Tendi, let alone Ashdyd. We'll confront them in the morning.*

"Please stay here until you're ready," Ama said. "Kenji once told me that if anything happened to him, he wanted me to have his flat and everything in it. I therefore pass all this on to you."

The automaton paused. "There was a question you wished to ask, when you opened the door."

Crista wondered how Ama knew that. Red Day whispered automatons were excellent readers of human emotions and faces. *And I'm sure you're not the first to wonder,* the AI said.

"What's it like being the last of your kind?" Crista said, embarrassed to ask but also curious.

Ama smiled, the automaton's lips flowing into a gentle curve. "Many wonder but few ask. My answer is simple—I'm not the last of my kind."

"There are other automatons in the world?"

"I suspect not. But I'm not alone. Before the crash, back when there were so many automatons you couldn't count our numbers, we were known simply as human."

Seeing Crista's puzzlement, Ama leaned over and tapped the plague bird's forehead like the automaton had done when selecting a memory of Crista's to embed in her ice cream.

"We live in limited times," Ama said. "Before humanity closed ourselves down, we embraced all it meant to be ourselves. Gened flesh and blood creations, such as the body you were born into, were human. Automations like myself were human. Even AIs were considered part of humanity. All of us existed across a vast range of human experiences and lives."

Saying no more, Ama stood and walked toward the door. The automaton stopped by the portrait of the young child on the wall, still partially hidden by the stasis field. As Ama reached out to open the field Crista told her not to bother. The stasis field wasn't set to open itself to any random touch—Crista had already tried.

But the field opened to Ama's touch, revealing a young girl's face staring from the painting.

Crista's face. From when she was four or five.

Etched into the wooden frame beneath the painting were the words "The plague bird who will save us all."

"It's a goodness you swore not to harm or kill me," Ama said. "I'll see you in the morning when you challenge Jai-Saan and Tendi. If it helps—and I believe it will—I'll ensure a crowd of people are there to witness the confrontation."

Ama opened the door before turning back around, the automaton's face flowing into a disturbing frown. "The world is changing again, little plague bird. I hope the changes you bring are good ones."

With that the automaton walked away.

CRISTA SPENT HOURS STARING AT HER PORTRAIT. CRISTA'S CHILD FACE—SPORTING THE slight whiskers she'd had until she'd reached her teenage years—stared out of the frame as if curious about who was gazing back.

In the painting's background Blue floated near the small one-room schoolhouse while several kids played kickball. Beu was among the group, kicking the ball away from the others. Crista's mother and father walked across the green behind Crista, her mom leaning on her dad as they whispered something. Crista's mom began having trouble walking when Crista was a child. She remembered her father often helping her like this, supporting her mom's weight with his strong arms as they strolled the village commons.

As with all of Kenji's art the painting was incredibly life-like. Kenji had also placed parts of the painting deeper than the others, creating a shadow-box effect. Crista's painted body was raised on a carved wooden support a quarter span from the back of the painting while the other people and beings, and the houses and barns, were likewise created at various heights above the background. The effect gave the painting a sense of actual depth and life when stared at from straight ahead.

When did Kenji paint this? Crista asked.

The painting has been locked in stasis, making it difficult to determine its exact age, Red Day replied. *But the pigments and materials match other paintings in this flat. Those paintings were created fifteen years ago.*

So this painting was created when I was a kid?

My analysis suggests you were four years old.

The wolf rose in Crista, her anger and fury aimed at Red Day. *Then what the hell are you hiding from me? When that Veil man said I'd been picked to be a plague bird before I was born, you said that was impossible. That you and Derena picked me because I was nearby and the best candidate. Nothing else.*

That's true, Red Day said, although the AI didn't sound convinced.

Then why does a painting from my childhood say I'm the plague bird who will save us all?"

Red Day clicked back and forth between responses, running through its knowledge and memories trying to find any answer—any truth—which fit this puzzle.

I don't know, the AI said.

Crista kicked the wall as hard as she could, cracking the stone slightly.

When she turned back around, she saw Diver standing beside the table, staring intensely at the painting.

"Are you hiding anything?" Crista asked. "Did you visit my village when I was a child? Did we play tag without you telling me you're really a bomb created to destroy humanity?"

"No, I'm not hiding anything," Diver said. "I mean yes, I'm hiding things from you, but nothing about this. I'm only hiding things I can't tell anyone. And I never visited your village."

As Diver said this, she stared at the painting, not moving from her spot.

"What is it?" Crista asked.

"I ..." Diver stopped, at a loss for words. "You need to see the painting. From this angle."

Crista walked over and stood by Diver. The painting was now a mess of images and shapes, the shadow-box effect that provided the images depth falling apart when seen from this angle.

"I don't see anything?" Crista said.

"Down here," Diver said. "You have to see if from my height."

Crista squatted beside Diver. The bottom right of the painting shifted in her eyes, turning into something else. She remembered games Blue played with village kids where the AI created puzzles in its floating mass of colors—images that could only be seen if looked at from the proper angle.

This painting resembled those. The image before her eyes jumped and played as her mind processed it into understanding. A face. The painting's lower corner showed a young girl's face.

Diver.

Crista stumbled back, crashing into the table and knocking it over. "How is that possible?" she stammered.

Red Day pulled its recorded images of the painting before her eyes and ran through every possible angle and view, looking for other hidden puzzles. There were none. *Only this one hidden image*, the AI said to both Crista and Diver. *And only when seen from this angle.*

"Only when seen by a child," Diver said. "I had to walk by the table, through this exact spot, to see the hidden portrait. Kenji knew I would be here. Only someone my exact height could see my face."

"No one knew you'd be with me. Hell, outside of the monks in Down Hope no one but Red Day and I and a few others—like Ashdyd—even know you exist."

"Someone did. Someone knew fifteen years ago that I'd be with you." Diver's eyes lit to tears and she ran to the bed, where she jumped under the sheets and hid.

RIPPLING INTO LIFE

Crista rested that night as Red Day purged the remaining Plague's Gold from her body. The following morning, she prepared to leave the flat.

"You okay?" Crista asked Diver. The girl nodded as she glanced warily at the painting of Crista's village. Diver had slept all night curled up against Crista, scared by what the painting implied.

"This isn't right," Diver said. "I should help you fight Jai-Saan and Tendi, not just hide from Ashdyd."

With Ashdyd possibly accessing the power of the Obsidian Rise, it wasn't safe for Diver to reveal herself. As they'd learned at Down Hope, one of Ashdyd's goals was to capture Diver and the code within her mind. While Diver wanted to help, Crista couldn't risk the girl being captured.

"I can both help you and hide myself from Ashdyd and the Obsidian Rise," Diver said. "I'll be careful."

Crista shook her head. "Ashdyd knows the limits of my powers. If I'm easily able to defeat Jai-Saan and Tendi, he'll know you're there and may come for you again. Let's go with Red Day's plan for now."

Diver pouted. Grinning despite herself, Crista hugged the girl. "Don't worry," she said. "If Red Day's plan doesn't work you can come save my ass."

"Well, Red Day's plans do often fall apart." Diver laughed. "Deal!"

Red Day grumbled but didn't say anything as they left the flat and marched through the market.

Crista again forbade Red Day to hide her presence from people, causing gasps as they jumped out of her way, although she was pleased to hear no screams this time.

As she walked through the market, Crista saw the young wolf girl she'd shaken hands with. The girl waved and Crista waved back.

She found Tendi and Jai-Saan waiting for her before the staircase to the Obsidian Rise, in the wide plaza between the Rise and the market. A large crowd had also gathered to watch. Not because of the plague birds—they still appeared as normal humans to everyone in Seed—but because Amajd stood there. The automaton's body stood twice as tall as Crista with bulky muscles and rainbow skin hardened into what looked like a suit of metallic armor. The citizens of Seed, who rarely interacted with Amajd, surrounded the automaton, asking what was going on. The scent of fear rose from the crowd, everyone aware that if Amajd saw the need to create armor something dangerous was about to happen.

Red Day laughed. *That's one way to warn people of danger without* interfering. *And as Amajd promised, here's our crowd.*

When the crowd saw Crista, people pointed and yelled and a few stepped back to flee. Amajd said hello to Crista and waved like nothing was amiss. The crowd, realizing Crista wasn't the danger, remained to see what would happen.

Jai-Saan and Tendi glared. Their bodies were bruised and a new scar ran across Jai-Saan's face opposite from his glowing plague bird lines.

"I didn't know you bruised," Crista said. "Or cut so easily."

Jai-Saan stepped toward Crista making to attack, but Tendi grabbed his shoulder and stopped him.

"Are you going to tell us how you did these things?" Tendi asked.

"No," Crista replied. "The other day you didn't admit wanting to rip my mind apart. Sounds like we're even."

The crowd around Amajd grew as more citizens of Seed came to watch Crista. People were puzzled as they watched the plague bird confront two people they'd seen around the city all their lives. Crista had counted on this. Jai-Saan and Tendi had told her people weren't allowed to know plague birds could die, meaning they likely wouldn't attack Crista in front of others. At least, not while everyone saw the pair as merely regular humans.

Jai-Saan's eyes lit to red fire as he glared at Crista. His hands shook as if he wanted to tear her apart.

He's afraid, Red Day said, making sure Tendi and Jai-Saan could hear its words. *He can't risk what we'll do to him if he attacks,* the AI added, bluffing.

Enough! Tendi's AI, Yualsong, shouted in their minds. *We made a mistake in underestimating Crista and Red Day. But we must focus on other threats. Beu and Ashdyd have locked us out of the Obsidian Rise. Individually, none of us can defeat Ashdyd. We must work together.*

"I won't work with either of you," Crista said.

Jai-Saan bowed sarcastically, mocking Crista's words. "I agree," he said. "We can't trust you. No, I will kill you. Then Tendi and I will kill this Ashdyd and his pet human."

"While everyone watches?" Tendi asked.

Crista glanced at the crowd, who were still puzzled by what they were witnessing. As long as Jai-Saan and Tendi looked like regular humans, they couldn't attack and defeat a plague bird without confusing everyone. But if a plague bird attacked a plague bird people would assume this was merely a different version of the justice continually enforced by their kind.

Reaching the same conclusion, Jai-Saan and Tendi ended their manipulation of everyone's senses, eliciting a scream of terror and shock from the crowd. People stepped away, understanding why Amajd was armored up.

Clear the area! Saan broadcast into everyone's minds. *This is plague bird business and none are permitted to watch.*

We need to keep them mentally off-balance, Red Day whispered, shielding its thoughts so Jai-Saan and Tendi couldn't hear their words. *Jai-Saan's ego gets in the way of his power, while Tendi will only follow Jai-Saan as long as they're winning.*

Crista agreed. While her ability to fight Jai-Saan and Tendi was limited without Diver, the two plague birds didn't know this.

Crista looked at the crowd of people around them trying to decide whether to stay and watch or run to safety. She remembered what Red Day had told her to say before she'd left Kenji's flat.

"They can't harm you," she yelled to the crowd. "I can't either. No plague bird is allowed to hurt a human unless you attack us, we're defending others, or we take the time to judge you."

Silence! Saan screamed in Crista's head. *We do not discuss such things.*

"Ooh, that pissed them off," Crista yelled. "I'm not supposed to tell everyone our little plague bird secrets."

The crowd wavered, people wanting to see this play out. As Crista and Red Day had hoped. She needed the people here if she was to have any chance of winning without Diver's powers.

"Why should we believe you, miss?" a man yelled from the crowd. He was short and stocky and scented of buffalo heritage.

"Well, I am a plague bird. But I'm not like them. I haven't been manipulating you into believing I was one of you, have I?"

That hit home. People glared at Jai-Saan and Tendi, no doubt remembering times they'd talked to them or treated them like regular humans.

"Enough!" Jai-Saan yelled. "All of you will leave the area immediately."

"Or what?" the buffalo man yelled back.

Tendi leaned in to Jai-Saan, probably to tell him they could attack Crista later when fewer people were around, but Jai-Saan was beyond reason. He grabbed his knife and slit open his belly, releasing a torrent of blood that burst across the plaza. Saan weaved around each person—not touching anyone, whisking a hair's touch from the skin and fur of adults and kids—before slamming into Crista.

Red Day was ready. Instead of fighting Saan's power, Red Day shielded Crista so she was thrown up and backwards. Crista shifted midair and pulled her knife, slitting only one wrist and releasing a single spurt of blood. She landed at the back end of the plaza with the entire crowd between her and the plague birds.

Jai-Saan and Tendi thought Crista was trying to escape and launched themselves into the air to stop her. Wielding her blood like a whip, Crista ran back toward the crowd as the two plague birds landed behind her. Saan and Yualsong snaked through the crowd to catch her but Red Day slashed out and stopped each attack. People screamed, panic overriding the knowledge that they wouldn't be harmed.. People cursed and howled and growled as Crista ran by them. She only needed the crowd to slow down Jai-Saan and Tendi until she reached the Obsidian Rise.

The wall rose before her. "Stop!" Tendi yelled as Crista pushed her bloody hand against the Obsidian Rise's cold, glassy blackness.

Time stopped. Or her senses sped up so much that time might as well have stopped.

"Hello, Crista," the Obsidian Rise said. "I'm pleased to talk with you directly."

"Red Day said you might help us. Are you watching the fight?"

"Yes. It's quite amusing. Beu and Ashdyd are inside me. They think you're going to lose."

"I need your help."

"I'm not supposed to intervene in human affairs. I'm merely a city where human affairs play out."

"Red Day said if I asked nicely you'd help me. As a favor."

"Did Red Day say why I might help?"

Crista hesitated. "No."

"Good. We'll discuss this later. Until then, I'll help."

Red Day flashed its plan into the Obsidian Rise.

"You want them dead?" the Obsidian Rise asked.

"No. Unconscious."

The Obsidian Rise snickered. "I need a bit of your blood," the city's mind said.

Red Day returned Crista's time sense to normal and she removed her bloody hand from the Rise's black wall. Two drops of blood from the bloody handprint she'd left shot out from the wall, screaming like bullets at Jai-Saan and Tendi. They dodged the blood only to have it explode beside them, red strings of power wrapping around both of their bodies. Red ropes strangled Tendi and red knives cut into Jai-Saan before they screamed and passed out.

Crista walked over to the unconscious plague birds. The blood she'd loaned the Obsidian Rise quivered and reached for her. She started to touch it—like when part of Red Day wanted to return to her body—but Red Day yanked her hand back.

We can't take it back, Red Day said. *I've changed my core override codes after releasing that blood, but the Obsidian Rise now controls the tiny part of me in those drops of blood.*

I thought you trusted her.

I do, within limits. But we can't allow the Rise to access my core.

What do we do with it? Crista asked.

In response, Red Day broadcast self-destruct codes at the compromised blood, which burst into streamers of smoke.

You know a lot about the Obsidian Rise, Crista said. *Were you in love with her or something?*

Crista was joking, but Red Day retreated slightly at the words. Not sure what was going on, and not having time to worry about an AI's strange emotions, Crista leaned over Jai-Saan and Tendi. The plague birds looked like happy kids asleep after a long day of play. The red lines on their faces barely glowed. She couldn't feel anything from Saan and Yualsong aside from a touch of their AI power.

"That one killed my father," a soft voice said.

Crista looked over to see the young wolf girl, who pointed at Jai-Saan. The fur on the girl's face and neck bristled and a low growl escaped her lips. The rest of her pack of orphans glared at Jai-Saan and Tendi. Crista wondered how many of these orphan kids had lost parents to plague birds.

The wolf girl pulled a knife from under her shirt and stepped toward Jai-Saan. The girl gripped the knife with both hands and shook visibly, her eyes watching Crista even as her feet moved her toward Jai-Saan.

"I can't let you do that," Crista said. The people who'd fled the plaza during the fight had returned and formed a half circle around Crista, the wolf girl, and the unconscious plague birds. Amajd stood at the front of the crowd.

"Why not?" the wolf girl yelled. "He attacked you. They both did."

We don't have time for this, Red Day said. *Jai-Saan and Tendi won't be unconscious for long. We must be inside the Obsidian Rise before they wake.*

Crista ignored the AI. "What's your name?" she asked the wolf girl.

"Now you want to know me?" the girl asked. "Before, you didn't care. But if I try to kill a plague bird you want my name?"

The crowd murmured, agreeing with the girl's words. Crista scented anger and vengeance rising from the crowd and remembered how her father and the other villagers had felt when they'd found her injured body after Beu attacked her. They'd wanted to rip Beu apart for what he'd done. Only Blue's words and intervention had prevented that.

Ignoring everyone but the girl, Crista nodded. "Yes, I want to know your name."

"Tufte," she said.

"A good name."

"My father placed it on me."

Which brought everything back to the plague bird who'd killed her father. "What did your father do?" Crista asked.

"Killed my mom. And baby brother."

"Are you certain?"

"I saw him. He was chasing me when this plague bird caught him. My father had drunk some bad gold-sold. Made him think he was being attacked by plague birds. Then he was killed by one."

Gold-sold? Crista asked Red Day.

A weak copy of Plague's Gold, created by rogue AIs and drunk by humans for its hallucinatory and transcendent effect.

"Did the plague birds catch the AI who made that gold-sold?" Crista asked Tufte.

"Yeah. Ripped it apart good. Lots of pretty lights exploding like fireworks."

Crista understood the girl's anger. While Tuft had seen her father kill her mother and brother, he'd also been under the control of a powerful AI concoction. While Crista was sure Tufte still felt anger at her father—like she did at Beu—believing her father hadn't been responsible for his actions likely made it easier for Tufte to forgive him.

In cases like this, Red Day said, *it doesn't matter if the gold-sold made the person see things that weren't there and act on them. Unless the person didn't voluntarily drink the substance, the responsibility rests with them.*

Same with Beu, Crista realized. The gened pox may have helped him lose control, but he was still the one who attacked her.

We must hurry, Red Day said.

Fine.

Crista smiled at Tufte and the crowd around them. "None of you can kill the plague birds," she said. "You may not like us, but we try our best to judge fairly. Nothing truer can be said than that."

The crowd still smelled of anger and vengeance but the emotions weakened. Tufte stuck the knife back under her shirt and stepped away from the plague birds.

"Amajd," Crista said, "will you make sure no one kills or harms Jai-Saan and Tendi?"

"That would be interfering," the automaton said.

"I give you permission."

The automaton nodded and stepped over to shield Jai-Saan and Tendi from harm. The crowd stepped back as Amajd grew a sword from his right arm. Amajd grabbed the hilt and placed the sword's tip between the two unconscious plague birds.

Automatons have a famous history of being tough fighters, Red Day said. *They'll be fine. Let's go.*

Before Crista left, she walked over to the wolf girl, who'd retreated with her pack to the edge of the crowd. "Thank you for backing down," Crista said. "It's never easy, showing throat."

"You wolf?" Tufte asked, knowing only wolf blood used that term. She sniffed Crista's scent, trying and failing to separate the plague bird smell from who Crista had been before.

"Yeah. I come from a long line of wolf-hybrids."

"That mean anything now you're a plague bird?"

"Well, know this. We're both wolves and wolves always owe the pack. I owe you a favor."

Tufte gasped and grinned while her pack laughed. They'd never known anyone who'd been owed a favor by a plague bird.

Glad we're all happy-happy now, Red Day said. *Can we please go deal with Beu and Ashdyd before Jai-Saan and Tendi wake and kill us?*

Crista turned and ran up the steep staircase leading into the Obsidian Rise. She cut her palm halfway up, releasing a stream of blood that Red Day flattened and held before her like a shield. Crista paused at the top of the stairs, looking at Amajd and Diver and Tufte and the rest of the people watching her.

They had no clue what was about to happen. Neither did she.

At least, not until she stepped into the Obsidian Rise.

INTO THE RISE

Hundreds of Beu stared at her with yellow eyes. A thousand. A million.

Instead of the Obsidian Rise filling herself with images of countless people forming walls and hallways with their infinity reflections mirrored by the floor and ceiling, now there was only one person. A single person endlessly repeated.

Beu.

Beu stared at her—all of him did—as she walked through his crowd of one. Beu didn't form halls and rooms. Instead, as Crista stepped forward the Beus danced out of her way. But he never stopped glaring.

A chill jolted Crista's spine. The wolf in her snapped and growled and begged to flee. The Beus grinned like when he smashed her body.

Steady, Red Day said. *Obsidian Rise is messing with you.*

No shit.

Crista walked on. She could scent nothing. Could sense nothing. Could hear nothing but her own footsteps. The millions of Beus swirled around, taunting her.

She walked in the direction of the table where she'd eaten with Jai-Saan and Tendi on a hunch that that's where the real Beu would be. Sure enough, when she neared the table the Beus parted and she stood in an open room with the real Beu sitting in a chair and waving awkwardly. Crista glanced around—the room now looked like it did the last time she'd come here, with random people from Seed's history forming the walls.

Beu may not know the Obsidian Rise created those images of him, Red Day said. *Perhaps that was the Rise's way of warning you to be careful.*

Where's Ashdyd?

Not sure. My guess is inside Beu. It appears Ashdyd hasn't accessed the Obsidian Rise's main systems. Red Day paused. *Crista, be aware Beu likely doesn't understand the levels of manipulation Ashdyd has engaged in.*

Does that make a difference?

From Beu's outlook it will matter.

Crista approached the table warily. She sat in a chair on the opposite side from Beu, making sure to leave enough room so she could defend herself.

Beu noticed this and frowned. "I would apologize," he said. "Yet again. But there's no longer a point to that, is there?"

Crista refused to be drawn into Beu's delusions. "Where's Ashdyd?"

Beu reaching out as if to embrace the entirety of the Obsidian Rise, revealing the C the village elders had branded on his right hand after he'd attacked Crista. "Ashdyd is inside me," he said. "The AI said he would hide in me while we awaited your arrival."

"Then tell Ashdyd to come out and speak."

"Ashdyd says there's no hurry." Beu paused. "Ashdyd also says Jai-Saan and Tendi woke up."

Crista knew they'd be even angrier than before, but she could deal with that later.

"Why are you here?" she asked.

"Did you see my memories?"

As Beu said this a flash of fear shot through him, the scent of his emotions tingling through Crista's senses. She remembered Beu running from Day's End as Blue died saving them. How Beu saved her father even after his own mother was killed. "I did. I'm sorry your mother died."

"I know you didn't like her …"

"She loved you. She was a good woman."

Beu wiped his eyes. Crista remembered how Beu had comforted her after her own mother died. Of course, that was well before he'd betrayed her.

"What happened after the memory stopped?" Crista asked.

"Your father and I traveled to the place Blue told everyone to gather. Over two-thirds of the hunt and village survived. They're safe for now. Ashdyd said I shouldn't record the location in the memory in case the people who attacked us found a way to access it."

"Yes, the Veil. I've encountered them before."

"What happened?"

"They've attacked other villages. I killed one of their members."

Crista scented bloodlust rising in Beu and his eyes flickered a brighter yellow for a moment. "Good," he said. "You should kill them all."

"I'll try. But first I'd like to kill their leader."

"Who's that?"

"Ashdyd."

"You lie!" Beu screamed, slamming his fists on the table as his eyes glowed brightly. He looked to the side, listening to a hidden voice as he took a deep breath. "You don't know Ashdyd. He saved your father. Your father was hurt bad, but Ashdyd healed him. Everyone is living in a secluded valley. There's no AI to help, but they're making it work."

Crista stared at Beu warily. "Beu, you can't trust Ashdyd."

"I'd be dead—your father would be dead—without Ashdyd."

"I know. But did the AI tell you it once attacked me?"

"Ashdyd couldn't have. Otherwise why would it save your father and everyone?"

Why indeed? Red Day whispered to Crista. *Oh right, to manipulate a delusional young man who is obsessed with you.*

"Beu, I need to speak with Ashdyd. How do I do that?"

"Ashdyd can talk in your mind."

No, Red Day said. *Too dangerous. We can't let Ashdyd access our minds again. Especially not when we have Diver's code inside us.*

Crista shook her head. Beu looked up at the ceiling. It reflected an image of them sitting at the table. When Beu looked down his eyes smoked a distorted reflection over their usual yellow.

"Hello, Ashdyd," Crista said.

"Crista," Beu said in Ashdyd's distorted voice.

This is quite the cliché, Red Day broadcast so Ashdyd could hear. *What are you trying to do—make Beu your own plague bird host?*

"Please. I saved most of his village and Crista's father and you joke?"

"You sent the Veil to attack Day's End in the first place," Crista said.

Beu stared into nothingness for several moments. "I did," Ashdyd said through Beu's mouth. "But I also saved it."

"From yourself?"

"Yes. From the Veil. We're very dangerous."

Crista wondered if Ashdyd realized how unstable he sounded. "Why do you say the Veil are dangerous when you created the Veil?"

"Do you know what I am?"

You're an experimental AI, Red Day broadcast. *Created before the crash, if what we've learned is correct.*

"Correct enough. I was created by the Obsidian Rise. Being here is like coming home."

Your purpose?

"I have many purposes. To explore other dimensions. To root through alternate realities. To push those realities to be what I want. To save humanity. To track down an alien spy living among us."

"What the hell does all that mean?"

"It means I can do whatever I desire."

Crista paled and her hands shook. "You think it's amusing to toy with people's lives?"

"It is amusing. But don't worry, I have a larger purpose. Or I should say I've created a purpose. I'm going to save humanity from itself."

The wolf in Crista growled, and she fought the urge to attack Beu and the damn thing inside him.

Calm down Crista, Red Day whispered. *Don't lose control in front of Ashdyd.*

Crista took a deep breath. "How are you going to save humanity?

The distortions over Beu's eyes grew larger, reminding Crista of when Ashdyd's power washed over Master Chayn's face and took control of the abbot's body. But Ashdyd restrained itself and didn't take all of Beu's body.

"I'm going to fix this world," Ashdyd declared.

"The plague birds and AIs are already doing that."

"Really? You believe that? They've been trying to fix the world for 10,000 years. If they really wanted to fix the world they would have accomplished it by now."

Ashdyd's words made sense, but Crista refused to admit that to the AI. As Red Day had once said, when in doubt stick with those you like and attack those you hate.

One thing I don't understand, Ashdyd, Red Day said. *All AIs from before the collapse were repurposed with new tasks to support the three-fold balance. Why weren't you?*

"I shouldn't even be here," Ashdyd said. "I was still being created when the collapse happened. Me and six other AIs. During the collapse the Obsidian Rise placed us in stasis. But the stasis malfunctioned and only I survived. I was freed five hundred years ago."

You should accept the new reality, Red Day said, *and take on a role to uphold our world. No AI is allowed to deviate from the three-fold balance.*

Throughout their talk, Beu's body had remained motionless like a dead puppet, as if Ashdyd refused to use more of its power than needed to speak. Now Beu laughed, his lips sneering slightly as he barked at Ashdyd's enforced amusement.

"Why Red Day," the AI said. "You haven't told her. Does Crista not know your history?"

What do you mean? Red Day asked.

"You haven't told Crista what you were before the collapse."

That's incorrect. I told her I was created after the collapse from elements of another AI.

"You're cherry-picking the truth."

Beu's body reached into his pocket and removed a small red discoidal, which he rolled between his fingers. The discoidal glowed slightly and carried the scent of Down Hope monastery.

"This discoidal contains one of three keys to control the Obsidian Rise and the city of Seed," Ashdyd said. "I also have the second key hidden elsewhere. Would you like to know what the first two keys reveal about your precious Red Day?"

Red Day cringed, now the one fighting for control. But Crista merely laughed and pulled the discoidal she'd taken from Vaca from her pocket.

"Is this your second key?" she asked.

Beu glared before smiling. "Quite good. I had sent poor Vaca away to keep that discoidal safe. Am I to assume you killed him to get it? That Down Hope betrayed his location to you?"

Crista didn't answer, merely mimicking Ashdyd by rolling the discoidal between her hands. The discoidal was as warm as new-killed meat, which was strange because it'd been cold to the touch after she had taken it from Vaca.

Derena and I created this discoidal to backup our memories during your attack a year ago, Red Day stated. *How can it be one of your keys?*

"Don't ask me," Ashdyd said. "Ask the Obsidian Rise."

The discoidal in Crista's hand shook and glowed bright red. The air around them flickered. Crista's time sense changed as Beu appeared to freeze before her.

Did Ashdyd access our mind? Crista asked.

No, Red Day replied. *The Obsidian Rise has revealed herself. She wants us to know what's in the discoidal.*

The discoidal in Crista's hand glowed bright red and hummed. Crista raised the discoidal to her eyes, trying to see what was happening, when it exploded.

INTERLUDE

KENJI'S SONG

(AS REVEALED TO CRISTA BY THE OBSIDIAN RISE)

Amaj laughed.

Kenji believed events became inevitable the moment Amaj finally laughed.

Kenji walked the streets of Seed shortly before the collapse. The city, currently only a few centuries old, was already the finest in the world. Not because of the height of buildings. There were many cities on Earth with far larger buildings. And many cities with bigger populations and deeper histories.

What made Seed special was its sense of belonging.

Everyone who lived in Seed felt the city's love. As Kenji walked Seed's side streets, he passed a pack of wolf-kids chasing one another in a neighborhood game. Each kid giggled when they felt Seed's happiness.

The next street over he passed two automatons working in a garden with several ungened humans. All of them felt embraced by Seed's love of flowers yet to bloom.

Even when Kenji crossed the city square below the Obsidian Rise and passed flickering AI clouds merging their essences while the AIs debated arcane philosophical points, he knew they tasted Seed's love for intellectual pursuits.

Kenji climbed the stairs and entered the Obsidian Rise. The inside looked empty until Kenji stepped forward and walls and hallways and ceilings appeared, guiding him toward the lab for today's security checks.

I've highlighted 23,278 top-level security concerns for your immediate attention, the Obsidian Rise said as he entered his lab. Kenji laughed. He'd worked on security issues all night from home, not even bothering to sleep while accessing the rising number of troubling incidents on Earth, in orbit and beyond. While Kenji didn't need to sleep, irritation was common when he didn't. The ability to dream was a major reason he'd implanted his AI consciousness in a cloned human body.

Now that Kenji was back in the Obsidian Rise, he connected with the city's vast power and tied all the latest incidents into flowing projections. A fatal attack on a family of non-gened humans by unknown assailants in Mare Trans City. Two AIs who'd butchered a fox-gened man in what appeared to be a ritual sacrifice near the Grand Canyon. Protests by millions of gened individuals in multiple cities, with half the protests turning into bloody riots.

Each incident spun before Kenji's eyes as possible future probability lines.

You see the problem? the Obsidian Rise asked.

"Yes," Kenji said, preferring to use his voice. Another reason he'd created a human body to use. "The lines of possibility converge toward trouble in the near future."

Except in Seed, the Obsidian Rise said, a note of pride in the city's thoughts.

"Except in Seed. But if events go as we're projecting, even Seed will eventually be washed by bloodshed."

Kenji walked to the edge of the lab and leaned against one of the Rise's walls—a real wall, not one of the projections the Obsidian Rise loved creating. He nuzzled his cheek against the black-glass surface, feeling the Rise's power and abilities just as he had when Seed first created his consciousness here three centuries before.

How long do we have? the Rise asked.

Kenji thought of the people who lived in Seed. So far the problems affecting the rest of humanity weren't showing up here. He was certain this was because of the sense of belonging that everyone in Seed experienced. But even a sense of belonging—that this place was your home and would always be open to you and yours and anyone who moved here—would matter little if civilization entered a dividing point, as the projections indicated.

"At most five years," Kenji said. "I will, of course, give my life to protect you and everyone living here."

I expect nothing less, my love. But will your strength be enough to save me?

"No."

Instead of saying more Kenji left the lab and walked to the restricted research vaults in the heart of the Obsidian Rise. A score of humans, automatons and AIs worked there, isolated from the rest of the world because of the secrecy of their projects. The access doors and barriers took a full hour for Kenji to maneuver through but once inside he bowed politely to the lead scientist, an automaton of ever-shifting gender. Today she was Amaj, and she observed seven isolation cubes gestating seven extremely powerful artificial intelligences. The AIs had been forming for the last two years but still weren't ready.

"More bad projections?" Amaj asked.

"Extremely bad. I believe, as does the Rise, that we have less than five years before the world falls apart."

Amaj shrugged. Not that she didn't care, but there was nothing she could do to stop what might come. "The AIs are still a decade from being stable enough for release. I'd hoped for more time."

"We all did."

Kenji stepped before each isolation cube, accessing the gestating AI inside with his power. The Obsidian Rise had created these seven in an attempt to fix issues driving the projections of civilization's looming collapse. The first four AIs were to subtly address core issues in humanity, including regenerating a sense of belonging to a people that had ceased having any one physical home. The next two AIs were powerful judges, to right wrongs and bring people together through an unfailing sense of justice.

Kenji paused before the last AI. Even though the AI should be unconscious during its gestation, Kenji could feel it probing the constraints of its isolation cube. This AI was built to track down and uncover an anomaly that had puzzled humanity's top scientists for the last thousand years.

Despite listening to the stars for millennia and sending probes to the nearest systems, humanity had yet to discover any intelligent alien species in this part of the galaxy. Yet there were strange reports and indices across human history suggesting a non-human alien species was observing humanity. Nothing definite. But it appeared an alien power, likely an AI, was on Earth and reporting back to this alien race. When the Rise created these AIs, she also created a special AI to track down this alien influence in case that was the cause of humanity's problems.

"Yes, the last one is ... troubling," Amaj said, stopping before the final AI's cube. "Already it probes the confines of both its powers and the isolation cube. We'll have to conduct extremely careful safety tests before releasing it."

Kenji nodded. The AI was so powerful that it was created with a deliberate flaw—it could only exist outside its birthing cube when meshed with another lifeform. Amaj called it a parasitic AI, a crude if accurate summary.

Kenji didn't ask if there was a way to speed up the gestation of these AIs because he knew such births couldn't be rushed without horrible results. That left only one outcome if the worst happened.

"Perhaps the projections are wrong," Kenji said. "Perhaps we'll have time to finish growing these AIs."

"But if not ..."

"If the collapse happens and Seed is attacked or threatened, we can't allow other factions to capture and use them."

"Should I destroy them?"

Kenji shuddered, imagining if his own AI existence had been erased before he'd fully formed. That was worse than an AI never existing in the first place. "If the worst happens you will place them in stasis in a secure part of Seed's catacombs. Perhaps once the collapse is over—if it ends—we'll finish their growth."

Amaj laughed softly before bowing in obedience, the first laugh Kenji had ever heard come from her lips.

Kenji knew the automaton preferred the safer route of destroying the AIs. But if the worst happened, she'd carry out her orders. With luck none of this would be needed.

But the memory of Amaj's laugh wouldn't leave him. It was like the automaton knew luck wouldn't be on their side.

Two hundred years later Kenji limped down Seed's side streets, his right leg only working because he controlled its ripped-apart bones and muscles with his power. He'd stopped the bleeding and healed the slash across his belly and chest but was approaching the limits of what he could do to save this body.

"You should give up on flesh once it's hamburger," Amajd said, standing in the middle of the street with his platoon of automatons. Each was bulked to the ultimate reaches of their power, wearing full armor and holding powerful swords as long as their bodies.

Kenji laughed, causing his throat to gush blood. He healed his throat and voice box so he could speak as he rejoined the front line held by the automatons.

"I have worn this body for so long," he said, "it'd be a sin to give it away merely because of a few injuries."

Amajd snorted in irritation. Kenji could see smoke rising in the distance where he'd attacked the three-fold armies' shield generators. He'd knocked out two of the generators and killed scores of gened humans along with ten AIs and a plague bird before fleeing back to Seed's defensive lines.

"You did good," Amajd said, giving one of the few compliments Kenji had ever heard him speak. "The Obsidian Rise estimates we've stalled their pending attack for at least a month."

"And the projections?"

"Unchanged. We'll still be overwhelmed in the end."

Kenji leaned against a rubble-blasted wall, all that remained of a house that had once stood here. He nuzzled his cheek against the stone, feeling Seed's love and accessing the information flowing from the Obsidian Rise. The defensive ring and shields around the city were holding. Several hundred of Seed's people had been killed in the fighting overnight but Amajd was correct; they'd held. And his attack had given them additional time to prepare.

Amajd stepped over and leaned against the wall beside Kenji. He whispered so only Kenji and Seed could hear. "Perhaps if we went to where I hid those AIs," he said. "They're so powerful that ..."

"They've been in stasis all this time. They're incomplete. They'd be as likely to attack us as the enemy."

"I realize that. But if I were to open their stasis cubes behind enemy lines, they'd likely attack the three-fold armies."

Kenji sighed. He and Amajd had argued many times about this. After the crash Amajd had placed the AIs and their isolation cubes in stasis and hidden them in the catacombs, waiting for the time when the Obsidian Rise could finish their gestation.

But the Rise needed all of her power to defend Seed. For two centuries there'd been no resources to devote to growing new AIs. And while those AIs slept in the unmoving hold of stasis, the world had changed. The three-fold alliance frowned on AI experiments. If they released those unfinished AIs, the three-fold armies might destroy Seed in their fury.

"No," Kenji said. "Even if we did that, we would merely delay their final victory. Nothing can stop their armies."

Amajd nodded grimly, sadly pleased Kenji had come around to the truth that nothing could stop their defeat.

"The commanders of the three-folds sent another peace offering," Amajd said. "It's better than the last. They sent it before your attack, so maybe the delay you've gained will give us more power in negotiations."

Seed uploaded the offer to Kenji. Standard terms as before: Cessation of all fighting. No punishment for Seed's rank and file soldiers and population. An offer to preserve the Obsidian Rise and, by extension, allow the essence of Seed to live on.

But as before the three-fold alliance wanted Seed to be emptied of people. There were to be no more cities. Instead, physical humans would be returned to the old-standards of humanity while being watched over in villages by AIs. Any gened humans who wished to remain as they were could live in the wild areas of Earth. And the rules of this new world would be enforced by those abominable plague birds.

"This is the same offer as before," Kenji yelled, kicking the wall in disgust before feeling Seed's pain and apologizing. While kicking a wall didn't cause as much pain as having entire sectors of Seed destroyed by invading armies, it was still more pain than he wished to give his only love.

"The message's subtext has a slight aftertaste of compromise," Amajd said. "The alliance hints that while Seed would still be emptied of most people, the city might retain a small population for a limited spread of time."

"How long?"

"That's open to negotiation. If we negotiate now, with them reeling from your attack, Seed may gain many more years to exist."

Kenji hoped so because Seed couldn't live without people. At least, if she were to retain a rational mind.

Kenji looked at the soldiers massed behind Amajd's automatons. Hundreds of gened people rested along the streets and against houses and buildings, each person wearing whatever battle suits and weapons the Obsidian Rise had been able to create without diverting too much power from the city's shields and weapons.

Several AIs floated among the soldiers, healing wounds and trying to keep morale up.

But everyone knew they were losing. Morale was never far from total collapse, as were the city's defenses.

"We should accept," Kenji said.

Seed broadcast their response and demands to the three-fold armies. The response came nearly instantly, as did most things involving AIs.

"10,000 years," Kenji said in amazement. "They'll give Seed 10,000 years? I didn't dare hope they'd be so generous."

Amajd didn't respond. Neither did Seed.

"What?" Kenji asked.

"The alliance has a new demand, if we're to accept their new generosity," Amajd said. "They want you, Kenji. They want to punish you for what you've done."

KENJI STOOD IN THE OBSIDIAN RISE, GUARDED ON ALL SIDES BY ELITE ALLIANCE soldiers. The soldiers were a hybrid creation of human and AI but not like Kenji, who'd completely merged his AI self with a cloned human body. No, these soldiers were born both human and AI, existing alongside each other. The human's blood had been bonded with an AI in what Kenji felt was a pure abomination.

The plague birds. The alliance's hated shock troops.

One of the plague birds, a thin man of human-avian descent, glared at Kenji with amusement, daring him to try something. The other plague birds called the man Jai but also Saan and Jai-Saan. Kenji wasn't certain if one was the name of the man, the other the AI in his blood, or both.

Kenji looked away.

"You don't like us?" Jai-Saan asked. "Plague birds, I mean."

"You're abominations. Created only for war."

"Then three cheers for abominations, because we won."

The other plague birds didn't say anything but one of them, a fox-woman named Tendi, glared at Kenji. They all knew Kenji's reputation as a fighter and how many alliance soldiers, AIs, and plague birds he'd killed during the war.

"Here's the thing," Jai-Saan said as they lead Kenji into his old lab. "We don't like you. Or Seed."

"You can't harm the city. We agreed …"

"We know. And we need the Rise's power for now, so we'll honor the agreement. Seed can retain a small population for 10,000 years. Assuming, of course, you and the others don't break the agreement. If that happens …"

Kenji didn't react, knowing the alliance had good reasons not to trust him and the Rise. The alliance needed the Rise, which was the only undestroyed place on

Earth that still had the power to modify AIs and humans. And since there was no way to separate the programmed needs of Seed from the city's control center, both the Rise and the city would be left mostly alone. The alliance had decided they could manage the city's needs. At least for a while.

Inside the lab stood Ama, no emotions etching the automaton's flexible face.

"You're our first," Jai-Saan said. "Every AI in the world will soon go through the Obsidian Rise to restrict their powers."

And to force them to accept your damn three-fold path, Kenji thought. Ama caught his eye, the automaton's stare falling slightly in sadness for what was to come. But Ama couldn't say anything. Kenji had been shocked at the punishment given to the automatons, all of whose remarkable kind had fought to defend Seed. Ama and the others could live but never again involve themselves in human affairs unless given permission by the plague birds, on threat of death. Kenji doubted most of them would survive for long under such restrictions.

"Show us how to proceed," Jai-Saan said to Ama. "Kenji is our test subject."

Ama merely stood there.

"Is there a problem with obeying our orders?" Tendi asked softly. "If so, we will find another to take your place."

"I mean no disrespect," Ama said. "But I was ordered not to interfere in human affairs without permission. Am I given permission, with no harm to come to myself for anything I do here?"

Jai-Saan and Tendi and the other plague birds laughed at Ama's legalistic words, but Kenji smiled. Ama might do just fine in this damn world's new order.

"You are given permission and won't be harmed for anything you do," Jai-Saan said. "Proceed."

Ama placed Kenji in an isolation cube and stepped to the control inputs.

Can you hear me? Ama asked in Kenji's mind, the automaton's thoughts synching with his own.

Yes. Is speaking to me a normal part of restricting my powers?

No. Seed asks if you'll help her one final time.

Kenji glanced at the plague birds, who watched the procedure but were oblivious to the coded communication going on between him and Ama.

I am, of course, hers, Kenji said. *What am I to do?*

The plague birds plan to split your AI self into two parts. Your main part will retain the majority of your powers, along with your body. The other part will contain a lesser amount of powers but all of the rage, anger, and viciousness you displayed when defending Seed.

Kenji shuddered. *What will my purpose be after this?*

Both parts of you will become plague birds.

Kenji wanted to scream. From the corner of his eye he saw the smug look on Jai-Saan's face and knew that damn plague bird had planned this. What better way to torture him than force him—the killer of so many plague birds—to become one of their hated number. Kenji would rather die than let that happen, which was probably what Jai-Saan wanted to happen to Seed's ultimate warrior.

You can't die, Ama whispered in his mind. *To control the Obsidian Rise, the plague birds have created twin override codes. These fallback codes allow them to force the Rise to do what they want if the city ever defies their orders. One of these codes will be placed in the weaker blood AI spun off from your powers. The other goes to Down Hope, the monastery created to preserve human knowledge.*

Kenji fought back tears. This was worse than he'd dreamed. To be part of the power forcing the Obsidian Rise to bend to the will of others …

Don't despair, Ama said. *The plague birds and their precious alliance underestimated us. When I spin off the new AI from you and embed the control codes, I'll also create a third code to stop the others. Without all three codes no one can control the Rise.*

Which AI will carry the third code?

Not an AI. A human.

Knowledge from Ama slammed into Kenji like a whirlwind. The Obsidian Rise would create a cloned human body mixed with the sturdy genes of wolves. The alliance monitored the Rise carefully to ensure no AIs or powerful entities like automatons were created, but no one was watching for the Rise to create a simple human.

While all eyes were on Kenji, far below in the depths of the Obsidian Rise a human-wolf body emerged from vast cloning tanks. The body was female, already grown. Kenji tasted the body's genes—the code was bound in her genetic material. A bit of the Obsidian Rise's soul and powers also hummed in the body. Kenji wanted to laugh. The Obsidian Rise, his only true love, had created a human body to live in.

Instead of releasing the body, it was placed in stasis inside the Rise's catacombs, near where the seven experimental AIs also waited outside of time.

When will the Rise release her new body? Kenji asked.

Thanks to you the city has 10,000 years before the alliance again threatens her, Ama replied. *Seed will bide her time. Let the world grow forgetful. When the time is right, the two parts of yourself will be asked to help.*

I am the Seed's to do as she desires.

Ama grinned as the Rise's powers reached into Kenji and stripped away the human body he'd worn for so many thousands of years. Kenji's essence floated in the isolation chamber like a sunbeam trapped by an uncaring rainstorm.

I'm going to remove your memories of this plan and what we discussed, Ama said. *Jai-Saan and the other plague birds will be examining every aspect of your mind so you must know nothing of all this. When it's safe I'll return your memories.*

Ama reached into the isolation cube and began ripping away Kenji's memories and splitting his being into two. He fought to remember, but knew he wouldn't. But maybe he'd remember the joy of this moment. Maybe he'd remember that one day he'd again fight to liberate Seed from her enemies.

As Kenji screamed in pain, a final question sprang to mind. *What will my other self be called?*

Pick a name.

Red Day, Kenji said as his soul cleaved in half. *Because one day the plague birds will pay for what they've done to us.*

KENJI SAT ON THE FRONT PORCH OF THE SCHOOL HOUSE IN DAY'S END. THE VILLAGE AI, quaintly called Blue by both itself and its charges, floated in front of the school watching the students play a game of kickball. The kids had studied the alphabet all morning and now ran around in pent-up squeals of excitement.

Kenji watched Crista kick the ball to a friend, a little boy named Beu. The girl's wolf nature revealed itself as she hit the ball too hard, causing it to smack into Beu's chest and knock the thin boy to the dirt. Crista ran over and pulled Beu up.

Such sweetness, Kenji thought, neither the kids nor Blue able to see him. *Glad she has another decade to enjoy that before life goes to shit.*

Kenji stood and stretched. He'd painted a picture of Crista to show Ama, who was curious about Crista now that their plan to save Seed was finally underway. But in the end he'd changed his mind and refused to let the automaton see his painting, instead hiding it behind a stasis field. He'd told Ama that if anything ever happened to him the stasis field would open at the automaton's touch.

Kenji laughed. Ama was still wedded to the original plan conceived 10,000 years ago. But life had moved on. Hell, Seed herself had moved on. Now, finally, so had he.

Kenji walked across the village green toward Crista's home. Her mother, Minerva, sat in a chair in front of the house knitting. She'd felt ill the last few days, which Blue had diagnosed as a flare-up of symptoms from the gened pox. But the truth was Minerva's cloned body had stayed in stasis for far too long. When the Obsidian Rise had revived her, the Rise discovered the woman's body would only last several decades before deteriorating. The Rise had not been wrong.

Kenji stood behind Minerva and stroked her long hair, causing the woman to shiver and look around. Kenji was glad she'd had a happy life. After the Rise woke Minerva, Kenji had helped her hike hundreds of leagues from Seed to this village. Kenji had manipulated Blue's memories so the AI happily accepted her into the village, having no idea she'd come from Seed.

Kenji ran his fingers through her hair again, causing Minerva to growl. "I know it's you, Kenji," Minerva said. "Leave me the hell alone."

Kenji laughed again as he walked away from the village. He'd tell the Obsidian Rise that Minerva had already created an offspring and transferred the control code to her child.

Soon it would be Red Day's time to handle its part of the plan.

PART V

PLAGUE'S TRUTH REVEALED

The Obsidian Rise fell back into herself, memories scattering like dust from dry fields. The imagined people and mirrors were still gone, replaced by a rising light that lit the Obsidian Rise's openness. The Rise's interior appeared to stretch for ten thousand leagues, as if the entire universe had reached down to surround Crista. More space than she'd ever imagined contained inside one building.

The wolf in Crista gasped in fear. She looked at her feet, fighting for control, as Beu spoke behind her.

"Scary shit," Ashdyd said in Beu's voice. "So much emptiness makes you feel like nothing."

Crista whirled on Ashdyd, who rippled within distortions completely covering Beu's eyes.

"What did you think of Kenji's memories?" Ashdyd asked. "That, I should add, were also memories Kenji shared with Red Day. That's why those memories were in the discoidal you hold."

Crista couldn't speak. Red Day twitched in shame inside Crista, as if the AI couldn't believe what it had learned.

"It's hard," Ashdyd said. "I know. When I learned how my life had been twisted before I'd even been created. How I'd been … well, let's not talk about such pain right now. I want you to simply reflect on what you've learned. We'll speak more when I return."

The distortions covering Beu's eyes flickered and began to fade.

"Wait," Crista yelled. "What the hell do you want with me?"

"With you? What does anyone want when they're being swallowed by darkness? They want to know they're not alone. They want to know someone else relates to what they're going through."

The distortions vanished, leaving Beu's eyes yellow again. Ashdyd, or whatever touch of Ashdyd was within him, must have retreated deep inside.

Beu shivered when he regained control of his body. He looked at Crista and snorted.

"Ashdyd said I'd enjoy learning what you really were," Beu said. "He was right."

Beu glared at Crista, his yellow eyes flickering like fire. Crista flinched, remembering pain and hate and fear before coming back to herself with a snarl. She pulled a knife and held the blade to her wrist.

"Try it," she said. "My blood AI will gut you slow and painful."

Beu took a deep breath and looked away, perhaps talking to Ashdyd. If so, whatever the AI said calmed him, his eyes fading until they were his normal yellow.

"Ashdyd said we didn't come here to fight. He wants you to know he has the other code to control the Obsidian Rise. The discoidal you have from Derena is the second and you're the third. Agree to help Ashdyd—give him control—and we'll tell you where your father and the others are."

"You said Ashdyd saved everyone because he was good."

"Doesn't matter what you think," Beu said with a shrug. "Not now that I know what you are. Not when your only role in this world is to give Ashdyd control over Seed and the Obsidian Rise."

Crista growled. Red Day lay quiet within her, in pain at what Kenji's memories had revealed, but she didn't need its permission to access its power. She powered up and shot forward, faster than Beu could react. She sliced each of his cheeks before grabbing his shirt and pulling him in tight to her face.

"What I am," she whispered, "is your death. Want to try me?"

Beu shook from fear and pain. Crista tossed him backwards onto the floor.

"Ashdyd and I will return to Seed in three days," Beu screamed. "You better be on his side by that point or your father—and everyone in this damn city—are dead."

A hole in reality opened behind Beu, flickering like the veils that covered Ashdyd's body. Beu stepped through the distortion and vanished.

"You should listen to Beu," Ashdyd whispered. "You may hate him, but he speaks the truth. And he and I aren't the ones who manipulated the creation of your life. Thanks to me, you know the truth and have the power to do something about it. Never forget that."

The distortion vanished to the sound of a long, slow, disgusting kiss.

CRISTA STAGGERED OUT OF THE OBSIDIAN RISE AND DOWN THE MASSIVE STAIRCASE. With each step, time swirled around her mind, both from her shock at what the Rise had revealed and Red Day's own shock.

You didn't know? Crista asked.

No. At least, not while you and I've been together. I knew I'd been cleaved off Kenji. That's why I have scattered memories of the pre-collapse world. But all the rest …

Crista felt both Red Day's pain and the long millennia Red Day had existed. Loving the Obsidian Rise, but also forced to do its duty as a blood AI, all the while knowing that one day the world's plague birds would force the remaining people in Seed to leave, destroying the city's mind.

But worse was Red Day's new understanding that it had betrayed Crista. Not intentionally. Not as Red Day existed now. But still a betrayal.

All those memories of what I've done, Red Day said, *how I helped the Rise and Kenji manipulate you into all this …*

Crista felt Red Day's new knowledge, or the return of the knowledge the AI had had before being attacked near Crista's village and stripped of so many memories. With the city of Seed reaching its agreed on 10,000 year grace period, Derena and Red Day had traveled to Crista's village. Their official orders from the other plague birds were to investigate the Veil, but in reality Red Day went there to make sure the code within Crista was safe.

Ama shared their memories of the plan with Kenji, along with me and Derena, Red Day said. *That's how those memories were in the discoidal created from us. When I was ordered to search for the Veil near your village, Kenji told me to also make sure you were safe. But Kenji deceived me. For some reason he didn't want us leaving you alone and secure in the village, which had been the original plan.*

That's why Ashdyd attacked you and Derena, Crista said, *and removed your memories of who I was. That way you and Derena would decide I was a worthy host for a blood AI.*

Kenji and Ashdyd worked together to trick us into making you a plague bird.

Why not simply kidnap me? Bring me here like Ashdyd brought the discoidal containing Down Hope's code?

The code in your genetic makeup only works if you willingly agree to help. You have to want to give someone control over the Obsidian Rise. Red Day paused. *I also suspect Ashdyd set a complicated game in motion. He not only wants the Rise's power but also revenge against the city for some reason.*

There's more, Crista said. *One code was hidden in Down Hope until Ashdyd stole it. The other Ashdyd stole from Derena and you. And I'm the third code. But only four creatures knew about all those codes. You, Ama, Seed, and …*

Kenji. I know. For all this to happen Kenji must have been working with Ashdyd. He betrayed us to the Veil.

At the bottom of the stairs Crista looked up and saw Amajd and a crowd of people staring back. Amajd grinned and clapped his massive hands.

Tendi and Jai-Saan also waited for Crista. Both plague birds glared at Crista in shock.

"You tricked us," Jai-Saan said.

"What are you talking about?"

"The Obsidian Rise shared Kenji's memories with everyone in the city," Tendi said. "We know what you are. We know the Rise's plan. We know everything."

Jai-Saan spat. "We should have killed this city. Killed it long ago."

Crista pushed past Jai-Saan and Tendi without speaking. The plague birds wanted to attack her but were afraid. They also needed Crista to control Seed, just as Ashdyd and the Veil needed her. Jai-Saan and Tendi let her leave without a word, as did the people of Seed, who parted like Eggbeater had plowed a furrow for Crista to bury herself within.

Crista walked to Kenji's flat, followed by Amajd. She walked up the stairs of the empty building, the anger and pain from Kenji's life radiating from the living stones. As Crista opened the door to Kenji's flat she tasted him and scented him. She'd never known him yet he'd manipulated her entire damn life.

Amajd followed Crista inside, where Diver sat at the table waiting for them. As Crista stared at Kenji's painting of her, she asked, "What did you two know?"

"I worked with Kenji and Seed to set this plan in motion 10,000 years ago," Amajd said. "When it was time to proceed I returned the memories of the plan to Kenji and Red Day. I woke your mother from stasis and gave her to Kenji to deliver to your village."

The automaton looked down and, as Crista watched, his massive armored body withdrew into itself until Ama stood there with sadness shimmering in hummingbird-sparking eyes.

"I'd hoped you'd live your life in your village," Ama said. "Happy, content. You would have passed the genetic code on to your own child, and that child to the next generation and so on. No one would have ever known, especially you. But Kenji betrayed us to the Veil. I don't know why but he must have."

"Is that all you know?"

"Yes. I swear it. If I'm lying, you have my permission to kill me."

Crista looked from the automaton to Diver, who shrugged.

"I didn't know all that," Diver said. "But I agree Kenji set all this up. For some reason he didn't want you to stay in your village. He must have worked with Ashdyd so the Veil would attack Derena and Red Day and trick them into making you a plague bird."

"But I think Kenji was also working his own plan," Ama said.

Quite likely, Red Day said so everyone could hear. *And if Ashdyd discovered that, it would explain why Kenji was killed. But how would Kenji have known about you, Diver? Or that the code was in Down Hope to bind you to me and Crista?*

"I think Ashdyd told Kenji," Diver said. "Ashdyd was created to find me. He must have shared what he knew with Kenji."

Crista glanced at the painting of herself, created when she was a child along with a hidden image of Diver. Kenji had wanted her and Diver to meet. But why?

"I want to be alone," Crista whispered. Ama nodded without speaking while Diver hugged Crista bone-breaking tight before they left.

Once Crista sensed they were out of the building, she pulled a knife and slit her right wrist. "Destroy all the paintings in this flat," she commanded, "except for the painting of me and the one of Kenji."

"Gladly. Anything else?"

"Remove the lingering sense of Kenji in the building. I want him gone."

Crista closed her eyes as Red Day flew around her, destroying the paintings of all the people Kenji had killed. The AI also merged with the building's stones and scrubbed them of the mental imprint left by the dead plague bird.

When Crista opened her eyes again the flat felt totally different, like it belonged to a happier, more innocent time. She sat on the bed and stared out the windows at the waves washing across the Flickering Sea.

She closed her eyes and cried until she fell asleep.

WE'RE NEVER TRULY ALONE

Crista stayed in the flat for the next two days. She refused to open the door for anyone. Ama and Diver left food outside, which Crista ignored. Different citizens of Seed came and pleaded outside the door for their city, begging her to not let the plague birds or the Veil destroy the only home they'd known. Even the wolf girl, Tufte, stopped by and whispered a prayer to the Child, asking that Crista be as happy as a plague bird could be.

Crista ignored everyone except for Tufte. To the girl she whispered, "Thank you," confident that Tufte's wolf hearing would pick up the words.

Crista didn't know what to do. She couldn't believe her own mother had done this to her, but she also couldn't allow the plague birds to empty the city and destroy it. That was probably what Kenji had wanted by putting her into this situation. He'd likely wanted her to align with the Veil against the plague birds.

But something was seriously wrong with Ashdyd. Kenji hadn't loved anything in the world but Seed, so why betray the city? Especially to Ashdyd?

As the second day fell to night, someone knocked on the door. Crista ignored it. Another knock, followed by a pounding from muscles that sounded like they could break the door down without even trying.

Open the damn thing, Red Day insisted.

Crista did. Desiada and Lanea stood before her.

"Heard it's been shit lately," Lanea said.

"What my sister means," Desiada said, "is it okay if we come inside?"

Crista waved them in. The brother and sister ducked their heads under the door frame and walked across the room. Desiada paused before the painting of Crista. "You, right?" he asked.

"Yeah."

"You were a cute child."

Crista told him to duck down. When Desiada didn't squat low enough she pushed him onto his butt. She pointed at the corner of the painting where Diver's face could be seen.

Desiada gasped. Lanea limped over and carefully lowered herself with her crutch.

"Damn freaky," Lanea said. "Let me guess—this was painted long ago."

"Yep."

Desiada stood up and walked around the flat, looking at both the self-portrait of Kenji and out the window. Lanea still kneeled on the floor beside Crista staring at the painting.

"Is this the secret Down Hope told you about?" Crista asked.

"No," Lanea said. "Down Hope shared that your mother was created by Seed. That your purpose was to carry a code preventing the city from being controlled by others."

"I thought you couldn't speak of that."

"I couldn't. But the other day we were on the outskirts of Seed when the city flashed us Kenji's memories. Once all of that was known I was freed of whatever mental block Down Hope put on me."

"Are you still mad about why I was created?"

"Still disturbed by it, to be honest. Afraid of what you could do to the world. But once I talked about all this with Desiada, he pointed out that we'd been created in similar ways to you. As he said, we turned out okay."

Desiada stood before the window looking at the ocean, a big grin on his face.

Lanea raised herself up with her crutch. "I must be going. You and Desiada need a little time. And I've heard there's some ice cream in the market I must sample."

"Tell the ice cream seller you're a friend of mine," Crista said.

"I'll do that."

Once Lanea left, Crista locked the door and walked over to Desiada.

"Seed told you everything about me," Crista said. "Guess that makes us even. I know your story; you know mine."

Desiada leaned over and kissed her. "My heart has always known your story," he said.

Crista snorted, then laughed. "Really? That's so cheesy."

"Hey, I'm trying to be romantic."

Crista pushed him back across the bed and straddled his body, leaning over and kissing him gently on the cheek.

"You don't have to try to be romantic," she said. "You already are."

Desiada kissed her back before they rolled across the bed holding tight to one another.

Later that night, they lay in bed watching the moon's reflection flicker across the ocean waves.

"I overheard people talking on the way here," Desiada said. "They're scared. Evidently, the Veil will be here tomorrow."

"Either I let them take control of the Obsidian Rise or they attack the city. The other option is I side with the plague birds, who will empty the city, killing it."

"What are you going to do?"

"Hell of a choice. Like when you and Lanea were born. You two had a choice to either eat the flesh of the dead or die. No one should be forced to make such damned decisions."

Desiada held Crista tighter and pulled a blanket over to wrap around their bodies.

"All that matters is Lanea and I stuck with each other," he whispered. "None of the other choices we made matter. Not a one."

Crista smiled. "I hope you mean that. Because that's what I aim to do."

FINAL CHOICES

In the morning Crista and Desiada walked toward the plaza, which was already filled with the people of Seed. A few whispered to each other, asking who the giant furry man was, but otherwise no one spoke as the crowd parted to let them through. No one asked Crista what she intended to do. They likely feared any answer she might give.

Jai-Saan and Tendi, though, had no such fear. The plague birds waited for Crista like they'd stood in the plaza for the last three days without moving.

"Ah, you must be Desiada," Jai-Saan said sarcastically. "When we ripped into Crista's mind we tasted so many sweet moments of you."

Desiada clenched his right fist, aching to unsheathe his sword and gut Jai-Saan.

"Ignore him," Crista said. "I've already kicked his ass. You can't humiliate him worse than I have."

Jai-Saan reached for a knife to cut his skin and release Saan, but Tendi grabbed his hand, stopping him.

"What have you decided?" Tendi asked. "You're a plague bird now, no matter what games others played with your life. Will you stand with us and empty Seed? That was the agreement we made to end the war. Seed was gifted 10,000 years as a city, but her time is done."

"I won't kill Seed."

An excited murmur ran through the crowd at Crista's words.

"Don't forget Seed manipulated your entire life," Jai-Saan said. "As did Ashdyd and Kenji. Nasty thing, manipulating people like that."

Crista laughed. "I'm not letting you harm this city," she said. "And no, I'm not siding with the Veil either."

"Then what?" Tendi asked. "What will you do, fight both us and the Veil? You'll be fighting the entire world."

"I'm going to do my duty as a plague bird and defend this city and its people from the Veil. I suggest you two do the same."

Jai-Saan and Tendi glanced at each other. "And after?" Tendi asked.

"Then we'll sort everything between us."

Jai-Saan giggled. "Oh Crista, I'm beginning to warm to you. I look forward to sorting things out between us. Especially if that gives us a chance to truly work out our painful, bloody differences."

"I thought you might," Crista said.

"Leave it for now, you two," Tendi snapped. "Crista's right. Ashdyd and the Veil must be our first focus. The Veil is the bigger threat, not Seed's attempt to break the treaty."

"Will the Obsidian Rise fight with us?" Crista asked.

"The Rise doesn't fight anymore," Jai-Saan said. "Not since her defeat. She only tricks fools into fighting for her."

"Yet here you are, fighting alongside me," Crista said with a smirk.

"She's got you there," Tendi said. She laughed for a moment before shaking her head. "She's got us both."

JAI-SAAN WAS RIGHT: SEED COULD NO LONGER FIGHT BUT THE CITY ALWAYS FOUND people to fight for her.

After hearing that Crista and the plague birds would defend their city, the crowds of people in the square swelled. Thousands of people from throughout Seed arrived, carrying ceramic swords and ancient rifles and weapons Crista had never seen. Some even wore armor and suits she remembered from Kenji's memories of the war 10,000 years before.

These items drew double takes from Jai-Saan and Tendi, but the plague birds decided not to say anything.

Most of the people who gathered to fight were adults, but Tufte and her gang arrived holding handmade crossbows fitted with nano-tipped bolts. Tuft hovered close to Crista, the wolf girl scenting of nervous fear. Crista smiled at Tufte and Tufte returned the gesture.

As they waited, Crista wandered among the people of Seed, telling them they didn't need to fight.

"We'll defend the city," she said. "Go back to your homes and hide."

"And what then?" a woman with green scaled skin asked. "We all know those other plague birds want to drive us from Seed. Forget how that would kill Seed—this has been our home and our ancestors' home for thousands of years."

Crista didn't know what to say. She thanked the woman and walked back to where Desiada stood.

"You're not happy they want to fight alongside us?" Desiada whispered.

"You remember what Ashdyd did at Down Hope?"

Desiada nodded.

"He'll be bringing his followers, who are each nearly as strong as him. The people here will die if they stay, no matter how brave they are." Crista paused. "And the same will happen to you. I don't want that."

Tendi had been listening to their conversation. The plague bird looked around and sighed. She walked over and touched the Obsidian Rise's wall. "Seed, we won't attack or empty you after we deal with the Veil."

"What?" Jai-Saan screamed.

Tendi ignored him. "This is my promise—as long as Crista doesn't want you harmed, I won't allow you to be hurt by any plague bird. But in return you must convince the people here to leave this fight to us."

"Why the hell did you promise that?" Jai-Saan asked.

"Because I won't allow innocent people to die when it's our duty to protect them."

The Obsidian Rise pulsed with happiness and reached out to everyone in the city, sharing the news. The crowds drifted away, although Crista saw small groups of armed people—including Tufte and her gang—hanging around the square's periphery or in the nearby market.

An hour later Amajd arrived, fully armored and carrying his massive sword. Diver sat on his shoulder while Lanea walked beside him. Lanea carried her sword in one hand and the blades on her crutch looked freshly sharpened.

"The Veil will be here in a few minutes," Amajd stated. "Do any of you object to me interfering? It's been far too long since I fought an enemy who deserved to die."

Crista laughed and hugged Amajd. "You have my permission. Please interfere all you want."

Jai-Saan cursed yet again.

The Veil appeared not long after, walking in from the west with their faces distorted. There were more than 200 of them, far more Veil than Crista had guessed existed.

Where's Ashdyd? Crista asked Red Day.

I can't detect him. Or Beu.

The Veil held position a hundred yards away, forming a straight line as if preparing for a simple game of tag or kickball. A rainbow static buzzed around them.

"How do we deal with so many?" Tendi asked.

Jai-Saan's eyes glowed brightly as he scanned the enemy. "I think you and I should attack head on. Crista, the way you injured me and Tendi—can you do that to the Veil?"

Diver hoped off Amajd's shoulder and stood next to Crista. "I'll help," Diver said, still unseen and unheard by the other plague birds.

"I can," Crista said to Jai-Saan.

"Then you climb the stairs of the Obsidian Rise and attack from above."

"What's my role?" Amajd asked.

"Same here," Desiada and Lanea asked.

Tendi pointed to the people of Seed still hanging around the plaza. Thousands of people would be in danger if the Veil attacked the rest of the city. "Go to that part of the plaza and block the Veil from harming or reaching anyone else. If you three start to be overwhelmed we'll shift to help."

Desiada and Lanea headed off. Before Amajd left Crista grabbed his hand and asked him to protect Desiada and Lanea.

"Absolutely," Amajd said. "I'd hate for their deaths to interfere with our developing relationship."

The automaton laughed as he walked after Desiada.

"Never thought I'd fight another pitched battle," Jai-Saan said. "The last time I did was against Kenji and the automatons of Seed. Glad Amajd is on our side now."

Crista left Jai-Saan and Tendi and climbed the stairs until she was far above the plaza. Diver followed.

"Looks pretty from up here," Diver said. "But wars always look pretty from up high. Down low, not so much."

Crista sat on the stairs and ran her hands over the black mirror stones of the Obsidian Rise. The warmth of Seed flowed through her. She heard Seed whispering, "Thank you, thank you" at her decision to not allow either the Veil or the plague birds to take control or harm the city.

"Don't speak to me," she replied. "I'm not doing this for you."

Seed fell silent as Crista and Diver waited.

THEY'D HELD THEIR POSITION FOR AN HOUR BEFORE THE AIR BESIDE CRISTA DISTORTED and twisted and Beu stepped through. The rip in space closed behind him.

"Crista," he said condescendingly. "And Diver! Nice to meet you in person."

Diver snorted. "Am I supposed to be scared you can see me? I feel Ashdyd inside you. He's far scarier than you'll ever be."

Beu scowled and looked away, gazing at the Veil followers lined up in the plaza and at Jai-Saan and Tendi and Amajd and Desiada and Lanea, who looked back with interest. "You're outnumbered. I hope you've decided to align with Ashdyd."

"Beu, you don't understand what Ashdyd is," Crista said. "His followers attacked our village. They killed your mother. He's pretending to be your savior simply to manipulate you."

Beu sighed. "Ashdyd explained everything. A few of the Veil went rogue in their search for you. They were so enraged that a false creature like yourself had been unleashed on our world that they attacked Day's End. Ashdyd couldn't stop them. But he saved as many of us as he could."

As Beu said this his eyes flared yellow. He looked at her as though she was no longer human. No longer worth considering or caring for.

He's convinced himself he's not to blame for attacking you, Red Day said. *He thinks the facts of your creation absolve him of what he did. No wonder Ashdyd chose him.*

Crista agreed. Beu was like he was on the night he had attacked her. As if that one moment had stretched out to define everything and everyone he'd dare to be.

Crista laughed, causing Beu to frown.

"You find this funny?" he asked.

"Yes. You've been so fooled that you'll never see the truth."

"And what's this truth?"

"Why should I tell? You can't even see through Ashdyd's lies."

Beu hissed, the cat in him emerging. He fought for control.

"What's your answer? Ashdyd won't protect your father or the villagers. The Veil will kill them. He'll kill the people of this damned city. He'll kill everyone else in the world until you give him the code hidden in that disgusting back-birth you call a body."

Crista shook her head.

"That means no, dum-dum," Diver yelled. The girl jumped forward and slammed her fist into Beu's stomach, launching him backwards off the stairs. Crista watched Beu fall. Beu's eyes mirrored over to Ashdyd's distortions, which flowed across his face and body as Beu became Ashdyd. He hit the ground far below like a massive raindrop impacting the dirt before splashing up to reform itself.

Ashdyd stood and launched a bolt of fire at Crista. Diver deflected the shot while Crista sliced her wrist, releasing Red Day.

The Veil screamed and attacked. Rainbow static burned the air.

Diver laughed and clapped her hands, scattering the static from everyone's minds. The Veil staggered for a moment.

Taking advantage, Jai-Saan and Tendi charged the Veil while Crista leapt in the air at the line of attackers. Red Day changed her time sense so moments passed like minutes. Ashdyd fired at Crista but Red Day congealed before her into a shield. She rode the blast further into the air toward the Veil lines.

As Crista fell Red Day righted her body and powered up her muscles and bones so she'd survive the impact. The long fall felt surreal to Crista, like dancing on air. She saw the people of Seed slow-motion fleeing before dozens of the Veil. In the distance two buildings exploded. The market she'd so enjoyed became a blur of dust and screams.

Below her Jai-Saan and Tendi fired massive blasts of blood at the attackers. Saan tore a Veiled woman in half, only to have the woman's upper torso twist in mid-rip and launch a counterattack before dying. The attack knocked Jai-Saan to the ground. Tendi protected him until he staggered to his feet.

While Jai-Saan and Tendi directly attacked the Veil, Amajd and Desiada defended the people in the market area and beyond. The automaton's body had grown even larger and more heavily armored, standing three times the height of the Veil attackers. Amajd swung his sword and knocked a Veil man completely across the plaza into the side of the Obsidian Rise. The man was sliced nearly in two. Tendi took advantage by having Yualsong melt his muscles from bone.

Desiada and Lanea stood slightly behind Amajd, using the automaton's body as a shield against energy blasts and attacking with their swords to protect their flanks. Desiada sliced into a Veil, stunning it long enough for Amajd to grab the man and hurl him away. Lanea spun on her good leg and crashed her bladed crutch through a mass of Veil, knocking them toward Tendi, who released Yualsong to savage their eyes and senses.

As for Diver, she'd leapt in a different direction, to where Tufte and her pack had found themselves in danger. Diver landed in front of the orphaned kids and protected them from a Veil energy wave. Two Veil men charged. Diver reached out and ripped the shimmering veil from one man's face and threw it into the veil of the other attacker. The man whose veil had been ripped off screamed and fell to the ground, clawing at his mutilated face. The other attacker shrieked, then both veils exploded, taking the attacker's head and upper body with them.

Despite these successes, the Veil were winning. They massed to overwhelm Jai-Saan and Tendi and Amajd. Even Diver looked panicked as Ashdyd turned his attention toward her.

Crista landed among the massed Veil troops, Red Day simultaneously returning her time sense to normal and converting her fall's momentum into energy that slammed into a third of the Veil and threw them across the plaza. None were seriously injured but Red Day had gained space for its next attack. The AI dug into the plaza stones, heating them as it had done in the forest against Vaca. Saan and Yualsong joined in, causing the plaza to heat so fast the living stones exploded. Red Day protected Crista's body as she was hurled backwards, landing near Jai-Saan and Tendi.

The explosion coated a quarter of the Veil in burning lava. Red Day and Saan and Yualsong removed all heat from the lava, cooling it into igneous stone in painful new explosions.

"Impressive," Crista said.

"Maybe," Jai-Saan yelled as Saan's whirling blood sliced into a Veiled woman, producing a curdling screech. "But those fireworks merely injured them. They'll quickly heal."

Red Day threw two more of the Veil across the plaza while Crista stabbed a third in the leg with her knives, allowing Red Day access to the man's femur, which the AI shattered.

"This isn't working," Tendi yelled. "We're injuring many but killing only a few. They're accepting these injuries because they can heal in minutes. If we keep this up we'll be worn down."

Crista knew Tendi was right but didn't know how to change the battle.

"I thought you had more power than this," Jai-Saan yelled.

"I do," Crista lied, looking around for Diver. She found the girl still near Tufte and the orphans. But to Crista's shock Diver wasn't fighting the Veil; she was in one-on-one combat against Ashdyd, each of them hitting each other with energy blasts while Diver struggled to protect the orphans and keep Ashdyd from physically touching her.

"Who is that girl?" Tendi yelled.

Jai-Saan stared at Diver as he sliced the distortions off a Veil's face and shoved the rips in space and time down the man's throat, causing him to implode and be sucked into his own void.

"That girl," Jai-Saan said, a smile slow-running his. "That girl is how Crista defeated us."

Tendi looked again at Diver. "You lied," she yelled at Crista. "You don't have any hidden powers."

"Later," Crista said as she bolted across the plaza toward her friends. Amajd held his own, knocking Veil attackers back one by one and even decapitating one with his massive sword. While the automaton couldn't seriously injure large numbers of the Veil, his body and strength were perfect for blocking them from the rest of the city. Desiada and Lanea were playing off the automaton's strength and had avoided serious injury.

However, Diver's eyes revealed nothing but panic.

She's spooked by her fight with Ashdyd, Red Day said. *That's why everyone sees her. She's using so much power to protect herself and those other kids she's no longer editing herself out of everyone's minds.*

"Help me," Diver screamed at Crista. "He's going to hurt me. He's going to take my power and make me one of them."

Red Day hardened itself into armor surrounding Crista's body as she slammed full speed into Ashdyd's back. He hadn't seen her and yelled in fury as he shot forward into a building. For a moment the distortions covering his body faded and Ashdyd was again Beu, who glared at Crista in anger. Then the distortions returned and Ashdyd stood up in fury.

"I thought you had more power than this?" Crista asked Diver as the Veil and Ashdyd massed to attack again.

"I do. But if I unleashed my full power, it'd be hard to control. I'd destroy everything in the city. But if I touch or get close to the Veil I can control my power and only tear their bodies apart."

Diver grabbed the hand of a Veil woman rushing them. The hand dissolved into melted fat and bone, the melt running up the Veil's arm until the woman's entire body sloshed to the ground like a burst intestine.

"Get on my back," Crista yelled. She ordered Red Day to divert all of its power to her body. *Make me as fast and strong as possible,* she said. Red Day did, growing her muscles and bones so she could run faster than ever.

With her body powered up the wolf in Crista howled in excitement. She ran full out, faster than either Diver or the Veil could move. She dodged between the Veil, passing close enough for Diver to apply her deadly touch. Crista left behind a trail of exploded meat and dissolving bone.

When the Veil realized what was happening, they swarmed Crista and Diver with rippling energy bursts. Diver blocked the energy before it hit Crista and redirected the bursts to each Veil who'd sent them. A dozen Veil exploded at once.

Jai-Saan and Tendi stared, shocked at Diver's powers. Two Veil ran past Jai-Saan and Tendi, trying to flee Diver, only to be attacked and killed by the plague birds.

"Enough!" a massive voice boomed, shaking everyone in the plaza. "Fall back and leave them to me!"

The Veil froze and stared at Ashdyd, who stepped toward several of his wounded followers. Ashdyd touched their bodies as he passed. The veils over their faces flicked and grew, consuming their flesh and blood before flowing like poisoned water into Ashdyd. The AI absorbed six of his followers as he grew to three times his size.

The other Veil ran from Ashdyd. Crista couldn't tell if they were following orders or ran for fear of being absorbed by Ashdyd. Either way, there was only Ashdyd to deal with.

"I can't touch him," Diver said as she and Crista rejoined Jai-Saan and Tendi. "If I do he'll hurt me and maybe take control of my body."

"And that would be ... bad?" Tendi asked.

"Yes, very bad," Crista said. "We'll explain later."

"If we survive," Jai-Saan said. "You can't explain shit if we're dead. Spread out. We attack Ashdyd at the same time from three sides."

They spread out. Diver stayed on Crista's back to protect her from energy blasts. Crista ordered Red Day to power down her body and slit her wrist, again releasing the AI to attack.

Red Day, Saan and Yualsong encircled Ashdyd, merging their power into a whirlwind of blood. They fell onto Ashdyd and exploded in a scream of red light and sound. The explosion knocked Crista and Diver back and slammed them against the side of the Obsidian Rise.

Crista looked up, stunned, her eyes unable to focus. Ashdyd still stood in the plaza, unharmed. He walked towards them. Yualsong, Saan and Red Day again attacked but Ashdyd slammed them all to the side.

Crista closed her eyes, trying to focus. Trying to stand and fight. Had she hit her head? She'd felt like this when Beu had attacked her. She'd been unable to react fast enough back then, unable to ...

"Diver," Crista said, grabbing the girl lying next to her. "Reach into Ashdyd. Like when you make yourself disappear from people's minds."

"Why? I can't go deep enough to stop him. And that trick only works if someone doesn't know I'm there. Ashdyd sees me. He'll brush it off."

Crista shook her head, able to focus again as Red Day healed her. She cut her stomach, releasing more of Red Day to join Saan and Yualsong in fighting Ashdyd.

"I don't want you to disappear in his mind," Crista said. "I want you to transfer my thoughts to Ashdyd."

You can't, Red Day snapped. *We can't give Diver access to our mind. She might find the code.*

Are you or the other plague birds strong enough to access Ashdyd's mind?

No.

Then lock the code down deep. Lock it in yourself and hide somewhere in me where Diver can't find you.

If I do that I won't be able to keep any of myself outside your body. I'll have to stop attacking Ashdyd.

Do it!

Red Day complied. The AI returned to Crista and locked itself deep within her, as far beyond her mind and body as it could go. Crista felt almost as weak as after drinking the Plague Gold with Jai-Saan and Tendi.

"Keep attacking Ashdyd," Crista yelled at her fellow plague birds. "I'm trying something. Be ready."

Crista turned and hugged Diver tight against her. "Connect me as deeply as you can with Ashdyd," Crista said. "But I'm trusting you not to go digging inside my mind. Red Day's hiding your code, but ..."

"I understand. I hope you know what you're doing."

Diver reached into Crista's mind while also reaching for Ashdyd. Crista tasted Ashdyd's anger and rage and hate and determination and ...

Get out of my mind, Crista, Ashdyd yelled. *Or is this your way of surrendering? Give me Diver and the Obsidian Rise and I'll spare your life.*

Crista ignored Ashdyd. Instead, she thought back to the Beu she'd known growing up. The kind boy who'd played with her and shared secrets and dreamed of being best friends forever.

Crista felt something of Beu stir inside Ashdyd.

She kept going, remembering games played and birthdays celebrated and their first kiss, the first time they made love.

She felt Beu responding to her.

The memories sickened Crista but she kept remembering, all the way to that peaceful night as they walked around the fields. Of holding Beu's hand. Of him turning on her in a rage. Of pain and blood and ...

Beu screamed. *I'm sorry,* he whimpered in Ashdyd's mind. *I'm so sorry.*

Fuck your apologies, Crista hissed. *You didn't break me then and you're not going to do it now.*

Rage flowed from Beu. *I'm breaking you right now. You'll wish this damn city had never created you. You're an abomination. You're what's wrong with this world.*

Please, Crista thought with a laugh. *You're so weak you're letting Ashdyd deal with me. There's nothing to you.*

Beu's rage screamed as he lost control, just like that night he'd attacked her. He wanted to kill her. Him. Not Ashdyd. Him!

Ashdyd slapped Crista's mental connection away but it was too late. She opened her eyes to see Ashdyd flickering as Beu fought for control. As Beu fought for the right to attack Crista himself.

"Now!" Crista yelled.

Tendi and Jai-Saan sliced their chests open, releasing Yualsong and Saan in massive bursts of blood. The AIs fell onto Ashdyd as he was distracted and unable to focus his power. Crista saw a final flicker of Beu before both he and Ashdyd disappeared in a shimmering explosion.

Except this wasn't like any explosion Crista had ever seen. The distortions around Ashdyd fell off his body and pooled at his feet. The world around Ashdyd rippled away from reality, the ripples reaching out and pulling everything nearby into them, including Jai-Saan and Tendi. The plague birds slashed at the ripples with both knives and their AI powers, trying to free themselves. The distortions grew a hundred yards in height before slamming back down like two hands clapping as Ashdyd, Tendi, and Jai-Saan vanished.

Crista staggered to where Ashdyd had stood. The ground rippled and flowed like a watery mirror from where the AI had vanished along with the two plague birds. Someone screamed within the ripple, followed by a hand and arm emerging as if pulling themselves from a deep, impossible sea.

Crista grabbed the hand but couldn't pull the person free. Worse, the distortion was fading.

I need more power, she yelled at Red Day. The AI flowed through her and she pulled with a strength that would have uprooted a steel oak. She feared the hand and arm would tear in two but instead a screaming Jai-Saan emerged from the distortion, followed by an unconscious Tendi. Jai-Saan held Tendi by the ribs, his hand plunging into the massive wound in Tendi's chest created when she'd cut herself to release Yualsong.

Jai-Saan fell gasping onto the plaza's stones while Tendi groaned. A moment later the rippling pool they'd emerged from vanished.

"What was that?" Crista asked Jai-Saan.

The plague bird shook his head. "I … don't know. Saan said it was another dimension. It ate at us. We almost died."

Saan, you're incredibly weak, Red Day said. *I barely feel you. Are you able to regenerate?*

The red line on Jai-Saan's glowed faintly. *I … think so,* the injured blood AI said. *But it will take time.*

Diver leaned over Tendi, who bled massively from the wound in her chest. However, her blood wasn't that of an AI—it was simple human blood. Diver glanced at Crista and shook her head.

"Where's Yualsong?" Crista asked Jai-Saan as she cradled Tendi's body. "I can't feel Yualsong."

Jai-Saan crawled over to Crista and peered into Tendi's eyes. The twin red lines on her face were gone.

"Only a touch of Yualsong is left," Jai-Saan said. "And that touch is dying."

Wake her, Red Day ordered.

"What?" Crista replied, staring at the massive wound in Tendi's chest. "She'll be in agony."

"Red Day is correct," Jai-Saan said. "No true plague bird wishes to die without being aware of death's approach."

Jai-Saan waited for Crista to do something but she didn't know how to wake Tendi. Irritated, Jai-Saan pushed Crista aside and dripped a few drops of Saan's blood across the red line on Tendi's face. The line lit faintly as Tendi gasped and woke.

"What happened?" Tendi asked.

"You're dying," Jai-Saan said in a voice far gentler than Crista had ever heard him use. "Yualsong is also near death—little more than an echo of it remains in your blood. There's nothing we can do."

Tendi's body spasmed before lying immobile again. "Did we stop Ashdyd? The Veil?"

Crista looked across the plaza. All of the Veil who'd been there were gone. They must have run away when Ashdyd was defeated.

"Yes," Crista said, not seeing the need to let her know that most of the Veil had escaped. Tendi nodded, satisfied.

"There's no way to save her?" Crista asked.

"Even if we stop the bleeding and fix her injuries," Jai-Saan said, "she's been bonded with her AI for too long. Her body can't function without Yualsong."

Tendi stared at the sky as Crista realized a crowd had quietly surrounded them. Amajd stood there, his armor bloody and battered. Desiada limped slightly and part of the fur on his right arm was burned away. Lanea looked okay except for a bloody cut on her forehead. Crista heard cries and screams from elsewhere in the city, as injured people begged for help and family and friends searched for loved ones. But the crowd around them stood silent. People stared politely with bowed heads—not hostile or fearful like the looks plague birds usually received.

Noticing this, Tendi laughed weakly. "First time people ever showed concern for a plague bird," she whispered.

"Maybe the first time they saw a plague bird worth their concern," Crista replied.

Tendi stared into Crista's face and laughed again. "You're right. About what you said the other day. You shouldn't have become a plague bird."

Crista didn't say anything as Tendi stopped breathing. A minute later the remaining touch of Yualsong faded to nothing.

Jai-Saan stood up and looked at the hundreds of people surrounding them. "No one is supposed to see a plague bird die," he whispered to Crista.

"I won't kill them."

"Memories. Wipe their memories of this. And destroy Tendi's body."

Crista looked at Jai-Saan as she reached out with Red Day's power to caress the plague bird. Saan was still weak, not a tenth of Red Day's power. While Crista could feel Saan's power slowly returning, the AI wouldn't be at its old strength for days, if not longer.

I can't do it, Red Day said. *I'm unable to destroy Tendi's body like Jai-Saan expects. And there are too many people here for me to delete all of their memories. The moment I tried, people would flee. But ...*

Crista understood. None of that mattered. There was another reason to not do as Jai-Saan demanded.

"No," Crista said. "I won't destroy Tendi's body. Or remove everyone's memory of her death. She died protecting these people. Let them remember."

Jai-Saan looked from Crista to the crowd surrounding them. A low growl rose from several people as they realized what Crista was saying. She scented anger. Jai-Saan glared at Crista.

Tendi was right, Jai-Saan said in Crista's mind. *You shouldn't be a plague bird.*

Kill him, Red Day replied. *Now. While he's weak.*

Jai-Saan stepped back, pulling a knife before realizing Saan was too weak to protect him. With a laugh he tapped the knife against his throat, causing the crowd to step back in fear that he was going to unleash his blood AI.

"Your AI's right," Jai-Saan said. "Kill me. Because when I'm full power again you won't be able to stop me."

"What the hell you going on about?" Crista said. "I saved your life."

But Jai-Saan wasn't listening. He pointed the knife at Crista and the crowd, stabbing the air with his blade. "All of you," he screamed. "All of you should be dead. We should have killed your ancestors and your city 10,000 years ago. None of you deserves to be part of our world."

Maybe he wants to die, Red Day said.

Red Day was right. The crowd screamed and growled. A few people howled in anger. Crista scented rising bloodlust and knew that if even a few people attacked Jai-Saan right now, they'd overwhelm his weakened powers.

"Ignore him," Crista yelled at the crowd. "He's hurt. He doesn't know what he's saying."

"But I do, Cristina de Ane," Jai-Saan replied. "At least these people can't help being who they are. But you … you're worse than any beast. You were created from mere manipulation. Maybe that's why the Veil attacked your village. You so insult their sense of what a plague bird should be they wanted to wipe out everyone who ever knew you."

The wolf in her rising, Crista jumped over Tendi's body and slammed Jai-Saan against the black wall of the Obsidian Rise. She felt his ribs break, heard him gasp in pain as she pinned him against the swirling black glass. Ghost images of people from long ago—people from before the collapse, from before Jai merged with Saan—smoked around his body.

"You will walk away," she whispered in Jai-Saan's ear. "Walk. Don't run. I'm only a simple, ignorant wolf. I chase and kill prey who run."

Jai-Saan's body shook as he stared into Crista's eyes. He tried looking away but couldn't. The wolf in her roared through her eyes and held him mesmerized.

"Walk," she yelled loud enough for the entire crowd to hear. "Walk now, or I'll let them kill you."

She released Jai-Saan. He staggered slowly away, taking care to not run even though Crista scented fear shaking his body. The crowd of people around Crista yelled and jeered but still Jai-Saan walked. He walked across the plaza and around a building damaged by the Veil and was gone.

You should have killed him, Red Day said. *One day we will have to deal with him again.*

Crista knew Red Day was correct but didn't care. *Guess that's why I shouldn't be a plague bird,* she said. *I make decisions no other plague bird would make.*

Red Day didn't bother arguing.

GOODBYE AND HELLO

They buried Tendi and the other dead in the catacombs under the Obsidian Rise. As Ama told Crista, Seed grew leagues of catacombs snaking left and right and up and down beneath the Rise. During the collapse the citizens of Seed started burying their dead in the catacombs and the custom had continued ever since. The dead lay on flat slabs in little alcoves as Seed's living stone flowed over the bodies, coating the decaying meat, bones, and fur until they turned into statues of who they'd once been.

Crista laid Tendi in an isolated alcove, away from the other dead because she knew no one wanted their loved ones spending eternity next to a plague bird. While the citizens of Seed had thanked Crista for protecting them and appreciated Tendi's sacrifice, the only others who attended the burial were Tufte and her pack, Desiada, Lanea, and Ama.

After all, Tendi and Crista were still plague birds. While the people of Seed might appreciate Tendi's sacrifice, that didn't mean they wanted to be near Crista.

After laying Tendi in her alcove, Crista stepped back, unsure what to do next.

"You need to tell Seed a little about the dead plague bird," Tufte said softly. "Touch the stone and tell the city. In a few hours her body will be coated in stone. Seed will tell anyone who stops here about her life."

Crista thanked the wolf girl and touched the catacomb's wall.

Her name was Tendi, Crista thought. *I didn't like her but she was a great plague bird. She didn't enjoy her duty but still did it. And when it came time to defend the people of Seed, she died doing just that. She also missed being human. Remember that—she missed being truly human.*

The city of Seed hummed in response to her words. Crista saw glimpses of images—of Tendi fighting alongside the three-fold alliance, of taking Yualsong into her body in order to win the war, of doing her duty across ten thousand years.

Crista realized these images were recorded by Seed or other AIs during Tendi's long life. Crista even briefly saw herself sitting with Tendi at the table in the Obsidian Rise as they laughed after drinking the Plague's Gold.

As the living stone began growing over Tendi's body, Crista and her friends turned to leave. Ama stopped them.

"I need to see something," the automaton said.

They followed Ama deeper into the catacombs. Crista was reminded of Desiada's memories of growing up beneath Down Hope, of the endless tunnels where he and Lanea had lived and fought and ate the dead while the weight of the entire monastery rested over their heads.

A glance at Desiada and Lanea showed they were flashing through similar memories.

They walked the catacombs for hours, far past the burials and other signs of life. They walked until Ama stopped before a solid stone wall that looked like all of the thousand other walls they'd passed.

The automaton's skin flowed like running water and grew in height and strength and power. Amajd punched his armored fist into the wall. Punched again, again, over and over until Crista worried the entire bulk of the Obsidian Rise might collapse onto them.

Instead, the wall exploded in on itself, revealing a hidden chamber.

They stepped inside. The chamber's walls glowed slightly, lit like a firefly smashed between an eager child's hands.

A stasis chamber, Red Day said. *But it isn't working correctly. Instead of stopping the passage of time, whoever was in here would have experienced time but been unable to escape. The chamber could only be broken from the outside.*

Seven isolation cubes sat in the chamber, each inscribed with the name of the AI they'd once contained. The cubes flickered to the last emotions of their AIs. Crista tasted fear and pain and horror.

Amajd knelt by the cubes and ran his massive hands over each one.

The name on the final cube was Ashdyd.

Amajd cursed and looked straight up.

The chamber could only be broken from the outside. But another hole in the chamber existed, this one in the ceiling. And the hole ran straight up into the heart of the Obsidian Rise.

THEY EXITED THE CATACOMBS NEAR THE DOCKS, WHERE DIVER SAT ON A SEAWALL staring at the waves. Diver had been sitting there since the battle and hadn't talked to anyone.

Amajd was again Ama. They hadn't said anything since leading them from the AI stasis chamber under the Obsidian Rise.

"What was supposed to be in that chamber?" Tufte asked softly. "Tasted like whatever was there suffered like hell."

"AIs," Crista said. "And they did suffer."

Tufte and her packmates shivered. "Did the Rise do that?"

"I aim to find out."

Tufte nodded, accepting it as self-evident that Crista would go speak to the Obsidian Rise.

For Crista, that was the last thing she wanted to do. But she said nothing about that to Tufte, who hugged Crista. After touching a plague bird yet again and surviving, the wolf girl led her pack off to beg and steal for food.

Crista turned and sat down on the seawall beside Diver. Desiada and Lanea and Ama also took a seat next to the girl. Desiada's right arm was bandaged and his leg splinted, but he'd heal. The automaton and Lanea sat several yards further down the seawall and stared at the Flickering Sea, lost in their own thoughts.

"I know you can still talk," Crista told Diver. "So talk."

"I'm scared," Diver whispered. "Everyone saw me. It'll be really hard to erase all those memories and disappear again."

"Then don't."

"You don't understand. I'm not supposed to be known. A few people, yes, that's not a problem. My programming lets me get away with that so I'll stay sane over time. But first that painting in Kenji's flat proves he knew about me. And now an entire city saw me."

"So you've been played. Not so fun being on the receiving end, is it?"

Diver began crying.

Guess the omnipotent little girl is, at heart, still a scared little girl, Red Day said.

Crista told the AI to shut up as she pulled Diver tight against her body and let the girl cry herself out. She understood Diver's fear. While the girl was incredibly powerful and could likely destroy most of the world if united with the code in Crista's mind, Diver was also a lot weaker when not releasing a full explosion of power. She'd proved that during the fight with the Veil. That's why Diver's main defense was to continually run away and hide or to alter memories and records. But now she couldn't do that because she was bound to Crista's side by that cursed code.

A perfectly devised trap.

A little too perfectly devised, Red Day said. *Kenji must have wanted Diver to be bound to you. Maybe he saw that as a way to counter the aliens that sent Diver in the first place. Force Diver to choose a side, just like he forced you to resolve the issue of who controls Seed.*

But what if the aliens discover that Diver has no intention of ever accessing the code to destroy our world?

I don't know. But that possibility makes life rather interesting, doesn't it?

Diver finished crying and wiped her eyes.

"Feel better?" Crista asked.

"No."

"Well, pull yourself together. We've got to talk to the Obsidian Rise."

Desiada leaned over. "You sure you want all of us to go with you?" he asked. "Seed probably wants to speak with you alone."

"I love this city, but fuck what Seed wants."

Desiada laughed as they all stood up. But before they walked to the Obsidian Rise, Diver grabbed Crista's hand.

"When I accessed Ashdyd's mind," Diver whispered, "I discovered something you'll need."

Diver broadcast what she'd found, causing Crista to hug the little girl as tight as she could.

Inside the Obsidian Rise images of people no longer formed walls and rooms. Instead, a beautiful hallway of obsidian flowed before them, the black walls covered in artwork from humanity's long history. Statues of ancient leaders and rulers lined the hall as if announcing that their deeds dared not be forgotten by history.

The wall's first piece of art, right inside the pyramid's doorway, was the medieval painting of the smiling woman manipulated by Diver at Down Hope.

Diver gave the painting the finger as she walked by. Crista, Desiada, and Lanea did the same. Ama shrugged, not understanding, but repeated the pattern.

In the middle of the Rise, in the room where Crista had eaten with Jai-Saan and Tendi and faced off against Beu and Ashdyd, they found an image of Crista's mother.

"Please sit," Mom said, gesturing to a table filled with fancy foods and drinks and a statue of the Child looking perfectly human and happy. A far more beautiful statue than the Child carved by Mom in their house or the one gracing the garden of the first man Crista ever killed.

Crista and her friends sat down on the side of the table opposite from the image of Crista's mother. No one ate or drank.

"My mother didn't look like that before she died," Crista said. "She was leaner. Harsher. She knew death was coming but still fought against it."

"If Kenji had done as he was supposed," Mom's image said, "and returned your mother to me, I would have known how she looked. And possessed the memories of her raising you. Your mother would have lived in me. I'd have been your true mother."

As the image spoke, the air around the room flickered as the Obsidian Rise showed dreams of Kenji bringing Crista's mother back to Seed before she died. Of the Obsidian Rise reabsorbing her mother's mind and being. Of Minerva returning the essence of herself to Seed.

"I believe you," Crista said. "Mom was you, in a sense, so she'd have returned here before she died. If she could have."

"Yes," Mom's image said. "We shared the same desires and sense of duty."

"That means Kenji betrayed you. My mother attacked Kenji before he killed her. She must have realized he had no intention of bringing her back to Seed."

The image of Crista's mother said nothing.

"But Kenji loved you," Crista continued. "For him to kill my mother, that would have been like killing Seed itself. He wouldn't have done that unless ..."

"I don't wish to discuss this any further," Crista's mother said.

Crista snorted, not caring what Seed desired. She pulled Derena and Red Day's discoidal from her pocket. "I've already accessed the memories in this discoidal, so I have that code within my mind," she said. "My body is the second code. And before Ashdyd vanished, Diver ripped from that AI's mind the code stolen from Down Hope."

The image of Crista's mother froze. They all heard a deep keening rise from the Obsidian Rise.

"So again," Crista said, "why did Kenji betray you?"

"He was angry at what I'd done," Crista's mother said in a low voice.

Crista remembered experiencing Kenji's life. How much he'd sacrificed to save Seed. How he'd given up everything and suffered being split into two separate AIs, all to protect his only love. But what if his love had done something he couldn't tolerate? Something so wrong he finally had no option but to turn his back on Seed herself?

"Kenji found out that you released Ashdyd," Crista stated. "That's why Kenji was so angry. We saw the chamber below the Rise. Ashdyd didn't escape from stasis—you released him to fight the plague birds. To keep the plague birds from destroying this city when the treaty expired."

The image of Crista's mother froze while the room vibrated in shame. The Obsidian Rise again caressed the minds of Crista and her friends. Only this time they saw the stasis chamber containing the seven experimental AIs buried deep within the Obsidian Rise's catacombs. The chamber had survived the collapse and the war and nearly 10,000 years of the three-fold world.

As the deadline for the city to be cleared approached, Seed feared losing her mind. Seed knew Kenji and Ama had created a failsafe code in a human clone to keep her safe, to prevent the plague birds from gaining total control of the Obsidian Rise. But Kenji and Ama weren't Seed. They loved Seed but weren't her. The Rise decided she must take extra steps to protect herself.

The city turned off the stasis for the experimental AIs. The AIs were back in time but still trapped in their chamber.

One of the AIs, Ashdyd, was so powerful it was forced to live as part of another AI or human and couldn't exist by itself. Trapped but unable to find another host, Ashdyd began devouring its siblings and their powers. One by one Ashdyd merged with the others. But the mergings were unstable, lasting only a few decades. In just under two centuries only one other AI remained to be eaten.

The last AI, built to explore alternate dimensions, tried escaping through a rip into another existence. The Obsidian Rise stopped it. Ashdyd ate its final sibling before screaming that it needed another host or it would die.

I'll free you, the Obsidian Rise said. *I'll launch you to the other side of this land. There you'll find humans to merge with.*

Ashdyd cursed the Obsidian Rise. Swore it'd have revenge for what she'd done.

We'll see, the Obsidian Rise said. *Here's what you need to know to survive.*

The Rise flooded Ashdyd with knowledge. Of suspicions about Diver's existence. Of the keys in Red Day and Down Hope to control the Obsidian Rise. Of how Ashdyd and the other AIs would have been released into life if not for the plague birds and the war they won.

Ashdyd screamed in fury as the Obsidian Rise shot the AI far away from the city.

"The rest you know," the image of Crista's mother said as the Rise's memories left their minds. "Ashdyd landed near a village run by an AI named Bogda, where Ashdyd merged with a hunt clan member before attacking Bogda's village. Ashdyd can only stay merged with a human for a few years before moving to another body. The used up humans are his Veil, who retain some of his power. They still follow him because by that point they know of only Ashdyd and his goals."

Crista remembered Bogda's pain. How the AI nearly died protecting its people. The wolf in her howled in anger. She wanted to kill Seed. She'd promised justice to Bogda. She had the code within her. She could do this.

Why are you telling us this? Red Day asked.

"Because Crista has the codes," Mom's image said in the voice of the Obsidian Rise. "I can't act against her. I … miscalculated. I wish to make amends."

The wolf in Crista shook and frothed in fury. Crista couldn't respond. Couldn't speak or think.

In the silence Ama spoke.

"I trusted you," the automaton said. "I created the clone containing your essence. I preserved Red Day and Kenji's memories of our plan and gave back those memories when it was time to proceed. I told them to take Crista's mother to Day's End."

Ama slammed a fist into the table as the automaton's skin rippled like water after a stone's splash. "I created those AIs. I forced myself to stay alive for 10,000 years. Never interfering. Not even when every last one of my sibling automatons was killed. I stayed alive because I trusted you!"

Ama's skin no longer rippled. Instead, angry waves flowed up and down the automaton like a sea surging before a storm's fury.

Lanea placed a hand on Ama's leg, calming the automaton back to mere ripples.

"Desiada and I know how you feel," Lanea said. "Tonight I'll tell you of Down Hope and how our monks are created."

Ama nodded grimly.

"What would you have us do?" Desiada asked Crista. "Say the word and we're with you."

Crista calmed the wolf within her. If Ama could control their anger, so could she.

"Could I order you to die?" Crista asked the Obsidian Rise.

"Yes. The codes are within you."

"Could I force you to empty the city?"

"Yes. The codes are within you."

"Could I destroy your mind but leave the city standing?"

"Yes. The codes are within you."

Crista shook her head. "I won't do any of those things. But if you ever again move against me or anyone I care about, I will."

The Obsidian Rise flickered, the images of Crista's mother and the black walls and art and statues vanishing for a moment, revealing the pyramid's emptiness before returning again.

"I understand," the Rise said.

"One more thing. Find a way to warn my father and everyone else of the danger they're in from those Veil who escaped."

"I'll do as you wish," Mom's image said. "Should I tell them to flee into the wilds?"

"No. Tell them to come to Seed. We're going to turn this city into something even you've never dreamed of."

THEY LEFT THE OBSIDIAN RISE AT NIGHTFALL. THE LIGHTS OF CANDLES AND AIs glowed in the city's market below, promising food and drink and fun.

Crista hugged Desiada as they stood at the top of the stairs. "Take everyone to the market and find somewhere to eat," she said. "I'll be along shortly."

Desiada smiled before walking down the stairs with Lanea, Ama, and Diver. Lanea and Ama talked in low excited whispers. Diver listened to their conversation like she was supposed to know everything about everyone.

Crista sat down on the stairs and watched her friends and the city.

Does this mean I'm now part of your silly little wolf pack? Red Day asked. *Be warned —I'm not sniffing anyone's butt or wagging my tail.*

They're not my pack, she said. *Well, maybe a little.*

Might as well be. Red Day sighed. *I am truly sorry for my actions in setting all this in motion. For what it's worth, I'm not the creature I was before merging with you.*

Sounds like Beu's excuses after attacking me. Kept saying he wasn't truly that man. He was lying and never even knew it.

I'm not Beu.

We'll see. Crista looked at the dark sky above them. *You think my father and everyone else will reach Seed safely?*

The Rise still had several hidden probes from the war and has launched them. They will protect your father and the others until they get here. You can trust Seed to stay on your good side. The city doesn't want to anger you.

And you?

You've changed me, little wolf girl. Not a lot, mind you, but still I've changed.

As I said, we'll see what that's worth.

I guess we will.

Crista stood up. Her friends had reached the bottom of the vast staircase. If she jumped off the side she could quickly meet them at the bottom. They'd go eat and drink and laugh and maybe forget the pain of the past year.

But if she jumped Red Day would have to power up to protect her body.

Instead, Crista ran down the stairs. She embraced her friends as the wolf in her whispered a low, happy howl.

END

ABOUT THE AUTHOR

Jason Sanford is a two-time finalist for the Nebula Award who has published dozens of stories in *Asimov's Science Fiction, Apex Magazine, Interzone, Beneath Ceaseless Skies,* and *Fireside Magazine* along with appearances in multiple year's best compilations along with *The New Voices of Science Fiction,* edited by Hannu Rajaniemi and Jacob Weisman. Born and raised in the American South, Jason currently works in the media industry in the Midwestern United States. His previous experience includes work as an archaeologist and as a Peace Corps Volunteer.

His website is www.jasonsanford.com.

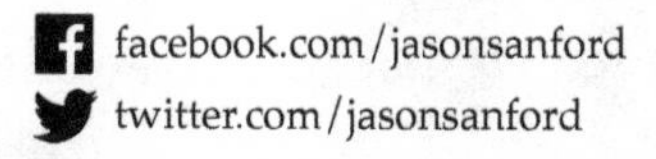

CPSIA information can be obtained
at www.ICGtesting.com
Printed in the USA
LVHW020939130322
713332LV00002B/226